This series is a work of fiction.
Names, characters, places and incidents are either used fictitiously or are the product of the author's imagination.
Any resemblance to actual persons, living or dead, is coincidental.

This publication may only be reproduced, stored or transmitted with prior permission in writing from the author, or in accordance with the terms of licenses issued by the Copyright Licensing Agency.

The right of Emmanuelle de Maupassant to be identified as the Author of this Work has been asserted by her in accordance with the Copyright, Designs and Patents Act 1988.

Viking Thunder - first published in 2017
Viking Wolf - first published in 2018
Viking Beast - first published in 2019

www.emmanuelledemaupassant.com

EMMANUELLE DE MAUPASSANT

NOTES FROM THE AUTHOR

Welcome to my 'Viking Warriors' steamy romance series.

Svolvaen and Skálavík are fictitious, as are my characters.
While the superstitions and rituals related in this series are based on true Norse beliefs, I've taken liberties in shaping them. You'll recognize the Norse myths, though with many omissions and told with my own emphasis.

Daily life and habits are based on my research, some of which is drawn from the 'Hurstwic' online site.
I've described the longhouse much as we believe it would have appeared, with deep benches along each interior wall (used for sitting and sleeping). Central firepits provided warmth and a means of cooking, with smoke drawn through a hole in the roof.

While it's commonly believed that most longhouses were 'windowless', the sagas of *Brennu-Njáls* and *Grettis* both mention openings akin to windows (without glass but using skins which could be drawn back).
I used this device most prominently in Viking Wolf, as it served my plot.

You might notice that I've chosen to use British spelling, but US punctuation… and there's a short glossary, to explain the handful of Norse words I've included.

Happy Reading
Em

CAST

Brought from Northumbria, by Eirik
Elswyth

Svolvaen residents
Eirik ('eternal ruler') – brother to Gunnolf
Helka – sister to Eirik and Gunnolf
Guðrún and **Sylvi** – Gunnolf's thralls (slaves who undertake household duties)
Astrid – a village woman who befriends Elswyth
Ylva - Astrid's daughter
Torhilde – Astrid's neighbour
Bodil – a former lover of Eirik
Anders – the blacksmith
Halbert – the blacksmith's son
Olaf – friend to Eirik

Svolvaen residents (deceased)
Hallgerd – the previous jarl (uncle to Eirik, Helka and Gunnolf)
Wyborn ('war bear') - father to Eirik, Helka and Gunnolf Wybornsson
Agnetha - sister to Hallgerd, married Wyborn
Gunnolf ('fighting wolf') – Eirik's older brother
Asta - Gunnolf's wife

EMMANUELLE DE MAUPASSANT

PROLOGUE

I dreamt the moss was damp beneath my feet and the trees shimmered. A roaring bear lumbered towards me and I fell in terror, my neck awaiting the heaviness of its great paw.

Instead, a hand soft and pale raised me up. A woman spoke my name and her eyes were the mirror of my own. She bid me stroke the bear's mane and I climbed upon its back, its fur warm beneath me.

ॐ I ॐ

June, 959 AD

I remembered what my grandmother had told me. *If they come for me, I'll kill them, or myself.*

Villages were being burnt along the coast, men slain, women raped and taken onto the boats. Such stories travel quickly. But it had been years since any Northman had landed this far south.

It was before dawn when they came, following a night of wind and thunder. The cockerel had not yet crowed and most of us lay asleep in our beds.

There was no one to fight for us. What time was there to pick up axe or knife? Those who stirred first from their beds were cut down. It was over before it had begun.

My husband grunted and rolled from the mattress, the thud of his body on the floor bringing me back from my forest dreams. My blood knew, before I heard any cry of fear, that the monstrous uninvited were among us, that the men standing guard beyond our doors had been slain.

He tried to hide under the bed, our brave chieftain. They dragged him out, and me, too, from under the covers, to stand barefoot in my nightshift.

"Take her," he said, that husband of mine. "Elswyth's young and strong. You'll see."

He crawled like a worm.

"Take anything you like."

Their eyes had spied the goblet and my jewelled brooches, those which pinned my hair and cloak.

"Anything," he pleaded, raising his trembling face.

ment. All they knew was anticipation of the next jump. It was the same for all their tomorrows, their bodies singing with the pleasure of being alive.

I'd pull off my tunic and leap alongside them, the air cool against my skin, the water chill yet thrilling.

I thought I could be the same. What did it matter that I had no pizzle? Such a little thing, I always thought. Though they were proud enough of them: their pikes, ploughs and pudding pricks. So many names for what lay between their legs.

As for mine, it was without name. *Your secret place*, my grandmother called it. What was inside? Not much that I could see. It was like another mouth, pink and soft, ridged and smooth, like the inside of my cheek, able to grip my fingers. I would lay my hand there, when I curled in my truckle bed, drawing strange comfort, but I didn't know what purpose it served.

Until my body began to change, and there was a tug inside me. When I touched between my legs, my fingers were bloodied.

"You're a woman now." My grandmother was as pleased as I'd ever seen her. Perhaps, now, she hoped I'd leave off from playing in the forest with the boys, and turn my mind to womanly pursuits.

I saw, once, two of the boys, chest to chest, hip to hip, legs wrapped tight. They thought they were unseen, but I was looking, from above, hidden in the branches of a tree.

I watched them.

Hands about their cocks, as if they had but one, not two, joined in stroking.

I touched myself and wished I too had a pike. How easy it looked, to rub that rod upon another's body, and gain pleasure.

My grandmother told me how my father died, when the Northmen came. They split him like we do the pigs, she said. Monsters. Gutting a man, to leave his entrails steaming.

She hid under the bed with my mother but isn't that the first place to look?

They laughed when they found them. Made my grandmother serve her stew, and when they'd eaten it, each took a turn with my mother.

She didn't cry, my grandmother said. She lifted her skirts and submitted. Brave, some might call it. It kept her alive.

I was born when the January snows fell, and who can say which of those Northmen was my father. What does it matter? I'm half-monster. Half-murderer. Half-something that does not belong. Because of the colour of my hair, and eyes palest blue. Do those things make a person beautiful or ugly? I'd as soon cut the gold from my head.

When I was too small to know her, my mother took a fever and died. My grandmother is strong. It's her hand that's raised me. Her hand, and the watchful eye of my aunt; she married our chieftain, and bore a girl, Faline, as dark as I am fair. I was old enough when my aunt passed, for his eye to wander to me, to covet what lies beneath my dress. Men cannot hide their hunger any better than the wolf or the bear.

"Accept him as your husband," urged my grandmother. "You'll be safe, and have everything you desire."

I took her counsel. It appealed to me to dress in finer clothes, and to be admired. My husband would be old enough to have fathered me, and there was something in that which drew my curiosity. He must know so much more than I. What would I learn in his bed?

My days of climbing trees and setting rabbit traps were gone but there were new skills to be learnt, were there not? New pleasures?

On our first night, I laughed when I saw his wrinkled pizzle, tiny beneath his belly. He didn't name me wife as he pushed me down. I was his teasing whore, a stinking cunt. He wrapped my hair thick about his fist. He had once, I recall, admired the gold of those curls, calling them sun-spun threads. He yanked them from my head as he spurted into me.

I said nothing, and I understood, at last, why my mother had kept from crying out.

3

I'd vowed to kill them, or myself, but had chance for neither. What could I do but endure, and hope I'd live another day. I knew that look, as they took the gown from me.

The first, having placed his hands in my husband's freshly-spilled blood, smeared it, crimson, across my belly, across my breasts. They laughed to see it. He drew his tongue across my skin, tasting death and life. It excited him, for his cock needed no help in finding its way.

I lay upon the bed as they each took their turn. What good would struggle have done? Better to lift my legs and make easy their pleasures. It meant no more than the ram tupping the sheep, or the bull mounting the cow. I'd been bedded enough to take a man, and these were but three.

I was nothing to them, and they nothing to me. They were more vigorous than my husband, their thrusts harder, faster. They were younger, of course, and stronger. Beyond that, I saw little difference in the act of sex. I was a sheath for their sword, a hole into which they might rub to the desired end.

I thought of my mother as they bedded me.

Had they been older, these Northmen, I might have wondered if one were my father. Doesn't fate play these tricks? To send my own father to rape me would be jest indeed. Such were the ramblings of my mind as they grunted through their labours.

As the last spent his seed, the others thumped his back, in congratulation.

It was then that she entered. No Northman, but woman, speaking as sharply as a mother to errant children. They stood a little straighter, those men, at her command, and left.

She stepped closer and reached out her hand, to touch my cheek. Her face was older than mine, but it was as if I looked into the lake, at my own reflection. Her hair, her eyes, the length of her nose, and something set in the lip. I saw another part of myself, another me, born in another skin.

And then she spoke, and though her words were awkward, I understood.

"I'm Helka," she told me. "I'll help you now, and you can help me."

4

What can I tell you of that day, when all about me wept, for husbands, brothers, sons slain? Every family, it seemed, had lost someone dear. I shed my own tears, giving the appearance of a grieving widow, though my sobs were not for my husband.

I had no love for him. He was less than a pig or a goat to me: unworthy to be called a man, let alone the chieftain of our village.

My tears were rather for the boys with whom I'd spent my childhood. Some had received injury, some were dispatched to the next life: Daegal, Nerian and Algar.

And how many women had been bent across their table or held upon their bed, as their uninvited guests made their welcome? Had they bid their children hide their faces, or turn to the wall, so as not to see?

Before the Northmen had arrived, my grandmother had taken to her bed with aches in her legs and, thank the Lord, they'd left her there. It was a blessing, for she remained ignorant of much that had passed.

The strangers would leave surely, if they had what they'd come for. There would be no reason to stay.

"We want to go," said Helka, turning those eyes upon me that were my own. "We were on the sea, when the storm came. The other boats sailed on, but it blew us here, and tore our sails. Our oars too; some are broken."

If we helped them, they'd leave.

I was the chieftain's widow. What could I do but urge our people to help repair those sails? Make haste, and send them on their way. They were too strong for us to fight.

The Northmen, having ensured that no man, or woman, would be inclined to do other than submit, ate, slept, and gathered whatever was of value. I thought them brutish in their manner, and their language rough upon the ear.

Their hair was long for the most part, and plaited like that of a woman, but their bodies were those of men — tall and broad and strong. They were unafraid to pierce you with their gaze.

I found myself looking, at the muscles beneath their leather jerkins and furs, at the size of their hands. Such hands had slid beneath my buttocks to hold me upon the hammering of lust.

There was one, taller even than the rest, a giant almost, with a long scar through his cheek, wearing the green and blue of their skin decorations all down his arms, and up his neck. Eirik, I heard them call him. He took our blacksmith's son by the scruff of the neck, and shook him like a doll. Only when Helka argued with him did he stop.

He laughed, but ceased his torment of poor Grindan.

Like all the others, he held her in respect.

Were they married? I wondered. It was a relationship like none I'd seen.

"Come, Elswyth," said Helka. Our women had stretched out the sails and had begun threading sheep gut to mend them. The Northmen would make their own oars.

"Take us into your forest?" she asked. "Show us where to find wood that is hard?"

They needed oak, the strongest, and I led them: Helka and ten of her Northmen. I know the secrets of the forest better than most.

I took them through the meadow, while the eyes of the village women bore upon my back. They'd been jealous of me, no doubt, as chieftain's wife. I'd always been thought to set myself apart, taking satisfaction in making myself different. Now, they were suspicious of me. I was too helpful, too placatory; the Northmen were our enemy, after all.

"How do you speak our language?" I asked, as we entered the first shade of the trees. My curiosity was too great to keep silent.

"Our father came here years ago, when Eirik and I were little. He brought back slaves, who lived with us."

She spoke of slavery as easily as we might have remarked upon the fatness of a sow, or the ripening of barley.

"Eirik and I laughed at their strange words. We wanted to learn. It was a game. When we wanted to speak secretly, without our mother knowing what we said, we'd use those other words."

"So he's your brother, Eirik?" I asked, "Not your husband?"

"Ha!" She laughed at that, slapping me upon the back so hard that I near fell under the force of it.

"As if I'd marry him! He drives me to madness and back again."

We moved on in silence for a while, I directing us to avoid where the brambles grow thickest. It was too early for the fruit. Only the thorns were abundant.

When she spoke again, her voice was quieter.

"I was married, but my husband is in Valhalla now. I'll marry again, when my body and mind desire it."

She paused in walking, touching my arm. "I'm sorry, for your husband, for his death. I understand some of what you must feel."

My retort was out of my mouth before I could stop myself. All the resentment I'd felt towards him. "I'm not sorry. I dreaded his bed. He wasn't a man. He was like vermin in the barn. I'm glad he's dead."

I spat the words, spewed them out like so much poison. The sweat prickled on my forehead. I'd kept that hatred inside me for too long.

I looked about nervously, as if expecting the Northmen walking behind us to turn on me in anger. What sort of wife was I, to speak so of my husband?

The first rested his hand upon his axe. Of course, he must have supposed my fury to be directed at Helka.

She shook her head at him, and placed her hand upon my shoulder, as if to soothe me.

"We have many of the qualities of the animals inside us. To be human is to be animal, whatever else it means. Sly as the fox, brave as the eagle or steadfast like the ox, each man has his animal kindred. Our *fylgja* accompanies us through life: that part of ourselves which is more animal than human."

It was an idea I'd not entertained before. Our people had long been of the Christian faith, as the monks had taught us. This said we were above the animals, made in God's image. It was something I'd tried to believe in, but I couldn't help feeling closer to the animals in the fields and forest and lake, closer to them than to any man I'd met.

"When a baby is born, their animal spirit comes to find them, to accompany them. My mother told me that, on the day of my birth, an owl flew into the room and sat upon the end of the bed. She wouldn't let anyone shoo it out. It sat for an hour before flying away."

A strange story, but there was something of the owl in her, it was true. I wondered if there was an owl somewhere in the trees, watching us at that moment.

Helka picked up a stone from the ground, and a leaf.

"Even these have knowledge and life, because the gods are in them. Freya is in the soil and trees, just as Thor is in the thunder. We know that Odin and his brothers first shaped the world, but it's reshaped every day by us. We all play our part."

It's just a rock, I thought, *just a leaf. I'm a Christian,* I reminded myself, *watched over by one God, who made the world, and the sun, the moon and stars, and who sees the blackness of our hearts, alongside the good.* And yet, I listened.

"Does the tree perceive the world as I do? I cannot know, but it and I share this world," said Helka. "Perhaps we cannot know ourselves but by imagining how other beings see us, not just men but the animals, the soil, the sea and mountains."

Helka told me more as we walked, of how her gods created the world, of how they continue to live in every part of it, from the smallest grain of sand to a drop of water. She told me also of trolls and dwarves, frost-giants and storm-giants, sea-serpents and sorcerers.

My grandmother had entertained me with tales of elves and dragons when I was little, of sacrifices to the old gods, and the old ways, as her grandmother had told them to her. But they were just stories. I know there are no giants in the woods, or any other magical creatures. I don't believe in magic, or that offering human blood will make the crops grow better. I believe, mostly, only in what my own eyes see.

However, such a teller of stories was Helka that I was almost regretful when we came, at last, to a place where the storm had brought down some oak branches.

As they selected the best in size and girth, to drag back the way we'd come, I stooped to pick a Death's Cap from where it grew on rotten bark.

No one saw me.

6

The Northmen had an appetite, and not just for food. There was plenty to go round in their eyes: for their stomachs and their cocks. They bid us cook for them and lay a feast in the banqueting hall. The surviving men they placed under watch in the barn, and the old women they sent home to sleep. It was the younger ones they wanted, to serve them ale and ensure a night of carousing.

Several had spent the afternoon carving new oars, telling each other jokes as they worked. It seemed incongruous, that laughter, considering the earlier events of the day. While I'd been in the forest, they'd lit a fire, upon which to pile the corpses. It was summer, so they couldn't be left, and the Northmen had no time or respect for our burial rituals.

Their mothers busy about their tasks, the children peeped through their fingers, watching the strangers sculpt animals from the wood we'd collected. Small hands reached out shyly to receive them.

They're skilled, these Northmen. You've only to look at their boats to see that. I wondered if one of these men had carved the dragon's head at the front of their boat, eyes bulging and teeth bared.

Helka advised me to stay in my room. My husband's body had been removed, his blood clumsily wiped away. I mopped the rest with rags, all the while listening to the roar of the hall, the squeals of the women as the Northmen laid hands upon them. Their lust was unleashed with the ale, their blood quickened beyond all reason. A table was not just for eating from but for fucking upon, and woe betide any woman in arm's reach.

The thought was terrifying, but those imaginings stirred me too. I blushed with shame, though I was alone, with no one to condemn me.

I fingered the mushroom in my pocket. How easy it would have been to place in the stew eaten by the Northmen. One Death's Cap held enough poison to kill ten men, to incapacitate all.

Yet, I had not. I'd kept it hidden. What had I been thinking? I regretted it now.

It was well into the evening when he came for me, the Northman Eirik, lurching through my door, thick-headed.

When he grasped me about the arm, I bit his wrist, but he swung me up over his shoulder as easily as I might a pheasant or a hare.

The sight of him filled me with hate, but something else too. Some strange jolt through my body, and the quickening of my pulse; fear and excitement in equal measure.

"Join us," he declared. "Drink with us."

It wasn't the bed he took me to but the hall, pausing on the way to relieve himself, pissing in the mud. He sang as the urine spattered, some song of his people. His shoulder rested awkwardly against my stomach and I wished he'd hurry up, so that he might put me down, despite my wariness for what lay ahead.

There was a cheer as we entered, and Eirik paraded me, still balanced on his shoulder. Helka rose and gave an apologetic smile, as he placed me in the chair she'd occupied. It appeared that even her influence had its limit. She whispered in her brother's ear and he nodded, before she left. So much for her friendship, if that's what we'd begun to share. She was as bad as any of them.

Eirik passed me his cup and gestured for me to drink. I'd have as soon thrown it in his face, but that I was thirsty. He looked at me as I drained it, taking the plait of my golden hair in his hand, stroking its length approvingly.

Untying the cloth that secured its end, he unravelled the strands, so that my hair hung free.

"Up now," said Eirik. "Dance for us."

He gestured, pushing beneath my elbow, but I refused to move. I was no performing minstrel, to entertain. Impatient, he lifted me about the waist, to sit where his plate had been. I slapped him: a good blow across the cheek that must have smarted. His men laughed all the harder to see it and, despite my fear, I thrilled with my own bravery. Whatever happened, I would not simply lie back and open my legs this time.

His look was stern for a moment, but reverted to indulgence, and amusement.

He called for his cup to be replenished and raised it in a toast, speaking his own language, addressing the hall at large. The words meant nothing to me, but were clearly at my expense, for his declaration raised a mighty chorus, and much stamping of feet.

Eyes glinting, he moved closer, to where I sat upon the table's edge. As he began to unbuckle his trousers, I raised my knee, giving him a crack to his tender parts. At that, there were more cheers but, this time, I knew they were for me. Jumping from the table, I grasped Eirik's cup, holding it aloft to be refilled, claiming my own victory. If I showed fearlessness, would I not earn their respect?

It was Faline who approached, my own cousin, the only child of my recently departed husband. I'd not seen her since that morning, and had noted then that she, of all the women, was most composed. She had no tears for her father and I'd wondered then if the rumours had been true, that he'd visited her, unbidden, in her bed before my body became his. I'd heard my aunt and grandmother whispering of such things, long ago.

Faline's bodice was unlaced, her breasts half exposed above, the fabric of her chemise torn. I could only guess at how the preceding hours had been spent. Her eyes were as wild as her hair, dark and dangerous. She filled my cup and then set down her jug.

She climbed, barefoot, onto the long table in the centre of the room, and began to sway her hips, all the time her eyes upon those of Eirik, who had sat back upon his chair, face red with annoyance.

Faline had never been married. She'd been promised to someone of importance, from the garrison town, under her father's instruction. Inconveniently, her betrothed had fallen fatally from his horse a week before the wedding day. Her father, my husband, had been obliged to plan anew, and no suitor wealthy or influential enough had yet been found for the match.

Yet, Faline moved like a woman well-familiar with the marriage bed. She raised her skirts as she danced, stepping ever closer, towards Eirik, until she was no more than an arm's length from where we sat.

She dipped low, bending her knees and sitting upon her haunches, her skirts swept aside to expose herself. Her bush, thick and curling, and the slash of her cunt, red, open and wet. She splayed her lips with her fingers, inviting him to look into her, and to see the salted-slickness of the men who'd entered her already.

I'd never seen inside another woman, not even in childbirth. It was the older women who helped with such things, not I.

Eirik's expression was intent. What man would not have been caught under her spell?

He released himself, letting his trousers drop to the floor, displaying his cock, fully erect, glistening at the tip. It matched the size of him: giant in stature, and giant of pike. No doubt, he was proud of it, for he gave a thrust into the air, which raised another cheer from the men around us. There was much banging on the table, and the serving girls were beckoned to refill cups swigged dry.

Eirik cleared the table all before him and invited Faline to approach, one hand already on his member, stroking it in readiness.

I shrank back, pushing my chair as far from them as I could, appalled at the brazenness of her. As she leaned in, she glared at me and I realized it was a look of triumph, as if I were her rival, and she had won a victory over me.

I had known always of her dislike, her jealousy of the attention shown to me. As a child, she'd often run to join us, in the forest, wishing to share our freedom. She'd not been welcomed. She was the chieftain's daughter, and none wished to incur his displeasure. They'd sent her back, told her to attend to her spinning wheel and loom.

Now, she was free, or perhaps she thought herself so. Free to take attention where I had spurned it.

As Eirik held her waist, she wrapped her legs about him. He pulled her forward, so that her buttocks rested on the edge.

Once more, I found myself looking where I could have turned away my gaze. I watched as the Northman pushed his ruddy cock into her, in one swift motion. She cried out, in pain I thought, jolted by the piercing of him. Then, he withdrew slowly, and I could not keep my eyes from it, veined purple, and slick, emerging from between Faline's legs.

He plunged again, and wrapped his arms all the tighter about her, holding her fast to his groin. She shrieked and moaned at the taking of him to the hilt, but, whatever discomfort she endured, it appeared tempered by her pleasure.

As she arched her back, her breasts were revealed in all their fullness from the confine of her bodice. Eirik let out a wolf howl, and grinned to the room, as if in performance to those watching. He dipped her further as he gave his next thrust, her breasts shaking with the force of him. His mouth lowered to her flesh, opening wide about her nipple, taking it first between his lips, and then his teeth, tugging at it, as he made three rapid thrusts, one upon the next.

Faline cried out once more, her hair falling behind her, her throat exposed.

Eirik laughed, the sound coming deep from his chest, and closed his lips once more to her nipple, rubbing the roughness of his beard upon skin I knew to be tender.

Faline took his head in her hands and held him there, like a babe suckling at her breast, her fingers knitted through his long locks.

Her pelvis, angled upwards, ground against his, as if she were in torment, and only his fucking of her, this animal fucking, watched by every Northman present, would assuage her.

Eirik surveyed the room, making eye-contact with the men about him, and then began in earnest, his buttocks clenching and relaxing as he waged war between Faline's legs.

The cheers were deafening as he laboured, faster now, his breath catching. He held her to him, impaling her, letting her feel the full hammer of his cock.

Her cries had become a keening wail, punctuated by gasps, as of a creature caught in a trap, yet with no desire to escape. Her hands clasped at the great muscles of his arms, to steady herself.

Eirik gave a roar with his final thrust, met with a squeal from Faline, who fell back, limp upon the table, as he let her go.

He threw back his head and gave another roar, as he slid out of her. From the floor he grasped a weapon and raised it full about his head, uttering a war cry, which the room took up, chanting with him as he punched the air with that great axe.

It was only then that he turned to look at me, as if he'd forgotten I was there. I felt horror, wondering if he'd bring the blade in one swift motion upon my head, for the entertainment of it, or in some fit of fury. I could not read the expression on his face. It was lust-demented, as if some madness had overtaken him.

The look upon my own must have amused him, for he threw back his head and let out his wolf howl again, and laughed.

Faline lay still upon the table, panting from her exertion and spent. An ocean had flooded over her, and she had been no more able to fight it than a pebble may stand against the crashing waves of the tide.

7

Eirik picked up his cup and gulped down its contents, wiping his mouth with the back of his sleeve.

His cock had retreated a little from its full stature, but remained broad in girth, the eye of it pointed now at me. He grasped the base, where the golden hair met the shaft and tugged it twice, in encouragement.

He looked at me, and the room grew quieter. Without looking, I knew that all gazes were upon us, upon me.

"In your mouth."

Eirik's accent was thick, his vowels longer than Helka's, but there was no denying the meaning.

He stepped closer, so that the tip of his cock rested almost upon my lips. I was repelled, and yet there was warmth between my legs at the thought of him inside me, in my mouth, and in my cunt.

He leant forward, nudging my bottom lip, but moving no further, waiting. I opened my mouth a little, darted out my tongue to lick the moisture resting there.

It was all the encouragement he needed. I closed my eyes as the smooth, wet head entered. He moved back and forth, gently, as if testing how far he might go.

I braced myself, expecting his hand upon the back of my head and his cock shoved hard into my throat. What would he care if I choked, if I couldn't breathe?

But he did not.

He let out another long, resonant howl, like a wolf baying to the moon, which the room took up, and he withdrew.

As I opened my eyes, I saw that he was drawing up his trousers.

He took my hand, and Faline's in the other, and led us past the jeering, cheering, cavorting crowd. His men, spurred on by Eirik's performance, had begun their sport anew, grasping the serving girls about the hips, raising skirts, bending them to receive what was coming to them.

I tried to tug my hand away but his grasp was strong. *I'm not your trollop,* I thought. *I'm not here for your pleasure.*

With each step, my heart beat faster.

8

Outside, the moon was high, illuminating dark clouds. There was the unmistakable roll of thunder approaching; in the distance, small flashes of light.

From one of the other huts, there was a baby's wail. Its mother, I supposed, was providing service to the Northmen. Some other's arms would give comfort: those of a woman too old to be of interest to men's lust.

My room was as it ever was, the bed piled comfortably with furs, some scattered on the floor. Eirik closed the door behind us and bolted it down.

The embers of the fire had dipped low. I bent to rekindle them, blowing gently beneath, coaxing with twigs and straw.

My hands trembled as I worked, knowing what surely awaited me. I knew that I should wish for it to be over quickly, that I should think only of enduring, but a flame was licking inside me as surely as those growing in the hearth.

Although we could hear the Northmen's revelry, the room seemed quiet, but for the crack of the fire.

We stood, Faline and I, and he looked at us, dark and fair, as he began to shed his clothes: furred jerkin, and woven leather vest, his shirt.

I saw the power of his body. His head almost touching the cross beam of the ceiling, his shoulders double the width of most men. His abdomen was hard, muscled. Most striking of all, his upper body was thick with dark blue-green patterns, interlocking, covering all his arms, as if he wore sleeves upon his skin. Designs stretched across his upper chest, and continued up his neck.

I'd never seen such a thing, such a man.

He smiled to see me look, and his cock gave a small leap. When he laughed, it was not as before, to command the approval of a crowd, but because the amusement was his.

Faline wasted no time. With a toss of her head, she stripped herself and climbed into my bed, pulling the soft furs to her neck. There was malice and mischief in her defiance.

Outside, the thunder rolled closer and, when Eirik spoke, it was as if his voice were a continuance of its resonance.

"Here."

I was drawn to the strength of him, to the force of his body and the power that I knew was his.

Once close enough, his fingers pulled at the laces of my costume, dexterous, despite their size. One by one, the garments dropped, or were pulled over my head.

I shivered in my nakedness, feeling the touch of his eyes upon me, their roaming of my skin, and the nearness of his body.

My husband had been a perfunctory lover, interested only in his own satisfaction, and as likely as not to give me a clout about the head as he entered me. Moreover, his bedding was a quick matter, over almost as soon as it had begun.

My grandmother had told me that I must be patient. Love would grow with time and, with it, pleasure, but it had not.

I'd loved a dog we kept from a puppy, and the lambs I'd raised one spring, when their mother had abandoned them. I'd felt more for those animals than I had for any man.

I'd heard the girls talk of the boys they liked best: the urgency of their kisses, of their own responding desire. I'd felt nothing similar for a man: not for my husband most certainly.

As for this Northman, his arrogance was insufferable. Yet, I burned for him.

He knelt, pressing his mouth first to one breast and then the other, taking not only my nipple but the whole orb into his mouth. His warm tongue worked with his teeth, to pull and tease, sending a spasm through my cunt. His hands grasped my buttocks and I felt a rush of desire. His warriors had raped and killed and stolen, and yet I could think only of my need to feel him inside me.

And then he was lifting me in his arms, to lay me upon the bed, pushing my legs apart. His cock loomed above, and his balls, large and heavy. The muscles of my sex contracted in anticipation.

I'd quite forgotten about Faline, but felt now her hands upon my shoulders, pulling me further up the bed. I struggled, indignant, but she pinned me at the upper arms, placing her weight upon me.

Faline's legs were open behind my head, so that I smelt the fish-sourness of her.

She exchanged a look with Eirik, one of knowing, of encouragement. Whether I liked it or not, she was to be the third in my bed and take her share.

I'd expected Eirik to push himself into me, to begin the fucking he must intend. I knew the sex act well enough. Instead, he raised my hips to his waiting mouth.

I'd never felt a man's tongue inside me. I would have twisted away, but that he held me tight. His laughter hummed against my sex, and then he ran his tongue through my slit, finding the nub I would press when I lay quietly at night.

I sighed in longing, wrapping my legs about his head, drawing him down further. His tongue gave me more pleasure than my husband's member had ever done.

What a strange thing for a man to do, I thought. *For what enjoyment is there in this for him?*

But enjoyment there must have been, for his mouth ate me as ravenously as the wolf will take a goose, feathers and all. And I, the goose, was only too willing to be devoured.

When he raised his face, I caught a glimpse of something darker: the desire to pursue his lust.

Keeping my hips raised to him, he aligned his cock to my gaping wetness, holding me firm beneath my buttocks. I felt the first nudge of his swollen head, and then he entered, as smooth and easy as a knife through freshly set butter.

I looked up and saw Faline watching Eirik, watching the long thrusts, each of which brought a responding moan from me, from the new voice which was growing inside, stoked by the fuel of this man's body.

She glanced down, into my face, and her expression seemed both gleeful, and filled with scorn: delighted to see me reduced, taken, constricted, I thought, yet resentful of my elevation into pleasure.

A crack of lightning broke directly overhead, so bright that it lit through the gap around the door. A deep, resonant rumble of thunder filled the room.

"Thor is watching us," gasped Eirik. "Beating his hammer across the heavens for all to hear."

He sank his cock into me once more.

"Hear Thor! He approves of our union."

I opened to the length of him, his girth stretching me sweetly as it slid deep. His thrusts rolled into me, swivelling and grinding upwards, his cock pressing where I most desired it. His abdomen flexed with each stroke, and then he was bellowing, sending his cock on a final thrust of pulsing victory, filling me with his seed.

My voice began to rise, as I approached a place of searing pain and pleasure. I could not retreat from the warmth travelling through my bones, radiating through my skin. And then, I was no longer in the room but carried from my body, seeing white light.

His head thrown back, Eirik gave a triple wolf howl and began to laugh.

I lay panting, light-headed, the world having been born anew.

9

I slept well, rising in the early hours to pass water, and to drink. Returning to the bed, I looked down upon them; Eirik and Faline, her dark head tucked under his arm, her hair tumbled across his chest. In repose, she looked younger, her face without its customary frown. And both so peaceful, as if our passions had been but a dream.

I'd rested as Faline took her turn, coaxing Eirik back to stiffness with her mouth and hands. She'd ridden him to her own wail of abandon. His moans had spurred her on, until she was shouting her delight and clenching her buttocks down upon him. I could read the rhythms of her convulsions.

I'd seen her in many moods, from fury to contempt, jealousy and irritation, but this side of her, her sexual nature, was unfamiliar to me. I wondered if my own expression of ecstasy had been the same.

Eirik had then lain quiet between us, facing me, with Faline curled into his back. I'd thrilled to touch his chest and the taut muscles of his stomach. I'd stroked the hair of his groin and fastened my hand about the base of his shaft, feeling it grow again in my hand, so thick that my fingers could barely encompass it.

I'd moved my leg across his, opening myself to him again, slick with his semen and my desire, touching the fat head of him to my ready lips. I'd rubbed my ache upon his length, claiming my own pleasure, my body awakened to its knowledge of sexual desire, of fulfilment.

His hand had found my breast, cupping it to his mouth, suckling as I rocked my hips. Each gentle bite and squeeze of his tongue had brought a returning clutch from inside me, from the soft passage encasing him.

I'd fought to control my breath, and heard the same raggedness in his.

Meanwhile, Faline had looked at me over Eirik's shoulder, her eyes glinting darkly. Her hands had appeared to work upon his buttocks, kneading, stroking. I fancied she placed her fingers between his cheeks as he moved within me. She'd bitten her lip to hear him gasp, and had pushed against him all the harder.

It was chill to stand without clothing, the fire having long extinguished. I returned to the warmth of their bodies, the smell of sex strong beneath the furs.

My hand stretched out to touch Eirik's body once more.

10

When I woke, it was Helka who stood looking down at me. Faline and Eirik has risen. I was alone in the bed.

She touched my shoulder.

"You are well?" she asked, her brow furrowed in concern. "No pain?"

Even in the first days of being wedded to my husband I'd not, in a single day, had such a volume of fucking. There was a dull ache between my legs, but it was more discomfort than pain. When the three Northmen had taken me, I'd tried to relax my body. I'd learnt that well enough during my marriage. To resist, to be fearful of pain, was most likely to cause it.

I thought back to Eirik: his mouth, his cock. I'd not known that I could enjoy the act as well as any man. I was under no illusion of love. It was Eirik's body that had given me pleasure, nothing else. No doubt he'd had many women, and would be between someone else's legs tonight.

Helka sat down beside me.

"I told him not to hurt you," she said.

I remembered her whispering in his ear. Her apologetic smile. I shrugged and looked away. I was angry with her.

"What about the other women. Go and speak to them."

She sighed.

"Men are men. They like their sport. I cannot change them."

I noticed then that she'd brought forward the washing barrel, and that the fire was lit.

"The water's hot," she said.

My body welcomed the warmth. I lent back, letting it cover my shoulders. Helka sat upon a rug, attempting to engage me in conversation.

Despite her apparent kindness, I no longer felt that I could trust Helka. Whatever pleasure I'd had from her brother, it was through little action of hers, that I could see. Her men behaved no better than animals, and she did nothing to stop them.

"How many other villages have you plundered?" I asked. "And how many have you killed? How many women taken against their wish? Will you put us in your boats when you leave, to be your slaves?"

I knew that the Northmen would take whatever they wanted once their sails were mended.

Helka lowered her eyes, giving no response.

"I won't come with you." I barked the words. "I won't be someone's slave."

Helka looked up. "What if you belonged to Eirik?"

I glowered.

"To belong to him is not nothing," she continued. "He's…" she sought the right word. "He's respected. A warrior. He can defeat any man. With him, you would have a place. You would not be nothing. You would be his bed companion, but more. You would have his children."

"And how many bed companions does he have?" I flared. "I'm surprised there's room for another. Are all your men the same? My husband's blood stains the floor of our bedchamber, and I cannot shed a tear for it, but even he never brought another woman into our marriage bed while it remained warm from my body."

"It is not men's nature to love only one," said Helka. "You know that, I'm sure… We, women, are obliged to be more steadfast, unless our husbands sanction us to behave otherwise."

Her face was impassive, while my own burned with shame and resentment.

"Men are beasts. All they know is violence and fucking," I retorted.

I dropped my head to my knees. If Eirik were to enter now and lift me from the water, were he to carry me back to the bed and ease himself between my legs, would I protest? Or would I wrap my arms about him, and draw him down to enter me, eager to lose myself in the heat of him again?

These men, these Northmen, were murderers, rapists, slavers. They took what they wanted. How many children had they fathered in their wake? I hated that some part of me was of their blood, that my true father had been like the men who killed my husband, like the three who forced me to take their cocks.

I looked up at Helka, into that face that was the mirror of my own.

"You see my hair?" I said. "Where do you think this hair comes from? Do you see my eyes?"

She nodded. "I knew from the first moment I saw you. Eirik sees that you're one of us. You belong with us."

Bitterness flooded me. "I don't want to belong to anyone, not even the mighty Eirik!"

My head was hot with fury as I began to sob. "I was born from violence, from a man taking my mother by force, raping her, even as others murdered the man I should have called 'father'. I should avenge them both by killing every one of you."

"Living in the past won't help you." Helka's voice was calm, soothing me as she might a child in a tantrum.

She took a cloth, wringing water over my shoulders.

"How can I forget the past? There are too many wrongs there," I said, through my weeping.

"You're not going in that direction," urged Helka. "Better to look at what's ahead of you, where your feet still have the chance to step."

I sniffed, wiping my eyes against my arm. "Eirik will grow tired of me," I mumbled. I knew enough about men. "He wants me because I'm a curiosity. He has no love for me. What am I to him? Another woman to fuck."

Helka was attempting to find the words she needed. "We judge by what we see, but there's more to the world. We cannot know the secrets of every heart."

Helka's face became more serious. "You have more than Viking blood; you have a Viking soul. This is where your bravery comes from."

My eyes narrowed. What did she know of whether I was brave or not?

"I saw you last night, in the hall," Helka said. "I was in the shadows, but I watched. I would not have let harm come to you."

I soaked a rag, watching the water trickle out.

"I don't know what I am," I sighed. "I'm neither hare nor rabbit."

Helka gave a brief smile.

"And I don't know where I belong. Not here, perhaps. I've never belonged."

"You feel restless," prompted Helka.

"Yes. Sometimes, I feel as if I'm so full of chaos and longing for something I can't name that I'll burst apart."

Helka leaned forward.

"This is what it is to be human. Our scream came before our speech, and it's still inside us."

She placed her hand on mine, stopping my fidgeting with the rag.

"Let me tell you one of our stories. At the centre of all things, is a tree, called Yggdrasil. It holds all that we know, and much that we do not, in its branches. It draws its water from a well and, inside, live three wise women. They carve into the tree our..." she paused, seeking the word.

"Our destinies?" I suggested. "What will happen tomorrow, and the next day?"

"Yes, our destinies."

I shook my head.

"If that were true we'd have no power to control our lives. I don't believe that."

She drew the pattern of a web on my palm.

"Life is like a spider's weaving."

She pinched her fingers, as if plucking a strand of the web.

"If we do this, the entire web trembles. Change one thing and all may change. The women carve our destiny, but destiny can be changed."

I shrugged.

"It's an interesting story, but it's not true. I don't believe in this tree, or the three women."

Helka closed my palm.

"The stories show who my people are. They help us remember that we all struggle, and we all desire. We fight for what matters to us."

I moved away from her, submerging my shoulders under the water again.

"I don't know if anything does matter to me."

It sounded petulant, I knew.

"I love my grandmother," I admitted, "But I don't know what I want, or what's worth struggling for."

Helka smiled. "It takes time to know. Our feelings change quickly, like the movement of clouds across the sun. But there will always be the sun, the sky. Perhaps in nature, you find your resilience."

This made sense to me. I felt most myself when I was in the forest, or swimming in the lake. I wanted to be free but I also wanted to know who I was. I came closest to finding that when I was outside.

I'd also felt most myself when Eirik had lain with me. I'd become more, in fact. I'd become part of him, feeling his strength inside me. It had been as if I was breathing with his lungs.

Helka interrupted my musing. "I'm making a decision today. We'll take no one from your village unless they wish to come, and we'll harm no one. We ask only that you continue to mend our sails. As soon as we can, we'll leave."

I'd just stepped from the bath when the door opened. Eirik entered and something caught in my throat, though it appeared that he'd come for Helka rather than for me. He paced straight to her, speaking rapidly in their Northern tongue.

Helka nodded and turned to me.

"There are men coming, on horses. We'll fight."

She paused at the door, looking back.

"Remember what I said."

Eirik noticed me then, standing naked, my skin risen in gooseflesh.

Two axes hung from his belt. A larger one was strapped to his back.

I waited for him to smile, in his lazy way. Instead, his expression was grim, intense.

In one swift motion, he was upon me, raising me into his arms. He grasped me under the buttocks and my legs wound about his back. With my body forced against his armour, he kissed me, my nipples rubbing on the knotted leather. I took his tongue into my mouth, wishing to devour him, as he was devouring me, with fierceness. A violent pang blazed in my cunt. He found the fur wet between my legs and pushed his fingers inside.

When our lips parted, I saw that his eyes were like the sky, filled with a storm waiting to break.

His men were calling him. He had to go. There was no time for consummation, though his cock stood monstrous. He returned my feet to the floor, where I found that I almost lacked the strength to stand.

He spoke hurriedly.

"I do not fear death. If I die, my axe will be in my hand, and I shall join Odin. I shall stand by his side when the time of Ragnarok comes. I hope that day is not today, for I wish to return to you, and I shall show you what it is to be loved by a Northman."

11

The village seemed strangely quiet as people crept from their homes, subdued, in sorrow and in shock. We who remained were a pitiful sight. Our strongest men had been cut down. We were mostly women, children, the elderly. The eyes of the girls who had been in the hall the evening before were downcast, their faces pale. Some limped, sore between their legs, I supposed.

Grindan's mother found a single shoe and cradled what had once been her husband's. Grindan comforted her, let her weep.

I went first to find my grandmother, still in her bed. Each time I'd brought her food and drink, I'd shared little, though she heard much.

Stroking my face, I could see her attempting to read the anxiety there, to surmise its cause.

"I'm well," I reassured her. "There's naught to trouble for."

She looked at me intently.

"There's something new in your expression, Elswyth. In your eyes."

I offered her some broth on a spoon, but she waved it away.

"There's a softness in you. As if you're in love."

I looked away, hardly knowing what to say. I wasn't ready to lay claim to that word for a man I'd spent mere hours with. A man into whose sleeping mouth I might have pushed a piece of Death's Cap mushroom. It lay still in my pocket.

Her brow furrowed and she shifted her position in the bed, wincing. Her legs had grown much worse of late.

Despite her suffering, she smiled.

"That look should have been there a long time ago."

My cheeks reddened a little.

"Be careful," she urged, placing her hand on mine.

"This change in you is not for love of your husband, is it?"

I hadn't told her.

Her nose, old as it was, had recognized the smell of burning flesh the day before, but she was unaware that our chieftain, my husband, had been among those corpses assigned to fire.

There was nothing now but charred bones, and little to distinguish between them.

"No, not for him," I said. "But, don't worry for me. I'll take care."

She lay back against her pillow, wearied from talking.

"Rub some flaxseed oil into my knees before you go Elswyth. And put a few drops of white willow tincture on my tongue. It eases the pain."

She took my hand. "I know you'll be cautious but, remember, there's a time for taking risks too."

12

The sound of metal upon metal reached us on the wind, the shouts of battle, and the wails of the wounded, of the dying.

The garrison, it appeared, having received news of a Viking landing, had sent its soldiers. Our own children, playing on the hill above the meadow, had seen them from some distance, and run back to shout of men on horseback. There was irony in that, those children having warned the very warriors who killed their fathers.

People had begun the slow resumption of household chores.

I approached those who'd been working on the sails, urged them to pick up their needles once more.

"Whore!" one muttered, spitting on my dress.

They turned their backs.

There was little I could say in my defence. Had I not, in the end, welcomed Eirik as my lover? Nevertheless, in my heart, I knew that it was not my recent behavior that brought their castigation. They had always sensed my difference, and wished to condemn me for it.

Faline kept her distance, her face troubled, as I knew mine to be. For the same reason? I couldn't have said. What did I wish? The death of the Northmen? It would be justice.

Yet I did not.

I could not wish harm to Eirik or to Helka. She too, shield in hand, had joined the battle cry, running through the long grasses of the meadow. I wondered what the wise women inside Helka's tree had carved for her fate, for that of her men, for Eirik.

Two of the children I sent to resume their place of watching, upon the hill, to return with news as soon as they were able.

I went to see the hens, but there were few eggs to collect, most of the chickens having been plucked and eaten.

The wind dropped as the sun rose higher, the cries drifting to us growing quieter.

I searched my feelings, and I could not deny that my thoughts were all of Eirik. His kiss remained inside me. I withdrew and lay upon my bed, seeking out the smell of him.

I could not help myself. I touched my breasts, where his mouth had been, and then between my legs. If he came to me now, I would not resist, even were he to stretch me out on the long table of the hall, and fuck me before every Northman's eyes. I would do whatever he wished. And I would do so as willingly as a new flower, opening to the sun.

13

The children's shouts brought me from my reverie. The Northmen had returned, bloodied and mud-spattered, skin split, eyes glazed in pain, clutching their wounds. There were none unscathed.

Eirik was not among them.

I ran from one to the next, repeating his name, my voice rising in fear, and then I saw Helka, her face weary.

"Eirik?" I asked.

"Still in the meadow."

I heard my wail as if it came from another's throat.

"No, Elswyth," she urged. "He's not in Valhalla."

And then I saw him, staggering under the weight of two men, carrying one upon each shoulder. Behind him, others too bore the bodies of those severely wounded, and dead.

His appearance was wretched, his face blood-soaked, one eye swollen red, already closing. He lay down the men he carried as tenderly as a mother might place her child in its cot.

I held back as he leant over them, speaking his farewell to the friends he'd lost, touching his hand to their heart, and their forehead. Despite their wounds, their faces were in repose. No further suffering for them.

Others were not so lucky. Helka asked for help in washing injuries and for cloth to bind them.

I wanted only to run to Eirik's side, to tell him that I was glad he lived, that his living had become as important at my own, but I knew also that I must aid Helka. Whatever the faults of these Northmen, they were of Eirik's blood — and my own.

"We should apply a garlic poultice before we wrap the wounds," I told her. "And smear a salve of calendula and chamomile, to help healing."

Clasping me to her, she nodded her thanks. She seemed unscathed, but for heavy grazing to her cheek. She'd feel the worst of it tomorrow.

We stood together, directing the children to fetch beer, for washing wounds, as well as for drinking. We added drops of valerian to each pitcher, to bring drowsiness to the men upon whom we worked. Needles which had mended sails were now scalded in hot water to sew flesh.

Our women, angry as they were, did their part. Perhaps there is something in seeing a man suffer that pulls at the heart of any woman, no matter the circumstance. In his face, she sees that of those she loves, and her instinct to alleviate pain outweighs her desire to inflict it.

Women instinctively seek to nurture, soothe and comfort. We are not the destroyers of this world. Our kinder nature wins out. Our strength becomes apparent when we have no other choice but to be strong.

At last, I applied honey and lavender oil to Helka's face. It would help the skin grow, and prevent too much scarring.

I hadn't spoken to Eirik, nor seen him for some hours, but briefly. He sat with his men, visiting each in turn, inspecting their wounds, speaking his own words to settle or cheer. I found him beside a man for whom I knew there was no hope. His stomach had been opened by a blade, too widely to be stitched. We'd wrapped it tightly, and given him a strong dose of Valerian. When he slept, he would not wake. Already, his eyes were heavy. He would soon let go.

"Come," I told Eirik.

In my room, I'd filled a bath for him, to ease his troubled mind, as well as his body. He had lost almost a third of his men in the battle. Many of the rest had suffered injury. They'd fought until the garrison horsemen were too few in number to continue. A handful had galloped off, no doubt to alert the fort further up the coast. In all likelihood, more would come soon.

There was no question. Eirik and his men would need to depart before first light.

I helped him undress, standing on a stool to lift off the heavy leather tunic. I was relieved to find that his own wounds were superficial, though I suspected that his ribs were bruised. He guarded them as we removed each piece of clothing.

A dark, crusted stain ringed his neck, though he had wiped most of the blood from his face. I tried not to think of the man it had come from.

I looked again at his body, covered in its patterns, dark green and blue-black. Those two sleeves, I noticed, were formed of the branches of knotted trees. Over one shoulder sat the head of a snake, its body extending down his back. Except that it did not look like any serpent I knew. Its scaled body curved down his spine, ending in a design of strange arrows through his buttocks.

He stepped into the water, one foot gingerly, then the other. I'd heated the water more than usual.

"That is Jörmungandr," said Eirik, seeing my perusal of the snake. "Child of the god Loki, sibling to the death-goddess Hel, and the wolf, Fenrir. Thor is destined to fight the great serpent, which stirs beneath the sea, ringing the world."

"But this snake is unfurled."

"It is Jörmungandr at the end of days, when it lets go its tail from its mouth, and Ragnarök begins."

I could not help but shiver. The solemnity of his voice, his belief in this story, frightened me.

"Until then, I fear not any man, for the gods within me are strong," said Eirik. "Although it was a man that gave me this battering today, and I do not thank him for it!"

I took a bar of soapwort, dipping it into the water, and rubbing it between my hands to make a lather.

I thought then of Valhalla, as I'd heard Helka mention. It was their name for Heaven, I supposed, as the monks had told us we should go to, if we were good and honest, and honoured God's commandments.

"And where will you go when you die?"

"The hall of the fallen," he replied, "Where Odin houses the warrior dead, who have shown their courage."

Eirik spoke slowly, pausing to gather the right words.

"The roof is golden-bright, made of shields, with spears for rafters. Its gates are guarded by wolves, and eagles fly above."

His eyes flickered brightly as he spoke. It was a story I imagined him having heard from the youngest age. I wondered how old he'd been when an axe had first been put into his hand and he'd been told to make himself worthy of joining Odin.

"All day long, they fight one another and, every evening, their wounds are healed, and they feast, served the finest food and drink, by beautiful Valkyrjur maidens."

"Of course," I interjected, rubbing at the grime upon his back. "There must be beautiful maidens."

He narrowed his eyes at me, before deciding to accept my banter.

"And are these maidens dark in looks or fair?"

I couldn't help but ask, although I wasn't sure I was ready to hear his answer.

"Both, of course," he replied, giving a lascivious grin. "For do not men wish variety in all things? You wouldn't have me choose between boar and deer? My mouth desires all flavours of meat."

I refused to comment. It was not a jest in which I felt able to encourage him.

Instead, I turned the course of our conversation back to what was serious.

"You don't wish to die?" I asked.

"We all die," he said. "Even children know this."

I nodded.

"Friends die, you shall die, and I too. Only our reputation remains," Eirik continued. "I will have men sing of me after my death."

His jaw seemed to set harder at that thought.

"We have a poem we call *Hávamál*."

"Tell me," I said. "I want to hear it." And I did.

Like Helka, Eirik was telling me of things I'd never heard. There was a strange thrill in knowing that there was still so much to learn about the world. I knew a lot — about hunting, and fishing, about plants, and medicines — but there was more.

"It says: *Wealth will pass, men will pass, you too, will pass. One thing alone will never pass: the fame of one who has earned it.*"

"And what of this one," I asked, indicating three horns interlinked on his arm.

"Those are Odin's, who makes men helpless, or gives his fierceness in battle."

I put my hand to the centre of his chest, where there was a strange circle of pointed arrows.

He raised his hand to meet mine, held it there, against his skin. I could feel the beat of his blood beneath, and the warmth of him. A familiar breathlessness began to grow in me.

"This is Aegishjalmur, which brings fear to our enemies."

His skin was a living cloak of his beliefs, giving him power. He related these things that meant so much and, as he looked into my eyes, I could see that he had power over me. His body radiated power. There was nothing I would not do for him.

"These pictures show us who we are, and where we come from," said Eirik, "Our roots, present and past."

I hesitated, scooping water into his hair. I was ashamed but I needed to ask.

"What about the future?"

At that, he let out a true laugh, and shook his finger at me.

"Only the gods know that."

I permitted myself a returning smile, dabbing the remaining blood from his face. I worked tenderly, pressing the cloth into the creases, rinsing through his beard.

I touched the old scar, which ran through his cheek, from his ear full to his chin.

"Long ago," he murmured, seeing a cloud pass over my face.

He took my palm and kissed it.

When he looked at me again, his eyes held that intensity I knew well.

I let my tunic and belt fall, stepping from them, and into the bath.

He guided my hand, still slick with suds, to his cock and, as I climbed across his lap, my cunt found him. He slid inside me as an eel will enter its pit, finding its true home, its place of safety.

I pulled his hair from his face, holding it behind as I lowered my mouth to his, meeting his lips, soft and yielding. He tasted of the honey the children had taken to the Northmen, spooning it into their mouths, squealing in half-pretended fear as those grizzled warriors had opened wide for more.

I rocked against him, my Eirik, now subdued, my breasts brushing his chest as I rose and fell, nipples taut with desire. His hands rested lightly upon my hips, his eyes taking in the undulations of my body.

It was I who kissed him, I who chose the rhythm of our coupling. My voice rose and tumbled in gasps and moans, pleasure coursing through me, not once, but in repeating, spiralling ripples, one crashing into the next, like waves building and retreating on the shore.

14

The Northmen took nothing more from us, asking only for food for the journey, and to fill their flasks with weak ale. Gudmund, Hagen, Ivar, Jerrik, Olaf, Sigurd. I knew their names now.

I sat with my grandmother, holding her hand, whispering to her of all that had happened. Her eyes grew wide, but she did not interrupt me.

How could I leave her, when I knew that she would not be long in this world? If I left, I would never see her again. I knew our village women would care for her; she was respected in a way that I could never be. My heart ached, however, at making my farewell, and I was suffused with shame at forgoing my duty to her.

Her tears came, but she insisted that I was to find my happiness with her blessing, wherever that lay.

"You're a good girl, Elswyth. He'll be fortunate to have you. And God will keep you safe, wherever you go."

I wondered if she were right, if God would accompany me, going as I was to a people who didn't even believe in him.

Helka came to find me, seeking out my answer. I reiterated that I would be no slave. If I returned with them, it would be of my own free will.

"I'll be your sister. You'll never be alone." Her promise warmed me. However, I was irked at her next declaration. "I've only to look into your eyes to know your heart's decision."

It seemed that I was unable to hide my feelings. Although I knew her to be right, it provoked me to hear her speak as if the choice had already been made.

"And what if I choose to follow my head," I answered, "I grew up here. These are the people I know, not yours." I only half-believed it. I'd never felt at ease here. I'd always been searching for something.

"Just as day follows night, and spring follows winter, our lives move from one state to another, sweeping away what is old, what has been outgrown," said Helka.

"And what do you see, when you look at me?" I ventured.

"You are water," said Helka. "You may take any form you desire. You can be the rain, or the lake, or the sea, or you may be water in a cup, if you wish it so."

I waited, in the pre-dawn darkness, by the boats, watching them make ready by the thin moon. True to their word, no woman had been molested since their return, and none was now taken against her will. Only one other joined me. Faline stood, refusing to meet my gaze, her eyes on the men loading the vessel. Whether she was there for Eirik I couldn't say. Perhaps some other man had taken her fancy. There were many who were handsome, and strong, many who would make fine husbands. Faline was a beauty. She would find her way.

I watched her splash through the water, before being pulled up, into the belly of the dragon boat.

The dawn was not far off when Eirik came to me. My feet had not yet committed to whatever lay ahead.

He spoke with the same seriousness as he had in explaining the markings on his body.

"My name, my blood, my honour, I will give to my children, and all those who come after. Just as I have inherited these things from my father, and those before him."

He took my hands, and I knew he spoke as honestly as he was able.

"Elswyth, I have lain with many women, and will lay with many more, but I ask you to keep my bed every night, to give me your body, for the bearing of my children."

It could not be said that I would leave without knowing my true position.

"Only for the bearing of children?" I asked, raising my chin stiffly.

"For that, and for my pleasure."

His hands crept about my waist.

"And I shall give you great pleasure in return."

He gathered me to him, enfolding me. In his arms, I felt that physical tug, the compulsion I was unable to ignore, at his touch, at the smell of him.

He carried me, that I should stay dry.

Wind filled the sails, and we were far away by the time the sun was full over the horizon.

I wondered what lay ahead, what adventure. I had already discovered so much.

EPILOGUE

We sailed through the day but, that night, the wind dropped and the men took up the oars. I slept, to the dip and sweep of wood through water.

I dreamt that I was running through a forest, running to escape some malevolent force, Eirik beside me. We ran until the trees opened, and we stood beside one another, looking down into a precipice.

In fear, I turned, to see a great wolf, black, with eyes blazing.

All at once, I was alone, and the beast stood over me, lowering its teeth, to close upon my throat.

VIKING
WOLF

EMMANUELLE DE MAUPASSANT

I

959 AD

With the midsummer sun dipping to the last portion of the sky, twenty men took the oars and pulled against the current.

We'd been three days on the open sea, travelling to Svolvaen. Some places on the rowing benches were now empty, for several of Eirik's men had fallen in the skirmish with the troops garrisoned near our village. As the ship battled fierce winds and my stomach heaved with the churning of the waves, I wondered if I'd made a grave error in leaving all that I knew to join these Norsemen. My thoughts turned repeatedly to my ailing grandmother, lying weak in her bed, left in the care of our neighbours. My decision had been selfish, borne of yearning for adventure and the chance to start anew, of my knowledge of kinship with these warrior men; borne, too, of my desire for Eirik, who'd pulled me into the protection of his hard-muscled body as the ship plunged across the vast sea.

At last, we sighted the mountains of the north. Reaching the calmer waters of their coast, sailing between scattered islands, the men's eyes raked the maze of inlets, looking for their own.

Gulls and gannets whirled above, cormorants and kittiwakes, as we followed the narrow channel of the *fjord*, as Eirik called it, past cliffs on either side, rising steep, pocketed with caves.

The crew's elation was plain to see and I shared in it, for I was now part of this world, although all in it would be new to me.

The other ships of the raiding party had returned some days before, survivors of the storm that had brought Eirik and his men to our coastline of Northumbria and the rocky beach on which my former village had nestled.

His people had been keeping look-out, horns blowing through the still dusk of the evening as we approached the landing piers.

What a press of bodies there was: comradery between men, as friends slapped and hugged one another, and received kisses from their wives, embraces from mothers, daughters and sisters. I no longer thought of those men as murderers, but as my kin. They'd shed blood, but I now knew my blood was also theirs. I recognized some part of their brutality as my own, for I was not as other women in the village in which I'd lived all my life. I was half-Viking: tall and golden haired, as the women of Svolvaen mostly were, and born of a wilder spirit.

Amidst the jumble of voices and the scramble of the crowd, Faline and I received little regard. We were no more than possessions, of Eirik's concern alone; curiosities, eyed briefly, then ignored. Whatever welcome I'd hoped for in my heart, whatever foolishness, I pressed it down and bit my tongue against disappointment. To earn my place would take time.

Eirik's sister, Helka, guided us away from the crowd, scanning for one who wasn't there: one who hadn't deigned to push among the common throng, who'd waited, instead, for Eirik to come to him.

We climbed the slope rising from the small harbour, past modest dwellings which appeared little different from those of my own village. The light had almost gone as we approached the summit of the hill, where stood a longhouse of great size, turf-covered upon low walls of stone. A sentry guarded either side of its door, whom Eirik greeted with clasped hands before we stepped inside.

The vaulted ceiling rose higher than that of the home I'd not long ago shared with my husband. The ribs reached up into the darkness, above a central fire pit, whose flames leapt, casting the farther reaches of the hall in shadow. The air was thick with the smell of stew, a great cauldron hanging over the heat of the pit, smoke curling upwards, to an open hole in the roof. Along the length of the hall were deep benches, sheepskins thick upon them; there was room enough to sleep the household and many more.

Faline and I stood behind Helka, who whispered a little of what was said, translating enough for us to understand. I was glad, too, that during our sea voyage, Eirik had begun to teach me some of his words.

"Jarl Gunnolf!" cried Eirik, "And my Lady Asta, who grows more exquisite than ever." He bowed to the pale beauty, sitting beside the man richly dressed in raven-black. She was beautiful indeed, with an air of delicate refinement, her fine hair hanging to her waist, a silvered cloak complimenting her dress of light-blue. Eirik was surely addressing his brother, the chieftain of their village, or *jarl* in their own tongue, and his fair wife.

So dark was his clothing, his beard and mane that I could not fully discern the man seated in that half-light. The shadows played over his face, concealing and then revealing. I saw him in pieces that did not resolve until I stepped closer, following Eirik's approach to the dais.

"You're returned then, brother."

Their features were similar, with full lips and a strong jaw; Gunnolf bore a livid scar through one eyebrow, deeper than that crossing Eirik's cheek. Despite the white creeping at his temples, I thought him yet in his prime, with shoulders broad and strong, and limbs muscular. As with Eirik, I imagined him taking whatever woman he desired, regardless of whether she was compliant. Yet the two were different. Where my lover was a stallion, his energy and passion scarcely contained, Gunnolf had a concentrated intensity to him. I found that I looked too closely and made myself lower my eyes.

"And Helka, my dear sister." Gunnolf rose from his seat, crossing the remaining space between us to kiss her hand. "You've brought prizes, I see."

Grasping above my elbow, he drew me forward, and looked at me directly; his eyes were the same icy blue as Eirik's, and my own. His scrutiny was piercing, as if penetrating to my naked skin.

Abruptly, he unhooked my cloak, letting it fall, so that I stood trembling in my worsted dress. It was not from cold that the shiver fluttered through me. His eyes took in the shape of me and lingered in careful appraisal.

With a shake of her hair, Faline jostled forward, pushing back her cloak to reveal the curves of her young body, wishing to capture the jarl's attention for herself.

My anger flared as it had when Eirik had taken us both to his bed. Faline was dark where I was fair, beautiful by any standard, and my rival for any man who showed me interest.

He regarded her with some amusement, and a nod of approval, before resuming his examination of me.

Eirik moved closer to my side, placing his hand firmly upon my shoulder. "Elswyth is a woman of former standing, and with some proficiency in healing." His voice, though level, was firm. "She is mine."

Gunnolf's eyes narrowed, and I saw him set his jaw as he squared his shoulders to Eirik. His fist clenched and I feared he'd reach for the dagger at his belt. The vein at Eirik's temple stood visible as he returned his brother's glare.

The two stood silent for some moments, before the tension broke, and Gunnolf's mouth twitched in a half-smile.

Gunnolf's gaze returned to Faline. "And this one?"

Eirik answered with all courtesy.

"Elswyth's step-daughter by her husband, now deceased. Both I offer for Asta's service, if our Lady wishes it. They come as free women but are willing to serve."

It was as we had agreed. I would need some occupation besides the tumbling companion of mighty Eirik, and my duties would be light, he assured me.

"For that, my Lady thanks you," said Gunnolf, replying for his wife. "No doubt, they will bend to the command of their betters, for all that you call them 'free'."

What next passed between them I never knew, for Gunnolf pulled Eirik close, and whispered in his ear. They laughed together and clasped each other about the back, thumping in brotherly embrace. However, as Gunnolf pressed his cheek to Eirik's shoulder, his expression was without mirth. If it was joy he felt at the ship's return and relief in knowing his brother to be safe, it was soberly tempered.

As Eirik led me away, I felt the jarl's inscrutable gaze upon us.

2

"No more waiting." He carried me to his bed, which would now be mine, in the service of our mutual pleasure. He cared not for the others, who would surely hear us beyond the meagre curtain of our boxed chamber, and nor did I. He lay me back and pushed up my skirts, freeing his erection from the rough wool of his trousers.

We'd been too long without consummation. Eirik would have taken me in the prow of the boat, but the roughness of the waves scarcely permitted it. How scared I'd been, sick with fear and the motion of the vessel. I'd believed I'd never see land again, but he'd pulled me to him, murmuring comforts, and bid me lay my head upon his lap. I'd been grateful for his strength, as I struggled with my own weakness.

Now, I watched as he reached beneath my buttocks, lifting me to his cock, nudging past the tightness of my initial trembling, for his size was enough to awe any woman. He pushed gradually within, easing me to accommodate his girth, voicing his pleasure in the warmth of my cunt and its constriction.

I drew up my legs, offering him deeper entry. Still, I held my breath as I prepared to take his full length. He slid to fill me with a groan of satisfaction, then began his steady rhythm, drawing back and forth, eyes bright with desire, bringing from me a returning moan.

His need would not allow him to hold back for long, his thrusts growing harder. Only his grip beneath me, pulling me upwards to meet the lunge of his cock, prevented him from pushing me away. With the force of his fucking, my voice rose. My fingers kneaded the muscle of his buttocks, urging him on; I'd known his lovemaking would be fierce, and I welcomed it.

At last, his voice broke in a Viking oath, and he shuddered, plunging with final fervour. I felt the flood of his seed and gave my own cry, part pain and joy, leaving me breathless.

With a low chuckle, he lowered his mouth to mine, kissing me gently. "A good beginning, my Elswyth."

His hands moved upwards, first to squeeze my waist, then to push down the fabric covering my breasts. He took each in his mouth, humming low as he suckled, rubbing his beard where it would most antagonize me. I wriggled, and clenched, against his retreating engorgement.

It wouldn't be long before he was again ready, his prowess being such as any man would envy. He pulled off my gown and the shift beneath, so that I lay naked before him. Stretched back on the bed, I opened my legs to him, awakened to desire and the certainty of fulfilment. There was nothing I would not give him.

His own clothing removed, he knelt above me, and I quivered at the sight of him. I knew all the scars of his body, and its markings, too: the intricate patterns of the inked sleeves upon his arms, dark green and blue-black, forming the branches of knotted trees; Jörmungandr, the snake curving down his spine, whose scales rippled as he moved, twisting its head over Eirik's shoulder, as if in an attempt to watch me. I knew the circle of pointed arrows on his chest, and those across the top of his buttocks: a cloak of beliefs that gave him power.

His erection was already rising. I wanted to feel him, to be naked under the insistence of his hands and mouth, coated with the sweat of his body, and mine.

He looked down on me with his customary confidence, tracing the curve of my belly, stroking through my soft fur. I held his gaze, wishing him to see me as clearly as I saw him.

"With just my tongue, little bird, I can trap you, and keep you, or make you fly." His voice growled low, speaking in my own language, his vowels drawn out as he formed the words.

He raised my hips again, and lowered his face, brushing my delicate skin with the bristles of his beard, kissing to the entrance between my legs. I felt the cream bubble from inside me, trickling out, in anticipation of receiving him.

He drew the flat of his tongue through my slit, before flicking against the sensitive nub, making me gasp before he pushed inside, to rub back and forth, moving expertly, to press where I desired, although never hard enough.

"Please," I begged, "Eirik…"

"More?" he whispered, his breath hot against my thigh.

I bit my lip as he penetrated more deeply, sliding through me in long, slow strokes.

He lifted his head and grinned, emerging from my slipperiness, sitting back on his heels. The firm, hard-muscled ridges of his abdomen led to the thatch of his groin, and the thickened root: full again, dark-veined, with the head pushed forward, glistening with arousal.

I reached for him, eager to pull him down, and into me, but he took both my hands and moved them to the base of his meat. "Feel me," he said. "Take it. Taste it."

Gripping the shaft, I rolled the skin back and forth, before guiding him to my lips, moving the velvet of my mouth over his smoothness, beyond the furrow and some way down his column, enclosing him tightly. I loved the solidity of him in my mouth.

He shifted and groaned, pushing one of my hands lower to cover his sac, closing his fingers over mine, rubbing himself through my grasp. I kneaded the heaviness in my palm, working him harder, extending my fingers to stroke the skin between his balls and his anus.

"*Völva!*" he groaned, calling me an enchantress in his own tongue, twisting under the pleasure I gave him.

I smiled as I took him from my mouth, for I fully intended to bewitch him. Shifting quickly, I moved to sit astride his lap. I was ready to lose myself in the heat of his body, but the devil in me wished him also to wait, as I had waited.

I was open, slick with his semen and my own desire, but I held back, rubbing only the tip of him to my ache.

"Now!" He growled, his hands firmly on my waist, pulling me down so that he slid inside in one long stroke.

Burying his face in my breasts, he pulled a nipple into his mouth, tugging hungrily, grazing me with his teeth.

"Faster!" Eirik groaned, wrapping his arms tight across my lower back.

I was soon close to the edge, rolling my hips, grinding my need against the base of his cock, crying out as I rose and fell.

As my tumult crashed upon me, Eirik pressed his fingers between my cheeks, pushing me to take him deeper and with the rhythm he so badly wanted, lifting me bodily up and down upon his shaft.

Three more strokes and his head fell back – his eyes wide and glassy, mouth open in breathlessness. His cock leapt inside me, pulsing to his final thrust and groan, and my own terrible delight swept me into the dark chasm.

I lay in the curve of Eirik's back, listening to the wind rise. I'd once told Helka that I was filled with longing for something I couldn't name; that I felt I'd die for want of it. Had I found what I was looking for, or had my search only just begun?

3

The barley ripened in the heat, dipping in the lazy winds of late summer. Eirik was a warrior leader of his Viking raiders, but a farmer too, toiling alongside his men to harvest the crop. With their muscle-corded arms and broad shoulders, they were built like oxen: necks thick, and bodies used to labour.

As the afternoon sun retreated, I would walk out to find Eirik in the fields. Among the scent of hay, freshly bundled, stacked beneath a blue sky, I would taste his sweat and the brine of his cock, and give myself, in whichever way pleased him. His men grew accustomed to our habit, slapping him upon the back at my approach, sharing bawdy comments. They nodded to me, in friendly fashion, for I made Eirik happy, and he was well-loved among his men.

Svolvaen was a fertile place, rich in apple orchards, pears and cherries, growing vegetables in abundance, and with good pasture for its livestock. Its people seemed to work for the good of all, without the jealousies and disagreements of my former home.

Gunnolf's methods of keeping law were both strict and fair. A man caught stealing a side of pork from the smokehouse was bidden to eat only from the trough for a week and to sleep with the pigs. It caused much merriment among the men, as well as having the desired effect upon the miscreant. He was duly humiliated: a punishment worse than any whip-lashing.

The jarl had a quick tongue, and a temper to match, which he made no effort to curb, as if he wished others to cringe and cower before him. As for those who showed their fear, they received his scorn. Where our paths crossed, I held my head high, refusing to give him the satisfaction of dominating me. Whatever attraction I felt, I pushed it to one side, for I had no wish to tread where my feet should not step.

My nature did not bend easily to service, despite the submission I'd endured under the hand of Faline's father. However, I found it no trial to wait upon Lady Asta, who was all gentleness. She was with child, but with many months ahead of her, she was able to attend herself in most matters. Faline and I did little more than heat the water for her bath and care for her wardrobe. Faline bristled under her diminished status, having been raised with servants of her own. Not being born to luxuries, I was more easily content, though my position had changed greatly since I'd sat at the left hand of my chieftain, with others to wait upon me.

Asta enjoyed our lively companionship, and we passed many hours in braiding her hair, sitting under the sun's warmth, the jarl's wife patiently teaching us whatever of the language and customs she deemed most useful.

There was no need for me to dirty my hem in the sty or to labour in the skinning of game for our stew. I knew how to tend livestock, and to cook, but these were Guðrún and Sylvi's duties. Nonetheless, I helped in small ways, for it seemed wrong to set myself above them.

With Asta's leave, I found a homely comfort in milking the goats and cows, and in churning the butter. Eirik said the cheeses I made were the best he'd tasted. With Sylvi, I went down to the shore to harvest dulse; the seaweed brought a briny tang to the fish stew she was adept at making. I learnt to preserve meat in vats of sour whey to prevent it from spoiling, and hung herring in the smokehouse, or outdoors, to dry in the brisk, northern wind. I refilled the lamps each morning with fish oil, adding cottongrass long enough for the wick.

I took on the language of my new home, word by word, reading my neighbours not only by their expressions – which were mostly of curiosity, sometimes of pity, or scorn – but by the phrases I began to unravel. I wondered how many years it would take for them to accept me, to look into my eyes and not see a stranger. I had Viking blood, violently conceived during a raid by the Northmen more than twenty years ago, but I hadn't been raised as one of them. Their rituals and habits were not yet mine but I wished to learn. For too long, I'd ached with the knowledge of not belonging; now, even within my diminished status, I yearned to be accepted.

The women of Svolvaen regarded Faline and I with envy, I could tell, for we enjoyed comparative leisure. They treated us with a certain reverence, too, for the Lady Asta was respected and loved, and she desired that others make us welcome.

"Her father was a jarl," Helka told me, "And his before. The marriage ensured an alliance with a settlement further north. She came with a rich dowry, of golden-threaded gowns and cuffs and rings set with gemstones traded from the East."

Even without her jewels and fine costume, she was a woman above all

The baby had just begun to stir when a young girl appeared behind Astrid, letting her mother know that she'd go to the lower meadow to bring back their goats from grazing.

"You're a good girl, Ylva." Astrid stroked her daughter's arm. "Keep on your shawl, remember, and hurry back."

I couldn't help but wonder at the linens Ylva had wrapped closely around her neck, for it was a fine day, and warm.

Astrid looked at me once more, and the infant I held, now balling its fists to its eyes and stretching in wakefulness. She slipped her boy to the ground, sending him to play, and reached to take the baby from me.

Her face was pale as she spoke. She was uneasy, but I sensed her desire to unburden herself, and speaking such things is sometimes easier with a stranger. There was no one near but she lowered her voice, nonetheless.

"My daughter suffers an affliction. She woke with an unsightly sore upon her shoulder several days ago, but now has two more, about her neck."

I listened with concern. I'd seen my grandmother treat various skin ailments. I leaned forward, telling Astrid of my skill, and that I might be able to help. She appeared disbelieving though, doubtless, she would wish my claim to be true.

"I've given offerings to Eir, washed the pus with mead, and applied honey. It seems only to have grown worse."

I commended her on her actions, but I was anxious, for I feared that the sore would spread its poison through her daughter's body and that contact might spread the affliction to others in the family.

"Will Ylva let me see, tomorrow, if I return?" I had already begun to think of remedies I might try, and which combinations of plants would be most effective. "I'll bring a salve, and we must hope for a cure. I'll do all I can."

Astrid smiled uncertainly. "She'll do as I bid her."

I rose to take my leave but had one more question to ask. Was anyone else in the village similarly stricken?

Astrid took my hands as she answered. The mothers of two other young women had come to her the night before, each under cover of darkness, having heard about Ylva's ailment, and eager to know in what ways Astrid had attempted treatment. Neither had admitted to their children suffering but she had known, from their faces, that they carried the same burden.

My mind raced ahead, wondering how many might be keeping their condition hidden, even from those closest to them.

These were my people now, and I would do whatever I could to rid them of this anguish.

4

The next morning, I mixed a salve of equal parts hazel bark and comfrey leaves, smoothed to a paste with honey.

Astrid was waiting for me at her door and her distress was clear. She hurried me inside, leading me to where Ylva sat trembling in her under-tunic. Her eyes appeared huge in her pale face.

I saw at once the cause for Astrid's fear; for a red welt was rising on Ylva's cheek.

"She woke with it." Astra wrung her hands. "And there's another appearing on her back."

The baby grumbled in the corner, but Astrid made no move to comfort it.

I helped in lifting off Ylva's clothing to reveal the oldest sore: angry red on her shoulder, the skin broken at the edges, oozing yellow pus. The ones upon her neck were little better. I wasted no time in applying the remedy, smoothing it upon the broken skin with a wooden spatula.

"Twice a day, apply a small amount. Tie a strap of linen over the top to keep the poultice in place," I explained. I'd brought several strips of cloth with me, which I laid on the side, beside the pot of salve.

I gave Ylva a smile. "We'll have you better soon. Be brave."

In truth, the rapid spread of the young girl's sores made me anxious. The fields were abundant in plants and herbs with curative powers, and I'd also begun cultivating my own, on the sheltered side of the longhouse, but the virulence of her affliction persuaded me that she needed a stronger remedy. There were many plants with soothing properties for the skin and I usually found the most potent growing in the forest.

Secreted in a leather pouch, I still had the Death's Cap mushroom I'd picked long ago and kept: its poison a talisman for my safety. I might have used it in those first days of the arrival of Eirik's men, when they'd plundered our village: might have killed them all, had I wished to do so. Some sense of humanity had stayed my hand. My role was to heal, not to harm. Yet, I'd kept it.

I'd ask Asta if I might accompany Helka into the woodlands, it being her custom to go hunting. She'd guide me deeper than I'd be able to venture alone.

I bid Ylva farewell, and Astrid walked me outside. I was reluctant to leave, knowing the troubles she bore.

"Avoid touching them, and keep them covered," I urged, kissing Astrid upon the cheek. "I'll visit again soon."

She nodded. I sensed there was much she wished to say, but there was no need. We understood each other.

"If anyone else needs me, I'll be ready. Tell them to watch for me."

I felt sure that Ylva was not alone. Behind closed doors, there would be others who fretted and feared. If I could help them, I would.

I embraced Astrid once again. Looking over her shoulder, I saw a woman standing no more than twenty steps away, watching with a ferocious expression. She carried a sturdy baby on her hip, fair-haired and with eyes of the lightest blue. The woman's own hair, plaited to one side and falling to her waist, was a rich auburn-red. Even from a distance, I could tell the child was a boy, his features being pronounced in the way they rarely are among girl-children. He looked back at me earnestly, chewing upon something hard clutched in his fist.

"Who's that?" I asked Astrid. "Has she come to find me? Do you think she suffers as Ylva does?"

She turned to look but spun back swiftly, moving her body to block the woman from my sight. Astrid's eyes darted away, not wishing to meet mine, but I persisted.

"She means to talk to me, surely?"

It clearly pained Astrid to tell me, but my squeeze of her hand persuaded her to be frank.

"It's Bodil, married to Haldor. Her oldest son was among Eirik's men when they went *a-viking*; it was his first trip across the sea, his first raid." Astrid hesitated, for it was a subject that grieved her. "Like my husband, he did not return."

I felt a pang of sadness on Bodil's behalf. No wonder she regarded me with such a damnable glare, for her son's death had been at the hand of my former people.

I looked again at the child in whose face there was something familiar to me. Astrid had not told me all, I was convinced.

"And that little one?" I asked.

Astrid chewed at her lip. I was sorry for it. She'd suffered enough but I couldn't let the matter rest.

"I know what you're thinking," she said. "He's a strong boy." Her eyes skirted away again. "He might be Haldor's… or he might not."

I could see for sure now. Those eyes were unmistakable, as was the bold set of the chin.

"Her husband knew, I think, but perhaps not." Astrid went on. "She weaves and sews well. There was a time when she was often at the longhouse, making clothes for Gunnolf and Asta."

"And for Eirik, too?"

Astrid's eyes told me all.

I kept to the other side of the way as I hurried past, but try as I might, I couldn't avoid the burning of her gaze. As I drew level, she spat fiercely upon the ground and hissed a fevered curse.

I knew not the words of her venomous oath, but their meaning couldn't have been clearer.

When Eirik took me in his arms that night, I thought of Bodil. She must have lain in this very bed, Eirik's weight above her as he uttered his deep groan of pleasure, shuddering to his release inside her. I imagined the imprint of her kisses, of her hands that had stroked and explored his body.

She must have looked for his longship even more eagerly than the others—anxious for the return of her lover. What jealousies she must feel. I wondered with what words Eirik had parted from her and whether he'd been to visit her since his homecoming. It would be too cruel for him to have said naught, allowing her to discover by word of mouth that I'd taken her place.

And what of the child? Did Eirik know him for his own? All these weeks I'd waited to feel his seed growing in me. I'd surrendered to his love-making countless times, but where was my baby?

My heart ached. I would have struck him, but he clasped me to his chest and murmured with his usual ardour. I was his love, his goddess, his enchantress, more precious than silver or gold, my beauty surpassing all other treasures.

His lips were soft and gentle and his body hard. I shivered under his touch and cried as I rode the waves of my ecstasy.

I wished there to be no past, for either of us.

Little good it would do me to think on Bodil or the other Svolvaen women who must have writhed in Eirik's embrace. How many, like Bodil, might follow me with ill-thoughts, borne of resentful rivalry? I could have spoken but I kept silent. To speak of my fears would be to make them real.

It was late into the night when I woke to a cool draught upon my skin and a figure looming above. I thought at first that it was Bodil, come to claim Eirik for her own and pull me from the bed. Her face twisted in malice and, to my half-wakened state, I saw her as some malevolent wraith. The horror of it choked me. Only when she spoke did I realize that it was no phantom beside me, but the ghost of another, living, lover: one who'd shared Eirik's bed even more recently than Bodil.

"I'm here for him," she said. "If he wishes it."

My anger overtook any fear I'd felt. Was there to be no peace for me, for us!

"Eirik is asleep, Faline, as you can see." I reached for the covers, which she'd thrown from me as I slept. "Go back to your own bed. You aren't needed here."

"Another time, then." She gave no apology. If anything, I sensed her amusement.

How long had she stood over me?

5

The next day, as Helka and I set out, it reminded me of the first days of our acquaintance, when I'd led her into my own woodlands, her Northmen wanting to find the best oak with which to make new oars. My heart quickened as we left the bright sun of the open sky, entering the half-light of the forest, canopied over with lush foliage. The season was turning but only a few trees had begun to alter colour and shed. The forest was alive, its uppermost reaches touched by the wind and the birds while small creatures moved beneath the leaves underfoot.

It had been some time since Helka and I had been alone, and I was gladdened to have her to myself. Upon less trodden paths, we walked briskly, Helka directing me to where dark sloes ripened on the bushes and the densest clutches of hazelnuts grew, for roasting.

It was upon the tip of my tongue to confide in her my meeting with Astrid, to seek her advice, but I kept the events of the previous day to myself. I'd tell her, perhaps, when I'd affected a cure; it would bring me greater pleasure to detail the challenge and my solving of it within the same story. Of Bodil, I resolved to make no mention, for I wished to hear no confirmation of what pained me.

Our sacks were soon brimming with docks, nettles and lambs-quarters, milk thistle, figwort and heart of the earth.

I'd always felt most content in the forest. It was where my childhood adventures had taken place, where I was free to climb and muddy my clothes, with none to tell me how a girl should behave. With the boys as my playmates, I'd learnt to be brave and to delight in the freedom of running wild. My grandmother had indulged me until I began the path to womanhood. With that change, my liberty had ended. How quickly my grandmother had placed me in my uncle's bed, a man three times my age. I'd cursed the day my aunt had followed my mother to the grave and left me to take her place.

"You've become quiet, Elswyth." Helka placed a handful of lingonberries into her basket. "Does ought ail you?"

I popped a berry in my mouth, wincing at the bittersweet taste on my tongue. "Just remembering."

"You miss your village?"

I watched her fingers pluck the crimson fruit. "Only my grandmother. Not much else."

"And how do you settle?" she asked.

I gave a small shrug. "I don't yet belong, but I will, I know. I must find my own way to being accepted."

"And Eirik is good to you?"

I nodded, squeezing a berry so that its juice ran over my fingers. As a bed companion, I was fulfilled; his prowess continued to leave me breathless.

"As it should be." Helka smiled. "I see that you make him happy."

She hesitated before continuing. "You know that others have shared his bed."

My chest tightened. Of course, I was aware, especially after my recent encounter with Bodil. It had been plain, too, from our first meeting—when Eirik had carried me over his shoulder into the Great Hall of my husband and had taunted me before his men. I'd thought he would strip and display me for all to see as he fucked me. Instead, he'd chosen another way, taking me to the chamber I'd shared with my husband until that morning, his blood still damp on the floor.

"Among the thralls, there are few he hasn't bedded, but there are others too… though their husbands may not perceive it."

Thinking of the child upon Bodil's hip and how Bodil had looked at me with such malice, I knew perhaps more than Helka realized. It made me wonder at the purpose of her conversation because she didn't usually speak in this rambling fashion.

Helka indicated a fallen trunk nearby and, brushing away damp leaves, invited me to sit. "I see that you wish to be more than Eirik's companion." She turned to look at me. "You wish to be his only one, his wife?"

I plucked at some soft moss growing on the rotting wood and sat quietly. As the weeks had passed, I'd become aware of my deepening feelings for Eirik. I saw him not as my master, nor captor, but as the husband that I yearned for—the man I wished to father my children. I fell asleep with the smell of him and woke to the pleasure of his kisses and the insistence of his morning desire.

I'd agreed to accompany Eirik to Svolvaen without promise of marriage. I'd asked for nothing beyond what he'd already given me. Nevertheless, it was true; I did want more.

"None has kept his interest as you do, but I say this to prepare you, Elswyth." Helka leaned forward, touching my arm. "It may never be."

As kindly as she meant the words, my heart gave a bruised leap. The wind rose at that moment and sent a wave through the branches, rippling the leaves, making it seem that they breathed with rustling sighs.

"His marriage is long overdue and, when it's made, it should be to a woman who brings not only a dowry but the promise of alliance. Svolvaen is prosperous, but we must grow stronger. As the ruling family, it's our duty."

I thought of Asta's arranged betrothal to Gunnolf. Was there already a woman of noble birth promised to Eirik? My stomach churned at the thought.

Helka drew me closer. "I see that you understand and that it hurts you, for I know the love that you harbour for him." She took my hand. "It's best for you to put these feelings aside. Eirik will let you go when the time comes, but he will behave honourably. You're strong, Elswyth, and will endure."

It seemed to grow quieter, as if the trees pressed close about were listening to us: not just to our conversation but to the whirl of my thoughts.

"When the time comes, you may continue serving Asta, keeping Eirik's bed when he desires it, or he'll find another man to be your husband."

Helka's face was all concern. I could see that she took no joy in telling me this. Nevertheless, a surge of heat and anger took hold of me. "And what of you, Helka? Where is your alliance? Your husband is gone, and you have no children. Where is your marriage of duty?"

Her expression grew cold, and she drew back as if I'd attempted to strike her. At once, I regretted my sharp tongue. I knew well enough that she mourned Vigrid, though he'd died a full two years before.

I reached for her, wishing to put right my unkindness, but Helka stood and moved several steps away, presenting her back to me.

My eyes pricked with frustrated tears.

"Forgive me, Helka," I begged. My disappointment had made me cruel, and I was ashamed. She spoke, I knew, only to warn me—to protect my heart.

It was some moments before she turned again. Her lashes were wet but there was steel in her voice. "You say this because you don't know…"

I was suddenly small and out of place, sitting among the dark ferns and twining roots. It had grown colder, and I felt myself an unwelcome intrusion in this ancient place. These were not the oaks and elms of my childhood forest, those I'd climbed, and under which I'd hunted for berries. Their shadows fell differently. Even the far-off birdcalls seemed strange to me.

Helka gave a rueful smile. "Vigrid is gone, yet he lies beside me at night. I sense him though I cannot see him." She looked at me directly. "How, then, can I bring another into my bed?"

I knew not what to say. Though I'd seen my husband murdered in front of me, I hadn't grieved for him. I'd given him little thought since leaving my village. Helka's devotion was altogether different, more akin to mine for Eirik. Should I lose him, I would lose part of myself.

"It's only a feeling…" Helka wiped her sleeve to her face. "There are many things that may be felt, though they pass unseen."

"There's no… malevolence?" I asked, suddenly fearful. If my own husband were to return to me, it would be in revenge or anger, not for love.

She shook her head. "I'm in no danger."

We walked on without speaking for a while, neither of us wishing to return to the subject. Whatever had passed between us, it appeared to have been set aside.

At last, Helka advised that we turn back, for it was growing dim. The autumn was fully upon us, and the light fading earlier each day.

I agreed, but we had gone only a few steps when I saw some funghi growing upon a nearby tree and beckoned Helka back for the use of her knife in collecting them.

Whether it was the ghost of our former conversation that lingered or something else that made her speak, Helka became serious again. "Elswyth, you feel an affinity with the forest, I know, but I must warn you not to venture too deeply, and never on your own, especially after dusk."

Nearby, an owl hooted, and I thought of the wild creatures that must live here—bears and boar. I knew there to be stag and wolves. Helka had brought her crossbow, though we'd come across nothing larger than a rabbit.

Helka took my arm, urging me to keep walking. "There are parts of the forest in which I would never wander for fear of what I might find."

"Or, what may find you," I ventured. I gave a half-smile, wishing to show I was unafraid, but her manner, so earnest, sent a shiver through me. The forest grew greatly darker, and it seemed that the trees pushed closer than before, twisting towards us in distorted shapes. Where there had been the noise of birds, it appeared eerily quiet.

Helka must have sensed this, too, for she lowered her voice. "It's said that there are mysterious lights in the forest; lights that will lure you to danger."

My own people had a similar tale but I'd never seen anything in our woods to frighten me. I'd hidden between the shadows of trees since I was very little. "I don't believe in such things," I said firmly.

"Whether we believe them or not doesn't mean they may not be true." Helka pulled her cloak tighter. "Our people have passed down stories through the generations, and the *skalds* tell them to those who will listen, as they travel from place to place. They tell of deeds brave and foolish, and the downfall of those who think themselves invulnerable."

She continued to hurry me onwards, and before long, we saw the forest's edge. Helka indicated for us to put down our sacks and baskets and rest.

The pale daylight was within sight, and the strange terrors that had risen up around us receded.

"There's something else I wish to say before we return," said Helka. "Among the things which live in the forest is a seductive, secretive creature. She hides her true nature, to lure men. Showing them only what is beautiful and enticing, she is the *huldra*: deceptive and vengeful."

"Many women must be part *huldra*, then," I added wryly.

"Does this creature not remind you of someone?" asked Helka.

I lifted my brows in response and invited her to speak.

"There's something in Faline which causes strife. I cannot trust her, and I wish she were not under our roof."

I couldn't deny that I'd often thought the same myself, but for some reason, I found myself unwilling to condemn her. After all, she was only looking after her own interests. I couldn't blame her for that.

She'd been the daughter of our chieftain. How different her life might have been had her promised betrothed not fallen from his horse. It seemed so long ago that I'd been married and suffered violence at my husband's hand. In Eirik, I'd found someone to give my love to, and received love in return, even if I were not his wife. What was Faline's lot without the benefit of tenderness or affection?

I remembered as a child her asking to join us in our play. We'd found a tree which enabled us to climb higher than ever we'd climbed before. The boys laughed at her, so small she barely reached their waists, and told her to go home to her father. Had I mocked her, too, and sent her, tearful, back to the village? Perhaps I had.

Helka picked up her basket once more. "It was a mistake to bring her."

6

Sylvi watched as I crushed valerian root in the mortar with petals of chamomile, cowslip and vervain I'd collected from the meadow. I steeped the mixture in hot water to create a draught.

"It's important not to use too much valerian," I warned, seeing her interest. "Jarl Gunnolf only wants to sleep well through the night, not fail to wake up altogether."

She nodded her understanding. If Sylvi ever wanted revenge on the jarl for the liberties he'd taken with her, I'd shown her the way. I hoped I wouldn't regret it.

Gunnolf had called me to him on my return from the forest. Eyes dark with exhaustion, he'd asked for something to bring dreamless rest. His need appeared genuine. I knew what it was to be troubled by perturbing dreams.

Eirik was also weary, but from physical labour rather than mental disquiet. He'd endured a long day in the fields, stacking the last of the hay into the barn. The harvest was drawing to its end—the fields dusty yellow and scattered with broken straw, the fruit trees stripped almost bare. The weather looked set to turn. The winter fodder for our livestock had to be harvested before it began to rot.

After we'd eaten the evening *nattmal*—a thick stew of mutton and root vegetables served with bread and mead—Lady Asta took her bath in the main hall of the longhouse, discreetly behind a folding screen, Faline ladling steaming water into the tub from the cauldron over the firepit.

When I approached Gunnolf, he'd already begun to undress, having retired to the boxbed he shared with my lady. Seeing Gunnolf in his undertunic, I did my best not to stare at his muscular thighs. His long hair, usually braided, hung loose about his shoulders.

He drank the sleeping draught down without hesitation, inclining his head in thanks. As I took the cup from him, he extended his finger to stroke mine. It was the lightest of touches, but I jerked away.

His cool eyes surveyed me. "What a nervous creature you are, as if waiting for me to pounce."

With that, he pulled off his remaining garment and cast it to the floor so that he stood before me naked.

I found that I wished to look. Like Eirik, he wore ink on his skin; so closely were the designs worked, I could barely make them out. I'd never seen a man with body hair so dense and dark, covering his shoulders and arms and down his back. It grew the full width of his chest and curled down the hardness of his stomach, joining his groin, so abundant it would have covered his manhood entirely had it been at rest.

There was no doubt that Gunnolf intended for me to admire him.

"If you wish to see my cock at full attention, you'll need to apply yourself with a warm hand… or mouth." He sat on the edge of the bed and opened his thighs in languid invitation. "Or sit upon it, if you prefer."

His lips twitched in amusement. I could not deny there was a wildness about him that was alluring. His mouth was full and sensuous, framed by his beard. His teeth, revealed as he smiled, were sharp; teeth made for biting.

I felt heat in my cheek, though from my own thoughts or from the jarl's forwardness I couldn't have said. I drew my eyes away, stepping back. Whatever I was thinking, it would be a dangerous game to play. Eirik had told me that he'd shared women with his brother when they were younger. He'd think less favourably of it now, I believed, as would Asta. I'd no wish to take that path.

Gunnolf rose and, for a moment, I imagined him lifting me to the ceiling, breaking my back in a single twist. I'd no doubt he had the strength to do so.

It was with some relief that I saw him stretch and pull back the goatskins, lowering himself between them. His taunting demeanour was gone, the lines about his mouth set hard. I saw something I recognized—a certain heaviness of heart from the burdens he was obliged to bear. It wasn't my place to speak, but the words escaped my lips before I thought to rein them in.

"Have you suffered long with these troubling dreams?"

His eyes narrowed.

It was impertinent of me to address him without him first speaking to me. I was no more than a thrall in his eyes, to be commanded or mocked. I felt sure it was only Eirik's claim upon me that had, so far, deterred Gunnolf from treating me as he did the other women serving in his household.

"What a presumptuous wench you are. My dreams are no concern of yours."

He seemed to consider raising his hand to me, but the moment passed, and he rolled his head wearily upon the pillow.

"Go fuck my brother," he said curtly. "And leave me to my rest."

※

Eirik would sleep as soon as his eyes closed, but he'd kept himself awake, waiting. A lamp burned on the shelf within his boxed chamber, the flame revealing his bare chest, in shadow and light, and the ridges of his abdomen, lightly coated in sweat.

He watched as I let drop my belt and unfastened the brooches at my shoulders. I stepped from each garment until I stood as naked as he, taking pleasure in his gaze upon my breasts and the roundness of my hips, down to the blonde hair of my sex.

Smiling lazily, Eirik pulled back the furs, revealing more of his body to me. His voice was low. "I need you, Elswyth."

He drew me to him as I entered the bed, finding the small of my back, bringing me close. I curved to him, my belly to his. Hardness pressed to softness, his mouth met mine. His palms cupped beneath the flesh of my buttocks and I moaned as he reached lower, his fingers brushing my cunt from behind, coaxing me to open to him. I gave a whimper of desire as his cock nudged between my legs. It required only the smallest shift of my thigh for him to push and enter.

Slowly, he began, clasping me firmly as he thrusted, one hand creeping between my cheeks, encouraging me to open further, to allow him deeper passage.

I surrendered to his lovemaking, wishing to make him part of my own body. In this act, he was my master in strength but we were equals in our hunger for one another.

"Elswyth," he murmured, trailing kisses down my neck. "My own sweet love."

Already, my breath was quickening. I arched against his steady rhythm, my fingers curling into his hair, guiding him to take my breast, wanting him to suckle hard. As he pulled me onto his hot stream of seed, I tumbled into my own chasm of pleasure. When he kissed me again, it was with tenderness.

"Was Thor watching us?" I teased.

"He's always watching. We give him something worth looking at."

Easing his cock from me, he rolled away, but I'd no intention of letting him sleep. Warmed by what he'd given me, I wanted more.

Straddling him, I rested my sex upon the root of his fading erection. I knew he liked to see me so, with my hair falling wanton and my breasts above him, my skin glistening with perspiration. He rested his hands on my waist, appraising through half-closed eyes. I rocked lightly and saw his lips part, wetted by his tongue.

Impossible that Eirik would desire another with this burning passion. He would never forsake me for a marriage of convenience. I wouldn't believe it. And yet, I recalled Helka's warning to me. I wished to hear some promise of Eirik's love, some proof of his depth of feeling.

I stroked the hair upon his chest, caressed his nipples.

"You wish to stir me again, my Valkyrie."

I licked where I'd touched, letting my breasts brush him lightly. Between my legs, I felt the base of his shaft thicken.

"We shall always be like this, Eirik?" Kissing his abdomen, I moved downwards, tasting the sweat of our coupling. "You would never send me from your bed?"

I took my tongue lower and closed my lips over his cock-head. Though not yet fully erect, he was reawakening. "Of course not," he murmured. "You please me better than any woman."

I enclosed him with my hand, squeezing, moving his skin back and forth, teasing the bulging helmet of his erection, sucking at the tender spot beneath its head.

"You'll protect me, always; love me, always?"

"Aye, I will."

I opened my mouth wide, taking Eirik deep, past my teeth, to the back of my jaw, humming against his growing hardness then drawing back, letting my tongue work the length of him.

"Odin's Valhalla!" Eirik gasped, opening his legs and grasping my hair. "Don't stop!"

I sucked upon him again, drawing forth his brine. He was watching my mouth moving on him, my tongue licking at the fluid that trickled from his tip, my hand cupping beneath.

"I want the taste of you, Eirik."

He groaned as I took his balls into my mouth, humming again so that he'd feel the vibration, letting him know how delicious he was.

At full arousal, it was more difficult to take him wholly in my mouth, but I returned to suck his length until I felt his tremor begin to rise. Swiftly, I diverted him into the warmth of my cunt; only just in time, for he cried out and pulsed inside me.

When I blew out the lamp, I lay my head upon his chest. "You love me, Eirik?" I ran my fingertips over the raised scar down his side, a wound from long ago.

"Aye, I love thee."

He wrapped his arm about my shoulders and I felt safe. He was mine and I was his.

"Forever?" I whispered.

In answer, there was only the soft, regular breathing of a man who had succumbed to sleep.

⚜

An old dream returned. I was alone with a wolf who'd long ago prowled my sleep. Circled by the beast, I didn't scream or run, but lay down and offered my neck. I bared my breast to its claws, watching as they peeled back the skin to reveal my beating heart. It lowered its shaggy head, licking the pulsing blood from my body.

It was still dark when I woke. I trembled—but not only from fear.

7

Late next morning, Lady Asta gave me my leave and I walked down to visit Astrid. I half-expected Bodil to be waiting, to block my path and lay vengeful hands upon me, so far had my imagination built upon my previous meeting with her. Though I passed several of my new kinsmen, I was relieved to see that she was not among them.

In truth, Svolvaen seemed extraordinarily quiet. The weather was turning cooler, the sky overcast, but fine enough yet to work outside and make the most of the good daylight. However, the street lacked its usual bustle.

Eirik had been pleased to close the doors on the barn, knowing the winter fodder was safely stored. He'd gone out with the fishermen soon after dawn, eager for the smell of the sea. The fields had claimed too much of his time.

The stacking of the hay had brought the harvest to its close and some of the older men sat in leisure, taking a pipe and a horn of ale. They paused in their conversation as I passed, nodding their recognition, which I returned in kind.

It was a simple gesture but it warmed me, and I was emboldened to address a woman seated nearby. She'd been following my progress down the hill, I was certain, but glanced away as I approached, to the embroidery in her lap.

"Good morrow." I wracked my memory for the right words with which to praise her needlework. Her fingers were nimble with the thread: a vivid red against white cloth.

"It's very fine," I settled upon, at last. "Your hands are clever."

She raised her head at that and thanked me.

"You've come to see Astrid?" she asked. "I saw her looking from her door, watching for you, perhaps."

Her face was kindly, but I only nodded. It wasn't for me to reveal why Astrid might be expecting me. I'd keep her confidences.

"You're a good girl." The woman turned back to her work. "Pay no heed to anyone who says differently; they're only wishing they were in your place."

I thought, wryly, that none really knew what it was like to be 'in my place' but her kind words touched me, since I'd had few enough from the women of Svolvaen.

Further down the street, two women were talking but stopped abruptly as I drew near, looking at me with ill-concealed distaste. I waved my hand in greeting but they turned away, retreating into the house without a backward glance. The door banged behind them.

It will take time, I reminded myself.

The kindly woman had been right about Astrid waiting for me. She appeared at my first knock.

"Thank the gods you've come." She shifted the baby to her hip as she drew me in. She'd been weeping, her eyes ringed red.

"What is it, Astrid?"

Ylva was sitting with her back to us, carding wool, her younger brother playing at her feet.

"It's been only two days. It's no worse, surely? You've been using the salve I gave you?"

Astrid's eyes beseeched me. "You'd best look."

As soon as Ylva turned, I understood Astrid's fear. What had been no more than a rising welt upon her daughter's cheek had begun to blister.

"Show your shoulder," Astrid directed her.

Ylva peeled back cloth stained yellow. The wound beneath oozed wet, the smell unwholesome.

"And those on your neck?"

"There's a throbbing in them." Ylva's lip trembled.

She was a beautiful young woman, her eyes the same delicate grey as her mother's, large and pleading, her hair long and flaxen.

"I'd hoped for improvement," I admitted. "But I've brought something stronger, today." I threw the old strip of bandage into the fire. "Don't try to wash this. Better to use new cloth each time. If you run out, at the very least, boil the old ones in the hottest water, then hang them to dry."

I took a pot from my apron pocket and spread a thick layer of green unguent onto the sore. "It's elm bark and yarrow, mixed with sage. It should bring down the swelling and draw out the poison."

"Thank you," whispered Ylva, her eyes welling wet.

I smiled but kept my voice firm. "Wash your hands before you change your dressing, and afterwards."

"I'll have water warming all through the day," promised Astrid.

As I removed the dressings, one by one, Ylva winced, the soiled cloth pulling at her tender skin.

"We'll soon have you better," I promised, doing my best not to grimace.

Astrid, too, was attempting to be cheerful, watching me closely and asking about the making of the balm. Despite her valiant efforts, I could see her distress. When all was done, I squeezed Ylva's hand and bid her be brave.

"Have you heard from the women who came to you before?" I asked Astrid. "Ylva can't be the only one suffering with this."

It occurred to me that it might be a reason for the relative hush of the street. How many families were harbouring a secret?

"I can't say," said Astrid. "If they share our troubles, they haven't told me, but I feel sure you're right. If they return to unburden their hearts, I'll tell them of your treatment. They'll need your help."

"And I'll be happy to give it."

I set the new pot of salve upon the table. "Twice a day, remember, and I'll come back soon, to see how Ylva heals."

Astrid placed the baby in his crib and walked me to the door, indicating for us to go outside a moment. She closed the door behind her and drew me close, speaking in hushed tones.

"I did have visitors but not the sort you're thinking of." She worried at her lip. "Ylva was betrothed to be married but the parents of the boy have broken the contract."

"They know?" It was a redundant question. Of course, they knew.

"Yesterday, when Ylva was shutting in the chickens. I'd told her to keep her face well-hidden, but the boy came to her. She tried to stop him, but you know how young men are. He wouldn't take no for an answer." Astrid gave a shuddering sigh. "He pulled off her scarf to kiss her and saw the soiled bandages at her neck, the blister on her cheek."

I imagined the whole of Svolvaen would know by now.

Astrid pushed aside a falling tear. "I can hardly blame them, but I fear for Ylva. What future is there for her? Even if we cure her of this, people have long memories."

My heart ached for the girl. No doubt, she thought herself in love. The breaking of her betrothal must seem the end of all that mattered.

I put my arms around Astrid's shoulders as she stifled a sob.

If I failed to heal her daughter it would be the end of more than Ylva's hopes for marriage.

8

The harvest was among the best Svolvaen had ever seen, a mild spring having encouraged orchard blossoms, followed by warm summer ripening the barley. This was safely stacked in the barn, with hay in another; no matter how deep the snow, the cattle would have their fodder. We'd laid down pears and apples for the winter, between straw, and conserved plums in their own syrup, packed tightly in jars. Every house had its provision of smoked herring, root vegetables and honey, its own store of mead and of ale. No matter what storms came, Svolvaen wouldn't starve.

When all had been gathered in, Jarl Gunnolf invited Svolvaen to join in a day of festivity, commencing with one to one combat, to be followed by falconry and then carousing, long into the night.

The clouds were thick overhead and the wind blew hard but the rain held off. The men outnumbered their womenfolk; perhaps the sport was not to their taste or they had other duties to attend to.

As I joined Helka, I looked among the crowd, for those who wore a cowl to cover their neck, my imagination thinking always of the affliction I believed was travelling among them. Astrid waved to me, with her toddling son lifted in her arms, that he might better see. The baby, I supposed, she'd left with Ylva, at home.

The jarl sat upon a raised dais, wearing his customary black, including a cloak of dark brocade, trimmed thickly in silver fur. Beside him, Lady Asta was radiant in a gown of palest white, embroidered in gold and yellow, smiling at her people, applauding each man who stepped forward to indicate his participation.

She rested her hands upon the growing babe within her, the swell of her belly visible. Gunnolf, too, appeared well content in showing off his lady's fertile condition.

"The jarl will preside over pairs of men, in successive bouts," Helka explained, "Until only one remains."

Eirik waited until all others had presented before showing his own willingness. Stripped to the waist, with his hair braided into a top knot, he stood taller than the rest. I'd seen him wield his sword and axe, and had tended to him on return from battle, streaked with other men's blood, but had never witnessed him wrestle skin on skin.

"Odin and Thor and all the gods are among us!" Gunnolf announced, slitting the throat of a sturdy hog. "Just as this life-force soaks the soil, so doth ours, shed in combat. May our deeds always be brave and glorious, so that all may know of the greatness of Svolvaen."

There was a mighty cheer at the squealing of the pig, and the gush of crimson that flooded at Gunnolf's feet. The animal would spend the rest of the day roasting, in readiness for the evening feast.

As the tournament began, I saw that agility counted for as much as strength. Each took up the great horn of honeyed mead, drinking deeply before they commenced, grappling within a designated square, no more than five steps wide; the first to pin their rival to the ground for the count of ten took the bout.

The shouts were deafening, roaring approval of each triumph. The outcome of some pairings was decided almost immediately; others left their opponents breathless, staggering from exertion, sweat glistening upon their hard-muscled bodies, sinews straining in pursuit of conquest.

Eirik seemed to win his matches with little effort, having not only skill in the various holds but the might to lift another man from his feet. Seeing him wide-legged in victory, the taut lines of his abdomen visible, I thrilled at the power of him, both as my lover and a warrior.

None seemed to mind his ascendancy. He allowed each a fair chance to demonstrate his prowess before asserting his own. Eirik helped them to stand tall, clasping his combatants about the shoulders in congratulation on a match well fought.

It was clear that he delighted in conquest as much as any man but valued fellowship above all, and these were his men, whom he had led across the seas, to return with riches and renown.

If Gunnolf was piqued to see his younger brother cast all before him, he dissembled well, giving his own bellows of approval.

When the final bout was declared, Eirik faced his old friend, Olaf, both men muddied from the many matches they'd already claimed. What Olaf lacked in stature, he made up for in lightness of foot, twisting repeatedly from Eirik's grasp, to the mirth of those watching. Eirik could have taken Olaf to the ground at any time but chose, instead, to revel in festive merriment, indulging Olaf's antics to avoid him.

Gunnolf followed closely, his eyes alight. Had Eirik been, at last, beaten, he would have had trouble concealing his satisfaction, I thought. There was another too, whose eyes were all for Eirik; Bodil had pushed her way to the front, carrying the fair child. She stood, neither cheering nor clapping but watching the vigorous performance of her former lover with quiet intensity. Was she recalling, I wondered, the sweat of their own bed-wrestling, her fingers pressed to the flesh of his buttocks, her body submitting beneath the brawn of his?

My temper flared at the imagining, for Eirik was mine, and the jealousy in my belly burned.

At last, with an indomitable cry, Eirik gripped Olaf by ankle and wrist, obliging him to bend in acrobatic fashion, curled upwards from the ground. As the count neared ten, Eirik gave his rival a playful tweak of the nose and pulled him to his feet.

The clamour was great indeed, with all shouting Eirik's name, and I saw a shadow pass over Gunnolf's face.

Eirik, however, played no more the fool, kneeling rather, before the jarl. "My victories or losses are in the hands of the gods. If I have strength, brother, it is through their grace, and I offer it in your service. Send me where you will, upon any mission, and I'll bring glory to your name and to that of Svolvaen."

It was a speech delivered from the heart; when Eirik lifted his head, his eyes were bright with fervour. Once more, the men received him with thunderous approval and it required the jarl's raised hand to gain the quiet he needed to reply.

"I accept your service, which I know is given in good faith. May you be an example to all men, in your allegiance to your jarl."

Gunnolf called Eirik forth and placed his own drinking cup in his hands but there was a tenseness to his jaw. I didn't wish to see the day Gunnolf believed Eirik's loyalty to be in question.

♛

We lifted down trestle tables from the rafters of the great hall, for a midday repast of smoked ham and cheeses, fruits and flatbread. The ale flowed and there was no man or woman whose belly was not full and whose spirit lacked contentment, for those hours at least.

I went to help in carrying jugs of mead but Eirik beckoned me to sit beside him. "There are others to serve," he assured me. "Today, everyone should see the regard I have for you and know you're mine."

Never before had he accorded me such public recognition; I was his consort, rather than his wife.

"You're worthy of their respect." Eirik placed his hand about my waist.

We fell to discussing the wrestling and I commended him on his performance, for it was as much that as a show of physical prowess.

"Aye, I won't deny it." He shared his smile with me. "There's little need for me to prove myself among my own men. They know my strength already."

"And what of Gunnolf's strength?" I sliced an apple. Its tang went well with the goats' cheeses before us. "Does he fear it would be his face pushed in the dirt, were he to take part?"

Eirik looked at me askance.

"Bold talk for such a little mouse under the jarl's roof." He took a piece of apple from my plate. "We're different, he and I, but no man had a truer brother. He would give his life for me, as I would for him."

I lowered my eyes, choosing not to answer. It seemed clear to me that Gunnolf might well be jealous of Eirik's popularity and his prowess. As jarl, he had authority but I doubted he had the men's love as his younger brother did.

The meal being taken, horses were brought, Gunnolf mounting an elegant, dappled grey, that shook its white mane as he took his seat. Eirik's was a golden roan, solid of leg and girth, with a deep barrel. There were perhaps twenty in all and Eirik led a mare for me to climb, chestnut in colour with a blaze upon its nose. It was Asta's, though I'd never seen her on its back, her condition preventing her from taking such exercise.

"You'd like to come?" he asked. "Join our hawking?"

It had been many months since I'd ridden and even longer since I'd joined in falconry, but I took my seat without difficulty. I looked back, to see Lady Asta waving. She'd want to hear all the excitement, later, and I'd no wish to disappoint her.

Of course, Helka was among the riders.

"The men will race on, in pursuit of the birds," she told me. "Stay close. Though the best hunting will be in the fields south of the forest, our ride may take us near the clifftops, where there are fissures hidden in the grass. A wrong footstep and your sweet mare would break its leg or fall. Some chasms are large—enough to take a horse whole, and the unfortunate rider."

I shuddered at the thought.

"You'll be safe with me," she promised. "Keep by my side."

Gunnolf took his falcon with the air of one who knows he is master, unhooding it and settling the bird. Its claws clutched the leather of his cuffed arm.

"Are you ready, brother?" he called, looking to Eirik, his eyes as wild and unfathomable as those of the dark-plumed peregrine.

"Aye, always," came Eirik's returning shout, taking his own bird, brought to him tethered on its leash. "Your hunter may be more powerful but mine has been with me since she was a chick." He stroked its soft, speckled breast and cocked his head to look into the hawk's amber gaze. "She's the better trained, I'll wager."

"And what do you wager?" Gunnolf called in return.

"Whatever you wish." Eirik grinned. "All that's mine is yours, after all. I can deny you nothing."

Gunnolf threw back his head and laughed to hear it. "Spoken well, brother. I shall think on it…"

With that, he let fly his peregrine and Eirik kissed the sleek head of his pretty hawk, before casting her to the wind. The jarl gave his mount a swift kick and set off toward the woods, leaving the rest of us to follow.

With the wind in our faces, we skirted the trees then dropped down toward the open meadows and the straw-blown fields.

The birds flew high, hovering to scan the ground then soaring and chasing one another. The peregrine darted so close, at times, I thought it would wing Eirik's hawk, but they flew on, swift and agile.

Gunnolf's bird was the first to catch sight of its prey, and he cried his delight to see it dive, talons outstretched at the final moment. The peregrine sat upon its prize, tearing fur and flesh with its razor-beak before Gunnolf's sharp whistle summoned its return.

Helka and I had been to the rear of the party, my own mare being less fleet than the others, but we now drew alongside.

From the peregrine's claws hung a hare, limp and bleeding, its neck broken, its eyes glassy in unexpected death. With a shake of feathers, the bird deposited its prize, resuming its place on its master's forearm.

"You've coddled your little hawk, brother." Gunnolf rewarded his own bird with a chunk of raw meat. "She seems not the mighty huntress you believe her to be."

Eirik held out his cuff, inviting his hawk to alight there.

"And what do you wish from me, my jarl?"

"Only the pleasure of an initiation."

Eirik frowned but bowed his head, and Gunnolf turned, looking about, until he found what he sought.

The jarl brought his horse so close that I felt the heat of its flank. My mare tossed her head away from the intruding muzzle of the dappled grey but I held her steady. Whatever was required of me, I must comply. I was a guest of Svolvaen and of the jarl's home; Eirik's promise was as good as my own. I could not break it without shaming him.

I'd never been so near to a falcon. It was a handsome creature, stately and graceful, but I felt myself shrink from its crimson-stained beak and its unblinking gaze. One of the men threw the hare to Gunnolf, who caught it in his free hand and pressed his thumb to the wound. The blood bubbled from the jagged tear at its throat, running thick.

"You may skit as swiftly as the hare but you can't escape."

Speaking low enough that no other could hear, he daubed my forehead before dropping the pad of his thumb to my lower lip, smearing blood there. The intimacy of it startled me. Instinctively, I licked the moisture away, finding it bitter upon my tongue.

"The first time is sweetest." Gunnolf's eyes lingered upon my lips, his own parting, full and sensuous. I found, somehow, that I'd bitten myself; he saw it and laughed, tossing the hare away again.

Gunnolf raised his arm and gave a soft whistle, sending the peregrine back into the sky. Eirik, too, released his hawk, and the two took the breeze under their wings, circling and swooping, lifting on the wild currents of the wind, daring one another higher.

The birds disappeared into the clouds while, down below, we craned to see them. The hawk emerged with the other on its tail. It was a game of chase, it seemed. However, the falcon's pursuit was relentless. The smaller bird skittered low over the field while its rival hovered above. As the hawk struggled to rise, the peregrine seized its chance. It dived, rearing up its claws at the final moment, knocking the air from Eirik's huntress, sending it tumbling.

The bird hit the earth upon its back and lay unmoving but for the flutter of one wing. Eirik rode to the spot, dismounting to take the hawk in his arms.

It trembled briefly, then lay still.

9

I'd long ago put away the garments I'd brought with me, for they marked me as an outsider. Helka most often wore tunics and trousers but gave me some of her aprons, woven from flax and dyed in shades of russet and green. They suited me well enough—engraved bone brooches fastened the straps over each shoulder.

She berated me for lack of skill in weaving cloth. Even she, whose time was spent more in hunting, knew how to work a loom. Her fingers were nimble but, when I tried, everything tangled. It had always been so.

"You're too impatient, Elswyth," she chided, showing me how to use the heddle rods to separate the threads of warp. She passed the weft through on its shuttle. "You desire to have all you wish without applying yourself to the labour of the task. All things worthy of attaining require our constancy."

I didn't deny the reprimand, knowing myself well enough to see the truth of it. I'd always been reckless, inclined to impulse and hastiness. I wished for action, not the monotony of hours at the loom. My stitching was little better, whether my needle was bone or wood. I preferred the dyeing of the cloth, knowing well which leaves and tubers produced the brightest colours.

Of course, I had one skill which rivalled these womanly pursuits, as taught to me by my grandmother—my healing knowledge of plants and herbs. However, I still hadn't found a cure for the sores which plagued Ylva.

The salve I'd made from elm bark, with sage and yarrow, had curbed the spread of the poison. The sores had become less aggressive but the skin refused to heal. Astrid told me that she heard Ylva sobbing through the night, for the loss of her young man. Though my treatment had prevented the blight on her cheek from becoming an open sore, the skin remained red and swollen, the infection lingering beneath the surface. I feared to lance it as I would a boil.

Not for the first time, I wished my grandmother were with me. How I longed to bury my head in her lap and seek her guidance. She always seemed to know the answer, even where the situation was most difficult. In likelihood, she was already dead and her home cleared of its simple possessions. If I returned, I'd find some other family living there, in the home I'd shared with her.

I attempted to put these thoughts aside, for they served no purpose and I wished to keep fair spirits, those being of best use to myself and to those around me.

The weather was full of the north wind now, and the first snow flurries had come to Svolvaen. "We'll soon be contained indoors. If the winter's hard, the harbour may even freeze over. We shouldn't waste this time," Helka urged. "Come—we'll go fishing."

Asta insisted that I take the opportunity. Her belly was growing fast but she still wished to attend herself in most matters. Faline would keep her company in my absence.

It was with some excitement that I sat in the rear of Helka's vessel. I'd not been upon the water since the great journey that had brought me to Svolvaen. I couldn't help a degree of apprehension but Helka assured me that I'd be safe in her care.

"Only move as I direct you," she commanded, "Or we'll find out how well you swim."

The air was fresh and the wind brisk, and I understood immediately why she liked to sail. There was an immense feeling of freedom, and it was beautiful, the sunlight quivering on the water. She took us between the cliffs and I gazed upwards, wondering at the height of the sheer rock.

"The men collect auk eggs in spring, climbing down from the top, attached to ropes."

The very thought of it made my head spin. It appeared too steep to climb. I could see no obvious footholds.

"You need a head for heights. It's not for everyone," Helka admitted.

"And you?"

"I prefer not to." She looked up at the whirling seabirds. A gannet dived not far off, emerging with a silver fish in its long beak. "The life of the chicks is precarious enough without us eating those eggs."

The tide was with us, taking us out towards the open sea, although the wind blew inland.

"The fishing boats go out in all but the worst weather. Mine too, although only as far as the mouth of the fjord. Beyond that, the waves are too strong." She patted the side proudly and pointed to the net folded at our feet. "You throw it out and let the wind take your sail, then pull it in afterwards."

"As easy as that?"

"You'll see." Helka nodded for me to take up the net. We fastened it to the rear of the boat before casting it a good distance behind. 'Now, we move the tiller and turn the boat so the wind is behind us. Our net will swell out as we move through the water, and the fish will be trapped inside.'

We spent the next few hours sailing back and forth, letting the wind carry us, the net filling with four or five fish each time, until we had quite a haul.

When Helka turned us back, she took us close to the cliffs, that I might peer into the caves. The opening of one was lower than the rest, and wider.

"I used to hide here when I was younger. There's a flat space, where it's possible to sit or lie down, and you can take a small boat right inside if you bring down the mast. You can tie it there, out of sight."

She steered us closer still, being careful to avoid the jagged rocks on either side of the entrance, where the waves splashed and split.

"Did you have cause to hide very often?"

"No more often than my brothers." Her lips twitched in a smile. "But not even Eirik knew where I went. It's good, sometimes, to have a secret place."

I conjured an image of the three of them as children, Helka playing with her brothers as I had with the boys of my own village. I suspected their rivalry had incited her desire for supremacy with bow and arrow, with sword, and upon horseback. I thought back to Gunnolf's marking of me with blood from the hare. He would have been a greedy sibling, hungry to take ascendancy; he would have thought it his due, as the oldest.

There was a rising in the wind, sending the gulls wheeling from the ledges above, to glide white upon the air. "I had something similar," I mused. "Part of the woods where the other children didn't like to go, and a particular tree I'd climb. One of the branches was wide enough to curl upon. I stayed there all night once. I'd forgotten to shut in the chickens, and the fox came and killed all but two of them."

"You were punished?" asked Helka.

"My grandmother smacked me, and I ran away."

"And how long did you stay hidden?"

"Only until the next day. I came home ravenous and was given three bowls of soup, with another clout for making my grandmother worry!"

"Ah!" declared Helka, "I was better prepared. I used to keep food in the cave, in a leather bag, and a bottle of mead."

I raised my eyebrows. How wonderful it would've been to have known Helka when I was growing up.

"I was a clever girl, yes?" She smiled in satisfaction, and I nudged her playfully.

"I still store some things there. We never know what may come… and a hiding place can be useful." Her face was serious again. "Although I'm beginning to think I should stop running away from what frightens me."

Her thoughts were evidently no longer upon childish things and I wondered what it was that Helka feared. She'd tell me, I supposed, when she had a mind to do so.

"If ever I need to hide, I'll come here."

"Except that I shall know where to find you." Helka smiled. "Not such a good hiding place!"

"But I shan't mind if you find me." I squeezed her arm. "I'll be waiting, knowing that you'll come and make everything all right again."

"Always, Elswyth, if it's in my power," Helka promised.

to endure three winters; none would miss what I took. Eirik, in any case, wouldn't refuse my request.

I took my leave and headed back, into the night, to those who awaited my return.

"Sing for us, my love."

I entered to see Gunnolf placing Asta's lute in her arms. He lifted her hair back from her shoulders, that her fingers might find the strings of the instrument more easily.

"What would you have me play?" she asked, her eyes lit by his touch. "I fear you know all by heart."

"Whatever pleases you, wife." Gunnolf dropped a kiss upon her forehead.

Despite these gestures of affection, his gaze strayed towards me as I joined them. He lay back on the goatskins about the firepit, taking up his horn of ale, and I felt him linger over the curve of my breast. I paid no heed, but Faline caught his look, her face drawn bitter. I hoped only that Asta did not notice such things.

We'd eaten well and the flames blazed. It was easier to bear the incessant moaning of the wind when we were comfortable inside. I closed my eyes and lay back my head upon Eirik's chest. We were a small gathering that night, only Helka and Olaf being with us.

I'd thought Asta would choose a love ballad. Instead, her voice filled the great space of the longhouse with an ominous tale, of the long winter coming, when all would freeze and wither. Her haunting melody unwound the threads of the doom of the gods and the horror which would overwhelm the world. The great wolf Fenrir would break its bonds and its jaws would ravage, until even the sun was dragged into the beast's belly. With the beast's last howl, the land would sink beneath the sea, into perfect silence.

We neither moved nor spoke as Asta's melancholy song rang out those dark prophecies of *Ragnarök*, but it seemed a shadow moved through the room, touching each one of us.

The last notes of the lute left us with the moan of the night wind beyond the safety of our walls, and we took our forebodings to our beds.

11

For so long, I'd slept against the warmth of Eirik's body and woken to his heated passion. My need was as great as his and not just by night. Eirik sought me out in whatever task I was engaged. Wrapping his arms about my waist, he melted me with his bearded kisses, his mouth hot upon my neck, before carrying me to his bed.

I watched and waited for my belly to grow, desiring motherhood as I never had with the husband I did not love, the husband Eirik's men had slaughtered. I remembered creeping from my bed as he snored, washing him from me to avoid a baby coming.

Eirik seemed blind to Faline's seductive glances, given as much to spite me as to gain him for herself. In this, and in his constant yearning for the comfort of my body, I saw love.

Helka ate with us most days, though she preferred her own company more often than not. She often retreated to the home she'd shared with her husband, Vigrid. Asta was sleeping a great deal and I'd just tucked the covers about her shoulders. Walking through the great hall, I passed Eirik, sharpening the steel of his double-bladed axe, sitting by the fire with Olaf and Gunnolf and several of the other men. I didn't need to glance behind to know that his eyes followed, that he was already thinking of the ways in which he would take me.

Later that evening, as I undressed for bed, I listened to their voices: raised in laughter, fists thumping upon backs in brotherhood—these Northmen who fought at one another's side. They were recalling some battle and their various braveries. It was the sort of talk Eirik loved, but he would soon come to me, I knew.

Lying naked upon the furs, my bare skin tantalized by their softness, I stroked between my legs. Dipping into the growing wet, I thought of Eirik's battle-born vigour, the hardness of his body and his warrior strength.

Blood-hungry weapons filled the chamber: his iron-headed spear, a light crossbow, feathered arrows as long as my arm, the helmet of leather and steel that fitted smooth to Eirik's head, and his chainmail tunic. His sword, wrought from twisted steel and iron, hammered into an unyielding edge, stood unsheathed. Even in the dim light it gleamed as if with its own vitality, remembering the many limbs it had severed and the crimson libations it had claimed. Heart of the Slain he called it, for its power over life and death.

When Eirik pulled back the curtain, he smiled to see me ready, my fingers starting what I wished him to continue.

"I shan't take you quietly." He unbuckled the belt upon which his dagger hung.

"My Lord," I answered, teasing him with a view of what lay inside me.

Grasping my waist, he pulled me to the edge of the bed. "Full of sweetness," he murmured, lowering his head to taste me, rubbing the flat of his tongue through my slit.

I shivered as he delved deeper, moaning at his upward caresses.

"I want them to hear you." He pressed the soft point of his tongue where I most desired it, sucking me between his teeth, letting his beard rub rough against the tender skin of my inner thigh.

I cried out as he pulled me more firmly onto his mouth, devouring my softness, penetrating me with the full length of his tongue.

"Louder, my love," he warned, "Or I'll invite them in, to hear you properly."

I squirmed beneath him, upon the very edge of my ecstasy. It was not the first time that others had been close during our lovemaking. There was little privacy, despite the wooden enclosure of our boxed chamber, and I was not ashamed of the noises I made. It excited me, even, to think of them listening, hearing the satisfaction of our bedding.

Dropping his woollen trousers, Eirik swiftly guided his shaft and I gave a wail of want as I took the glistening head.

"Yes, my sweet one." My body took the full length of his desire, delivered hard into my yielding flesh. I panted with the force of his thrusts, lifting my hips to meet him until my voice gave its final rising. Eirik groaned loudly and clenched, holding himself deep, pulsing his seed.

There was a cheer and laughter from the adjoining room, at which Eirik grinned, collapsing beside me.

"You wouldn't bring them in here, would you?" I asked, though the idea did not horrify me as perhaps it should have done.

"Nay, I would not." Eirik's hand found my breast, squeezing the nipple. "For they would not wish to stop at looking. Any man watching you writhe beneath me would want his share, and I've no wish to do battle in my own bedchamber. You are my woman, Elswyth. No other shall have you."

His answer pleased me and we made love again—slowly this time, rocking languorously until the end, and with Eirik's kisses gentle on my lips.

We dozed, and it was fully dark when I woke. All was quiet, but something had stirred me, and Eirik, too.

"Did you hear it?" I asked. "Someone crying out?"

I placed my tunic over my head and looked through into the great space of the hall, where the embers were glowing still. There was a keening from the far end, where Asta slept.

As I hurried through, I saw Guðrún peeking from the alcove in which we prepared food, with Sylvi behind her.

Another curtain swept aside and Gunnolf appeared, bare-chested; Faline was beside him, her fingers curled about his arm.

He inclined his head to me—in recognition, I supposed, for my having risen to attend his wife. My returning nod was brief before I looked away.

The lamp's wick was still lit on her bedside, though almost burnt to the quick, its illumination showing me the paleness of her face as she sat up in the bed, her eyes wild and dark. I wrapped her close, for she trembled.

"Did you hear him?" She clung to me, her cheek clammy against mine.

I thought she referred to Gunnolf and his wayward behaviour. It was a subject none mentioned in Asta's presence.

"Nay, my lady. I heard nothing. The house is quiet." I rocked her gently upon my shoulder.

"I couldn't find him, no matter how I looked."

"Only a bad dream," I soothed, encouraging her to lie back.

"Where do they go? The babies that die?" She licked her lips and I saw they'd grown cracked.

"Your child is well, my lady, growing safe inside you." I smoothed a tendril of hair from her forehead. "There's nothing to fear."

She cradled the curve of her belly, turning her face full to mine, her eyes pleading for reassurance.

"I couldn't watch when they put him in the fire." Her fingers fluttered, fretful. "The smoke carries them to the next world; that's what they say, but I don't know if I believe it."

"We all have dark thoughts, my lady, but no one will harm your baby. I'll make sure of that." Taking her hand in both of mine, I whispered softly, saying whatever I could to pacify her. "You'll always be safe when I'm near. You've had a nightmare. It's *draumskrok*: no more than dream-nonsense."

In her fright, she looked more like a child than a grown woman and I was reminded that she was little more than my own age.

"I'll mix a draught to make you sleep again; deep, so that the dreams won't come."

I attempted to rise, but she wouldn't release my hand. "Gunnolf promised not to burn my body; he'll bury me where we put the ashes."

"Ashes?"

"From my first." Asta lifted herself from the pillow, pulling me closer, crushing my fingers within hers. "He's alone, under the frost, in the forest."

In all the months I'd tended her, she'd never mentioned another birth. What pain there must be, to bind bones and flesh within one's own body, to feel the heartbeat of another, only to see that creation brought to nothing. It was little wonder her mind strayed to this lost child, despite her carrying a new babe. Perhaps the pregnancy had caused her mind to wander, but it would do no good to dwell on what was gone.

"We can't choose our time of death," Asta asserted, her voice faint, yet resolved. "Only the Nornar may do that."

I remembered Helka telling me of this legend: that the three women of destiny carved each life upon a stave of wood at the time of our entering the world. Nothing could change what happened. It was this that inspired the bravery of the Norsemen, Helka said, for what is there to lose when a man's fate is predestined.

"It's like *The Song of Skirnir*." Asta sighed. "My destiny is fashioned down to the last half-day, and all my life is determined."

"No more of that, my lady. Think of the new baby coming, arriving with the spring. How happy you'll be then."

The tension seemed to leave her body and she released my fingers, lying back once more.

"I think I shall never see it."

She spoke quietly but I heard every word, and an unsettling feeling overtook me, sitting there, wrapped in shadows. Looking at her face so pale, I saw the skull beneath her skin, and shuddered.

12

Winter continued, in snow-deep slumbering stillness. As the very darkest days approached and the festival of *Jul* drew near, some ventured forth with the full moon to gather mistletoe. The same scythes that had reaped maize and barley from the fields brought down the evergreen foliage, rich in white berries, dangling in great clusters from the trees.

I tied the bunches tight, passing them to Helka, who climbed on Eirik's shoulders to hang them from the rafters. Steadying herself against the great beam of wood above her head, her fingers worked nimbly to secure the thread. "The god of light, Baldur, was slain by an arrow of mistletoe and was sent to reside in the cold and misty Underworld, in everlasting night. The goddess Hel kept him, though he was a reluctant consort."

"And did he stay there for ever more?" I never tired of hearing these stories, though they didn't always make sense to me.

"Nothing lasts forever. It's said that he'll return when Ragnarok ends and the cycle of life begins again. From death, he'll be reborn. Until then, he must endure, as we do, through winter's grip on the frozen Earth."

"On the first night of *Jul*, when the daylight is shortest, we keep vigil until dawn," said Eirik. "No matter how fast Sól drives her chariot, fleeing Fenrir, the devouring wolf of darkness, she's doomed to be swallowed by his ravening jaws. We must wait and watch, to show our need for her to rise again."

There had been a time, long ago, when I'd hidden up a tree to escape a wolf. I remembered the saliva upon its fangs and the steady gaze of its pale eyes. Wolves were beautiful creatures but unpredictable, and always hungry. They were not to be trusted.

Helka reached down as I passed along more mistletoe.

"It's the night of Odin's Wild Hunt," went on Eirik, "When he leads the immortal souls of our ancestors, charging across the sky on Sleipnir, his eight-legged stallion."

The thought filled me with awe. "Have you seen this, Eirik?"

"No wise man ever has." Eirik moved a few steps so that his sister could reach further along the beam. "It would be too dangerous to meet the *Ásgardr* riders. The border between the worlds of living and dead is not always fast, especially when these winter days make the Earth resemble the dark and cold of Hel's merciless Underworld."

"We leave gifts of food and drink in the snow," Helka added. "So that they pass on without danger."

I'd been raised a Christian and knew my own people would be preparing to honour the day of the Saviour's birth. However, we had older stories not unlike these—of winter's darkness and the light that would come again. We decorated our homes with wreaths of green and mistletoe through the months of frost to remind ourselves of the waiting Spring. We had, too, our own rituals to deter the eye of mischievous spirits that roamed most freely when the Earth became a wild and inhospitable place for man.

Helka's stories spoke to my blood, and I sensed the truth of them.

With her foot, she nudged Eirik's shoulder to return her to the ground. He gave me a wink then made a purposeful wobble, pretending to drop his sister, for which she rewarded him with a clip to his ear.

"Have no fear, Elswyth." Regaining her feet upon the ground, Helka looked up to admire her handiwork. "The forces of the restless dead have no reason to harangue you."

"Indeed, not," I answered, but I thought of my husband, whom I'd never mourned, having never loved him, and of my grandmother, left behind across the sea. Had she passed into the next world? I had no way of knowing.

⚜

The men dug through the snow to allow passage up the hill, and the longhouse was soon filled with ribald laughter and boisterous sports. There were some I'd not seen before and some faces I knew well. Torhilde was absent but Ylva came with her mother, though she kept to the corner of the room and wore her cowl close. The blight upon her cheek was hardly visible in the dim light but I knew she would be conscious of its marking.

Eirik brought me a new gown to wear, the fabric fine spun in a becoming shade of violet blue, its bodice embroidered with pansies.

"Wear your golden hair loose, today, as Asta does." He placed a kiss upon my neck. His own tunic was of the same cloth, embroidered with sheaves of barley at the hem.

Gunnolf donned the skin and head of a goat, sacrificing four of the sturdy animals and a pig for the three-day banquet that was to begin. Several women helped Guðrún and Sylvi prepare the victuals. I understood, then, why our pantry had been stocked so full.

My mouth watered over the abundant pots of stew and the richly scented roasting meat. Eirik cut a slice from the pig's shoulder and fed it to me, hot and running thick with juices.

A huge log of oak burned beneath the spit, with holly sprigs and fir branches thrown atop.

"Rake through the ashes in the morning and save the largest pieces," Asta told me. "We'll hang them up to bring good fortune for the coming year."

Before closing the great doors, they rolled out a giant wheel, carved from wood kept dry in the barn. Gunnolf set it aflame, and Olaf and Eirik pushed it off, to whirl down the hill—a burning symbol of the sun, cutting through the darkness, its journey ending somewhere in the meadow.

It wasn't long before the drinking games began, the men competing against the women, while the jarl and his lady sat in judgment, deciding which rhymes and insults were most filled with wit. It was no surprise that Helka shone in weaving puns and riddles, easily gaining the better of the men who challenged her. Eirik soon held up his hands and surrendered before his sister, lifting her onto his shoulders as he'd done when they'd hung the mistletoe, parading her about the room as the victor in their battle.

It was good to see her laughing, and Astrid, too. In that atmosphere of merrymaking, the women linked me into their arms, united in sharing their drollery at the expense of their menfolk. My heart swelled with a new feeling of acceptance and, more than ever, I was glad to have made my journey to join Eirik, to begin this new life.

A tug of war followed, wives pitted against husbands, with the children watching wide-eyed as their mothers planted their feet and pulled with all their might. The women of Svolvaen were strong of arm, for the contest was a close one, though it ended with skirts flying, as they were brought to the ground by the superior brawn of their men.

"Come now, mothers, sisters and daughters," declared Asta. "In gracious forfeit, refill their cups and embrace these men beloved. Rejoice that their strength in sport is also the strength that protects us in times of war."

Eirik was the recipient of more kisses than seemed his due but I was content to let him revel in them, for it was a night of festivity and I'd no wish to be churlish. It was well into the night before the revellers nodded to sleep upon the benches ranged each side of the great hall, sleeping off the mead they'd enjoyed.

The dawn was thin and grey but I smiled to see it. If Odin's terrible hunt had passed over our roof, I'd heard nothing. Through the second day of feasting, we sat again around the fire and listened to tales of man-eating trolls, giants and the gods—their cleverness and trickery, jealousies and deceits. I laughed at how Odin dressed as a bride to retrieve his powerful hammer and shivered to hear Helka tell the full story of sweet Baldur's sojourn in the hidden world of the dead. There was much drinking and eating, the women sharing their gossip as they prepared the table.

Later, Gunnolf encouraged the men in games of chance and threw down a challenge. "Your hand, brother," he proclaimed, resting his elbow upon the table, "And we shall test your prowess." Filled already to the brim with ale, he slurred his words.

Eirik was no better, and the result was part comical, as each vowed to prove the superiority of their arm. Yet, there was an edge to the jarl's sport. With sleeves pushed to their elbows, laying bare their corded arms, it was clear that the contest was in earnest, at least on Gunnolf's part. His teeth clenched in grim determination as they pushed back and forth. Bringing Eirik's fist to the wood, Gunnolf gave a shout of triumph and there was a wildness in his eyes.

While his men cheered his conquest, I thought their hails lacked the fervour of those Eirik had received during the harvest wrestling tournament.

Asta kissed her husband's forehead then excused herself, pleading her condition.

"Brother, you have the better of me," conceded Eirik, gracious as he always was.

"Come, Faline," Gunnolf called. He indicated the jug she carried. "Our horns require attention, and you have the means to satisfy us."

His bawdiness inspired snorts of laughter but I took no pleasure in his lewdness, worrying that Asta may have heard her husband's remark as she made her retreat.

I knew Faline enjoyed attention and she seemed willing enough to claim Asta's place at the jarl's side, even if it were to play the whore rather than the wife. However, it was I Gunnolf looked at as he slapped her rump and drained his cup dry, drawing her to him as she filled it once more. My face must have shown my distaste but he gave no rebuke, surveying me with lazy eyes.

With the drinking of more ale, a round of ribald jokes began and I felt inclined to take my own leave, but Eirik bid me stay and sit on his knee. This I did, though I soon regretted it. He'd drunk more than usual and became lustful before his men, bouncing me harshly upon his lap and reaching beneath my skirts.

He acted towards me almost as he had in the days of our first meeting, in the demeaning fashion of a master commanding his thrall. "Come, wench, you'll not deny me. You like me well enough in our bed."

"And in the fields, too," chimed one of the men, to the guffaws of his neighbours.

Eirik pulled aside the fine linen of my bodice, taking my breast in his hand, for all to see.

"Nay, Eirik," I declared, endeavouring to release myself. However, even in his cups, he was too strong, grasping me all the tighter as I struggled, taking my nipple in his mouth and laughing at my annoyance.

Seeing the leering grins of those about me, my anger broke. I slapped Eirik's cheek to make my escape, pulling my clothes to cover myself.

"I'm to bed and you may join me if you wish. If you prefer to sleep on a bench with your ale then stay as you are."

Helka had sat aside, never being one to interfere in the jests of men, but she rose to my side, adding her voice in berating his lack of care.

Gunnolf howled with mirth, slapping Eirik upon the back, a wicked gleam in his eye. "Best do as you're bid, little brother, since these women are your masters." He waggled his little finger. "Perhaps you've lost your cock already and had better put on an apron."

At that, Eirik lurched to his feet and, within three steps, had grasped his axe. Helka reached to detain him but he shrugged her away, eyes suddenly blazing. In undermining Eirik's masculinity, Gunnolf's insult was the fiercest any man might suffer.

"What say you?" Eirik roared. "I am man enough for any woman, and none the master of me."

Gunnolf rose to his feet at that.

"None but I," he snarled. "Remember well that I am master of all Svolvaen and your allegiance is to me."

The hall fell silent as the words were cast.

"Unless you go to chop wood, you'd best set aside your axe." Gunnolf's voice was filled with its own steel.

Eirik lowered his arm. I'd never seen him so, seeming not to know where to look nor what to say. He knelt upon the floor, bowing his head.

"Forgive me, my jarl. In my haste, I did not see the joke. The ale unbridled my temper but my allegiance is yours, as ever."

Gunnolf reached down and took the axe from Eirik.

"Beware, brother." He scanned the faces of his men, as if addressing not just Eirik but them all. "Do not allow that temper to be your undoing."

He ran his thumb across the sharp edge of the weapon.

"To do so will be to find the blade upon your own neck."

told me that his mother had died when he was barely three years old but I didn't know the circumstances.

"We might join our blood with that of Skálavík." I heard Eirik say. "It would end the feud. Jarl Eldberg might accept Helka for his bride."

"Marry Eldberg!" she protested. "I'd rather lie with the hog in the sty."

"Nay," snapped Gunnolf. "Hallgerd is two years dead and I've waited long to overthrow the pact. I am jarl, now, and will have my revenge. I'll let the dogs feast on those Eldberg loves, then crush him beneath my foot." Gunnolf laughed but there was no mirth in it. "Besides which, the little birds I pay to tell me of our enemies have sent notice that Eldberg has some new wife in his bed. So, that alliance is no longer possible, brother."

I imagined Helka's relief at this news, as I watched her shoulders relax.

Gunnolf took another swig of ale. "He'll pay for the actions of his father, as will all Skálavík."

The silence hung heavy before Eirik nodded. "Aye, brother. I understand your wish." He took a long draught from his cup. "However, I've no desire to lead us to empty defeat. Jarl Eldberg's warriors outnumber ours fourfold."

"Asta's clan have pledged their help," added Helka.

"They have," conceded Eirik, "But the match was made by our uncle with an eye to her dowry. I don't trust her menfolk to fight to Valhalla's gates. They prosper only because they live upon an island easily defended."

"I'm ahead of you, brother, with an alliance strong enough to bring victory to our cause. Before the snows came, I sent a petition to Jarl Ósvífur of Bjorgyn, offering Helka's hand to his son, Leif. You'll travel as soon as the way is clear."

Helka's voice was edged sharp. "And I have no say in the matter."

Gunnolf growled in displeasure and I wondered, not for the first time, at Helka's boldness.

She would comply with nothing against her will but Eirik attempted to sway her, nonetheless. "Set aside your grief for Vigrid. Your unwed state is an insult to Freya and all the gods, who made women for the pleasure they bring to men and for the bearing of children."

I flinched to hear him say so for, if the bearing of children were a woman's duty, had I not also failed?

I couldn't see her face but I imagined her eyes blazing. "I'll never marry again, unless to a man of my own choosing."

"Enough!" Gunnolf's voice rose in a curse. He grasped her arm. "You'll have the man I put before you."

"The decision is wise, Helka," Eirik urged. "Leif Ósvífursson is renowned as a warrior and will become jarl in due course. It will be a good match."

Helka answered most coolly. "I might direct you to the same path, brother. I hear that young Freydís Ósvífursdóttir is in need of a husband.

Why not an alliance forged from your marriage? She's newly reached her womanhood, I believe, and comely. You should take an honest wife. You've spent too many years casting your seed in random fields. If you won't marry for love then do so for our people."

I choked back an impulse to step forward and rage at Helka. My blood turned to ice at the thought of Eirik laying this Freydís in the bed we shared, touching her hair, her skin. I held my breath, waiting to hear how he'd answer.

He seemed about to speak but the words did not leave his lips.

Helka tossed her head in frustration. "I see that I must decide for us, brother. Your bravery only runs to violence, and not to matters of the heart." She jabbed at the fire, but there were no more flames. The embers had lost their heat. "I make no promise of compliance but, as soon as the weather allows, we'll travel to Bjorgyn. One way or another, we'll return with an alliance."

Gunnolf lifted the jug and poured from it. "Here's to new allies, dear sister, dear brother," he toasted. "May you find them to your liking. If not, I suggest you do not return at all."

14

Helka donned her cloak and departed. Gunnolf too, rose, taking some steps towards the boxed room he shared with Asta before changing his mind. Turning away, he removed himself, instead, to the bench where Faline slept.

No doubt she'd heard all that had passed, as well as I. How gleeful she'd be. Not one word had Eirik offered to protest his love. Helka, too, had betrayed me. She'd rightly warned me against believing Eirik ready to wed, but I'd not expected her to urge his marriage to another. I'd thought her to take my part, to wish my happiness as much as I wished hers.

I could foresee how it would go. Once in Bjorgyn, Helka would persuade Eirik to seal an alliance of marriage, that she might be spared the contract herself. If Helka convinced him of her abhorrence to the match, Eirik's sense of duty would force his choice.

He didn't shift from the fire, continuing to stare into the embers. I watched him with neither the will to move nor speak. What could I say that would be worth the breath?

I'd struck a bargain and Eirik had kept his part. I wanted for nothing. He might have taken me against my will, making me his thrall. Instead, it had been my choice to accept whatever terms I found under his roof—not as his wife but as his consort. I'd made my choice willingly, to leave my homeland and travel to Svolvaen. I'd been eager to learn of my heritage from the father I'd never known—the Viking who'd raped my mother and conceived my birth. I'd embraced this path, eager to learn about all that shaped my nature, but I was not ready to learn that the man I loved thought so little of me.

Had I been born from my father's marriage bed, would I have been valuable enough to have my hand sought by Eirik? There was little enough chance of that, now, when he had the pleasure of my body and no obligation beyond my keep.

As it was, I'd found only another place where I was tolerated more than accepted. Were Eirik to grow tired of me, my position would be lost. I burned with the injustice of it.

It could do no good to dwell on my discontent, yet I couldn't set aside my heart's true yearning.

I walked to where he sat. When he looked up, I saw an anguish I'd not expected, though I couldn't tell if he was simply pained that I'd overheard or anguished at Gunnolf's insistence at an allied marriage.

Leading him to our chamber, I undressed him and myself, until our bare skin touched and my breasts brushed the hair of his chest. He guided my hand to where he wished it but I was not ready to lose myself in lovemaking. Instead, I lay him down and curled my body to his.

"If you take a wife, what will become of me?"

"You'll stay with me." Eirik's voice was firm. "You're mine."

"You won't send me away? Marry me to another man?"

"Never."

I fought to contain my tears. "But how can it be? I cannot watch as another woman takes what I desire— marries, where I have no hope. And what of her, this Freydís? How can you expect to keep us under the same roof?"

"If I take her for my wife, she'll do as I ask."

"But you don't wish it, Eirik?" I'd never begged, but I could hold back no longer. "You want me to have your children? You want me to be with you, always?"

"Yes, my love, yes." His soft mouth found mine and his fingers stroked my hair. I felt the caress through all my body, felt myself opening to him, seeking the reassurance of his physical love, wishing to believe that our lovemaking would conquer all that I feared.

Man and woman joined, we sated our need. I surrendered as I always did. There was unfathomable pleasure in his touch, breaking me apart until the world was tumbling and I was lost.

"You'll marry her." I whispered, afterwards.

"When the time comes for me to act, I'll know what I must do. You, too, Elswyth. You'll know."

"And why must we obey your brother? Can we not leave? There are other lands, surely. A place we might go."

"You don't know what you're saying." His reply was resolute. "We must do what's best for Svolvaen—you and I both."

He placed his fingers on my lips, bidding me listen.

"When my mother told us to hide, Gunnolf carried me," Eirik began. "We went to the forest, crouching among the trees. I didn't want to hear or see, but Gunnolf made me look, and Helka, too. We hid until there were no more flames. My uncle, Jarl Hallgerd, beat the Skálavík raiders into retreat, but my father fell, fighting." His voice caught in his throat. "They took several of our women, my mother among them. Svolvaen emptied its stores and coffers for their release, and the pact was signed."

He said nothing for some moments and I ached for him. I'd caused pain, making him remember.

"When she returned to us, she was changed. Grief for my father, I thought; perhaps something else I was too young to understand. A few months later, they found her in the fjord." His breath left him in a long sigh. "My uncle and aunt had no children so we became theirs and, on Hallgerd's death, Gunnolf received the jarl's mantle."

I kissed Eirik's fingers and moved them over my heart. "You serve him because it's what your uncle wished."

"And what my father would have thought right. It's my duty to serve Svolvaen and my jarl, even when I don't agree with his strategy."

"No matter that he wishes to lead Svolvaen into war against an enemy you may not be able to defeat?"

Eirik pulled me closer. "If it's my destiny to fight, I will."

"What if it's your destiny to die, Eirik?" Tears overtook me. There was so much I might say but I knew no argument would change how Eirik felt, nor the outcome. His bravery had won my heart, and the physical power of him. How could I change any part of what I loved?

His sense of duty was as real as the inked patterns upon his body—those markings that defined who he was, and where he'd come from. It was my history too; yet, half of me did not belong here, and I was not his wife. I was no better than his slave, albeit a willing one.

My voice trembled. "I can't lose you."

"Don't cry." He brushed my hair from my face. "I'll return, and we shall have many nights, my Elswyth."

He kissed me, murmuring his promises, but the words fell hollow, for what substance had they? I must take what was granted, having no power to demand more, but I feared an end to my happiness.

15

Weeks passed and the thaw came, until there was no more cause for delay. The evening before their departure, we sat about the fire as we'd done many nights before. The flames leapt, and the shadows with them. We were subdued in our conversation, each consumed by our own thoughts.

Eirik gave me an amulet to wear, engraved with the hammer of power. "Like Mjolnir, Thor's magical weapon, I shall return." He fastened the leather thong about my neck. "Gunnolf will watch over you." I smiled weakly at that, for I'd no doubt that the jarl's eyes would be upon me.

I'd been angry with Helka for a long time, unable to put aside my belief that it would be Eirik who returned with a bride, rather than she with a groom. But she was my friend, nonetheless, and I parted from her with a kiss.

The next morning, I watched them ride away. I wrapped my cloak about me to ward off the early morning chill, then went to rake the remnants of the fire. Nothing remained but blackened ash.

There had been other deaths over the frosted months, each accompanied by the same disfiguring blisters, but none spoke openly of the strange outbreak, which affected some and not others. The old and weak seemed to suffer most, and the very young. There was a rumour of dark magic, Astrid told me—of a curse upon Svolvaen—though such whispers bided behind closed doors. The confinement of winter had likely curtailed the spread of the disease but spring was on our heels, with all hands needed in the fields. There could be no more hiding.

"Show them your healing," Gunnolf demanded, bidding me visit every household. "Take whatever you need; do what must be done."

I gave my promise and hoped with all my heart to find a cure. With it would surely come the respect I sought. I might yet earn my place among these people.

With the jarl's authority at my back, Svolvaen's doors opened to me and I took my remedies to all who needed them. I prevented sores from festering and eased the sting of open wounds. Some regarded me with suspicion and were reluctant to accept my touch; others were grateful for my care. I gave my time to all, whether they wished me there or not, for the blight was no longer a private matter. What strength would Svolvaen have if half its people were lost to the disease?

I refused to give up hope. The blooms were flowering afresh in the meadows and plants' leaves unfurled in new growth. The answer, I felt sure, lay close to hand.

Despite this shadow hanging over Svolvaen, life continued. The fields needed ploughing, ready for their seed, and Gunnolf commanded that the fortifications of our settlement be strengthened. Men were charged with cutting branches for sharpening, and a second row of outward-facing spikes were added to our perimeter.

One day, around this time, I realized I no longer had the dried mushroom I'd picked so long ago, in my own forest, over the sea. I'd kept it in a leather pouch, convincing myself that I'd never need to use it. It seemed an age ago that I'd been tempted to put its poison to evil use, on the first night on which the Viking raiders had feasted in our hall, drinking my dead husband's ale.

It had been a foolish whim to bring it with me, and to keep it, secreted in my pocket. With the bright sun returning, it seemed best that it had dropped and fallen somewhere, without me having noticed. I imagined the pouch lay somewhere in the forest, long since covered by leaves and moss.

Meanwhile, I thought often of Eirik and Helka, making their way through the hills, to the lands beyond. Each day that passed took Eirik further away, but the needs of those about me called on my strength and were a distraction from the disappointment eating at my heart.

Both Gunnolf and Asta had need of my skill, for we were a house of troubled dreamers. My lady woke often with a mournful cry, though she shook her head when I asked her to unburden her fears. Whatever darkness filled her thoughts, she wished no longer to tell me of it. I was wary of giving her too much of my sleeping draught, lest it robbed her of her growing babe. Gunnolf, meanwhile, urged no restraint, drinking down whatever I gave him to chase away his own vile visions.

My own nights were filled with the faces I saw through the day. In those sleeping hours, I roamed the forest, searching for the plant that would bring our cure. The wolf of old still prowled the shadows of my slumbered world, its gaze upon me, though it did not approach. One night, Asta walked with me in my forest reverie, not by my side but following behind, her footsteps in keeping with mine. When I turned, she gave not her usual smile. Her face ashen, she looked with pained expression, clutching the roundness of her stomach, her eyes beseeching, though I could not discern what she wished from me.

I woke with beating heart and hurried to her chamber, fearing she suffered some further malady.

The jarl had risen early, it seemed, for she was alone. Though pale, indeed, she was still her own sweet self, refusing to grumble at any discomfort from the growing babe. I helped her in her toilette, then bid her rest.

"You're near your time, my lady." I unhooked the goatskin from the small window, placed where the roof met the low stone of the wall to let in the sunlight and the pleasant-scented air.

She nodded her assent, easing back upon the pillows.

"I'll bring porridge with extra honey, for you need your strength."

"How attentive you are, my Elswyth." She smiled her thanks. "I know not where Faline gets to…" She let the thought trail away and I did not take it up.

"It's good to hear the birds and feel the warmth of the new season." Asta rested her hand upon her belly and closed her eyes again. I wondered if there were not one babe but two within, so large was she. It worried me, for she was small of frame and such births were rarely easy.

"A fitting time for new life to enter the world," I said, pushing aside such thinking.

"Time to redden the *hörgr* with sacrifices for Freya," she replied. "'Twas my own hand that did so at the last *Ostara*, dedicating them upon the forest's sacred stone."

"My lady?"

"The sacrament of dying to be reborn," she murmured. "A time to give up old illusions and habits; to recognize the changes in the world before us."

"And to welcome the spring?" I asked.

"Of course." She yawned, and I saw that she would soon be asleep again.

"I'll bring your *dagmal*," I said. "Remember that you must eat, my lady."

I watched with interest as Svolvaen prepared for its festival. Unlike *Jul*, I sensed it would be a sombre affair. No one was willing to tell me what I wished to know, as if it could only be experienced and not explained.

I made my daily round, bringing more of my salve to Astrid. Torhilde had returned home at last—her husband finding he had need of her, after all. He'd become resigned to the marks upon her skin, having developed sores on his own body. Hers had responded well, as Ylva's had done—not fully healed, but not the unsightly blister they had first presented.

I looked to Ylva, who played with the baby upon the bed. The child was growing well, evidently of strong constitution. It had contracted not a single mark. The blight remained arbitrary in choosing its victims.

"Gunnolf has said that only those who are well are to attend the festival," Astrid told me.

"Do you mind?" I asked Ylva, but she blushed and turned away, leaving her mother to answer.

"I'm relieved, in truth," Astrid whispered. "*Ostara* is a night of mystery, when the gods bend close and whisper in our ear." Looking back at Ylva, she drew me to the door, then led me outside. "Its rituals take us back to the earth we came from, to the animal part of ourselves. It's not for children, or for girls who've never lain before with a man. There are no rules on *Ostara* night. No husbands and no wives; only men and women."

I guessed her meaning and was taken aback. Eirik had said nothing to me of *Ostara,* had given me no warning. I thought of the *Jul* festival and the many kisses he'd received. I'd refused to indulge my jealousy, but they held different significance now. I couldn't help but wonder if there were any women in Svolvaen who hadn't enjoyed the attentions of my warrior lover.

"It's up to you, of course," added Astrid. "The men won't touch you unless you invite them, but beware when you do, for the lust of the gods is in them and you'll feel it in your own blood, too."

"And you, Astrid? Will you go?"

She gave a small smile. "I will, indeed; *Ostara* brings power to the soil and to our own body, too. My husband isn't coming back and my bed is lonely. Who knows what *Ostara* will bring me…"

"Be still, my love," said Gunnolf, as he placed the dagger's edge to her ear. "You cannot attend but I'll burn your hair on the sacred altar, and Freya will accept our offering." He drew the blade carefully through her silken tresses, placing the cut strands in his pouch.

"Of course, husband." Asta accepted his kiss upon her brow.

"And I shall remain with you, my lady," I asserted. "You're too close to your time to be left alone."

As I knelt, Gunnolf's hand came to rest on my shoulder. Its heaviness prevented me from rising and stilled my voice against argument.

"I think not." The jarl pressed more firmly as he spoke. "The ceremony awakens us to the pulse of all that lives. It invigorates us with the vital energy of Freya and all the gods. How can you heal others if you don't allow that energy to awaken in yourself?"

I kept my eyes upon the hem of Asta's gown.

"Faline shall stay and tend to your needs, wife." Gunnolf's thumb extended beneath my hair and found the bare skin at the back of my neck. "Under my eye, Elswyth will come to better understand our ways."

16

As the sun climbed, Gunnolf lead us into the forest, the horse's reins loose in his hand. I walked behind, watching the swish of its tail. It was a path Helka had never shown me, light dappling through the canopy, patches of warmth alternating with the shade until the trees grew sparser. Entering the open glade, where the full heat of the spring sun reached us, I felt the impatience of those about me, eyes glancing one to the next, alight with unspoken excitement.

From branches cut and sharpened and driven into the soil, we set our make-shift frames, draping them with skins, above pine needles dry and deep. My gaze was drawn to the *hörgr*. The huge altar stone emitted power, flattened along its upper edge, bathed in the brilliant light of our unclouded sky.

The men lit a fire, stoked with debris from the forest floor and ringed with stones, to contain the flames. We'd brought food for feasting but none touched it. "For afterwards." Astrid gave me a sly wink. "That's when you'll be hungry."

She unwrapped the laces of her boots, to leave her feet bare. "Take off yours, and stay close," she directed, passing me a wooden bowl. "No harm will come if you're with me."

"Kneel, women of Svolvaen." The jarl bid us approach the *hörgr*, while the men stood behind.

The smoky aroma was sweet, as if from the burning of rosemary and heather, but with a bitter undertone. It enticed me to breathe deep, drawing the seductive smoke inside my body, leaving my head and body light. As the moments passed, the trees seemed to grow taller and the sunlight brighter.

"Give yourselves to Freya, on this day of *Ostara*," the jarl continued. "Revel in her blessings, so that your bodies may ripen under her favour."

From his pouch, he took out the long strands of Asta's hair, throwing them into the flames, where they disappeared, as if they'd never been. "This symbol of womanhood I burn, asking Freya to accept our *blót*."

At his nod, the men led the horse forward. "This animal I sacrifice, that Freya may bring prosperity to our crops, our livestock and our people."

The animal seemed to sense what was to come, its eyes rolling in fear, skittering away from the altar, obliging a tighter hold upon its rope. As Gunnolf raised his two-handed axe, I shrank back, wishing not to witness the fatal blow, turning my head.

"You must see," hissed Astrid, clutching my arm with surprising firmness, her eyes wide and bright. "Draw on our goddess Freya's strength."

I made myself look. Another of the men stepped forward, stunning the stallion just below its brow with a single stroke of his cudgel. Before the beast had time to fall, Gunnolf swung his blade to connect with its neck. The crimson spurt seemed almost to hang in the air, in that moment between life and death. Staggering, the horse let forth a rasping sigh and collapsed, the blood foaming to its mouth.

The slow arc of the jarl's second blow sliced through the thick air, meeting the neck once more and severing the head completely. I swayed, bumping against Astrid, who reached around my waist to support me.

"Life for life, we offer this blood to nourish the soil," declared the jarl.

"Do as I do." Astrid stepped forward, lowering her bowl to the tangled gore, catching the oozing scarlet. By the time I'd done the same, the pooled warmth upon the ground had stained my feet, sticky between my toes.

While we women assembled behind the altar, the men of Svolvaen ranged upon the other side. I'd never seen them so still in body, so intent in concentration, following all that we did—as if in their own trance.

"These women dedicate themselves to you, at this time of *Ostara*, great Freya." Gunnolf raised his arms skyward. "As your willing handmaidens, fill them with the desire that drives all creatures of our world and, in their pleasure, make them fruitful."

He came to us in turn, dipping his thumb to the viscous liquid we carried, daubing each forehead. Reaching me, he placed his hands over my own and held me within the steady gaze of his pale eyes. I trembled as he lowered his thumb into the dark crimson, as on that day of falconry, when he'd marked me with the blood of the hare.

I dropped my eyes at the remembrance, waiting for his thumb to catch my lip, for his hand to raise my chin, that he might better see me. I waited for the press of his mouth to mine.

When he moved on, I was left with the disturbing knowledge that I'd sought more of his touch.

The last of us was Bodil, and her eyes did not lower. Gunnolf brought her bowl to his lips and drank, leaving a smear upon them, a gash of red across his cheek. He placed his hands either side of her head and drew her into a kiss deep and long. I could almost taste the blood upon his lips, as if he were caressing my mouth, rather than hers.

Breaking their contact, he led her to the foot of the altar, where Bodil unclasped her apron, letting it drop. Having removed her tunic, she stood naked, auburn hair loose over one shoulder, her skin pale and freckled. She was slender through the waist and hip but her breasts hung large, swollen from the milk with which she still fed her baby.

Gunnolf helped her step up, to lie upon the great stone. At his nod, the women moved closer, knowing their role, familiar with the ritual. The first raised her bowl, letting blood drip onto Bodil's stomach, then tipping further, running scarlet rivulets. The second bowl splashed her breasts, trickling to her throat, while the third cascaded down her abdomen, bloodying her pubis. Bodil gasped and arched her spine as if in raptures of desire, craving more.

My mouth grew dry, observing her wanton freedom. She turned her head as I emptied my own bowl upon her stomach, her eyes filled with more secrets than the forest at twilight, mocking me with her womanliness, with her proven fertility, with her seduction of the man I professed to call my own.

What did I have? An empty belly and an empty bed. Eirik had left. When he returned, it would be to bring home his new bride.

My reverie was interrupted by Gunnolf's voice, thick and slow and deep with lust. "Ripen our seed, Freya, in the soil of this woman's womb, and inside all our women."

His face was transformed, eyes half-closed, while his palm stroked his erection.

Bodil cupped her breast and slid her hand through the slippery crimson, leaving a path down her torso. Her bloodied fingers reached inside her silken sheath, opening her lips.

A moment later, Gunnolf had gripped her raised knees, pulling her towards the edge of the stone to meet his penetration. It took but a dozen strokes before he groaned his release. Parting from her, his length bobbed wet, his lower torso marked with the blood from Bodil's body.

She stretched upon the stone as the next man stepped into the jarl's place, elongating her bloodied body, reaching her arms above her head. She took him willingly, lying still as he aligned his cock and thrust inside her. His strokes were more measured, deeper, bringing a quickening of her breath.

I could not look away, imagining the cold stone against my own back and the stretch of this stranger entering my sex. My mouth grew dry at the thought of taking Bodil's place, of surrendering myself to the same carnal abandon.

"Go, women," announced the jarl. "Find the men of your choosing. Take your pleasure, and may your coupling be fruitful."

None hesitated, setting aside their bowls, moving swiftly to claim their preferred partners. I watched them move away, quietly purposeful, leading their men through the trees or into the shelters we'd erected.

"Come," urged Astrid, tugging my hand and scanning the men yet to be taken, eager to make her choice. "I know who I desire. Who will you choose, Elswyth?"

I looked again at Bodil, beckoning a third lover to approach, opening her mouth to take him there as the other continued his slow strokes between her legs.

I fought the languor descending over my body. Stumbling to the edge of the glade, I heard Astrid call my name but, when I looked back, my eyes found not hers but those of the jarl.

His mouth curled in a lazy smile, revealing the bloodstains between his teeth.

17

I darted through shade and light, feeling nothing but my need to escape, to run from what I did not wish to recognize in myself, fearing all I'd seen.

Emerging from the forest onto the open cliffs, I gulped the crisp air, sobbing with relief at having left behind the strange enchantment that had threatened to overwhelm me. Burying my face to the cool soil, I slept.

He visited my dream, and we were wolves together, leaping through shadows. A night-wind rose through the trees and curled back again. A storm was coming, bristling dark. The black veil of clouds moved swiftly, claw-shredding the crescent moon.

When I woke, he was there, beneath the darkened sky. The beast in him had roused me and I could still taste the growling thunder on my tongue. Something in me was stirring, waiting to uncoil.

"No more running." He touched his fingers above the yoke of my gown, leaning closer. I caught the strange smoke clinging to him and the faint aroma of sex. His breath was upon my neck and I waited for the warmth of his lips.

He was not the man I loved but it was not love I sought from him. I wished for the roughness of a kiss given in the service of jealousy, anger and lust. A kiss which would declare myself to be my own woman—slave to no-one.

Despite my love, Eirik had abandoned me, just as he had so many women. He'd left me to fend for myself and so I would, without regard for him.

The crows were circling, cawing their alarm, before a blinding jolt of lightning stabbed jagged and I tipped back my head in surrender. There was triumph in Gunnolf's eyes, for he was about to take what his brother presumed to own. He placed his hands about my throat, lifting my chin with his thumbs, drawing me upwards to meet his mouth, his tongue. I was falling and there was no going back.

His hands pushed away my bodice, baring the swell of my breasts to the cool air, before covering them with warm palms, thumbing my nipples. Breaking off our kiss, he dropped to take one hard point between his teeth, devouring me with his suckling and his teasing tongue, until my cunt clenched.

"Mine now," he growled, laying me down upon the grass and lifting my skirts. I wrapped my legs around him, wanting him inside, making me forget that I'd ever loved Eirik.

He made me whimper, delving my wet sex with a clutch of fingers before drawing out the thick column of his cock. The sky cursed us with its rolling thunder as I returned the roughness of his lust: biting his lip, breaking his skin with the drag of my nails, pinching the underside of his buttocks to drive him harder. He was wild and thorough, taking me so violently that I cried out in pain, but I had only one thought—that he must not stop.

He crushed my lips to his as he came, pulsing thick, his hands clasping my body to the depth of his final thrust.

Held beneath the weight of him, I clenched against each spasm, and the first drops of rain began to fall.

18

The smoke from the sacrificial fire had affected my judgement. I'd had no warning of what *Ostara* would entail. If Eirik had given it any thought at all, what had he expected? Didn't he foresee that the jarl would take what he wanted and I'd be powerless to deny him? With such lies I tried to vindicate myself.

I'd proven faithless. Perhaps the village wives who'd looked at me askance had been right all along. I didn't deserve their respect, for I had little enough for myself. Wandering from room to room, I couldn't rest. I found duties outside and lingered in the barn. I willed Gunnolf to follow me, willed him to burn me again with his desire, to make me forget myself. Yet, when he had cause to pass me, I flinched away.

I could barely meet Asta's eye, though she treated me as she'd always done. Whatever she knew, or imagined, she did not betray it in her manner. Her heart seemed far lighter than my own, without the bitter burden of reproach, though her body grew ever weaker.

The baby, now grown large and eager to enter the world, appeared to be taking her life-force to feed its own. When her pains began, I prepared the room, bringing water and linens, preparing the knife. I knew what was done, having more than once helped my grandmother deliver new life.

And yet, no baby came. Instead, Asta clutched her stomach and wretched bile, perspiration stark upon her brow. "Can you hear it, Elswyth?" Her hand grasped my wrist with strength she couldn't spare. "It won't let me rest."

I soaked a flannel to cool her head. "There's no one here to hurt you," I soothed, raising water to her lips, but my comfort was not enough. She trembled and tossed, raking her skin so badly I had to bind her hands in cloth, tucking her nails inside her palms.

At last, she lay still but her eyes were unnaturally bright, following me about the room, until the black haw tincture I gave sent her into sleep. She woke gasping for air, thrashing in her sweated bed, wracked in body and mind.

Gunnolf watched from afar, fearing to come near yet unwilling to leave her altogether. His face grew hollow, watching her slip away. He could not look at me, nor I at him.

My dreams were filled with Asta, walking always behind me, through the dark shadows of the forest, her steps ever slower, hampered by her belly. Her eyes were filled not just with pain but with reproach, as if she knew that I'd wronged her and could not forgive.

On waking, I hastened to her side, ready to beg forgiveness for my offence, willing to do whatever she commanded to make it right. Except, of course, there could be no such remedy. No going back.

On the fourth day, Guðrún shook me at first light, for Sylvi wouldn't stir and her skin bore a speckled rash.

"Bathe her in cold water and ensure she drinks," I instructed.

As the village came awake, we saw that others had been visited by the same shadow, as if it had flown across the rooftops by night.

Had Svolvaen not endured enough? I'd seen this before, or something much like it. The pox had touched our village one summer in my childhood. I remembered my grandmother brewing birch bark, yarrow, elderflower and meadowsweet to ease the fever. Borage too, which grew between the brambles and nettles and fallen trunks, higher than my waist, its leaves rough and wrinkled.

Faline watched as I ladled the mixture into travelling pouches, bottles and jugs, but made no effort to help. Most of the time, she and I barely spoke, but the shared memory of our former home pressed hard on me. I knew her to be kin and regretted that we weren't closer.

"You remember how we came through the pox, years ago?" I prompted. "My grandmother treated us."

"I recall." Faline picked up one of the jugs, lowering her nose to the aroma of its contents. "Your aunt had taken my mother's place by then. She told me that, if I scratched, the scars would disfigure me and I'd never find a husband." She placed the remedy back upon the table. "I did everything they told me to but there never was a husband, was there…"

She and I, both, had been cheated, in various ways. I'd thought myself above her, of late, condemning her choices. I'd proven myself no better. I was worse, being a hypocrite. Faline, at least, made no pretence.

"Help me carry these?" I asked. "Lady Asta needs my tending, too, and it'll be quicker together."

She regarded me a moment, then lifted a hand to her cheek. "I'm feeling a little weak… and hot. Perhaps, I should return abed…" She turned back after a few steps. "If you've any sense, you'll do the same. Let them look after their own."

I lay upon the floor, listening to Asta breathing through the night. While I heard her, I knew she lived.

She would swallow neither fish nor meat—only porridge and honey, coaxed between her lips from my spoon, though even this her stomach would not keep. I told her stories of my childhood: of the trees I'd climbed, and the joy of leaping into cool water in the heat of summer.

Waking before the dawn, she whispered. "Look after my baby." I lit the lamp and its flame quivered thin. Her cheeks bore twin flushes, though her face was paler than ever. "You and Eirik."

Had she forgotten the reason for his departure? Forgotten that there would be a marriage but that it would not be I who stood beside the groom?

"Beautiful in your wedding gown…" she mumbled, in her reverie of a future that could not be.

"And you'll be there to see it." I went along with the 'make-believe', promising her everything she wished, bringing her jewel box at her bidding.

"To wear on the day you become his bride." She fumbled among the trinkets until her fingers plucked two brooches, carved in bone and ringed in silver. One bore a bear and wolf, gripping one another in battle, surrounded by looping serpents; the other, a soaring bird, its wings and tail hanging low.

She placed them in my lap before resting back against her pillows, letting me sing to her while she closed her eyes.

The wick burned low, then lower, until the flame guttered and I was left in the dark, Asta's hand cold in mine.

Somewhere beneath her ribs, the babe unborn pressed its fists to its blood-filled cage, in fluttering jabs of arm and foot. Its battle was over before it had begun.

19

Only one other grieved as I did, though he never showed me his tears. I'd never doubted that Gunnolf loved her, though perhaps only in the way men do when they believe a woman to be too noble for them—resentment and adoration in equal measure. Had he once believed her goodness would elevate his own nature? It was how I'd felt, each day, in her presence. Instead, we'd both deceived her.

Asta had never treated me as a stranger. She'd been sister and mother both; more even than Helka, whose adventures took her beyond my sphere. And how had I repaid this kindness? I'd fallen so easily to temptation, driven by anger, as much as lust.

Now, she was lost to me in every sense, taken to some realm beyond the living where she would surely know my sins. My self-loathing grew, for not only had I betrayed her trust but I'd been unable to save her from torment, dragged slowly, painfully, to the bitterest end.

Her symptoms had been strange. Not quite those of the pox, though she'd displayed many of the signs. Instead, her body had turned against itself without apparent cause.

I washed and dressed her for the final ceremony, for the burial she'd wished. One of her brooches I fastened to her robe of purest white. She'd given me so much, and I wished to place something I treasured in her resting place. The other I pinned to my shoulder. I hoped she'd find peace, embracing both her children in death—her son, and the unborn babe within her body.

Gunnolf carried her in his arms to the edge of the forest, to the hole he'd dug himself beside the resting ashes of their child; she weighed little, and he was strong.

It was a quiet affair, for so many in the village were affected by the pox, keeping to their houses in sickness or in tending others. Gunnolf said naught as he laid his wife's richest jewels upon her breast, and her lute beside her. He crouched down to whisper his farewell, for her ear alone, then took up the spade, his face hard in sorrow, casting the soil upon her body. I shuddered to see it fall, feeling its weight as if it were I who lay in the cold ground, buried slowly by the earth.

The men would later build a mound above: a resting place fit for the jarl to join his lady and their babes, when the time came, Guðrún told me.

In the days to come, I attended the sick, mixing salves and tinctures. There was too much death. Illness took several of the younger babes, too feeble even to cry their hunger.

Gunnolf did not come near, except to command stronger draughts for sleep. There was danger in increasing the potency of the valerian root. It would do more harm than good, I warned. Headaches and dizziness would plague him, however strong his heart. His mind, in anguish, would rebel, losing its former reason.

He cast my cautions aside, shadows beneath his eyes telling me of his need. I gave what he asked, understanding that longing to find oblivion, each waking bringing the misery of remembrance. I, too, wished to escape, to no longer know myself. My strangled remorse was more than I could bear.

I dreamt of rotting leaves and the drip of water through earth and rock, soil cold in my mouth and crawling things. I looked into the dark, and it slithered inside.

20

I knew that they talked about me, despite all I'd done for them. It wasn't enough that I'd treated their sores and tended them through the pox. I heard the whispers as I passed their homes, saw the narrowing of their eyes and heads turned from me.

Lady Asta had been under my care and she'd died. I was to blame.

Visiting Astrid, it seemed our friendship had grown cooler. Neither of us had spoken of *Ostara* night. I knew not what to say, ashamed of my fears and of my seeming rejection of the honoured ritual. Leaving her, I saw Bodil sitting outside her own door, a length of cloth in her lap, her fingers plucking with her needle. She raised her chin and met my eye, her lips drawn thin, unsmiling.

I wished suddenly to be far away, to be just myself, unanswerable to anyone. My feet took me through the fields of new shooting barley, rippling in the late afternoon breeze. The trees were already trailing long shadows, the swallows dipping and looping against a sky streaked through with violet cloud.

However far I walked, there was no escape from my thoughts—from all that had happened and what might be to come. I fingered the amulet at my throat. Eirik had vowed to return, had worshipped my body as he made his promises of protection and love. Did those promises have any worth?

With Asta gone and Eirik soon to return with his bride, what place was there for me? Was I destined to perform the most menial tasks, like Sylvi and Guðrún, without hope of a home of my own, a husband, children? And then I remembered how I'd lain with Gunnolf, willingly, knowingly, and I was filled with shame. What sort of woman was I? If I suffered now, it was no more than my due.

With dusk falling, I returned up the hill. Sylvi was still suffering from the pox, banished by Gunnolf to Helka's empty home during her recovery, leaving Guðrún with more work than she could manage. It was selfish of me to have stayed out so long. Faline, I knew, would help with only the easiest of duties.

I returned past idle-grazing livestock, skirting behind the huts. Before I rounded the corner, I heard them, sitting just beyond, not far from the longhouse. There was still much for me to learn of Svolvaen's language, but I understood the men well enough.

"… a whole houseful of women to comfort him now…"

"No wonder he looks like he doesn't sleep."

They chuckled at that.

"I'll take the dark one off his hands when he's bored with her…"

"The blonde for me," said another. "If she's good enough for Eirik, she'll be good enough to suck my old cock."

My face grew hot but I couldn't claim to be surprised. I knew men well enough—how they talked of women.

"He tired of her quickly, didn't he? Won't be long now before he's back, and with some other pretty wench to warm his bed."

"'Bout time… though she'll have to be more than pretty to keep his sword from finding other sheaths."

As they laughed again, the bile rose in my throat. I'd heard no more than I already knew—that I was but one of many lovers to have entertained Eirik for a short while, before his attention was drawn elsewhere. No doubt, he'd told Bodil he loved her, too… and all the others.

It was impossible to escape the truth. No matter my anger and my faithless deceit, I loved Eirik.

※

I lay awake that night and thought of the man who'd pleasured me in so many ways, pouring his desire into me. The bed was cold without him, despite the generously piled furs.

Whose body was warming his as I lay alone? There would be some companion—some thrall to pleasure him, or more than one. Perhaps he was already wed and his new bride spooned beside him, tasting what I'd so lately enjoyed. Such thoughts were fruitless, but they returned time and again.

The evening had not been a pleasant one. It seemed so long ago that we'd spent time in storytelling and song, the men bantering and the women teasing. Hardly possible that these walls had gathered Svolvaen's people so recently in festivity, at Yuletide.

Gunnolf's mood had become ever sharper, finding fault with each dish served to him. Even his favoured men from the village—summoned to keep him company, to play dice and share their news—had been unable to lift his spirits. He'd sent them away, his words harsh where there was no need.

Faline had dropped a dish of bread, for which Gunnolf had given her a clout, sending her to the floor. He raised her by the hair, saying she was a useless wanton—that he would cast her out and forbid any household to take her in, that he would tie her to a tree in the forest and let the boar and wolves find her.

Her eyes had flashed in resentment but she'd kept her silence. She'd pinned her fortune to Gunnolf just as surely as I had to Eirik, and what awaited us now? She'd shed no tears at our lady's passing; perhaps, she'd thought Asta's death would be her making. For all her wiles, Faline was no wiser than I, both now slaves to the whim of the jarl.

I dozed, at last, but was stirred by a creak and a sigh, a moan, long and low. From outside, I thought—some animal in pain, one of our livestock. The wall behind me adjoined the stable and there were two calves due to be delivered. The young lad who slept with them would call for help if it were needed. I strained my ear but there was no voice on the wind.

And yet, something was amiss.

Slipping on my cloak, I entered the main hall. The ceiling stretched above, a reaching chasm of darkness in which some bird or bat was trapped, flapping through the rafters. The embers glowed still in the firepit but cast no flame, no light to throw shadows in the gloom.

I paused to listen, looking into the recesses of the room. To my left, Guðrún was snoring. All else was quiet but for a sound like breathing, laboured, but muted. I could not discern what or who it might be but it was coming from outside, I was sure

I eased the door open, careful to avoid it creaking. The moon's illumination seemed unnaturally bright after the darkness of the longhouse, enough to show me the slope of the hill and the outlines of houses further down.

There was a screech from some night bird—an owl most likely—which drew my eyes to the edge of the forest. In the moonlight, it appeared closer, as if the trees had shuffled forward as we slept.

But there was no creature, huddled and wounded, lingering beyond; nor some scavenger, sniffing for scraps. No sound from the stable.

There was nothing but the breeze of the night hours, shivering the far-off trees. Nothing but my own breath, and the beating of my heart.

21

Faline filled the jarl's cup once more then withdrew to the corner of the room. Her cheek bore a bruise, her eye darkened above, the brow cut. I'd given it three stitches to close the gash, for which she'd grudgingly given her thanks.

Gunnolf had been drinking since that morning. We knew how this fuelled his moods. He was as likely to become violent as melancholy. I watched from the alcove of the pantry, Sylvi and Guðrún beside me.

He cupped the dice close, whispering to them before casting, but the outcome was the same as it had been on every throw.

"To Hel's realm with this!" He pushed back from the table. "There's Loki's trickery here, or one of you has replaced the dice."

"Peace, my jarl," soothed one of the *karls*. "'Tis but a friendly game. We may play some other if you prefer."

"Damn this foolishness and take up your weapons," Gunnolf commanded, staggering some steps to grasp his double-handed axe from where it hung—a monster of a weapon, heavier than many could wield. "It's been too long since we practised our skills. What manner of men are we if we forget how to fight?"

"My jarl, now is not the time," urged another of the men. He rose warily from the table, his gaze upon the blade in Gunnolf's hand. "We're in our cups and may not judge as we should. We wouldn't wish an injury on our brethren."

"A man should be always ready." Gunnolf planted his feet and raised the weapon above his head. "I'm not my uncle. I'm not weak, like Hallgerd."

"Of course not, my jarl," answered one. "You're the bravest and strongest of men. With pleasure, we'll polish our swords on the morrow and join you outside, but not tonight."

Gunnolf swayed where he stood then roared in anger, swinging the axe in a great arc that threatened to meet with their heads. Stumbling under its weight, he brought the edge down, embedding it with a mighty thud in the age-stained table.

All had risen, moving beyond the jarl's reach, looking wildly one to the other, as aghast as we women.

"I see into your hearts." Gunnolf spat the words, tugging fiercely on the weapon, cursing as he endeavoured to release it from the wood. "You've no stomach for battle. You're as slippery as eels, making excuses for your fear!"

Though he clearly spoke in drunkenness, the declaration was the greatest of insults. A man's honour was everything; not to be challenged, not to be ridiculed.

There was a grumbling of displeasure among the *karls*, but none raised his voice above the others, their eyes still upon the axe, which Gunnolf had now freed and was passing from one hand to the other, stepping towards the men who'd pledged their service to him.

"When I call on you to attack Skálavík, which of you will take your sword and bathe it in enemy blood?" Gunnolf almost lost his footing as he raised the mighty weapon above his head, lurching into the midst of his *karls*. "When I put Eldberg's head on a spike, what will you be doing?"

The men scattered, some bounding for the door, others dodging the jarl's swinging axe, leaping across the table to escape his rash attack.

"Run away, weasels," he shouted after them. "Get out of my sight. You're not fit to call yourselves men, let alone Vikings of Svolvaen!"

As the last scurried for safety, he crashed the door closed with his shoulder and flung his axe across the floor. Finding his cup, he drained it dry.

"More ale!" he shouted, but Faline did not step forward. Hidden far in the corner of the room, she shrank from him. I couldn't blame her, for I wished only to do the same, to escape his notice. He was in no state for company, his behaviour shameful. Yet, some compulsion bid me do as he'd requested.

"Are you the only one brave enough to face me?" Gunnolf's eyes were steely.

I said nothing, refusing to bow my head or look away. He was used to blind obedience but I resolved not to show meekness. He returned my unflinching stare, the silence a wall between us, tension heavy in the space dividing his body from mine. At last, he held out his cup, indicating for me to fill it, and I willed my hand to remain steady, vowing not to give him the satisfaction of seeing my fear.

His draught was deep, the ale brimming the edges, running down his beard. Wiping his mouth with his sleeve, he grimaced, tossing the empty cup to the floor.

"What is a man to do, Elswyth, when all about him are cowards?"

"You're tired, my Lord. Take the rest you need."

"Rest!" He flung back his head and gave a hollow laugh. "Sleep brings no rest." A shadow crossed his face. "Better to stay awake and find diversion."

He shrugged off his jerkin and flopped back onto one of the deep benches, propping his head upon his arm, his eyes still upon me.

"Do you wish diversion, Elswyth? Or do you prefer to sob to your pillow, thinking of the man who has left you?"

He inclined his head, waiting for my answer, but I gave none.

"You think you're Eirik's true love? That he'll forsake his duty and return to marry you? Are you still eager for some sign?" His smile was crooked, lacking mirth. "Have you not noticed that he's made no haste to return."

I twisted away, not wishing him to see the tears which had sprung, for he had hit his target, voicing what I was only too ready to believe. Anger flared in me, towards Eirik and Gunnolf, though I was most angry with myself. I'd been a fool to believe that Eirik could love me in the way I wished him to.

The jarl stroked his beard as he spoke and a new wickedness entered his eyes. "My brother and I always shared everything, Elsywth. Shall we not share you?"

"I've already tasted that wine, my Lord, and found it lacking sweetness." I lowered my eyes for, despite all, I felt the tug of my womb and cunt for him. The lust which had consumed me at *Ostara* had brought me shame and self-loathing, but I hadn't forgotten the satisfaction of that terrible abandonment, however fleeting.

"Sweetness isn't what I'm offering." Gunnolf's mouth twitched in a disdainful leer.

Under his scrutiny, the clothes peeled back from my body, the skin from my bones, showing all I wished to hide.

"What is it you want?" My voice trembled.

"I'll show you."

He rose from the bench and held out his hand, pointing to the corner of the room and clicking his fingers, summoning not I but Faline.

She came forward, knowing, I supposed, that to refuse would bring worse consequences.

"An obedient creature, when she wants to be." Gunnolf turned her face upward, surveying the injuries of his making.

He pinched her cheek roughly, then spun her round, pushing her to bend over the table, directing her to raise her skirts.

He must have beaten her quite recently, for the welts were still livid across her buttocks—blue, without any hint of yellowing. He unclasped his belt and pulled the leather through, releasing it from his trousers. "But, sometimes, the pleasure is in defiance." He looked back at me over his shoulder. "And struggle…"

My mouth grew dry, watching him, waiting for him to raise the leather to her poor skin. There was no love lost between Faline and I, but I had no wish to see her suffer.

"It's shameful for a man to harm a woman, or for him to take her body when she has no desire."

"You think this one has no desire?" Gunnolf slapped Faline's backside and I winced to see her flinch. "She likes to fight but she likes fucking even more… and she is made for fucking." He lingered over the last word and pulled the belt tight between his hands but, instead of raising his arm to strike her with its edge, he pulled her hands awkwardly behind her back, wrapping the belt's length around her wrists.

He lowered his mouth to the bruise on her rounded cheek and bit the flesh savagely, evoking her sharp intake of breath.

He kicked her legs wider, entering her with his fingers, then splaying her labia.

"You see this; made for my pleasure?"

It was not the first time I'd seen Faline's cunt engorged, waiting for a man. The last time, it had been Eirik burying himself inside her, upon the banqueting table of my husband's hall, cheered on by every Northman present. Faline had taken many that night, but her prize was Eirik—he the one she'd most desired.

Gunnolf let his trousers drop, revealing a full erection from the dark bush of his groin, the head beaded with excitement. He took it in his hand, stroking the skin, a smile playing upon his lips.

I expected him to jab inside, to take her brutally, forcing his penetration. Instead, he ran the slick head of his cock through Faline's slit. He teased her with half-thrusts, rubbing against the tender nub of her cunt. She lifted her rump to encourage his entry.

"Please…" I heard her whimper. "Please, my Lord."

He aligned himself, claiming with one smooth motion, pushing deep before easing back to enter again.

Faline moaned in response, whispering again, as if to herself. "Please…"

A heat began to burn me. The heat not just of anger but of desire, my own cunt filling with cream.

"There's more than one place to fuck a woman, of course." Gunnolf's voice was cold as he withdrew, slick with her juices, raising his cock to press against her anus. Faline gave a strangled cry but Gunnolf held her firm against the table. She squirmed only briefly before he pushed past her initial resistance.

As his buttocks clenched and relaxed, she uttered low groans, as of a creature caught in a trap yet with no desire to escape. He kept his rhythm until the end, culminating in his final convulsions of pleasure.

I hadn't moved from where I stood. I'd waited, with the growing knowledge that, when he turned to me, I would submit.

I'd pour out all my bitterness—at Eirik, and at Gunnolf too. I'd make Gunnolf roar, as his brother had done. Neither would be more or less than the other. Gunnolf was just a man; I'd use him to sate my need. Gunnolf wished a slave to command but I would command him, take him, own him!

I desired a man inside me again, but also hungered to lose myself in the act. We'd consume each other, in wrath and fury, rather than love.

He withdrew from Faline's body, presenting a cock no longer fully rigid yet still emboldened.

"You're an animal," I hissed, picking up the nearby jug of ale and casting the contents to drench his groin, knowing it would fire his passion all the more.

In a single step he was upon me, his hands wrenching my shoulders, growling his ire and laughing low.

"Exactly as you wish."

He yanked the front of my dress, breaking the clasps, then dragged down the shift beneath, tearing the clothes from me as I stood. I did nothing to defy him, my own hands helping until I was naked, revelling in his palms moving over my breasts, cupping my buttocks, squeezing my flesh. I cared not that Faline watched as I gave myself to him, nor that her eyes burned with displeasure.

I clasped the great muscles of his arms, steadying myself against the roughness of his mouth, opening my legs even before he lay me upon the table. His piercing brought a moan of pleasure I couldn't conceal, my cunt eager for his violence, my skin hungry for his raking teeth.

He crushed me to his chest as he ejaculated, with a cry to match my own bursting wail. The sparks flared, broke and collided, dazzling me with their light and sending me, once more, tumbling into the abyss.

2 2

Gunnolf had become brutal, rough and ravenous. I knew his soul ached and there was no remedy, his anger another version of my own. We sated mutual grief and savage passion. Each bruise he gave me was a brand for my many sins, marking the slow death of my heart.

His moods continued, volatile and violent. He lashed out before burying his head upon my lap. He told me of the first days of his wedded life, and before. His uncle had arranged the marriage. A contract of alliance, of course; not planned for love but for her rich dowry. Nevertheless, Gunnolf had marvelled at Asta's loveliness, her composure, her grace. She'd been his prize.

Now, he lamented all he should have said and done. "She carried my child but it was not enough to keep her in this life. Did she die, Elswyth, because I failed to show my love? Is it this she cannot forgive? Her beauty is buried and rotting, yet she is beyond the door, beyond the curtain. She does not rest; nor will she allow me peace."

Mixing the sleeping draught he demanded, I said only that intended to soothe him. Even then, he tossed, restless, thrashing from haunted dreams.

Fingers bone-white, eyes hollow and searching; I saw her too.

Each moment of sleep took me to the forest, through which I ran, the trees leading me in circles, so there was no escape. She was always there; now close at my shoulder, then behind. It was no longer her belly that she clutched but a bundle in her arms, which she thrust towards me. Within was the grey face of her swaddled baby, without breath or life. Her expression held the pain and reproach for which I blamed myself, and great sadness, too, for all that might have been and was lost.

I couldn't shake the fear that I'd never been asleep but had been looking through the darkness at her face.

※

The rising sun brought the promise of summer and its warmth should have lifted my heart, as it did those of the children who ran outside, eager to make up for lost days.

I'd done my part in helping Svolvaen recover from the pox, easing raging itches of the skin and debilitating fever, but I could scarce rejoice; Asta's death, and my betrayal of her, remained a torment to me.

I'd been remiss in many ways, seeking to avoid what was difficult. I'd retreated so far into remorse and self-pity that I hardly recognized myself. My body remained healthy, despite all that had happened around me, but I no longer believed in my purpose, nor my skills. I hadn't saved Asta; nor had I found a cure for the disfiguring sores. My treatments were but a temporary salve.

There was only one person I could turn to, though our friendship had floundered. We'd spoken but briefly since *Ostara* night. Astrid had confided in me during her anguish; I'd pulled away in mine.

She looked tired, answering her door. Pursing her lips, she kept me on the threshold, inclining her head at last, shifting the wriggling baby from one hip to the other.

"Take a seat, then." She lowered the little one to the floor. "You know you're welcome."

I deserved the sharpness in her tone. I'd neglected her, and Ylva.

"Fresh pulled an hour ago." She poured some milk and handed me a cup. "Ylva's taking the goats down to the meadow, so it's just us."

I sipped the creamy liquid, still warm, and smiled my thanks.

"You've been occupied, I hear." Astrid took the stool across from me, beside the hearth. She clucked her tongue. "'Tis no more than anyone would expect, of course, you sharing the same roof, and Eirik gone these many weeks."

All Svolvaen probably knew; there was little that could be hid. Astrid looked at me pointedly, waiting for me to unburden myself. We hadn't kept secrets from each other, in the past.

When I didn't reply, she rose to stir the contents of her pot, suspended over the fire.

"I didn't intend…" I couldn't bring myself to explain. Whatever was happening between myself and Gunnolf, I didn't know how to describe it.

"The other, that Faline, not enough for him; he's got to have you, too?" Astrid looked pointedly at the discolouration on my neck. "And both of you feeling the heel of his hand."

Gunnolf liked to restrain me, or to squeeze my throat when he took me. Only once had I blacked out under the pressure of his thumbs, awakening to the wetness of his cum streaking my thighs and the throb of my cunt.

I'd loosened my hair about my shoulders but the marks were difficult to hide. There were more on my wrists.

Astrid lowered her voice. "The jarl isn't what he was. Always strict, we knew, but fair with it. Now, the men are afraid. It's not only you that's suffering; the blacksmith's son took a beating off the jarl, yesterday, and not for anything that a cuff to the ear wouldn't have sorted. He's told the men to farm only in the morning. They're to fell timber the rest of the day, to extend fortifications by the harbour; on pain of flogging if they don't."

I frowned to hear it. Gunnolf had mentioned nothing.

Bringing the ladle to her mouth, Astrid sipped the broth. "He needs another wife, of course. Although that won't stop a man like him..." She lowered her voice. "They're looking for Eirik's return. It's him the men love; he who should be jarl."

I shifted uncomfortably. Having tried hard to push away thoughts of Eirik, of the state of my heart and his, I'd convinced myself that I'd stopped waiting for him.

Astrid leaned forward. "There's something else." She hesitated, glancing swiftly about, though there was no one to hear—only the baby. "Something not right."

She opened her mouth to speak, then looked away, busying herself with the poker, stoking the flames beneath her cooking pot.

"What is it Astrid?"

"I'm not sure I believe it. I shouldn't have said..."

She bustled to the pantry, returning with an armful of vegetables. Taking them to the table to chop, the knife trembled in her hand.

"It's not more illness?"

"No. Nothing of that sort." She frowned, keeping her eyes downcast, slicing into the pale flesh of a turnip. "Not any illness that can be cured..."

"What are you saying?"

"There are whispers, but I've not seen it myself... It was wrong of me to say."

I jumped up, rounding the table to stand beside her, reaching to stay her arm. "I must know, Astrid!"

Despite the warmth of the day and the fire lit, a chill fell on me.

"It's something affecting Gunnolf? Affecting me?"

"Perhaps, yes..."

My heart lurched.

"She was never strong but, still... we didn't expect it. We were waiting for the baby to be born. Even though she lost the first, we thought it would be alright this time. Asta wasn't one of us but everyone respected her—loved her, even."

Astrid's eyes darted to mine, her words tumbling, urgent. "You did, too, didn't you, Elswyth? You would never have hurt her…"

"No." My voice scratched in my throat. "I would never have hurt her."

Astrid shook her head. "Then it can't be you. She's come back, but it's not for you."

The room grew smaller in that instant, the walls moving closer. "Come back?"

Astrid let drop the knife. "When there's something not right—a hurt the person can't forgive, a betrayal, some wrongdoing…when they can't let go."

I grasped the edge of the table, biting upon my lip. I didn't trust myself to speak.

"That's what they say. It must be something terrible, don't you think, to bring her back? For her restless spirit to revive her body and make it walk again?"

I summoned all my strength. I had to know everything. "And someone has seen… her, in Svolvaen?"

"At the top of the hill, near the edge of the forest and…"

"You must tell me, Astrid!"

She flinched at my raised voice.

"Around the jarl's longhouse."

The room swayed. No matter what I told myself, I could not escape. My knees buckled and I fell to the floor, dissolving within the dark tide.

23

Their raised voices roused me, far across the room. I couldn't make out the words; wasn't sure that I wanted to. I was warm where I lay, in darkness but not asleep. Somewhere between—not awake either. My fingers found the goatskin beneath my body. I was comfortable. If only they would stop shouting, I could stay here and hide, drowsy and safe.

I remembered now; I'd fallen, in a faint, the floor hard under my cheek. Astrid had been telling me what I could scarce believe, yet which I felt to be true. The sins of the past were not forgotten, and Asta did not lie peacefully in her grave.

Who but I was to blame? I'd failed to save her; hadn't acted quickly enough, had overlooked something. I'd loved her… but had some dark corner of my being wished her to die? Hadn't I been envious? I'd wanted to bear Eirik's children, to be his wife, to claim the status that would bring. Instead, I had no choice but to rely on the good favour of others.

As for the jarl, I was no naïve maiden, my virginity seduced away. I'd known what I was doing. I'd become his willing lover, overtaken by a madness of self-loathing, fed by emotions I could barely fathom. He and I were alike in ways I'd not wished to recognize. We were capable of wild fury, stoked by grieving anger. Whatever excuses I conjured, I couldn't escape my guilt.

Someone was sobbing, someone shouting; words coming closer, louder.

"…dark forces, in the forest. Just like her grandmother." It was a voice filled with hate. "…goes out at night, looking for her creatures, picking plants for her spells."

There was a murmur through the room.

"…bewitched Eirik… made him bring her here… put magic on my father before that… been casting her enchantment on you, Gunnolf… she wants Asta's place… was chieftain's wife once and wants to be again."

"Wake her." The speaker was gruff, his voice commanding.

Hands raised me up, splashed water in my face. I shied from returning but those hands were insistent. Someone pinched the skin on the inside of my elbow, hissed in my ear. "Wake up, witch!"

Faline was holding something in her palm, raising it to my face, her serpent eyes lit. Her mouth was voluptuous even as she spoke venom.

"I found what you've been carrying in your apron pocket! A deadly mushroom, and one piece missing!"

I shook my head in confusion. I hadn't anything in my pocket. The mushroom had been lost weeks ago, before *Ostara* night. I couldn't remember when I'd last seen it.

"What say you?" It was Gunnolf's voice, full of pain. "Was it your scheme all along? To kill whoever stood in your way? To seduce whichever man could most advantage you? What mischief did you plan?"

What had I done? This looked much like the one I'd picked, so long ago, when I'd walked in the forest with Helka. The red rim beneath the cap was distinctive. I'd brought it with me, across the sea—a symbol of unused vengeance. I could have killed a host of warriors with this tiny mushroom. Had some part crumbled into Asta's food? Had I poisoned her? I thought back to her symptoms—the stomach cramps, nausea, vomiting bile, and the itch across her skin. Not the pox at all, but the gradual, agonizing failure of her body.

The horror of it jolted me awake, tore at my chest so I could hardly breathe, wrenched my gut like the devil's own claws. The mushroom was mine.

"The guilt is in her face!" Faline spat the words. "Look! I dare her to deny it!"

"It's true," declared Gunnolf. "I see it, now. Only a conscience wracked with shame could look thus."

"No…" My tongue was thick in my mouth. What could I protest against? Had I not wanted position and power? Had I not envied? Kept secrets? And who but I had tended Asta?

"Murderess!" Faline hissed, as they led me away.

24

Many gathered, watching as the jarl's men led me to the harbour, my hands bound. Wrongdoers were beaten, but what of murderers? What of witches?

They secured me to the whipping post, but not in the position for flogging. I faced forward, my back pressed to the old wood.

"If you're innocent, explain your actions. You assured me you would take good care of my wife and you proclaimed yourself a healer."

I was used to seeing Gunnolf in many moods; now, I saw the cold resignation of his heart. He desired another to take the blame, to ease his sense of guilt. It was of no matter that I hadn't been the only one to serve his lady.

"Was the death of my dear Asta achieved by your devious hand? Was it your hidden wish to take what was hers? Do you deny that you betrayed her trust?"

"You know I'm innocent." I tried to avert my gaze from the many who looked upon me, to focus only on the jarl. "I loved our Lady Asta, and did all in my power to care for her and the baby."

I endeavoured to hold Gunnolf with my eyes, to convince him of my sincerity, but he turned away.

Scouring the crowd, I searched for some sign of support. Had I not tended their children, treated them in their sickness? For that, hadn't I earned their trust? I hardly recognized them now, their mouths set hard. Women and men alike, ready to turn against me. I could hear their mutterings: '… not our kind… thinks herself too clever'.

"I've tried only to help; never to harm." My pleading voice sounded thin. The sun had already dipped low but sweat trickled down my back. My mouth tasted sour. "If I could bring her back, I would…"

I thought I'd escaped those who didn't understand me, to have found a new life, among new people. I'd deceived myself, for I remained as much a stranger as ever—mistrusted, suspected of ill-doing.

And then I saw Torhilde, pushing through, calling my name, and Astrid followed by Ylva, carrying the little one.

"What are you doing?" Astrid whirled to challenge the crowd. "Elswyth would never hurt anyone! Have you forgotten what she did for us?"

Torhilde's voice shook as she spoke but she planted her feet firmly beside Astrid's. "Elswyth showed me compassion when my own neighbours had none. Only Astrid took me in; only Elswyth would dare look upon my affliction."

"Didn't she risk her own health to be with you, to enter your homes, to treat you?" Astrid implored.

Drawing back the yoke of her gown, Torhilde revealed the dull redness of a still tender sore, part-healing. "How many of you have these on your body? Hasn't Elswyth tended you?"

A sob rose in my throat. I knew the defilement felt by those who suffered, knew the stain Torhilde carried. How brave she was, and in loyalty to me. Whatever was to happen, it gladdened me to know that I wasn't alone.

The young woman who next pushed forward wore her hair loose—a cascade of auburn-red.

"Your sores are not yet recovered, Torhilde. Don't they still disgrace you; don't you still rely on this woman, hoping she'll heal them?" The look Bodil gave me was arrogant, her eyes filled with enmity. "Perhaps she has you where she wants—reliant upon her to heal you, feeding upon your gratitude." She spoke with relish, as if she'd waited long to smear my name with the basest of accusations. "How many others are the same—hiding what shames them, dependent on this interloper, waiting for her cure? She has no noble blood or claim to higher status, yet she has you all as her thralls."

"She's a witch!" sneered Faline. "She probably caused your sores. Don't let her fool you. She cares only for herself."

Another took up the cry. "Caused the sores and the pox, too!"

I looked again to Gunnolf. Would he credit such slanders, based on nothing but Faline's word and the vindictiveness of Eirik's former lover? There was no softening to his expression but nor was there malignance. His thoughts were impenetrable.

"I trust neither of these foreign women," said Bodil, "But this dark-haired one knows the other well. If she warns us of this woman's ill-intent, I believe her."

Faline cast me a triumphant glance, barely able to conceal her glee. Running forward, she thrust her face close to my ear. "No Eirik to save you now, but don't worry; I'll keep him warm for you, when he returns… I've passion enough for both brothers."

It was suddenly clear to me. Another had sat with Asta, on *Ostara* night.

Soon after that, she began the cramps that convulsed her body. The mushroom had been lost not long before. Faline had found it, surely— had recognized its nature, or guessed why I'd kept it.

I'd been blind. If I'd seen what was happening, could I have saved Asta?

"It was you!" I croaked, my lips dry with fear. "It was you!" But the crowd's growing clamour drowned my words.

"Enough!" Gunnolf raised his hand. "What we cannot know, the gods shall decide. Tie her to the stacks at the end of the pier. If she survives high tide, it will be they that save her."

"No!" I struggled against the arms that carried me through the parting crowd. I caught sight of Astrid's stricken face, her cheeks wet with tears.

The stacks would be covered within a few hours. I'd be left in the dark, gasping for breath as the chill water lapped over my mouth, then my nose. There would be none to save me and I'd have no power to save myself.

25

The sun left the sky and the slim moon rose. My hope sank as I waited beneath the small stars sliding cold through the dark. The water made insidious progress, to my chest, my shoulders.

I'd wondered if someone might be brave enough to follow their conscience, to steal unseen through the village, to untie the cruel rope which wrapped awkwardly about my waist and hooked over the outer stack of the pier.

A few had lingered, to watch me lowered into the fjord's chill embrace, to call names from the safety of the shore. None wished to come too close. After all, I was a witch, was I not?

Even Gunnolf had kept his distance. Whatever we'd been to one another, whatever we'd shared, it had not been built upon love.

Eirik's amulet nestled still in the hollow of my throat. If I saw him again, in the next life, I'd swear my love and my regret; anger and resentment had brought bitter pleasure. I'd been fated neither for marriage nor the security of devotion.

The tide was almost fully in, and none had come to deliver me. The waters stretched from this place, across the great waste to the land of my birth, and I was solitary, in the shadow of the grey night.

I prayed to my old God and then to Freya, Frigg and Fjorgyn: the female gods. If they had no ear for my suffering then none would.

Would they punish Faline as I was being punished? We each had our sins. She'd acted from jealousy—from desiring what lay out of reach. Her grudge had long simmered, stored away until her spite could be indulged. Even in her wickedness I pitied her, for she'd find no contentment.

The clouds drifted over the moon, obscuring what little light was to be had. It was quiet, as if Svolvaen had melted far away. I was alone with the lap and splash of waves against the fishing boats, gently rocking in their moorings on either side of the pier. I thought back to what Astrid had told me—that Asta's restless spirit walked. No one wished to be outside, even to watch the final breaths of a witch, as the water claimed her life.

If Asta wished revenge, it was done, for my life could now be measured in gasping breaths. I tipped my chin and closed my eyes as the black waves stroked my lips, theirs the last caress upon my skin.

And then, something swept my leg—the smooth glide of a fish, or a feathering of seaweed. It skimmed silken against my arm, brushing lightly upon my wrists where the rope bound them, and passed around my waist. My body slipped beneath the water as the bonds loosened, and I tasted the briny sea. Kicking my legs brought me to the surface, gasping for air, with my heart pounding.

I knew not who, or what, had intervened. Some creature sent by the gods or their own divine hands reaching to save me. I could not think—only rejoice that the chance had been given for me to live!

My skirts were heavy as I swam, my shoulders stiff and my chilled body leaden, but force of will drove me onwards, towards the shore. The push of the waves helped bring me to the shallows until my knees scraped shingle. I dragged myself beyond the movement of the water, glad to feel the hard pebbles beneath me and the brisk nip of the night air.

There was barely a sigh of wind, the world quiet but for the breaking waves and a far owl calling. I was exhausted to my bones yet my heart beat in exhilaration, for I was alive.

I could not remain thus for long. One thing was certain—that I must take action. I might present myself to Gunnolf and all Svolvaen as having escaped the tide's reach. The gods had saved me, proving my innocence. Yet, I feared the malevolence of Faline and Bodil. They wouldn't rest until their spite was sated, and they'd have no trouble finding ears. The seeds of doubt had been sown, even among those who'd shared my friendship.

I needed time to plan and a place of safety from which to do so. My first thought was of Astrid; she, I could trust. Alongside Torhilde, she'd spoken for me when so many were ready to believe ill. She'd hide me if I asked, but this I would not do. How could I place her in such a position?

High on the shingle was Helka's little boat—the one in which she'd taken me sailing through the fjord. How long ago that day seemed, when I'd thrilled to speed with the wind and shared her delight in the success of our fishing. I remembered her showing me the cave—her own special place, where the ledge ran flat and deep.

Might I manage the vessel alone, with the oars rather than the sail? The moon's slender crescent was in my favour, breaking only momentarily through the cloud. None was likely to see me, even were they to look out. I couldn't delay; the fishermen would soon arrive, setting out on their day's work.

The pebbles shifted under my feet, loud to my ear and louder still as they tumbled before the boat. I hauled it by the bow, down the slope to the water's edge. Every part of my body ached but I made jerking progress. Finally, I was wading out, holding the boat's edge, light-headed with relief on feeling it float free.

My sodden skirts slapped the deck as I tumbled in. I caught my knee hard on the edge of the seat to the stern, cursing a good oath to control my tears. The sail had been rolled away but the oars were still inside, and I wasted no time in fitting them to the locks. The sooner I left the shore behind, the safer I'd feel. There would be time, later, to rest and to think; for now, I needed to send the boat through the water, taking myself away from Svolvaen, and danger. It was a struggle to breach the waves, tilting the blade to the right angle, but I was soon taking longer strokes, letting the boat glide onwards, with the great cliffs rising on either side.

I was shaken, weary and anxious but an old part of myself was awakening—the girl who'd climbed the tallest trees and swum in forest pools, who'd hunted rabbits and spun her own fate. If I were to survive, I'd need to be brave, and resourceful.

The moon appeared again, illuminating the sheer face of the crags. I was further along than I'd realized, moving parallel with the escarpment. Stilling the oars, I looked for an opening, wide and low and jagged either side— Helka's cave. I dipped the oars again, taking care not to drift close. Perhaps I'd gone too far. I might so easily have missed what I sought, in the faint, silvered light.

And then I saw it—the distinctive opening in the cliff and the narrow passageway through which I must pass. Another moment and I'd be level, relying on my oars to guide me, risking the little wooden boat on the jutting rocks.

I felt the swell rising as I approached, the upward surge as it pushed into the inlet, lifting the boat and tossing me towards the unyielding stone. I reached out my oar, endeavouring to push myself away, but the force of the waves was too violent. There was a judder as the bow connected, an alarming scrape and grind of buckling planks. I braced with a single oar, only to see it splinter and snap. Unthinkingly, I did the same with my hands, crying out as my palms scraped upon limpets. The boat swayed beneath me, spinning to rasp upon the opposing rocks. I whimpered as the hull creaked, waiting for a crack of rupture which would sink me. Water was about my ankles, the boat tilting. Grasping for the remaining oar, I pushed again off the rock and, with all my might, moving its blade desperately from one side of the boat to the other, propelled myself toward the cave's shelter.

26

Even as the sun rose high the next day, it remained cold within the cavern. I was drawn to the furthest ledge in pursuit of warmth, of some touch of daylight. Watching the surf swelling and surging beneath, I sheltered unseen. Only one would guess I was here, and for her I waited. Helka would know what to say, what to do. She, I felt certain, would take my part.

What could I do but wait? The boat had been damaged badly, sinking beneath me as I scrambled out. With the dawn's thin light, I found it had disappeared altogether. Only the splintered oar remained, its fragments floating out of reach.

I'd found Helka's provisions—leather pouches of water, cheese and smoked ham. The cave's cool interior had preserved them well and how good they tasted, filling my mouth not just with flavour but with their solidity, with the pleasure of eating. I made myself chew slowly, passing each piece over my tongue. I didn't know how long I'd need them to last. Even eaten sparingly, they dwindled quickly.

Lying on my belly, I caught a sliver of shattered oar from the water, thinking I'd use it to prise limpets as the birds did with their beaks, but the wood was already too soft to be of use. Eventually, I found a shell, the cast-off casing of a mollusc long-dead, the inside smooth. It was a better tool, affording me several tiny mouthfuls, but those soft creatures clung tenacious to the rocks. In desperation, I smashed until my knuckles bled.

Scraping slimed algae and pliant seaweed from the rocks, my nails tore ragged. I pressed my mouth where my fingers were inept, tugging with my teeth, eager for any nourishment. Each swallow made me only thirstier, my mouth brine-soaked, parched dry amidst so much water. I was steeped in the sea, the stinging spray penetrating not just my clothes but my skin and my eyes, its touch a torment to my cracked lips.

I fell to licking from the damp walls, my tongue raw against the rough formation of the stone, seeking respite from the salt, needing fresh water. Time dripped as slowly as that thin trickle upon which I depended. It dripped in the long darkness and through the muted day, falling like those beads of moisture on the rock.

I eyed the gulls soaring beyond the entrance of the cavern, wondering how they would taste, imagining the satisfaction of their flesh in my belly. None came near. It seemed more likely that they'd pick my bones than I theirs.

Nights passed in the cavern's embrace. I curled upon the gnawing ache of hunger, shivering, hiding my face in the crook of my elbow, wrapped in sweat despite the cold. The world had reduced to this damp place of stone and sea, to rock and water and the chill inside my bones.

Only in slumber was there relief. In my dreams, I joined the boys I'd played with in my childhood, swimming in the forest lake, gulping down great mouthfuls of sweet, fresh water. How we would run, and jump from the highest rocks above, falling deep before kicking up to emerge, gasping and laughing.

I saw my grandmother, kissing me goodnight, my aunt, and the mother I'd barely known. Would I soon meet them all again? And Eirik. I dreamed of his soft kiss and of his arms, strong about me.

I dreamt, too, of entombment and engulfing dark, and woke to find it real. My chest, seizing tight, choked the air from my lungs—too thick to breathe.

By the feeble light of day, I woke to an ominous, gnawing ache within my left hand. I felt the clutch of fear and willed myself to look. There was infection, as I'd seen so many times. My fever had not just been from the cold but from the affliction I'd avoided all these months, caring for others in the village. Across the width of my palm, the sore was livid purple, the centre beginning to blister, throbbing deep under the skin, seeming to spread out beyond the boundaries of the lesion.

How much time had passed? How long would it be until Helka came? Had she and Eirik been detained by Jarl Ósvífur, or been attacked by a rival clan on their return journey from Bjorgyn? The duration of their absence had been far longer than expected, even before I took refuge in the cave. I clutched Eirik's amulet and invoked the gods. I did not wish to die, but to stay here would be my end.

I'd been a strong swimmer, once. Shouldn't I try? Swim for the shore; find some other place to hide. With limbs heavy and my head light, I sat upon the furthest point of the ledge, waited for a lull between the waves, and lowered myself into the sea.

27

Closing my eyes against the brightness all around, I kicked hard. Dwelling in that cramped, underground space, I'd grown used to its gloom and the confinement of its walls. The sky now felt huge and the sun dazzling. I knew I must clear the perilous rocks. Only then would I have a chance.

Almost immediately, the swell lifted me high then plunged low, saltwater entering my nose and throat. I struggled and spluttered as the current swept me sideways. Scraping my elbow, I spun, reaching out my hands to stop myself. I caught my breath in pain but fought forward, almost dragged under before being hoisted upwards on a surging wave and pushed beyond the jagged granite.

I felt the difference at once and was filled with optimism. If I might now stay afloat, I could kick my way to shore. Yet, as I began to swim, I seemed to make no progress. The realization came to me in a flood of despair. How foolish I was! I'd never reach the shore, for the tide was on its way out, drawing me with it. I'd be swept out of the fjord, to the open sea.

In my panic, I kicked harder. I might, perhaps, make my way back to the rocks, drag myself hand over hand, returning to the cavern. That hope was in vain for the current was strong. Already, I was drawing level with the next opening in the cliff—a smaller hollow, without visible ledge but also without rocks. I might take refuge there and wait for the turning tide. Summoning the last of my will, I thrashed through the water. Turning my body, I swept close to the cliff face and braced myself. Knowing how easily the waves could crush me against the unyielding granite, I launched myself into the cave.

I entered green twilight, the water calm. It stretched back a long way, ending in a shelf wide enough for me to sit upon, perhaps to lie. Algae grew thick upon the walls, fanning like hair where it touched the brine. I clutched a clump, pulling myself by its anchor, to heave myself from the sea.

Had I the strength, I might have cried but my quiet despair lodged in my throat. I fisted my left hand shut, not wishing to see what I knew grew there. My head throbbed with the fever and my limbs trembled. I could think no further than to rest, to sleep, curling upon myself as animals do, knowing themselves in the grip of sickness.

She came to me in my dreams. I lay in a lush meadow, the cornflowers tall around me and the sun warm, my eyes closed to its glare. I heard her singing and then felt her gown brushing against my leg, from my ankle to my knee. There was nothing to fear for she was with me. I opened my eyes and saw her face, as lovely as it had ever been.

I woke to find my leg trailing in the water, long strands of green sweeping my skin. It had only been a fanciful reverie, yet I felt somehow comforted and renewed by Asta's appearance. And there was something familiar in the sensation on my leg. Had it been the same that I'd felt those days before, when I'd been bound to the pier?

Something else had brought me from sleep. Not touch but sound, for there was a rushing noise, the low rumble of a storm and, closer, the sound of trickling water. The light was dim, for it was the first of the day, but enough to show me rain upon the sea and a low mist.

My body had no wish to move. Scraped, aching and fevered, my inclination was to close my eyes once more. Too long since I'd eaten, too long since I'd been warm or dry. The struggle had left me.

The tide would be turning but it would do me no good. My legs were leaden and my body bruised; to swim seemed impossible. Straightening my arm brought a stab of pain. The abrasion on my elbow had crusted, then broken. The sore on my left palm ached and itched. I opened it partially and winced. I clutched still some algae, torn as I'd dragged myself from the water, its slender strands plastered to the lesion. I would examine it later, when I had the mind. There were nagging irritations elsewhere on my body that I refused to dwell upon. I'd no wish to look, for what good would it do?

I lay still, listening to a steady drip and splash. Helka had told me the cliffs were riddled with chasms and cracks, crevices through which water would travel. Perhaps if I could find the source, there would be fresh water to drink—enough to wet my mouth, at least. Turning my head, I saw the fissure and a faint slant of light. Would it be wide enough for me squeeze through?

I groaned as I found my feet, my back and limbs protesting, head reeling, but it was good to stand. If I allowed myself to sleep, the temptation would be to never wake again.

The first section of the opening was the hardest to breach, the bones of my hip chafing awkwardly. Had I tried even a week ago, my flesh would have been too ample. There was a curve, obliging me to bend then crawl. I shuffled on my knees and knuckles, hearing the trickle of water, telling myself it would be only a little further. If the tunnel came to naught, forbidding me final passage, it would be more than I could bear.

At last, the rock receded and I emerged into a narrow column of space. I felt a change in the air—only a fraction warmer but certainly brighter. What I sought was flowing down the wall, forming a clear pool beneath. I plunged my lips, drinking greedily until my stomach ached to bursting. Craning my neck to look upwards, I almost laughed with relief, for there was sunlight and a fresher smell—a hole through the rock, to the cliffs above. The gods had answered my prayers, showing me the way.

The rising granite had footholds and places my hands could grasp but it would be coated in fine algae, running with water. If I slipped, my bones would find their rest here, hidden in the heart of the rock.

My left arm was in pain and my right gashed. Could I take the rough treatment of climbing? I still felt feverish—my forehead hot and my hands clammy. I steeled myself to unfurl my fingers, knowing that I must inspect my palm. Algae had pressed into the tender flesh, preventing me from seeing the progress of the lesion. I lifted the strands, easing them from the sore. It was tender but there was no ooze of pus. The blister had reduced in size with no tinge of yellow, no appearance of aggressive infection. Pink and swollen though it was, it appeared to be healing. I flexed my hand and blanched a little but the discomfort was bearable.

Not only had divine forces watched over me but nature, too, offering her bounty. I rested my head against the rock and gave my silent thanks. Wasn't this what I'd been searching for, all these long months? I'd investigated many of the seaweeds along Svolvaen's shore but had never found this fine-threaded variety. The gods had led me here. This would be the remedy for those who'd shown me love, and those who'd doubted me.

It would be easy to return later, with other villagers, to bring a boat and fill it with enough to treat every person in Svolvaen many times over, but how could I reappear in the village empty-handed? The charge of being a witch would mar the miracle of my survival in their eyes. If I brought the cure which they needed, perhaps it would convince them of my true intentions.

No algae grew in this small space where the spray did not reach. I grunted my discomfort as I crawled back through the fissure but was driven by the thought of Astrid, Ylva, Torhilda and her children. I'd collect what I needed and climb from this place. I'd cure the affliction for which others had blamed me and, in the process, save myself.

My apron I tucked upon itself, creating a pouch in front and behind, to stuff with the algae growing plentifully from the walls. With the torment of hunger nagging me, I pushed some into my mouth, making myself chew the thin strands. I'd need what strength I could muster to make my climb.

A further length I twisted secure around my hand. My mind and heart were set.

28

Had the incline been steeper I would never have succeeded, but the tunnel provided ledges upon which I took respite, bracing my feet on the opposing side, allowing me to rest my heated forehead against the cool rock. Several times, I hit my skull and lashed the air with curses but an inner determination pushed me on. I'd come so far and would not fail.

No matter what lay in store, I'd perform this last act. Ylva would be released from the sores that blighted her young beauty, and Torhilde, too.

The sun was well past its zenith when my face met its warmth, the landscape bathed in soft splendour. Pressing my cheek to the moist grass, my tears welled. I'd been lost to love, had been entombed, but I'd emerged into the light again.

After the quiet of the subterranean passage, I marvelled at how the world hummed: bees hovering and dipping, grasshoppers in the clover, and the chirrup of birds. The breeze carried the sound of every rustling leaf. The grass was as I'd never seen it, each blade defined. A buzzard circled, sailing wild above the cliffs, observing everything in sharp detail, as I now did. Defiantly, I watched it, feeling my vitality returning. It would have to search elsewhere for its meat.

I set my jaw and inhaled deeply. Tempting as it was to lay in the late afternoon sunshine, to let it dry my clothes and revive my aching body, I needed to hide. Only after dusk would I creep down the hill, skirting behind the huts, seeking refuge in Astrid's home.

The last time I'd entered the shade of the trees, the wild strawberries had barely begun to flower; now, the fruits were ripe, staining my trembling fingers as I crammed their sweetness to my mouth. Beneath, the moss was soft—a bed waiting for my head. I found the oblivion of sleep, knowing that I'd soon be with those I cared for.

※

It was night when my eyes opened again. My body was stiff but my palm no longer felt tight and tender. My head felt clearer than it had in days, and the skin cool. Had eating the algae released the fever from my blood? I marvelled at its properties. Steeped in boiling water, it might make an effective brew.

A bird shifted in the bushes, disturbing a fluttering of moths, their flimsy wings flitting past my cheek. I thought I heard a sigh. I swallowed against the sour taste in my mouth, the pang in the back of my throat. Was someone here? My neck prickled at the thought.

There was no footstep through the undergrowth, no snapping of twigs. Peering deeper through the velvet dark, I saw nothing, but the conviction remained that someone breathed at my shoulder.

A rush of feeling overcame me. "Asta?" How thin my voice sounded—a quivering reed in this great forest. Huddling my arms close, I felt for the amulet at my neck. My hand brushed the brooch, still pinned high on my apron. Asta's brooch—the one she'd given me.

I'd dreamt of her, in the cave—had felt her touch. I'd feared her spirit's anger, but it had never been her way.

"Forgive me, Asta." My voice still quaked.

In the distance, an owl hooted and took flight, its hunting sights set. It was time, too, for me to leave, to rejoin those who'd shown me friendship.

29

On my second knock, Ylva opened the door.

"Who is it?" Astrid's voice carried from within.

Ylva gaped—at my wild appearance, I supposed, and at finding me still alive. I slipped inside, for it wouldn't do to stand too long. I'd kept to the woods then crept through the long grass of the meadow, before approaching the house from behind.

Though dusk had fallen, there seemed to be a gathering near the longhouse and I'd no wish to be seen.

"In the name of Freya!" Astrid leapt from her stool. "Elswyth!" In two bounds, she'd embraced me, pulling me tight.

My tears sprung, for I'd been too much alone in the cold and dark. I'd near forgotten how it felt to be welcomed into a friend's arms.

"Don't speak," she urged, looking me up and down. "Ylva, bring hot water and my green robe… and some broth and bread."

"I've never seen such a sight!" she gave a half-smile. "Let's get you out of these clothes, then clean and warm."

I let her nimble fingers unfasten the straps of my apron, then stayed her hand.

"You've been collecting again—from the shore by the smell of it." She poked at the long strands of seaweed wrapped in the tuck of my skirt.

I had to show her before she went any further, though I was loath to admit that I'd been unable to avoid the affliction. In that moment, I understood some fraction of the shame that Ylva had endured, and all the others who'd suffered with the blight.

Unfurling my palm, I picked off the strands of algae that clung, holding it out for Astrid to see. Even since that morning, it had improved, returning almost to its natural colour, the blister barely raised at all.

She nodded quietly. "It was a wonder that you went so long without succumbing to the illness. It's just begun, has it?"

I nodded, choking back tears that threatened to bubble over. "It was much worse, and I had the fever, too." It was relief I felt most of all—relief that I was healing. But it was more than that. The algae would change so many lives. My own recovery was proof of it.

"We'll soon have you feeling like yourself and, when you've some food inside you, it won't seem so bad. You can tell me everything when you're ready."

I did my best not to wince as she eased the damp tunic over my head. My shoulders were wrenched from the arduous climb, my arms still sore. Astrid tutted as she passed the warm flannel over my skin, so tenderly. There were other patches of skin, upon my back, which looked a little red, she told me, but none had blistered like my palm. I assumed it was my eating of the algae that had helped, preventing them from fully erupting.

Astrid soothed me as she worked, bathing gently where I was most bruised until the grime of days past was washed away. She wished even to spoon the broth to my lips but I insisted on doing that for myself. It was thick with vegetables and meat; with each mouthful, I felt my strength returning.

"I knew you couldn't be dead." Astrid stood behind to comb my hair. "Though you don't look far off it, I have to say!" She wetted the slatted wood, doing her best not to pull.

"I rowed the boat," I began.

"I know about that." Astrid dropped her hand to my shoulder. "I went down to the harbour before dawn—before the fishermen, even. I couldn't see you by the pier. Then, I realized it was gone—the boat. You told me, Helka took you out, and I remembered. No one else would have dared to take it."

A clutch of fear seized me, for if Astrid knew then everyone did, surely. Why hadn't they gone searching? Wouldn't Gunnolf have commanded it?

She must have felt me stiffen. "There's no need to worry. Some would see no harm come to you." Taking up the comb again, she continued freeing the tangles.

"Anders suggested that we say his son found you disappeared and took Helka's boat, to see if your body were drifting. Everyone knows Halbert's headstrong. He's always been one for mischief. Halbert agreed immediately, telling his friends he lost the boat on the rocks, sailing too close to the cliffs, then swum back. Some have raised an eyebrow but a piece of the hull washed ashore not long after."

My throat tightened again. The blacksmith, Anders, and Halbert. They were loyal to Eirik.

"What about the others? They still say I'm a witch?"

Astrid sighed. "Some do. Some don't. Some say the gods took you in punishment; others say they saved you. They spoke of little else, for a while…"

"And now?"

Pulling her fingers through my hair, she separated the lengths, making ready to plait them. "None can know the jarl's mind, but he's not himself. They're saying he's out of favour with the gods—that he's not the man he was and not worthy to lead us." Astrid leaned closer to my ear. "He's forbidden anyone to speak of…" she hesitated, dropping her voice lower, "the *draug*."

It wasn't a word I'd heard before but a chill passed over me. I turned, searching Astrid's face.

"The restless spirit in human form. I told you of it, Elswyth."

She had, and the story had haunted me. After all that had happened, I had my own tales to tell, but those would wait; now was not the time.

Astrid began passing strands of my hair over and under, her fingers working methodically as she spoke, following the rhythm of braiding that required little thought. "Others have seen her, at the top of the hill. No one wishes to venture out after dark."

"No one?" I frowned. "I thought I saw people around the longhouse."

"Why, yes; today's different!" Astrid exclaimed, then her hands froze and there was an abrupt silence. "Forgive me, Elswyth. I thought this was why you'd come out of hiding. Because you'd seen. Because you knew."

My heart jolted in that moment. I was aware of her fingers resuming their tidying of my hair, briskly forming a central plait and smaller ones either side.

Only when she'd finished, securing all with a strip of linen, did she again look into my eyes, offering me the truth though she knew it would pain me. "Eirik and Helka have returned to Svolvaen, with fine visitors. There's talk of marriage."

I'd grieved and prayed, despaired and believed again, that Eirik would return. He had, but not for me. If his bride were with him, my hopes were futile. However, I endeavoured to pull my thoughts away from Eirik. Whatever secret wish I'd harboured, it was my discovery that had driven me back to Svolvaen. Despair would only hinder me.

I pointed at my bundled apron, discarded on the floor, long strands of green spilling out, and indicated my palm again.

"I had to come back, to show you. It's the remedy we've needed all along. "It's from the cave I sheltered in. The algae will help. I know it will!"

Astrid's hands flew to her mouth. "You found a cure!" With a sob, she threw her arms about me.

Over Astrid's shoulder, I saw that Ylva was looking at us. As usual, she sat some distance away but she'd heard everything. I'd never known her without her affliction. Perhaps, once, she'd been talkative and carefree. If so, she'd soon be again. My own hopes for happiness had been crushed but hers might yet be recovered. I'd think of Eirik later. For now, I had a debt of friendship to repay.

I eased Astrid away from me, knowing it was time we got to work. I'd endured much but it hadn't been in vain. The gods had kept me alive, had given me time to reflect and the will to recover my courage, to escape my dark prison. Just as Eirik was performing his duty, I'd do mine.

"We'll make the treatment together. I'll show you."

Ylva gave her assistance, grinding the pestle in the mortar, releasing the seaweed's healing juices. The plant had worked well as it was but how much more effective it would be once we'd prepared it.

"Soak your linen strips in the liquid and place them on each sore," I directed. "Steep the rest of the algae in boiling water. Make a tisane and drink it down. Go afterwards to Torhilde and to the others. Act where I cannot."

Astrid's eyes shone wet as I borrowed her hooded cloak, drawing it close to my face to creep away.

I heard her as I closed the door behind me. "I knew you'd come back."

30

I took the path behind the main thoroughfare. Near the summit of the hill, the mist was creeping, emerging from between the dark trees of the forest, wreathing them, shifting and rolling, like a ghostly sea from which the ancient trunks rose.

No wonder that Svolvaen's people kept to their homes, for the landscape had an eerie hue. One might believe anything, see anything, on such a night. I, too, was afraid, yet I continued. With my own eyes, I was determined to inspect Eirik's bride—the woman he'd chosen over me.

Light glimmered from two low windows, where the longhouse roof met its walls. The skins had been partially hooked aside to let the breeze enter. At the main entrance, several men stood sentry, their voices carrying low. They'd rather have been inside, no doubt, imbibing ale.

There was one other opening to the rear and it was to this that I crept. Pressing close to the thatch, I knelt and raised my head, peering within.

The hall was full, with Gunnolf's men and those who'd ridden out with Eirik; strangers, too, from Bjorgyn, I guessed.

Faline was wearing one of Asta's robes, yellow cloth woven through with golden strands. It had suited my lady well. Faline's skin appeared sallow against its tone. For all the finery of the gown, she had no place at the table beside the jarl. Instead, she carried a jug, her mouth pressed tight as she filled each cup.

Gunnolf barely looked at her, nor conversed with those on either side. Instead, his eyes, hollowed-dark, darted to the corners of the room. It gave me no pleasure to look at him. I'd been another woman in those days as his lover.

Helka was seated just beyond Gunnolf but her attention was all upon the man to her left. He wasn't of the common build, being tall and slender. His arms were well-muscled but not in the way of Svolvaen's men. His ear was keen to the words she shared with him and, when he leaned close, she closed her hand around his. She'd always kept men at a distance; this one, she did not. He was certainly attractive, with features fine-drawn, his jaw strong and his movements lithe. They would make a fine pair if that was what she wished.

I searched for Eirik. Would he appear different now he'd chosen a bride? There were many men with blonde hair loose about their shoulders, with eyes sparkling in good humour, wearing the same sort of leather jerkin Eirik favoured. There were many men worthy of a woman's attention, but I didn't see the most brave and handsome of them all.

And then my chest constricted. The girl sitting beside Gunnolf was new-bloomed in womanhood and of the same, slight appearance as the man on Helka's left. Not yet ripe, as a woman should be on coming to her marriage bed, but with the promise of loveliness. This, surely, was Freydís, the daughter of Jarl Ósvífur—the alliance conceived by our jarl. The seat next to her was empty, though the place was set.

Helka rose, coming to stand behind Jarl Gunnolf, bending to his ear. Whatever she said, his expression remained distracted. He shook his head and waved her away, his thoughts seemingly on something beyond what surrounded him.

She frowned, looking uneasily about the room before resuming her place. Still standing, she lifted her cup and chimed upon it with her knife, to call attention for the raising of cups.

"Welcome, one and all, to the house of my brother, Jarl Gunnolf, and to Svolvaen—to the home of courageous men and comely women."

I shifted a little, not wanting to miss anything, yet wishing also to keep myself hidden.

Helka's merry aspect faded for a moment. "It seems my brother has some urgent business to attend to, but I know I speak for him also when I say we were too long absent from Svolvaen, from the home of our forefathers, for which we offer our regret." Here, she looked warmly at the man beside her.

"I half wonder if it were not Eirik's plan to be thrown from his horse, for our prolonged stay in Bjorgyn brought friendships which shall endure." Helka tipped her head towards the young girl smiling tentatively beside Gunnolf, and the man to Helka's left raised his cup to hers.

With eyes alight, Helka raised her voice to fill the room. "We look forward to the greatest of celebrations—the joining of our two clans through marriage."

At that, there was a resounding cheer and stamping of feet. I sunk to the grass beneath the window. I'd no need to see more. I'd heard enough to pierce my heart.

I could never return. Svolvaen's people did not want me; Eirik did not need me. Even were I to clear my name of the charges of witchcraft and poisoning, I could never bring myself to serve Eirik's new bride as I had Asta. If Eirik believed my innocence, he might find some man willing to make me his wife, but how could I live under that yoke? I'd never love another; would never be content unless the arms that held me were Eirik's.

I'd fought so long to prove myself worthy of others' regard; fought to survive when all hope seemed lost. What had all my struggle been for? I'd helped others with my skills but I couldn't heal my heart.

Perhaps contentment awaited me only in the next world. I thought of taking myself into the forest, letting the wild beasts find me, or of seeking the cliff edge—a quick end and no more suffering. But how could I do such a thing? I'd come too far to give up. Wasn't I stronger than that? Didn't I deserve my chance at happiness?

I wouldn't succumb to the easy path. My story would not end here. But, I needed to leave Svolvaen. I pictured myself wandering from place to place like the *skalds*, offering my healing arts to the sick, until I found those who would welcome me to stay—where I would find a hearth, a house, and eventually, a husband. I was still young.

There was only so much torment I could bear, and to remain here would be my undoing.

The night fog had unravelled and was moving fast, racing to meet me as I rose to higher ground. Laughter drifted up from the longhouse, sounds of shouts and clapping, dulled by the drifting mist.

I headed to my left, away from the sheer drop to the sea, but tumbling curls of white fast obscured the way.

Even in my plight, I was loath to step blindly, for a fissure might appear beneath my foot. I'd no wish to slip into some narrow crevice, wedging within the rock, or to break my bones upon each jarring ledge of a longer fall. What poor joke it would be, were I to find the chasm through which I'd so recently climbed.

Better to crawl, that my fingers would find any dangerous lip. From habit, I pulled up the hem of Astrid's gown, to avoid its dirtying. I suffered a pang of remembrance. I'd made no farewell, for which I hoped she'd forgive me. This time, I would not return.

How cold it had become in the thickening fog, chill tendrils passing over my skin and entering my very bones. I carried on, hearing the distant rumble of waves, the heels of my hands brushing bracken and the discarded nest of some hilltop bird, wincing as my knee found a stone's sharp edge.

And then all receded, and I was wrapped in silence.

My fingers touched something icy cold. I wasn't alone. My eyes fastened upon the slender foot before me and the hem of a white robe, stained with soil.

I had no power to lift my head, to look upon the creature who stood before me. A cry rose in my throat but froze as surely as the breath and blood within my body. I attempted to speak her name, knowing it was she, but my voice abandoned me. Choking back my tears, I recoiled further, retreating from the one who had always been true to me and whom I had repaid so poorly.

It was another who broke the blanketing of the enfolding mist, another who ran, heedless, his voice strangled.

"My love. My love. Forgive me."

Gunnolf's dark head bowed to kiss the foot, and her hand reached to raise him. In death, as in life, she was beautiful, but so pale, and her eyes no longer blue but black as the pit revealed behind her. As if risen from the grave, her hair garlanded with leaves, her cheek and hands earth-covered, she was a thing without the radiance of life, yet moving and seeing.

He stepped to embrace her then gave a single cry. Consumed by the mist, he fell, to whatever emptiness lay below.

At once, another passed swiftly by me, her scream filled with both fear and rage. I shouted in warning but it was too late. Perhaps Faline flung herself upon the ghostly form, or Asta reached to claim her. The outcome was the same. Locked in tormented embrace, they toppled as one into the gaping chasm.

Shadows seemed to sweep before me, like the cast of clouds on grass, drifting before the sun. Except that, as my eyes closed and the ground surged up to meet me, there were no clouds nor mist. Instead, the moon was high and bright, and the stars uncountable.

31

T he flame flickered in the lamp, showing me Helka's face.
"You're awake, thank the gods!" She lifted a cup to my lips, tipping it for me to drink. "Eirik found you, but no sign of our brother nor of Faline." She pushed hair from my eyes. "What happened, Elswyth?"

Where could I begin? Impossible to tell the whole story. Would it even make sense?

"I heard about Asta's death and their terrible accusation of you; of what my brother did." She squeezed my hand, resting above the furs on the bed. "How did you escape?"

I had no answer for that. The gods had saved me, I'd thought, or perhaps a hand had reached from beyond the grave.

"I knew it couldn't have been Halbert who took the boat. I guessed you must have gone to my cave."

I nodded but couldn't bring myself to recount what had occurred. I was so weary. What was to be gained from reliving those days? Couldn't I be left in peace?

"You're exhausted." Helka looked at me with anguish. "Forgive me, Elswyth. I would have come to find you in the morning…"

"It's of no matter." I sighed and returned the pressure of her fingers.

"Eirik wants to see you."

The mention of his name made my stomach lurch, made the breath halt within my chest. How could I face him? My dignity remained, if little else.

"He refused to believe you were anything but innocent, Elswyth. Sylvi came forward today; she'd been afraid to speak, but she said she saw Faline putting something from an old pouch into Asta's *nattmal*. She knew!"

It should have been some consolation but of what consequence was it? I could summon neither anger with Sylvi nor any joy for myself.

"You were gone so long," I said, at last.

"Eirik's horse threw him as we were entering Bjorgyn. The injury wasn't severe but I insisted travel was impossible. I kept him there far longer than was necessary."

"But, why?" This I couldn't understand.

"Selfish reasons." Helka's cheek reddened. "Leif... I needed to discover if there could be more between us... more than desire. I needed time, Elswyth, to know him, and for him to know me. Love comes by strange paths. I feel that he's been waiting for me, all this time. I still grieve for Vigrid but my heart has opened again."

"The man who sat beside you?"

This was something, at least. For Helka, I could be glad.

"You saw?" Helka shook away her confusion. "So, it was you he ran after? Gunnolf leapt from the table, shouted that he saw a face outside."

Perhaps it had been me; perhaps another.

Helka's voice was firm. "You must know, Elswyth, that Eirik was eager to return. The men of Bjorgyn have not his prowess; he might have bedded a dozen women but none interested him." She leaned closer. "I made him stay, and he could hardly refuse since my choice would give him freedom."

Nothing made sense to me. "But, Freydís?"

"Ha! What of her?" Helka stifled her laughter. "She's pretty enough but hardly a match for Eirik. Even had he wanted her, her father would never have permitted it. He believes a man must demonstrate horsemanship above all; to fall from his mount before we'd even been presented to Jarl Ósvífur hardly boded well, and I made such a fuss of the injury! The jarl declared that no groom with the prospect of a limp would be worthy of his daughter, no matter the strength of his sword arm!"

"Then the marriage..."

"Is mine, of course!" Helka squeezed my hand again. "To Leif! Freydís is young but she has a stubborn streak. She begged to accompany us, to see the lands with which Bjorgyn was allying. Her father saw no reason to keep her from the adventure. The weather has been clement and she carries herself well on horseback, as they all do."

"And, Eirik?"

The curtain separating the box bed from the rest of the great hall pushed aside and he was suddenly standing over me, broad and strong, filling the space with his masculinity.

Helka retreated as Eirik wrapped me tightly in his embrace, holding me close, my cheek pressed to the warmth of his chest and his own resting upon my head. My body remembered him and my heart ached with the knowledge of my loss.

"My Elswyth," he murmured. When he released me, it was to draw my mouth upwards, in a kiss so deep that I forgot all but my love for him. "I thought you were lost to me. All those weeks I was away from you, I came to know my mistake. My thoughts were with you, every day; my heart was yours, always."

I wished to speak but no words would come.

He pushed back the strands of my hair that had come loose. "What must you have thought and endured! And all because I was too foolish to see what was before me. If I'd been here, I would never have allowed them to accuse you." His brows knitted in anger. "By the gods! How you are alive, I know not, but I thank Odin for it!"

He held my face between his hands, his voice fevered. "When they told me how they'd treated you, I wished to strike down Gunnolf where he stood! Only Helka's insistence stayed my sword."

I placed my hand over his, searching his gaze as he continued. "I looked for you… I couldn't bring myself to sit at his table last night. I was in the stable while they ate."

There was so much I wished to say. Above all, I needed to tell Eirik of my errors and ask his forgiveness. I was not blameless. He had wronged me while following his sense of duty while I had chosen my path wholly in anger. My resentment and wounded pride had led me only into further pain.

He tightened his hold, as if never to let me go, embracing me with his body and the ardour of his love. His voice broke with emotion, husky with longing and all that lay unspoken between us.

"Elswyth, I must have you—for my bed, for my pleasure and your own, to bear my children as my wife, for all the time given to us by the gods. Whatever is past, we must forget. From this day forward, we shall promise to love one another and this will be all that matters."

In answer, I raised my face and took another kiss. For what the gods decreed would be, and I knew that I would always be safe in the arms of the man who loved me above all others.

EPILOGUE

It was to be a summer of marriages, not only mine to Eirik, and Helka's to Leif. Ylva was among them; she gave her hand not to the young man who'd spurned her but to Halbert, the blacksmith's son. I was glad of it, and for all the happiness that ripened, along with Svolvaen's crops. We were healing, in many ways.

I sometimes thought of Gunnolf, and Faline, free, at last—of ambitions and fears, jealousies and resentments. I hoped they were at peace, and Asta, too.

Svolvaen gained a new jarl, and Eirik's shoulders bore the honour well, though he mourned the loss of his brother. No matter the many grievances between them, they had been blood-bound.

It shamed me to admit my many follies to Eirik. I'd lost all sense of myself in trying to destroy the last ruins of my love and had been half mad with remorse over Asta's death. Gunnolf and I, both, had allowed the worst part of ourselves to reign in those dreadful weeks.

Eirik sat in silence as I spoke. I feared he'd be unable to forgive but he blamed himself more than I.

The cause of the sores was never known, but we'd found our cure. It would take time, as I'd foreseen, for me to earn respect, to counter mistrust. None called me 'witch' or 'murderess'; not to my face, at least. I told my story, as best I could, but not all of what had occurred could be explained. The workings of the gods and those places beyond our earthly realm are not ours to fathom.

Each night, Eirik stroked my hair until I fell asleep. In his arms, I believed there would be no bad dreams for, whatever the future held, we would face it together.

VIKING
BEAST

EMMANUELLE DE MAUPASSANT

I

ELDBERG

May, 960AD

He woke to the crackle of flames. Sparking and spitting, the thatch was alight, glowing dull through a veil of acrid smoke.

The end of the bed was afire. He sat up to kick at the furs, to draw breath to shout, but his throat closed against the foul ash.

"Bretta!" He choked out her name, shaking her, but she made no answer. Reaching beneath, he lifted her into his arms and, forced to inhale, was wracked by coughing.

By the gods! They had to get out.

With eyes smarting, he found the floor.

The blaze was moving quickly, the flames licking through the timbers.

Eldberg buried his face in Bretta's shoulder. She was limp, her head flung back.

Find the door.

He managed several steps, ignoring scorching embers upon his bare feet, scorning the fierce heat. Nothing mattered but to escape. He was almost there when something struck his head.

Bretta rolled from his arms as he fell. He called her name, or thought he did.

Bretta! My wife. My love. Mother of our child yet to be born.

And then, though the room was bright with flames, there was only darkness.

2

ELDBERG

May, 960AD

Eldberg lay three days and nights, his body not yet ready to wake. When he did, it was to searing pain.

The memory of that night returned with the force of all Thor's thunder, striking fear in Eldberg's heart. Already he knew his fate, but would not accept it, not until the truth had been spoken aloud.

Sweyn, the commander of his battle-guard, stood to one side, his face severe, flanked by Fiske, Rangvald, Hakon, Ivar, but none would meet his gaze—not even Thoryn, the most steadfast of his sworn men.

Only Sigrid—Bretta's aunt—summoned the courage, though her fingers trembled. "The great hall's roof lies smouldering." Her voice rose not above a whisper. "Ivar and Thoryn battled through the flames to drag you out." Sigrid drew a deep breath. "Thrice, Thoryn returned for Bretta, but the smoke was too thick, the heat too ferocious."

She bit her lip. "Rangvald and Fiske held him back from trying again. My Bretta! She is…"

Eldberg's chest constricted.

"She's gone, my jarl."

A shudder passed through him—a sudden, terrible despair. He lay still, willing command of his desire to howl in anguish. His wife! The woman he'd wed at her father's behest—a contracted marriage to tie his loyalty to Skálavík. The wife for whom he'd never expected to feel love. The wife who had adored him—inexplicably, and without reservation.

And the child.

His hands bunched the cloth upon which he lay.

His child. Six months in the womb.

Eldberg swallowed back sour bile and set his jaw. With renewed intensity, he scanned the faces before him. Motioning Sigrid away, he looked to Thoryn.

The man's misery was etched deep, his lips parched and white. Thoryn was brave and loyal; he would have given his life to save Bretta.

Eldberg turned to Sweyn. Of all his men, he was most like himself—ambitious and unforgiving, able to act without remorse or mercy.

Stolen as a child by marauding berserkers, Eldberg had been enslaved until his fifteenth year, when his height and strength and his relentless will had earned him a true place among them. He'd known only their ways—where brutality and savagery were rewarded.

As Beornwold's mercenary, paid to join his raiding trips to the West, Eldberg had fought alongside Sweyn these fifteen years, and had seen his jealousy—for Eldberg was soon favoured above all others. The old jarl had chosen him to marry Bretta, to sire Beornwold's line, and to take his mantle.

Sweyn obeyed through no sense of brotherhood, but because it brought him command over others—in his jarl's name.

Keep your enemies close, Beornwold had told him long ago.

Eldberg frowned. He'd heeded those words well; allowing Sweyn authority, satisfying the need that drove the other man, making use of it. Had Sweyn become greedy? Had he wished his jarl's death and that of his heir—yet to be born?

The Norns had unpicked only one strand of that thread upon their loom.

A mist of fury descended, a veil of red that brought his head momentarily from the pillow. He itched for the hilt of his sword, driving his nails into his palms. Through his left side, swathed in salve and linens, came a jolt of pain.

The conviction assailed him—Sweyn had planned everything. Had sought to kill him and take his place. Had murdered Bretta!

"How did the fire start?" Eldberg kept his voice level, addressing Sweyn alone. Despite his fury, he would seek evidence carefully.

"That I have learnt, my Jarl, and have the culprit shackled." He gestured, sending Ivar and Fiske from the room. "We captured him on the very night of his crime. A spy from Svolvaen, sent to murder you."

Summoning his strength, Eldberg raised himself a little. "Lift me, Sweyn."

As bid, his commander took him beneath the arms, hauling him to a seated position. The stab of pain was greater than Eldberg had anticipated, but he endeavoured not to let it show. He'd endured many wounds. This was no different.

Sigrid darted forward to place pillows behind his back, her face pinched. He nodded curtly, acknowledging her care. She, at least, he could trust.

Sigrid had raised Bretta as her own and respected the love between her niece and jarl.

The man dragged into the room, hunched over, was a head shorter than those around him. Fiske and Ivar supported him on either side, for he was unable to stand. His head and limbs hung limp, his wrists and ankles bent at unnatural angles. Both eyes were swollen closed within his bloodied face. His jaw hung slack—broken.

"The man has been beaten near to death." Eldberg fixed Sweyn with an icy stare.

"I interrogated him. It was necessary."

Eldberg narrowed his gaze. "And now he can no longer speak."

"I discovered all you need to know, my jarl. Hallgerd's successor, Gunnolf of Svolvaen, sent him. From a fishing boat he swam into the northern cove and climbed the cliffs hand over hand. Waiting until darkness, he entered the woodlands, watching several days before he acted."

"Undetected? All that time?"

Sweyn shrugged. "He is more weasel than warrior, adept at hiding."

"And why? What of the treaty? Nigh thirty summers have passed. Why should this Gunnolf act so foolishly? Svolvaen is no match for our strength."

"You answer your own question, Jarl." Sweyn dipped his head. "In fear of what we once were, and what we have the power to be, Gunnolf sent his man to collect what information might be useful." He glanced up again. "And to wound us most mortally, by causing your death."

Eldberg shifted, wincing. "Pull back his head. I would see him."

Sweyn grasped the man's hair at the crown.

In the heat of battle, Eldberg thought nothing of severing a man's limb or head, but the state of the prisoner made him grimace. Being unable to close his mouth, bloodied drool hung from his chin. His cheek and nose were likely broken, the flesh bruised and raw.

Eldberg liked to look a man in the eyes—to judge by what he saw within, but the swollen flesh prevented him from doing so. He returned his gaze to Sweyn, whose own granite-grey eyes remained impassive.

"How was it done?"

Sweyn gave answer without hesitation. "He learnt of your chamber's position within the longhouse. He carried a bow and was able to fire flaming arrows to where they would have most effect. By the time our watchmen saw the flames, your chamber was already imperiled."

Eldberg was assailed, most suddenly, with the memory of Beornwold's funeral. Sweyn had soaked a strip of linen in fish oil and wrapped it about the arrow, dipping the head into the fire cauldron before setting aim for the pyre upon the old jarl's longship. Sweyn was not only adept with sword and axe but one of their most masterful archers.

Eldberg stared meaningfully at Sweyn. "The cur was well-prepared. Were he able to answer me, I would ask him much." If his sworn-man related the truth, the assassin before them had been cunning and courageous, and favoured by the gods—for the guards under Sweyn's command swept the perimeter of Skálavík daily.

The town's trade in metals and weapons, made from the ore dug from the mountains, had made Skálavík wealthy. There was hardly need for raiding to bring bounty to their coffers. Many from across the region came to them. Their warriors engaged now in protecting the town's commerce, ensuring its security.

"What now, my jarl?" Sweyn wet his lips. "A few blows of my axe and we may toss him by parts to the pigs."

A gurgle rose from the prisoner's throat, and his feet scrabbled momentarily before he hung limp again.

"'Tis fitting," Eldberg declared. "If a man is willing to inflict pain, he must expect like for like." He held his commander's gaze, but Sweyn did not flinch.

Signaling his wish to lie down again drew Rangvald and Hakon forward. Eldberg blanched as they aided him but did not voice his discomfort. The burns would take time to heal, but they were nothing compared to the wounds that tore his heart. The grief would become part of him. He would focus on that pain—would feel it and remember.

And a day of reckoning would come.

He closed his eyes, leaning back. "Hold the wretch's head in the fire pit, and keep it there until I no longer hear his screams."

※

Eldberg

At last he slept. In his dream, he clasped her close. Her skin was soft and her hands caressing, though her fingers were chilled.

Don't leave. I need you. Stay with me. Bretta!

But his arms could not hold her.

Waking, he was soaked in sweat, alone, and his chest so tight he could hardly breathe. She was gone forever—his only love. His wife, and the child she carried—his son or daughter.

He wanted to howl to Odin and Thor, to swear vengeance by all the gods for what had been taken from him. Casting back his head, he gave a mournful cry. Let others hear and quake to know his anguish. He would find no rest until he'd devoured his enemies. Let them know the beast he was and fear him—a man disfigured not just in body but in soul: The Beast of Skálavík.

3

ELSWYTH

July 30th, 960AD

The fjord was filled with shimmering light and the squawk of gannet chicks. Eirik pulled deep on the oars, the warmth of gold-veined summer on his back.

His shoulders flexed as he rowed—entirely naked, bronzed, lean-muscled. The waves lapped softly.

Letting the boat glide, he lifted the oars from their cups, safely stowing them. He made a show of placing his hands behind his head and resting his gaze where I'd hitched up my gown of green linen to enjoy the sun on my skin.

"You're slow to catch up, wife."

"Not wife, yet." I suppressed a smile. "I'm free to do as I please until the vows are spoken."

"You wish to disobey me?" Eirik's eyes flickered with mischief. "If it's punishment you desire, raise your skirts and I'll gladly redden your backside."

"And what of you, husband?" I pulled my dress higher and opened my legs, offering him the view he sought. "Will I need to punish you? Or will you forsake your wickedness once we're wed?"

In a single movement, he knelt before me. "I have eyes only for you, wife." He winked, making clear where he directed his admiration.

Wrapping his long hair around my fingers, I tugged back his head. "Helka's been teaching me how to use the bow. Give me cause, and you'll need to guard your own behind."

He pretended to ponder, and I jerked harder, laughing, but eased my hold as his hands came to rest just above my knees. His palms were calloused from wielding not just sword and axe but hoe and spade, from farming in the fields, but they were warm, and his touch gentle.

"You need not doubt my fidelity." He sealed his promise with a kiss upon my inner thigh. "There will be only happiness." He continued upward, his golden beard grazing soft against my skin. "And many children."

His voice was husky as he brought his mouth to my curls. His tongue found me, the tip flicking back and forth, and I moaned, feeling my wetness grow. The familiar ache stirred low in my belly. Eirik had shown me what it was to be desired and to crave in return.

His heart was mine, he said. Yet, I held back some part of me—afraid of him seeing how much I needed him.

Not so very long ago, he'd left Svolvaen at Gunnolf's command, to make a marriage of alliance. Duty was stronger than love, he'd told me. Even now, on the eve of our wedding, I didn't know if I could trust my heart to his care.

Nor did I know if I could trust myself.

On the night of Ostara, when Gunnolf had seduced me, hadn't I welcomed that strange, consuming oblivion? I'd believed myself betrayed—that Eirik had never loved me, that he'd come back wedded. Piece by piece I'd died, letting Gunnolf claim what Eirik had so carelessly cast away, until I barely remembered who I was. I hadn't wanted to remember.

I pushed against Eirik's shoulders, suddenly fearful, unsure of myself, but he grasped my waist and pulled me firm toward his mouth.

"I want you." He buried his tongue deeper, reaching where his cock would soon follow. "And this—forever."

I struggled only briefly, holding fast to the raised portion of the deck until I could think only that he must not stop. It had always been so, from the first days, when he'd come to Holtholm as a raider, and I'd been powerless to deny him.

I slid my fingers through his hair, yielding to the urgent hunger of his mouth. With yearning pain, I wanted him, but he took his time, for it aroused him to see me so. He teased me long and slow, until my belly tightened with sweet pain and I shuddered, blinded by brilliant light.

Unfastening the brooches that held my gown, he pulled all that I wore over my head, until I lay as naked as he, and he moved to cover me.

He pressed his lips to my eyelids and my forehead, and to the hollow of my throat, scooped back my hair to nuzzle behind my ear.

I twined my arms about his neck, welcoming his weight and the long sliding push of his penetration—lost to the sensation of being filled and stretched.

"So tight. So warm." He buried his face against my breast, suckling with each thrust, then grazing my nipple with his teeth, yielding sharp pleasure.

I could not lie still. I wanted all of him. Caressing his buttocks, I pulled him deeper, wrapping my legs around his. "Eirik!" I breathed his name, gasping for air, trembling, while he clasped me tight. A searing jolt seized me, white-hot and blazing. I raised my hips to receive him, crying at the depth of his final invasion, arching as he spurted his seed—desiring all that he would give.

※

I rubbed my cheek on his chest, listening to the slap of water against the side of the boat as we lay together.

Eirik cradled me. "You're mine, Elswyth." His lips touched the crown of my head. Tenderly, he stroked my hair. "I wish only…"

I raised myself to my elbow, wishing to know what troubled him, but he shook his head.

"'Tis foolish— for she is dead these thirty years."

Sitting up, I placed my hand over his heart. He'd spoken of his mother only once—of her abduction when Eirik had been but three summers old.

"Do you wish to tell me of it?"

A shadow crossed his face. "It changes nothing to dwell on the past."

I brushed the hair from his eyes. "But it may ease your heart and—"

He caught my wrist and turned my palm to meet his lips, holding it there for several moments. "You wish to know what pains me, wife, that you may share in understanding."

"I do."

Eirik returned my hand to his chest, holding it there with his own. He breathed slowly, his brow furrowed, gathering his thoughts.

"For many years, I had no knowledge. Only later did I discover what no one wished to tell me. My grandfather, jarl in his time, married Ingrid of Skálavík and two children were born: first Hallgerd, then my mother, Agnetha. When Agnetha reached the age of betrothal, they promised her to Beornwold, Ingrid's nephew—Jarl of Skálavík."

I bit my lip, for I knew that such a contract had never been fulfilled.

"Hallgerd became jarl on his father's death and spurned the contract, giving Agnetha to his closest friend, Wyborn."

"A love match?"

Eirik nodded. "Half of the dowry that would have come with Agnetha was sent to Beornwold in recompense, and it seemed the matter was settled. My mother soon bore Gunnolf, followed by Helka, and myself. More than six years passed."

I frowned, knowing that blood feuds began over far lesser offences. "But Beornwold had not forgotten."

"No, Beornwold neither forgot nor forgave. After my grandmother's death, he came to take Agnetha by force, saying that what he'd been promised should not be withheld.

"And Hallgerd beat the Skálavík raiders into retreat."

"Aye," said Eirik, "but not before my father fell, and my mother was taken by Beornwold." He squeezed my hand. "Svolvaen emptied its stores and coffers for her release, and a pact was signed. The boat maker and his two oldest sons went to Skálavík to build three dragonships. In return, there was to be no further conflict."

I swallowed, wondering if I was brave enough to ask more. "And did she speak of what passed during her captivity?"

Eirik made no reply, merely looking out over the fjord. At last, he said, "When Svolvaen sent a ransom for her release, Beornwold sent her back, but she wasn't the same. I woke up one morning and she was gone again. Everyone was searching. It was the next day that a fishing boat found her floating, out there."

"Oh, Eirik!"

I regretted having asked at all.

His mother had taken her life, grieving for the husband lost to her, and for the lost part of herself taken by Beornwold. The saddest part was that Eirik, Helka, and Gunnolf had lost them both.

Eirik gathered up my under tunic, passing it over my head, then held out my green gown, helping me into it before pulling on his own clothes. "My brother grew up thinking Hallgerd weak for having signed the truce. He always spoke of revenge for our parents' deaths but knew we lacked Skálavík's strength. An attack would have brought the end of everything."

"And what do you wish, Eirik?"

"I, too, have hungered for justice, but I won't ask others to lay down their lives to appease my sorrow. We all live with wounds from our past. It's wisest to find a way to see beyond them." Moving to the other end of the boat, he fitted the oars once more.

"We'll complete the fortifications begun by Gunnolf once the summer's crop is harvested, but I intend no feud with Skálavík. Beornwold is dead these four seasons past, and the bad blood has ended."

We said no more as Eirik turned the vessel about. The sky had grown dusky—a soft twilight before the brief hours of darkness.

My heart should have been filled with joy but a secret lodged there, held close these weeks past. I hadn't been sure at first, but my conviction had been growing, and I needed to tell Eirik. He would soon notice himself, and I must speak afore that time came.

For so long I'd desired a child, and Freya had answered me, but my past clung upon my shoulder like the darkest shadow.

Gunnolf had died on the night Eirik had returned to Svolvaen, yet I remained in his power, for I feared the babe I carried had not been sired by the man I loved.

Just another few weeks, and I will tell him.
But tell him what?
That his own brother, having made me his bed thrall, had planted his seed where

Eirik had failed? That his heir might be born of that lust, rather than the love between us?

Eirik had sworn forgiveness of all that had passed in those precarious days—but would he forgive this? Surely better for me to pretend certainty and claim the conceiving to have occurred only after Eirik's return. It might even be true.

I'd wanted a marriage built upon trust and honesty.Instead, it would begin with a lie.

4

ELSWYTH

July 31st, 960AD

"A toast to our jarl and his good lady," bellowed Olaf. He towered above us, standing upon the table. "May the gods give us all such wives—clever and resourceful, and with beauty exceeded only by Freya."

Eirik grinned and inclined his head in thanks as our guests drank, and there was much banging of cups for them to be refilled.

"You'll need to go looking in the forest to find your sweetheart, Olaf!" Anders hollered from the other side of the hall. "Some bear is sure to be willing to embrace you."

"No need to go so far," guffawed Halbert. "The sheep pen is right outside. Half a dozen darlings to choose from there, Olaf!"

The others roared in laughter, men and women alike, making ribald gestures. Guðrún, walking amongst them with her jug of mead, was tossed from one lap to the next, until she landed upon Olaf's—to much cheering and her own blushes, for all knew she nursed tender feelings for him.

I couldn't help but feel content. Since my arrival in Svolvaen, I'd fought for acceptance and approval. Now, seeing how I made Eirik happy, his people had granted me their blessing. I'd played my part as hostess that day, taking many kisses upon the cheek.

Only Bodil, standing apart, scowled as I glanced her way.

You can keep your sour looks, I thought. *For I am married now, and Eirik will have no more of you!* I gave her an innocent smile, but she continued to glower, and I reprimanded myself for pettiness. Though she'd once been

Eirik's lover, he'd shown no inclination for her since bringing me to Svolvaen.

I resolved to enjoy the merriment, which had moved to the bracing of elbows for arm wrestling. With so much mead drunk, the bouts quickly escalated, until there were several men tumbling on the floor, red in the face. They tasked Eirik with taking on every one. The losers of each bout received a light punishment—a horn of ale brought for drinking in one long draught, to more cheers.

I'd lived in Svolvaen a full year, but I was yet to grow accustomed to the boisterous nature of such gatherings. With some relief, I retreated—it being a bride's privilege—asking Sylvi to set aside the platter she carried and come with me to comb my hair. I'd worn it loose today as Eirik liked best, falling to my waist.

From beyond the wooden partition of Eirik's chamber, there came the sound of stamping feet and shouts of encouragement. I closed my eyes as she drew the carved bone through my hair, letting her attention soothe me.

"My congratulations to you, my lady," Sylvi spoke softly as she worked. "And may the gods send you their blessings, and all the happiness a bride may wish for."

I murmured my thanks, but no more—for I knew she referred to the getting of children. She'd guessed already, perhaps, at my condition, but I knew she would say nothing. Sylvi had always been adept at keeping secrets.

"'Tis beautiful you look. The bride's scarlet is becoming on you."

Sylvi had dyed the wool herself, steeping it in the bark of mountain alder, and the colour had sprung vivid. I touched her hand in gratitude. "You've always been kind, Sylvi—a good friend."

She squeezed my fingers in return, then drew the comb again. She gathered back my hair from my shoulders, being careful not to dislodge the copper brooches clipped to the looped straps of my gown. I tilted my head back and absentmindedly fingered the adornment on my bodice. Not just any brooch, but the ivory pieces Asta had gifted to me before her death.

Asta.

I could still see her face so clearly.

Since the night of Gunnolf and Faline having fallen into the chasm upon the cliffs, the rumours of Asta's spirit walking had ceased, and I was glad— for that other realm had no place in this.

Gunnolf's body had washed ashore after some days, though Faline's had never been found. With his sword and shield upon his chest, we'd sent the jarl to the next life upon the pyre of a burning ship.

I wondered if he and Asta had found the peace that had eluded them in this world. There had been too much death and too much unhappiness, but Eirik was right—we would begin anew.

We'd spoken our vows that morning, upon the shore of the fjord, alongside Helka and Leif, with all Svolvaen bearing witness to our marriage.

Helka would soon return to Bjorgyn with her new husband, there to enjoy further rites before Leif's own people, but, until then, we'd celebrate together.

Eirik's gaze had not wavered as he'd made his promise to keep me as a husband should—to care for me, feed and clothe me, protect me, and give me children. The last he'd spoken with a smile, which I'd returned even as my heart trembled, aware of the babe growing already in my womb.

With two pigs and a goat offered in sacrifice to Odin, the animals had been promptly carried off for roasting. The feast couldn't begin in earnest until the meat was cooked. There had been merriment at the tables nonetheless, each set with the abundance of our mid-summer harvest, and every guest given a loaf baked in the shape of a sun wheel.

Though Eirik had desired our marriage without delay, we'd chosen to wait some seemly time, and to conduct our festivities to coincide with *lithasblot*—giving thanks to Urda for the bounty of Svolvaen's lands. The weather had been kind in ripening the crops and, thanks to the algae I'd discovered in the cliff caves, we'd cured the ailment that had plagued our people. We were strong enough again to tend the fields. The first fruits were gathered, and the livestock were faring well.

"There. All done, and 'tis like a golden cloak, my lady." Setting aside the comb, Sylvi knelt to retie my slippers. They, too, were new, crafted from softest leather and sewn to match my bridal garb.

It felt strange, still, to have others wait upon me. For so long, I'd been little more than a thrall—first as the plaything of Eirik, brought from the far western shores of my homeland for his pleasure, and then at the mercy of his brother, Gunnolf, in those dark days of Eirik's absence. In name, I'd been 'free', but there had been few choices before me.

We were fortunate in having Alvis, the lad who tended our livestock, to fetch water and firewood. But I'd always helped Sylvi and Guðrún, for there was much work to be done—cleaning hare for the pot, kneading bread, churning milk for cheese and butter, smoking and salting meat and fish, and working at the loom. With the harvest safe, we'd be busy preserving for weeks to come. No matter my position as the jarl's wife, I'd vowed that those duties would not change—though I'd be spared the more burdensome tasks.

Another roar of laughter rose from within the hall. As Sylvi glanced up, she caught my eye. I sighed, somewhat wearily, knowing that the revelry would continue long. There had been much to prepare in the past weeks, in readiness for this celebration, and we were both exhausted.

However, Sylvi only smiled. "'Tis been too long since there was merriment, my lady. We must let them have their fun."

She was right, of course, but I was reluctant to face again the men's rowdy jests and foolery. The door of the longhouse was wide open this night, and it would be easy for me to slip out, just for a while.

Filled with so many, the longhouse was warm, and my arms were bare, but Eirik had given me a wedding gift—a knee-length cape of finely woven cloth, trimmed with the russet-coloured pelt of a fox he'd hunted this winter past. I draped it about my shoulders, glad for it as I stepped out. A breeze shivered the forest leaves.

There were only a few hours of darkness, for it was high summer still, but the true night was upon us now. Further down, there was the distant light of torches. Even tonight, the watch were keeping guard, and I imagined them impatient at their posts, waiting to be relieved, that they might join the carousing.

I walked some way up the hill, eager to leave behind the unruly celebration. It was my habit to seek the evening air, for I was oft disturbed by fretful dreams, and they'd plagued me much of late. Perhaps that explained my tiredness.

I breathed deeply, willing myself to let go my fears. Eirik and I were married, and nothing could prevent our happiness. Soon, I would tell him of the babe, and he would want to believe that it was his.

Yet, something gnawed within me. I knew not what the gods of my new home would make of my falsehood, but the omniscient God of my old life would not approve. In my heart, nor did I.

I looked skyward, as if seeking the answer there, and the clouds parted to show me the moon. Full and low hung, it filled the sky with so much light, I was dazzled, but only momentarily. No sooner had the orb revealed itself, than a shadow passed over from which a skull seemed to form, the jaw open in a leering grin. I wanted to look away, but the vision held me transfixed.

Never before had I seen such a thing, though I knew the summer skies were said to play tricks in the same way as the winter borealis.

The next moment, from the corner of my eye, I saw some movement, or heard a footfall, but whoever was there was quicker than me.

A hand of steel closed about my throat, while another clamped over my mouth. My shriek of protest came to naught and gained me only rougher treatment, for I was yanked from where I stood, my ribs crushed as I was dragged away, my arms pinned and my feet skimming the grass.

It's just a prank! One of Eirik's men come to carry me back.

Except it could not be, for whoever this was, his handling of me was far too rough. He made no attempt to speak, nor to return me to the ground, and we were not heading toward the longhouse but away, in the direction of the forest.

I lashed out, punching his leg, then raking my nails. Wriggling one arm free, I jerked my elbow hard into his thigh, then again. With a curse, he turned me upright, and I twisted to claw his face, but I merely scratched the tough leather encasing his chest. His fingers were still pressed to my mouth, and I bit them, only to have my head shoved back violently for my trouble.

At last he spoke and with deadly calm. "Try that again, and I'll snap your neck." His eyes were cold, his face one I'd never seen before—a face without emotion.

And then I saw the flames.

My abductor had brought me some distance, but I could see clearly that the turf of the longhouse was alight. The moon was clear once more and the scene well-lit. There were perhaps thirty men, some still tossing their torches upon the roof and through the door.

It had happened so fast. I'd walked outside and had seen no one, but they must have been hiding behind the houses, crouching in the shadows.

The night had filled with screaming and desperate shouts. Several emerged from the longhouse door. They were in no state to defend themselves—unarmed, disoriented, as stunned as me. Their attackers let them blunder, lurching with blinded eyes, but their weapons were already drawn.

No!

My own shout of warning was muffled by the hand that held me fast, fingers digging into my cheeks.

More of our people emerged through the door, falling to the ground, gasping for breath.

Eirik!

I saw him, and Helka, too, coughing through the billowing smoke. The hem of Helka's gown was alight. Eirik threw her to the grass and rolled her, sprawling across to stop the flames. He did not see the man who approached, who stood over him with a raised sword. In his wedding finery, none could doubt my husband's status. He was the Jarl of Svolvaen.

There was a rushing, crackling sound as the timbers beneath the turf caught light and large chunks of the outer covering fell into the space below.

No need for moonlight now. The oil-soaked torches tossed upon our home had made quick work. The whole sky seemed to burn.

Amidst the horrible glow, I saw the man loom over Eirik, taller than those around him. The flames illuminated his face.

Terror struck my heart. Beneath that amber blaze, his skin was red and puckered, framed by a mane of hair that glinted copper, and his eyes were dark with hatred. With both hands, he brought his blade high and plunged it downward, piercing Eirik's body.

I screamed so loud, that even the iron hand upon my face could not silence my cry.

Eirik!

Without seeing his attacker, without chance of defending himself, he'd been struck down. The brute placed his foot on Eirik's back, levering upward to withdraw his sword, then kicked him over so that Eirik's eyes were upon the stars.

If those eyes were still capable of seeing, I couldn't tell, for there was no movement, and my heart froze.

No! It cannot be. You're not dead!

Eirik!

You must get up!

The sob that rose in my throat choked me.

I must go to him. Help him.

I struggled again, knowing I had to get free. Though my arms were pinned, I kicked back against my captor's shin.

"*Bikkja!*" He spat the curse and wrenched me about, letting go only to slap me hard across the cheek.

The world spun, and I felt the brute's shoulder in my belly.

"Eirik." I tried to raise my head, to make him hear me, but there was no breath in my lungs. I could see nothing through my tears.

We were heading away from the settlement, skirting along the edge of the trees, down toward the meadow, then cutting through branches that tore at my hair. Still, we pushed on, until I heard the river.

Deposited on my feet once more, I found my knees wouldn't hold me.

I couldn't think, couldn't move. Nothing made sense.

If they would only leave me, I would curl up under the trees and close my eyes. Perhaps it wasn't real. If I went to sleep, wouldn't I wake later and find it all to have been a horrible dream?

But I wasn't to be left. There were four small boats sitting low in the glimmering water. Around us, others were slithering down the bank and jumping aboard.

I was yanked too hard and landed on my behind. We slid together over half-rotten leaves before I was swung over the side of the last vessel and shoved into the bow.

This was how they'd come, unseen, but from where? And with such stealth.

For what purpose? To capture me? It made no sense.

To destroy Svolvaen? We'd harmed no one.

To plunder our stores? They'd taken nothing.

I looked at the faces surrounding me—men like those who'd been feasting in our hall. Men with blood on their hands. They reeked of smoke.

The boat was near full, and those closest surveyed me. One, whose eyes were gentler than the rest, inclined his head in my direction. "What's this, brother? We were told to take no one. He'll break your arm for it, or your neck."

"None of your business, Thoryn." My captor sneered. "Besides, there's different rules for me. I do as I like."

The other man frowned.

"Cast away. We're done." The call came from the front.

The one who sat beside me brought a length of twine from under the seat, and I watched mutely as he bound my hands.

"Say a word or give me any trouble, and I'll sling you over." He pulled the final knot tight, then grinned, showing two teeth missing. "I might do it anyway, but I won't think twice if you don't keep your mouth shut."

As we cast off, I looked back, hoping I would see Eirik—wanting to believe he was unharmed and had managed, somehow, to follow.

But he was not there.

There was no one in the trees above us.

The breeze carried only distant screams.

ELSWYTH

July 31st, 960AD

The boats were shallow and narrow, and the men rowed carefully. In one place, where the waterway curved, they became stuck in the mud and had to use all oars to be on their way again.

I saw only the dark shape of the other boats ahead, and the men crouched before me, pulling steadily homeward. We passed through meadows until the flatlands became hills, and the river wound through a wooded valley.

I was alone, and those I loved were dead. Svolvaen's people were not mine by birth, but they had become my family. Shivering, I grasped the edges of my cloak, pulling it closed as best I could. My hands had grown quite numb from the rope.

My eyes grew heavy from the constant sound of the splashes from the oars, but there wasn't room to lay down or any soft place to rest my head. Nevertheless, I dozed, and woke to find us passing between steeply rising rock, the river narrower than ever. Within the scree and crevices grew overhanging trees, the branches of which oft brushed the men's heads. Each time, they stilled their oars and lowered their shoulders so that the vessel glided silent beneath the foliage.

High above, the moon had faded within a sky of lifting violet. We were followed, but not by human eyes. A pack of wolves leapt over the crags above, looking down. Fortunately, there was other prey. Only winter drove them to reckless hunting.

The sun rose steadily, and my lips grew parched. My captor drank his pouch dry and refilled it from the river but pushed me away when I indicated my thirst. Only Thoryn offered me water, which I gulped gratefully until the other man snatched it away.

At last, the chasm opened on one side, and the forest came down to meet us, bringing the sound of birdsong and the rustle of small creatures moving beneath the ferns. The men had hardly exchanged a word in all our journey, but they seemed to grow easier as the trees became sparse, smiling to one another—glad, I supposed, to be not far from their beds.

Though my hands were tied, it appeared not to be enough for, nearing our destination, my captor knotted a second rope, which he looped about my neck. Weary to the bone, I made no struggle. What little fight remained within me I'd conserve for when I needed it.

I was surprised to see the tree line give way to jagged peaks. Fierce mountains loomed above. When the first vessels threw their ropes ashore, the men disembarked without delay. One stood taller than the rest, his shoulders broader, and his hair flaming red and wild, reaching past his shoulders. He barked at two who'd been waiting on the landing pier and, as he turned, a new wave of sickness engulfed me. The left side of his face was puckered with coarse scars. It was the man who'd killed Eirik.

Instinctively, I ducked low, not wishing him to see me, for nothing good could come from drawing the attention of one so brutal.

My captor waited until all others had left our boat before lifting me onto the platform, then tugged on the rope tied about my neck, leading me uphill. I could hardly keep up, stumbling behind, but he seemed satisfied to let the others outpace us.

It was not until we breeched the summit of the meadow that I smelled the salt air and saw the fjord below—a strip of glittering silver with mountains dominating its far side. The settlement was far larger than Svolvaen, with buildings sprawling the full width of its harbour. Most of the men peeled away, downward to those dwellings, until there was only my captor and I, climbing still, away from the main bustle of the town, the forested slopes to our left.

Ahead of us was a homestead—a building large enough, I guessed, to hold several hundred people, and newly thatched, the reeds not yet weathered. There were pens and byres for livestock; a horse was being led from its stable; someone was hanging fish in the smokehouse; and women were churning butter in the dairy. From one building came the distinctive smell of skins being tanned—rich and earthy, and slightly sweet. From another, a blacksmith's hammer rang clear.

It seemed a wonder to me that, while the heart of Svolvaen had been destroyed, and my own with it, here, life continued as normal.

I expected us to approach the longhouse, for I would be just a thrall, brought to serve. If I were lucky, I'd be permitted something to eat and drink, at least, before being given work to do.

"Not there." Seeing the direction in which I looked, he tugged harder on the rope, chafing my neck as he guided me onward, further up the hill.

There was another hut, high on the headland, set apart. Coming closer, I saw that it commanded a view not only of the fjord and the town but the far mountains and the open water to the north, dotted with small islands. It was a watchpoint, with a brazier upon a great pole, ready to be lit in warning.

Three men sat, their weapons laid to one side, intent on some game. They looked up as we approached.

"What's this, Sweyn?" called one. "Entertainment?" He grinned, pulling on his beard.

Sweyn merely grunted and gave the door a kick. I hesitated, but the rope was firm about my neck. He jerked it maliciously, hauling me over the threshold, and I swallowed a sob. My legs threatened to collapse beneath me, and my neck was rubbed raw. I was hungry, thirsty, frightened, and sick.

The light from the open door revealed a bench along one side and a large chest, bedding piled in one corner. Sweyn pulled on the rope, hand over hand, until there was no distance between us.

His face bore an expression of delighted cruelty as he reached for my breast, squeezing roughly, thumbing my nipple. "Fine clothes for a fine lady." He pushed closer. "And you're just as fine underneath, I'd say."

I tried to twist away, but the rope around my neck made that impossible. I stood very still, aware of his sweat and the sourness of his breath.

He slipped his hand inside the wide neck of my gown—calloused fingers coarse across my soft skin, taking possession of what he now thought was his. He took my breast into his palm, kneading the flesh, then found the point of my nipple and pinched it.

I did my best to remain expressionless, refusing to show my fear. Instead, I spoke as forcefully as I could. "Why did you come to Svolvaen? Why did you take me?"

"Because I could. What does it matter?" With a leering smile, he removed his hand, then snapped, "Take it off. I want you naked when we're fucking."

"I won't."

Grasping my face, he turned it upward. "We'll take this outside. You won't be so haughty when you've three holding you down. I'm a generous man. Once I've filled you, they can each take their turn. Then we'll see if you're worth keeping alive."

"No!" The word emerged strangled, and he laughed, his eyes alight with malicious mirth.

I was alone, with no one to help me. No one to care whether I lived or died—and I wanted to live. Not just for the sake of the child I carried, but for myself.

If I could run fast enough, past the men outside, I might reach the homestead. There, someone would take pity on me. I'd be at their mercy, but the women of the house wouldn't let them use me as a whore. This I told myself, summoning what strength remained inside me. Knowing I'd have only one chance, I drew up my knee.

Sweyn must have sensed my intention, for he recoiled as I acted, managing to turn half away, so that I caught him only partially in the groin, but it was enough to wind him. Cursing, he released me and staggered backward.

With a hammering heart, I ran. He would be only a few steps behind, and I would feel his fist for what I'd done. Blindly, I raced for the door, lifting my hem to avoid falling. But I must have misjudged, for the doorway grew dark and I collided with a hard wall. A wall standing three heads above me, wearing a leather breast plate with an axe hanging from its belt. A wall of pure muscle, whose hands had grasped my shoulders to keep me from toppling.

My head fell back, and I lost all power to move.

It was the demon, his wild hair a fiery mane. The side of his face was scarred. His left eye had barely healed. The burns were recent but, long ago, some blade had cut deep across his cheek, leaving a gash through his beard.

Unblinking, he looked down at me, and I was drawn into his eyes. Even in that dim light, I saw how unusual they were—green and gold. There was power in those eyes, as if he might demand anything, and others would obey.

I witnessed his surprise at the way I stared at him, and his grasp tightened, as if he were unsure that I was real. His voice rose deep from his chest, rasping, as if it were difficult for the sound to emerge from his throat.

"I commanded that there be no prisoners."

I couldn't see the brute I'd been fleeing from, but I heard the shuffle of his feet.

"The gods threw her easily in my path, Jarl. They meant for me to take her."

In reply, the red demon touched the ivory brooch on the bodice of my gown. He surveyed the rope about my wrists and the thick noose hanging from my neck. "Take as many bed thralls as your cock needs, Sweyn, but not this woman."

My heart beat strangely. Was I to be saved, after all?

And then my blood turned to ice, for those eyes, so intense, were upon mine again.

"It is I who will own her—for I am owed a debt."

6

ELSWYTH

August 1st, 960AD

I received a mug of buttermilk, gulping it down greedily, and a hunk of bread. With my hunger appeased, my will was restored.

More than once, I'd faced death, but still I was here. If the gods had a plan for me, I was ready to hear it. For some reason, I'd been brought into the hands of this murderer; the man who'd killed my husband, who must have ordered the torching of our longhouse.

The remembrance filled me with a desire to empty my stomach, but I needed to be stronger than that. The sorrow that filled me was already turning to anger—a more useful emotion to harness, for it might keep me alive.

The jarl had commanded that I be washed, and so I'd been brought to the bath-house. The thralls had not looked at their master as he gave them his orders, nor had they wished to look at me, at first.

The hut was large enough to house a family but contained a great wooden tub, braced like a barrel. I'd never seen the like of it, nor the manner in which it was filled. Above the fire pit, the cauldron was suspended on chains, hung from a braced rod of metal, and a long spout emerged from its side. Those who'd brought me inside had only to push the lower half of the bowl for it to tip water into the tub.

It must have taken eight cauldrons' worth to have brought the water to its current level. The bath had not been intended for me, of that I was certain. A table stood beside the tub, upon which rested linens and soap.

The two women helped me to undress and to climb the steps, holding my hands as I lowered myself into the steaming water. Gradually, they grew braver, and I saw them glance one to the other and back to me. They'd seen the slight roundedness of my belly, the distinctive curve sitting low. Eirik had thought me only to be eating well, but I could see they knew better.

I must gain their trust. Perhaps they'll know a way for me to escape.

Or, if I were to remain and lived long enough to see the babe's birth, they might find a place of safety for the child to be reared. I didn't want to think of that. I couldn't think of it—for such a thing seemed too distant and too sad with all that had happened in the past day and night.

But I needed them, so I smiled as they scrubbed my back and tipped my head for them to wash my hair. I murmured my thanks and asked their names and from where they'd come. They only shrugged at that. Both had been born here—Thirka and Ragerta—and had been slaves, always.

The name of this place? Skálavík.

I fought down my fear when I heard it.

Only two days ago, Eirik had told me his tale, of the dark deeds of Beornwold of Skálavík. But this jarl, the demon, wasn't Beornwold.

I wracked my memory. Months ago, I'd listened as Gunnolf had plotted the alliance that would strengthen Svolvaen. Eirik had suggested marriage between Helka and the new jarl of Skálavík. She'd protested vehemently, but Gunnolf had dismissed the idea anyway, for the jarl was newly wedded, he'd said.

That was something! If I might speak with his bride, she'd be sure to take pity on me—for I'd lost so much. Any person with a heart would feel my pain. I would ask about her, when I had the chance. But first, I wished to know more of my enemy, of the man who'd wrought destruction on all I loved.

"The Beast, they call him—*Aifur*," said Ragerta. "Though his birthname is fearful enough."

"The mountain of fire—that's what it means, Eldberg." Thirka dropped her voice low, as if saying it would conjure him in the room.

"And what has he done to earn this reputation?" I turned the soap over in my hands, pretending a nonchalance I did not feel.

Ragerta glanced at the door. "They say he was taken by berserkers as a boy and raised among them as a slave—but that his bravery earned him his freedom and he fought among them for a while."

"You've heard of those men who are more like beasts?" added Thirka. "They wear only the pelt of bears or wolves and live like them, in the forest."

"They can even jump through fire without being harmed." Ragerta's eyes were wide.

"He claims he can do that?"

"No. He never speaks of that life." Ragerta shifted uneasily, her eyes darting away. "Only once did I hear a man mention this—a merchant, years ago, before Eldberg became jarl. He made some joke, about him going into the forest not to hunt wild animals but to mate with them."

"What happened?" Part of me did not wish to know, but still I listened.

"It was as if he were possessed." Her voice grew quieter. "His face grew hot and swollen, and he began to shake all over, so great was his rage—as if he meant to turn into a true beast before us."

"And his teeth!" Thirka squeaked. "He bared his teeth as if to bite."

"And the merchant?"

"I've never seen anyone more frightened. He froze, cowering, then came to his senses and fled. Eldberg followed him outside." Thirka pushed her fist to her mouth, unable to continue.

I looked to Ragerta, encouraging her to finish the story.

She bit her lip, adding quickly. "When he came back, he was holding something small, which he threw to the dogs."

I swallowed back a sudden taste of bile. It was a foul thing, to desecrate a body.

"His boat became Eldberg's, of course," said Thirka.

The next moment, I felt a draught upon my back, and the two women shrank away, their faces transformed by fear, a terrible fear.

Hugging my knees to my chest, I kept very still. Though I couldn't see him, I heard the heaviness of his tread and felt his presence behind me.

Thirka and Ragertaboth scurried to depart, leaving me alone.

"Stand up." That rasping voice again, the words spoken abruptly, expecting to be obeyed.

I didn't reply, nor did I move.

It took but two steps for him to reach me, placing his hand against the nape of my neck, and my heart leapt in my chest. He was not merely a stranger touching my bare skin, but the man I'd watched murder my husband—a man I had every reason to hate.

I was too afraid to look at him, nor did I wish to comply, but what should I do? Could I reason with such a man?

Before I had the chance to decide, the pressure on my nape increased. Slowly, he raised me up. The realisation had me splashing, then spluttering in shock. My feet floundered to gain purchase while my hands flew to where he grasped me, but there was no fighting his strength. Water streamed from my hair and down my body.

Only when he had me standing did he let go, spinning me about to face him. My humiliation was immediate, and I brought my hands to cover myself, though the gesture was ridiculous. He grasped me by the chin, turning me to the firelight.

"You will look at me."

I'd lowered my eyes out of shame, but I raised them now.

The room was warm with steam, yet I shivered.

As before, he studied me intensely—not my body, but my mouth, nose, and eyes. His brow drew tight in concentration. "You look like someone…" His voice trailed away. "Impossible, of course, for you are no Skálavík woman—nor even a woman of Svolvaen."

"'Tis true," I stated plainly, determined not to be cowed. "I come from Holtholm, far to the west, and would be there still had Eirik and his men not sought haven with us in a storm. I went willingly to Svolvaen, not as Eirik's thrall, but as a free woman." I held my chin a little higher. "Yesterday, he made me his wife." As I said it, the memory of what had happened rose in a white-hot flash.

He said nothing.

"Is it your habit to kidnap women from your allies and burn their villages? What sort of man are you?"

I shook away from his grasp. He had no right to touch me.

"I saw you! You didn't give Eirik a chance to stand. He didn't even know who was attacking him."

"It was no plan of mine to abduct you. That notion was Sweyn's alone, and I believe he knew not who you were—only a woman who took his fancy. But the gods brought you to my hands, just as they brought the good fortune of my finding all Svolvaen gathered in one place, and your cur-of-a-husband to my feet. I wished him dead, and he is. I regret only that his passing was too swift. As to allies, I recognise no treaty!"

I drew back in horror, for I'd never heard a man speak without honour. "He was my husband. The man I loved!"

The right side of his mouth curled into a sneer. "You were his thrall, submissive—and to that of his brother, I hear, when this Eirik abandoned you."

His statement shocked me into silence. Dropping my head, I felt the shame of those dark days. "Eirik loved me, and he returned. He wanted no other woman." I stumbled over my explanation, knowing that nothing could excuse the choices I'd made. "I believed I was forsaken, but I was wrong."

I had to live with my sins and, still, they wrenched my heart. Perhaps I was faithless, my will to survive stronger than my fidelity. Even becoming Eirik's bride, I'd failed to speak honestly, making no confession of my fear that the child I carried was Gunnolf's.

Yet, for all that, I needed honesty from this man. I needed to know why he'd attacked Svolvaen. Though I wished to spit in his face, I calmed myself. Curling my arms tighter about my body, I framed my question carefully. "You broke our treaty of peace. For what reason?"

Eldberg's reply was pure ice. "You see my face, caused by the assassin your jarl sent to Skálavík."

I didn't understand. "Eirik wished for peace. He would never have—"

Eldberg cut me off before I could say more. "And yet my wife and unborn child are dead at your jarl, Gunnolf's, order."

His wife and child? Dead?

In his last days, a strange madness had overtaken our former jarl. He'd trusted no one. He'd been violent and cruel, even to those who wished to serve him. Could he have sanctioned some terrible deed?

But Eirik bore no guilt for his brother's action.

I began to explain, but Eldberg lunged toward me.

"It changes nothing!" With each word, he shook me. "Your husband did naught to curb his brother's evil—and for that, he deserved death. His kin took what I held most dear, and I shall repay in kind. His end was quick, but your punishment shall unfold at my leisure."

I sobbed, for he was crushing me painfully.

"You are nothing now but my slave and shall serve in my bed—willing or not—until you call me your master, forsaking any allegiance you gave to your Svolvaen jarl."

"Never!" I raised my hand to strike him, but he caught my wrist and twisted back my arm. I cried out, struggling.

My instinct was to escape his hold—to flee, though there was nowhere for me go. I was naked and friendless, and never more alone. But could I submit as he asked? Every beat of my heart protested. I was to be humiliated and kept in fear, knowing that any dissent would bring worse punishment.

I gasped through my tears. "I beg your mercy. Know that I plead not just for myself but for the child I carry. It is innocent and should not be punished."

Releasing me, he stepped back and, this time, it was my body that received his appraisal by the firelight's glow: my breasts, then my belly, lingering between my legs, and down their length.

With a mocking smile, he cupped beneath my breast, measuring its weight and smoothness, grazing my nipple with the coarse print of his thumb. His other hand, he laid across my womb. His touch was gentle, but I shuddered. Tears of shame pricked my eyes as I stood helpless.

I'd withstood much—marriage to my pig-of-a-husband in Holtholm, submission, even at Eirik's hands in the earliest days; torment in the long months of his absence when Gunnolf had become my lover. Couldn't I bear this, too?

There was a dark glint in Eldberg's eyes as he moved his hand lower, brushing the curls of my cleft. His finger parted me, and I flinched. Slowly, he pushed one finger inside. I turned, not wishing him to see my face, but he growled, commanding me by that feral sound to meet his eyes. They were filled with shadows.

Impaling, merciless, they contained something far more consuming than lust.

An emptiness.

His voice was a cruel whisper, even as he curled his finger inside my flesh. "Perhaps in the spring, I'll take you to Kaupang or Hedeby and sell you in the slave market. Some rich old man would buy you and the child—or one of the higher-class brothels. I might find a trader from one of the eastern harems; they prize a pale complexion, and hair such as yours."

I could not hold back a strangled cry.

He wouldn't!

But of course, he would. What did he care?

Withdrawing his hands, he brought them to my cheeks, commanding me again to look into his eyes. "Or in payment for my murdered child, should I not kill this baby when it's born?"

God help me, and Freya, too.

Could I live with myself if I became his willing whore? Whether I allowed it or not, he would take what he wanted. Wasn't it better to accept what I couldn't fight? To stay alive? If I pleased him, might I gain favour? Perhaps even my freedom?

The fight left me. For now, I would say whatever was necessary. I would do what he asked. I would endure.

"I swear on the life of the child I carry, I shall serve you. I will be your thrall and submit to whatever you command." I made myself hold his steely gaze.

There was a last flash within his eyes before he smiled, and I felt a wave of sickness. I knew not to what I'd agreed.

7

ELDBERG

August 1ˢᵗ, 960AD

"Be quick about it." Eldberg threw her a cloth. She clutched the linen to her chest as she rubbed herself dry, attempting to cover her nakedness.

Rather late for that.

She was trying not to cry.

He watched as she stepped out of the washing barrel. It almost made him bark with laughter—her pleading mercy on account of carrying a child. The fact had only stirred his rage from a deeper place.

Three months had passed, and the pain was forever etched on his soul. He felt it constantly. The darkness. The despair.

He lived for only one purpose now.

Revenge.

He'd torched Svolvaen and cursed them all to Hel as they'd screamed. He'd seen the men responsible for Bretta's death pay for it with their lives. He'd stood victorious over his enemies. And still the venom flowed through his veins.

Elswyth was fastening the brooches at her shoulders, elegant fingers working the pin. That dress! So very like Bretta's had been on the day they'd wedded.

Something about her made him uneasy. Was this Loki's trick? Some would believe it was the work of the gods. Their humour could be crueler than any man's.

Sweyn must have seen the likeness. It was why he'd taken her, surely.

The same silken hair, falling thick over her shoulders, the same upward tilt of her eyes, the same indented curve to her upper lip. More than that, the way she moved her hands and tilted her head.

She was an echo of the wife lost to him. Coming upon her in the watch house, seeing her in that half-light, just for a moment, he'd thought it was Bretta found again, not dead at all.

The reality of it had brought a hammer blow—as if he'd not suffered enough of those. Not his wife, but that of his enemy, delivered into his hands.

Ah, yes. Odin had presented him with the opportunity for a different sort of revenge. The possibilities were almost overwhelming.

She knew it, too.

His enemy's most prized possession at his mercy, becoming his willing thrall. He could destroy her in a single night if he wished or in a single hour. But there were sweeter paths to the end he sought.

If Svolvaen's jarl looked down from Valhalla at this scene, what would he see? His beloved flogged and raped?

Nay.

There was a better way.

Piece by piece, he would reduce her, until she submitted to him as she never had to her husband. Fearing the worst treatment, she'd be grateful for what she received, and he would offer not just the torment of anticipated pain, but pleasure, too.

She was standing in the wedding dress donned for his enemy, waiting for him, Eldberg, to command her. Given time, he would make her yearn and plead. He would make her beg for him. He would make her betray what she thought she believed.

This would be his true vengeance.

※

The air was thick with the smell of roasting boar; a feast for the returning men—in reward for a mission well-accomplished. Eldberg let them see his prize, leading her by the rope Sweyn had tied around her neck, though he left her hands free.

She walked steadily behind him, her footing sure and her head high, though she cast down her eyes. A hush had fallen amidst the revelry, as they watched their jarl compel his acquisition to the far end of the longhouse. Sweyn watched closest of all.

The partition was but a curtain. She would be aware of that, knowing that those on the other side would be able to hear all that passed between them. Would she know also that his men would be imagining what he was doing to her?

A new woman was always of interest. A new thrall always a possibility, and a temptation. He would make it clear that she was his— that, for the time being, he forbade any to touch her. But she would not know it. Let her fear and feel his mercy at the same time.

Out of sight, the noise from the feasting continued—laughter and lewd comments beyond the divide that separated his chamber from the rest of the hall.

Eldberg meant to begin immediately. How she spent her first hours would set the tone for what was to come.

He might let her spend the night upon the floor, her ankles and wrists bound, the noose tight around her neck, attached to a hook on the wall. The thought of seeing her like that sent a jolt to his groin, but there were other ways to make her suffer—not like a dog beaten and chained.

When he requested that she remove her clothing, it was without argument. Eldberg took a bolt of jade silk from his trunk. It was among the finery he'd traded on his last trip to Hedeby. Silk he'd bought as a gift for Bretta, that she'd never had the chance to sew into a gown—kept in Sigrid's chamber.

He gestured to Elswyth that she might lay her clothing over the trunk. He'd remove it later, so that she'd know she had nothing with which to cover herself. That privilege would have to be earned.

She brought her arms about her breasts, as if to comfort herself, but did nothing to cover between her legs. He made a point of looking at that part of her as he tore the silk into strips. The fibres gave way easily, ripping along the weft—his destruction of something that had been beautiful.

He motioned with his head again for her to lay upon the bed, to stretch out her arms and legs, to expose herself to him, so that nothing was hidden.

His palm met hers briefly as he tied his first knot. Her hands, small and graceful, clenched into fists. She watched wide-eyed, disbelieving then resigned as he tied her with the silk—each wrist, each ankle—then cast her gaze to the rafters.

How pale she was. Her hair clung damp to her skin—tendrils over each breast. Her nipples, large discs of pink, made his mouth dry. If he took the rosebuds between his teeth, tongued and suckled, would she moan in the same way as Bretta had done? Would she push forward, needing him to take her softness deeper into his mouth, needing him to take possession of her?

No. He knew the answer to that.

As his captive, she could do nothing to prevent him from taking her body, but she could withhold her mind. For his revenge to be complete, he wanted that, too.

There were many ways in which he could subdue her but, for now, he'd give her something to think about.

"Look at me." He leaned close enough that she would feel his breath on her face—close enough that his leather jerkin brushed her breast. She would be aware of his weight—would know that he could crush her simply by shifting his body over hers.

Still, she looked at the timbers, but he guided her chin downward, until she permitted their eyes to meet. He spoke softly, letting each word unfurl. "One day, soon, you'll give me everything."

Showing her the last strip of silk, he wrapped it around his knuckle, drawing it tight, then placed the width over her eyes.

She pressed her lips together, saying nothing as he secured it. Only when he brought his hands to rest on her ribcage did she respond with a shuddering breath. Her pulse quickened. She trembled.

What was she imagining?

That he would fuck her?

In this position, lying open, she could be certain of it.

What if he told her something else?

That he would send his men; fingers greasy with meat, mouths eager upon her, raising up her hips to meet their thrusts—one by one, until he decided her punishment was enough.

Yes, she would believe it.

Her chest rose and fell, and she swallowed, worrying at her lips. She shifted, testing the bonds. They were not so firm that she couldn't move. One foot flexed. She stretched her fingers, then curled them closed.

He told her nothing, knowing she would tell herself far more.

※

Eldberg had offered up daily sacrifices to the gods, and they'd looked favourably upon him. The scarring would remain, but he'd kept all the fingers on his left hand. The rest was superficial. Even where his hair and beard had been scorched, there was regrowth.

Still, the pain tested him—strange prickles where the tissue was knitting together; a sign of his healing. Only the eye on that side truly troubled him. The eyelashes were gone, replaced by blistered skin. Some vision remained but, with the eye half-closed, it was difficult to judge distance. When he grew tired, even his own hands refused to come into focus.

If the others knew, none had spoken of it, and if Sweyn or any other had thought to usurp him, they'd waited too long to act upon that ambition. Those closest to Eldberg served through fear but also respect. Who among them would dare claim themselves his rival, fit to take his place?

They hadn't expected him to pick up his weapons. Not yet. Nor had they expected him to lead the attack on Svolvaen. He'd pushed himself to do both —to show them that he was tenacious, a man whose life-force burned stronger than the flames sent to consume him.

This evening, Eldberg was plagued with sparks of pain down his side. In answer, he drank more mead than sat well in his stomach and let the carousing continue longer than he'd intended.

Fiske and Hakon tried to draw him into conversation, avoiding any questions about the woman, though their curiosity was evident.

Sweyn said nothing, sitting apart, unable to hide his scowl.

Eldberg let it pass. The man was entitled to nurse his discontent—as long as he didn't show outright disrespect.

It was a trial to sit so long, knowing she lay in his chamber, but the waiting would do his work for him. Only when most of the men had passed out on the long benches did he return.

The wick had burnt low, but the light was sufficient for him to see her slender body, pale as moonlight, stretched out on the sheepskins, occupying the bed he would have thrown himself into had he been alone.

Jerking at the sound of his footstep, she twisted against the restraining silk, straining to identify who was in the chamber.

He stood beside her, letting her feel his presence. She would know the smell of his body and the rhythm with which he breathed.

She raised her head, and he thought for a moment she would say something, but she lay back again.

His cock grew hard. His body remembered the satisfaction of entering a woman.

In the hours that had passed, he'd had time to plan. From the trunk, he drew out the smaller of the marble columns and the harness that went with it. The leather straps were stiff, being new. Another gift for Bretta—one she'd never seen. He rubbed his thumb over the stone.

A strange thing, he'd thought it, but the merchant who'd sold him the device assured him that the noblewomen of the southern Mediterranean all used them. There were five pieces of marble, each slightly wider and longer than the last, chiseled, then polished smooth. Only the final rod bore any resemblance to his own organ, but the trader had explained the thinking behind the progression.

Something about it had aroused him—the idea of watching Bretta touch the thing against that part of her that was designed for his pleasure. Watching her push the cold stone inside her warmth—moving it in and out and thinking all the while of what she really wanted instead.

That she'd desired him, Eldberg had never doubted. He'd served Beornwold for over ten years before the old man had settled the contract. In that time, Eldberg had watched Bretta grow from a child to a woman, and he'd seen how she admired him. Shyly at first, for she'd been innocent. Later, with an intensity that spoke of the passion she would bring to her husband's bed.

He'd waited, taking no other in marriage, making himself indispensable to the old man. There was no one stronger, no one more formidable, no one better able to take command of Skálavík. Once Beornwold had realised that, the settlement had been straightforward.

And Bretta—so beautiful, so eager, and so in love—had been his.

Eldberg frowned. Always, it came back to this—what had been his, and what had been taken from him.

Moving to the bed, he brought his hand directly to her—his palm against soft curls, his fingers pressed to the opening of her sex.

She jolted, attempting to avoid his touch. Her belly, softly rounded, moved rapidly with her breaths. Against the fat pad of his thumb, her skin was cool. But not so for the flesh between her legs. There, it was hot.

How would it have felt for her—to lie here, exposed, all this time?

No doubt her shoulders were aching, though he'd tied her flat and given enough slack to allow her to flex her elbows.

What had she most feared?

A subtle shift located her swollen nub.

Just like this, he'd given Bretta pleasure—with his fingers and his tongue. There was a way to stimulate a woman, just as there was a man.

Dipping inside, he brought out her cream and rubbed lightly upon that part she would be incapable of controlling. She wrenched away, but then her hips pushed forward, meeting the caress again.

His captive.

He played the game patiently, letting her resist with murmured protest, withdrawing, then bucking toward him until the wetness covered not just his fingers but her thighs.

Something inside him tightened.

Splaying her with one hand, he touched the marble rod against her slickness.

"What is it?"

"It's what you agreed to, slave. Nothing more."

With a single push, he slid the column inside her.

"I don't want it." She thrashed her hips, then bore down, trying to expel the thing that filled her.

"An ungrateful way to behave when you've been given a gift."

As she raised herself again, attempting to shake away the rod, Eldberg slipped the leather harness under her back. His fingers were not as nimble as they had been, and the wick had all but burnt away, but he didn't need his vision to fasten the strap around her waist.

"What are you doing?"

In the near dark, he wedged the rod into its leather cup and brought the holding straps over her lower abdomen, knotting them onto the front of the belt. These, he pulled tight, so that the marble shaft was drawn fully into her body, held securely in place.

"I don't want it!" she hissed again and thrashed, then made another angry sound and went still. "When I move…"

Satisfied, he pulled one of the sheepskins from the bed and tossed it on the floor. She'd have all night to simmer.

In the morning, he'd ease her discomfort—at least for a little while.

"Take it out," she said quietly. "Please."

He smiled.

"Pleading already?"

8

ELSWYTH

August 1st, 960AD

I imagined all the ways I might kill him. A blade through the heart or sliced across his neck. Perhaps an axe through his skull, or a swift-acting poison. Even beating him to death with the thing he'd left inside me.

When I tilted my hips, it sent an ache of yearning through my sex. It was provoking and demeaning in a way I couldn't put into words.

And how long was I to be tied?

The restraints only chafed when I struggled, so I lay still and tried to divert my thoughts.

I'd agreed to obey him for the sake of the babe I carried, and for my sake, too, since I didn't wish to die, but my blood grew feverish.

I'd have my revenge—not just for myself but for Eirik and all Svolvaen.

He was an ugly brute, who'd murdered the man I loved, and, whatever he thought, I'd never belong to him.

In his madness, Gunnolf had sentenced Svolvaen to its cruel fate, and we had all paid the price. Eldberg had been wronged, but we weren't to blame, and there was no justice in the retribution he'd brought upon us.

The beast had bedded down on the floor, the smell of mead strong on his breath. While I lay awake, he snored.

At last, I must have dozed, for I woke to the dim light of dawn filtering through the smoke hole in the rafters, and the man I loathed standing above me, holding the sash that had covered my eyes.

"I need to pass water." I made no effort to hide my scowl. "And drink some," I added with less abruptness. I wasn't in a position to show my temper.

He'd been fearsome and brutal the day before, but he appeared subdued this morning, his face grey. He said nothing and moved as if he were in discomfort.

A bad head, I hoped, from too much drink. Perhaps his back was stiff from his night on the floor.

He unfastened the belt and straps about my waist first, drawing his hand down my belly, letting his fingers brush my damp curls before pulling out what had tormented me. I couldn't help but gasp as it left my body.

Thank the gods!

Relief, and something else.

I was slightly sore from being stretched, but also very wet. Having held the thing inside me for so long, it felt strange for it to be gone.

With the untying of my wrists, my impulse was to claw at his face, but I wasn't a fool. Whatever state he was in, he remained stronger than me. If I wanted to inflict pain upon him, it would have to wait until I'd better knowledge of this place and an ally to help me escape.

Even with all four limbs free, I couldn't right myself. My immobility had left me stiff, my hands and feet full of pinpricks. I rubbed at my wrists, shook them, rotated my shoulders, then my ankles. Everything hurt.

With a grunt, Eldberg raised me to a sitting position and fetched a bowl from the corner.

More humiliation!

A prisoner in this room, tied to the bed, impaled, and made to piss in a pot.

I gritted my teeth, bringing myself to the edge of the bed. Gingerly, I squatted over the bowl.

"Turn away, can't you!" I cast him a black look.

He grunted again and called out for Ragerta. She must have been waiting, for she appeared promptly.

"Food and ale for both of us." He passed his hand through his dishevelled hair. "Hot water and a cloth."

As I pushed myself back onto the bed, he picked up the pot and passed it to her.

"Get rid of this."

She glanced at me, showing no surprise at my naked state. Of course, she would not. Everyone would know my purpose in the jarl's chamber.

There were voices and movement in the main part of the hall already.

Damn the lot of you, I thought. They were the men who'd burnt Svolvaen. The men who'd carried me away to this place. I hoped the rich food they'd eaten the night before turned their bowels liquid. I hoped they felt as bad as Eldberg looked.

Curling my feet under me, and my arms about my body, I shrank to the corner. Thanks to the season, I felt no great chill, but I wished to cover myself and regain some dignity.

He sat heavily on the mattress edge, his head in his hands, and I thought again about caving in his skull. But I had no weapon—nothing of sufficient weight. The harness and the stone thing were upon the trunk, out of reach.

On Ragerta's return, he took the mug from her and drank it down, wiping his mouth, and nodding for her to refill it. Being thirsty, I did the same.

There was porridge—just like the grøt Sylvi used to make, sweetened with honey. I ate hungrily, scraping round with my spoon.

"You don't need to tie me again," I ventured. "You have my oath that I'll do your bidding."

Eldberg glanced over his shoulder, wiped his mouth again, then tossed his bowl away.

"I'll do what pleases you." Let him think it! I glowered behind his back but, kneeling forward, touched his hair, gently raising it above his left ear, revealing the scars that ran across his neck.

He moved quicker than I'd imagined him capable, grasping my wrist, twisting it away.

I cried out, but he only pushed back harder, rendering me flat upon the bed again, his bulk bearing down on me.

"I can't b-breathe!"

His other hand came to my throat. "Think not to seduce me with lies, thrall." His thigh came between mine. "I shall know when you truly desire to please me." Releasing his hold on my neck, he brought his hand lower, squeezing my nipple hard—making me gasp with the suddenness of it.

"When that time comes, you'll take me into your body and plead for my seed. You'll fuck in all the ways a woman can take a man and the viper in you will writhe for more. You'll ride me until your cunt aches, and still you'll beg."

Pinned beneath him, I seethed. I'd never beg.

He was growing aroused. Through his clothing, he was hard against my stomach. I was all too aware of my nakedness—leather and chain links against my breast and belly, woolen serge between my legs.

Before I had the chance to reply, he flipped me onto my front. With my cheek pressed to the covers, I faced the wall.

"Fuck you!" I couldn't help myself. The man was an animal. Again, he was tying my wrist—looping the silk and knotting it, pulling me forward to secure the sash to the far bedpost.

I could do nothing to prevent him from tying the other hand.

"Please." I couldn't let him do this again. "You don't need to—"

"Quiet, thrall." He dragged my legs apart.

Though none of the bonds were drawn tight and the sheepskins were soft to lie upon, I could not bear the thought of being made to remain still again.

"Don't do this."

And then I felt the dampened cloth, drawn gently up my inner thigh. Hot and then cool, along both sides. Eldberg dipped it into the water again, then wrung out the excess. He held the cloth to my sex then eased apart my cheeks, drawing it along the crease, pressing to my anus.

A trembling fear was taking hold of me—that he would enter me there. I'd felt the size of him when he'd been pressed to my stomach.

He put aside the cloth and rested his palm upon my behind.

"You won't hurt me." My voice sounded so small.

The bed creaked, and I heard the chest lid open. I caught a glimpse of what he withdrew. Another of the stone columns, though larger and carved differently—its head more bulbous, the shaft slightly curved, and studded with protruding nobbles.

"No!" I protested, fighting my tears.

"You agreed to all." He sat again and parted me.

I could offer no resistance and awaited a cruel thrust to the hilt, but he eased it inside me. With each nobble sliding into me, I could not help but gasp.

"Bastard!" I hissed, but he said nothing, only holding the thing still. My own will counted for nothing.

After some moments, he withdrew it—just as slowly, until it left me altogether. It was to be a slower torture, and one that amused him regardless of his ill night's sleep. He rubbed the rounded head where I was swollen—nudging, teasing, before penetrating me again haltingly with its full length.

I kept my eyes on the wall and bit my lip.

It would soon be over. Soon.

Next, he twisted it, so that it touched in new ways, and moved his other hand low beneath my belly, palm hot. I drew breath sharply as he extended his thumb to press against my most sensitive place.

I was unable to move or resist as he simulated the act between a man and woman, using the shaft of stone to slide into me, back and forth, and the pad of his thumb to taunt me.

I pushed into the bed, but he raised me on his palm so that his impalement became deeper. I buried my face in the sheepskins, refusing to let him hear me moan. Despite all I felt—my hatred and humiliation, anger and disgust—I knew what he was coaxing from me. A burning warmth was overtaking all thought. Pain and piercing pleasure were building. When it broke, the wave sent me tumbling, rending a cry that tore from my throat and had me straining against the bonds that held me.

Eldberg's voice was almost weary. "Mine already, thrall."

He left me tied all day, but without the harness—without the invasion of his toy. Twice, Ragerta came to hold a cup to my lips, helping me to drink. For my other needs, she slid the pot beneath me.

My chest was tight with refusal to weep.

I'd crossed a threshold, betrayed by my body. Though the secrets of my heart were my own, Eldberg had won some small part of me, and so easily.

I listened to the working sounds of the hall—hushed chatter, and a woman's voice giving orders. From outside, there was the sound of cows and the bleating of ewes. There was hammering, the thud of butter churning, flapping wings, and sudden squawking.

Ragerta brought me the *nattmal* of vegetable broth, spooning it into my mouth with swift efficiency. I asked her if Eldberg had done this before and what had happened, but she merely shook her head without answering, as if worried who might hear her.

Afterward, I lay quietly, knowing he would come soon.

By the time he did, the room was full dark, and he lit the wick in a dish of oil, as he had that first night.

He did not come near me at first, and I remained turned away as he undressed. I did not wish to look on him as he removed his clothing, though I had no doubt his eyes were upon me. I heard the clink of his weapons and the soft fall of his tunic and leggings to the floor. Much time passed before he said, "Do you wish me to touch you?"

I kept my face turned. "I've agreed to serve you, but I'm your unwilling whore. Whatever happens is your wish, not mine."

It was an insolent answer and ill-advised, but he spoke no threat of punishment. Instead, he untied the sash about one of my ankles and rubbed the skin, his calloused hands firm in their kneading, restoring the flow of blood.

Climbing upon the bed, he removed the restraint from my other leg and caressed me in the same manner.

A lump formed in my throat, but I gave no thanks. Whatever kindness he showed me was for his own ends.

Being partially free, I should have felt better able to defend myself, but there was no truth in that. He'd merely gained power to position me in other ways. My hands were still bound, after all.

I resolved to do nothing to help him.

Fuck me, and it shall be as if I were a corpse.

His leg brushed mine as he ran his hands along my calves and thighs, keeping my legs parted around him, until he clasped my hips.

Leaning forward, he brought his lips to my buttock—his breath as warm as his tongue.

"You feel nothing?" He grazed me with his teeth, moving from one cheek to the other, devouring my flesh with open mouth, sucking and biting—though without force enough to hurt me—all the while holding my hips fast.

I squirmed, but kept silent.

Moving one hand to the small of my back, he used his other to probe my wetness. "You desire this." He pressed with his thumb, circling, teasing. "You want me inside you."

My head buzzed with fury even as I writhed under his caress, still giving no answer.

He laughed low. "What have you been thinking of, waiting for me?"

"That you want to torture me," I hissed, "—to punish me for something of which I'm innocent."

"Punish you." He withdrew his hand. "Is that what you desire?"

"Nay! That is not what I said!"

He rose from the bed, and I heard the chest's lid open.

I dared not look, but heard the switch pass through the air. The pain was immediate—a burning sting across the crease of my lower buttocks.

"This is what you want, thrall?"

"Nay!" I cried, fearful that he would strike me again.

I attempted to push my legs together, but his hand intruded upon me. Three fingers slid easily inside.

Against my will, liquid rose from deep within the flesh that he sought to make his own.

"You deny this pleasure, but soon, you'll think only of the man who masters you now."

Kicking my feet, I tried to wriggle away. "If I take pleasure, it will be my doing—not yours."

Withdrawing again, he struck me twice with the switch, across the fleshiest curve of my behind.

The moan from my lips came unbidden. I abhorred him, yet there was a tug inside me. My body opened to him, despite the rebellion of my mind.

I was alone and frightened, aching, angry, and aroused. To say what he wanted to hear would make all easier, but I could not yet surrender this piece of myself.

"I do not wish it," I sobbed, burying my face in the covers.

I waited for him to punish me again but felt instead his hand smoothing my hair.

Without speaking, he untied the final sashes. As I curled up, he brought his arm across my body, pulling me into the warmth of his chest.

I was aware of his nakedness, of his arousal pressed to the crevice of my cheeks, but he made no move to force his penetration, nor did he ask again what I wished from him. I lay tense, aware of him behind me, his breathing becoming that of a man who slept.

Wearily, I closed my eyes.

I no longer knew myself, nor understood the man who held me captive.

9

ELSWYTH

August 3rd, 960AD

Ragerta woke me, helping me sit up, placing a bowl of *grøt* in my hands.

"Where is he?" I hadn't felt him rise from the bed. If he were close by, would he tie me again, now I was awake?

"At the harbour. There's a new trading boat in," she whispered. "But he won't be long." She indicated the pail standing by. "I've water for you to wash. He told me to help you quickly."

"Ragerta." I placed my hand upon her arm, wanting to say something, wanting to explain away my shame, make her understand that I was here against my will. It was unnecessary, of course. What did she care? I was her master's bed-thrall, and there was nothing to excuse or judge.

"Thank you," I said simply.

The water was hot and welcome—not as refreshing as the barrel in the bathhouse, but I could hardly expect that privilege, unless it was Eldberg's wish that I be taken there.

"He said I was to watch you." Ragerta gave an apologetic smile.

There was naught for me to do but await his return. He'd take whatever pleasure amused him, I supposed, then leave once more. I could try again to persuade him that he didn't need to restrain me—that I'd be compliant.

This was my best hope, wasn't it? Only if I were free could I hope to escape. Not yet, perhaps, but as soon as I had a plan.

But what did compliance mean? Resigned acceptance? No.

Submitting was not enough.

He wished more than that—to bend me to his will, to have me writhe and beg for him, and disavow the love I'd borne Eirik.

This I still could not bring myself to do, but there might be another path.

I would not be passive like a slave.

I would invite his passion, but on my own terms.

⚜

Ragerta was right; he was not long in returning. Entering the chamber, he immediately dominated all around him. Ragerta scurried away, leaving us alone.

I'd thought carefully of how I would present myself and what I would say. Already, I'd wasted almost two days and nights. The sooner I made him believe I was pliant, the sooner I might escape.

I lowered myself on the sheepskins, raising my arms and parting my legs in simulation of the position in which he had tied me.

His gaze was wholly upon my body as I did so, and I felt a new energy fill the room, as if there was nothing else but my nakedness and his desire to possess what he saw.

"You await me, thrall." It was a statement rather than a question, but I nodded, parting my legs a little farther and turning one knee outward, that he might see what I offered him.

Neither of us spoke as he unstrapped the leather at his waist, from which his short-bladed dagger and axe hung. He pulled his tunic roughly over his head and jerked open the drawstring of his trousers, kicking them away.

With the mid-morning sunlight filtering through the central opening in the longhouse roof, I was able to view him as I had not before.

The burns which marred his face travelled the length of his body, but only upon his left side—from his neck, across one shoulder, and down the muscles of his arm.

Ugly, raised welts broke the contours of his body ink, scars dappling the hard plane of his chest and the ridges of his stomach, reaching the deep crease of his abdomen and continuing down his thigh, even to his foot.

His arousal was already prominent, springing from the russet hair at his groin. The sight made the breath catch in my throat.

Stepping closer, he took my hand and guided me to encircle him.

Rubbing my palm to his thickness, he said, "Now, you see what I will thrust inside you."

My punishment, and your revenge. My mouth was suddenly dry. *Will you be happy when this is done?*

With his hand over mine, he stroked upward from the root, squeezing hard so that my fingers were nearly crushed beneath his own. It took nothing more for him to become rigid as iron, a bead of moisture glistening at the tip.

He gave one final stroke and released me. "Another day I shall teach you how to take me into your mouth. For now, I wish to discover fully what I own."

Leaning close, his voice was huskily soft. "Hold nothing back." He nodded to the curtain that divided us from the greater chamber. "Let them all hear that I am your master—that you are no longer a woman of Svolvaen, but mine."

Touching my hip, he rolled me to my front. My cheeks were still tender from the three strikes visited upon me.

He knelt to retrieve his leather belt, and I froze in horror. Was this what it meant—to be owned by the Beast? He meant to flog me with the thick leather which carried his weapons?

Perhaps he heard my gasp, for he looked up.

Holding the strap in his hand, he watched me with curiosity. "This excites you?" He regarded my buttocks and then the belt. "You appreciate pleasure only when tempered with pain?" He appeared to think upon it, rubbing the leather between his fingers.

"I shall first give you pleasure and then we shall see."

He extracted a small pouch and then a vial from within.

A potion? I wondered. There were such things, I'd heard, that heightened sensation and passion. Only once had I experienced such a thing—breathing the sacred smoke of Svolvaen's Ostara celebrations. I'd not been myself that night—my inhibitions lowered, until I'd welcomed a coupling that should never have been.

Eldberg came again to the bed, sitting above me.

When he opened the bottle, it brought a strong scent—ginger and sage? I wasn't sure. Those could be drunk when prepared as a tincture.

"Neroli," he murmured, "and sandalwood. I paid a fine price this morning. You see, thrall, what I do to coax what I desire from you."

It made no sense. He had only to thrust himself between my legs and the act would be done.

His hands, though calloused, were rendered slick and slippery—caressing my shoulders, pulling my arms to my sides. His thumbs travelled downward, until he found the dimples of my lower back. There, he gripped my waist, and his arousal brushed against me.

Kneading, he rubbed the curve of my hips and the fullness of my cheeks, his fingers working the fleshiest part, moving to the crease where they met my thighs. Again, he returned to my buttocks, the fragrant oil aiding his movements. Back and forth he worked, his fingers dipping lower, slipping into the cleft of my behind, skimming my curls, encouraging me to accept his fondling.

All the while, I closed my eyes and tried to imagine that it was Eirik who touched me, but I could not deceive myself. These hands were not Eirik's.

Eldberg lowered onto my back, his cock nestling where his hands had caressed, between my cheeks. His thigh pushed insistently between my legs, obliging me to open wider.

He was breathing hard, rubbing, then nudging where he wished to enter.

No! I cannot! I'd taken a man inside me there before, but Eldberg was bigger than any lover of my past, and I feared what he was capable of—that he might use me too roughly. Suddenly, I feared taking him at all. What was I doing! In the throes of desire, he would tear me asunder.

He shifted, drawing my legs between his own so that he fully straddled my hips. In that moment, I turned swiftly and the slickness of the oil permitted me to slip onto my back.

In this position, at least, I would have a better chance of diverting him.

"My lord." I was aware of my voice quivering. "I beg you—" I tipped back my head, making myself look at him, saying the words I knew he wished to hear. "You shall own me everywhere."

Reaching for his fingers, I brought them to my breast. "But first, caress me here." I wetted my lips. "Spend your seed here, if you wish it—or over my belly. Let me rub you into my skin, that I may smell of you."

His expression was inscrutable, his eyes half closed. His erection rested on my stomach—a hard rod pressing where there was no entry to be had.

Drawing back, he sat on his haunches, his arousal above me.

Grasping my legs, he brought them on either side of his. Reaching beneath, he raised my hips, so that my sex rested upon his testicles.

Only then did he pour more of the oil into his palms.

His fingers, light and firm, swept over my belly, circling, moving ever higher, until he gathered my breasts in his hands—covering then revealing, holding their weight, then releasing. Rubbing my nipples until they ached.

Even through my fear, I did not wish him to stop. Beneath the rhythm of his caress, a strange languor overtook me, and a warmth low in my womb.

And, all the while, I was aware of his manhood—the head dark and swollen, the shaft, thick-veined.

At last, he brought his mouth where his hands had caressed, gently biting, grazing with his teeth, then suckling hard, so that I arched into his hunger. His mouth was fiery hot on my skin, his beard softly grazing, making me moan, even as I was repulsed.

When our eyes met again, his glinted darkly, and he touched his tongue to my lips.

I cannot! That intimacy is for lovers—not for what exists between us. I'm no more than a body for your pleasure, and for the perverse revenge you think to take.

I twisted away, but he threaded his fingers through my hair. I was helpless again, my throat exposed.

His mouth was insistent, kissing my neck and my jaw, then returning to my lips.

He had shifted, bringing his arousal to my core.

I'd known this moment would come, yet I struggled—only to have him capture my wrists and drag them above my head, palm on palm.

In the next moment, he entered me, gaining possession in a single stroke. I cried out, though more in shock than pain. My own traitorous arousal had helped him.

He held himself inside me, the soft hair of his chest pressing to my breasts, his breath soft on my cheek. I'd thought to have taken him all, but he pressed forward again, and I realised he was not yet at the hilt.

I bit my lip to keep from moaning. He was so deep.

Easing back, he paused before his second thrust. It came more easily, as did the next, and the next.

He lowered his mouth to my nipple, pulling the point into his wet warmth. Once there, he did not release it, consuming and demanding, drawing harder, sending a searing flame to my womb.

As he bucked and shuddered, his features contorted.

With the last throbs of his pleasure, he grew still, and the look upon his face was wretched. I saw there an echo of all I felt—despair and pain, and a chasm of terrible loneliness.

Eirik was dead, and I was slave to this man's bed—as I had been to Gunnolf's. I knew this path and the soulless, aching emptiness that would come.

10

ELSWYTH

August 4th, 960AD

The next morning, it was not Ragerta who brought me food. The woman who swept aside the curtain was no thrall.

"Stand up. Let me see you." I recognised her voice—one I'd heard many times since I'd been brought to Eldberg's chamber. In some manner, she was mistress here, though not his wife, I knew.

The room smelled of coupling—thick with sweat and the scent of sex. Scowling, she pursed her lips, and the lines it brought to her mouth made apparent her age. Her hair, worn in a thick braid, was a similar hue to my own, only slightly lighter at her temples. She bore the expression of one who'd seen too much of life's bitterness. It was etched in her face. Perhaps mine was the same, or would soon come to be so.

I rose from the bed, drawing my hair over my breasts and clasping my hands to cover my sex. That part of me was sore, for Eldberg had taken me twice more through the night.

She made no bones of surveying my nakedness, then my face, staring long and hard at each feature, as if there was some puzzle she wished to decipher. She met my eyes, and something flashed in her own.

"I've no wish to be here," I said quietly. "And I do not remain willingly."

The woman waved her hand in dismissal. "Were it up to me, you'd be thrown from the cliff and that would be the end of you."

Her mouth tightened again, and she frowned. "As it's not my decision, you'll make yourself useful. Not just in here—" she glanced briefly at the bed. "But in other ways."

My heart gave a sudden leap. I was to escape this confinement? To do so would be the first step toward my finding a way to leave this place.

"You can weave, I suppose? You know how to prepare meat, how to make bread and porridge?"

"Yes—all those things." I nodded.

"Then get dressed, and we'll find you work." From a sack at her side, she tossed a bundle of fabric. "It's too fine for a thrall, but he insists you wear it."

It was my own soft undershift and gown—sewn for my wedding day. Holding them to my chest, I felt a stark pang.

To have me wear the gown as I served in his household was a cruel joke. Yet, I was glad—for it was my own, and wearing it would keep to mind all that I'd lost. It would give me strength to make my escape and have my revenge upon the man who'd inflicted so much suffering.

The woman had not returned my cape. That, with its soft collar of fur, I imagined she'd kept for herself.

"You're not to go outside, and if you give us any trouble, he'll tie you again. Perhaps you'd prefer it, being used for whoring and none of the real work." She sniffed with obvious distaste.

"Nay, I only wish—"

"Don't speak unless I ask you a question!"

The glare she gave assured me I should avoid baiting her temper.

"And keep a civil tongue! Know your place, and call me mistress."

With that, she swept out.

I shook out the gown. There was still mud on the hem, but dry, it would be easy to brush out. Checking its deep pocket, my fingers closed over what I'd placed there when I'd undressed in the bathhouse: the amulet Eirik had gifted to me—the hammer, Mjolnir, Thor's magical weapon.

All those months before, Eirik had left with Helka on their mission to Bjorgyn and had placed it about my neck, promising to return. More time had passed than either of us had anticipated, but I'd worn the pendant, always, and he'd kept his word.

Did I dare wear it again?

It no longer had the power to bring him back to me. Nothing could do that. And Eldberg would likely take it from me if he saw it.

Better to leave it where it was.

They were all together now—Eirik, Gunnolf, and Asta.

Helka, too, and Astrid? Were they watching from that other realm? That I could not think about. While I lived, my concerns were in this world.

Entering the main hall of the longhouse, I was astonished again by its size—twice that of ours in Svolvaen.

The main door was open wide, and sunlight entered also through the hole in the roof, directly above the fire pit.

In the kitchen area, Thirka was pulling the skin from a hare.

At the far end, fleeces were stacked high, reading for dyeing. Ragerta was spinning carded wool into yarn, while the woman who'd come to me stood at her loom.

Fixing me with a glare, she jerked her head toward a wooden trough near the fire—a huge hearth bounded by stones reaching to my knees. Three iron pots simmered over its flames, one filled with water and the other two with stew—all suspended by chains, hooked high into the ceiling beams. A grid of iron bars covered one end, for the roasting of meat.

"When you've finished mooning about, there's bread to knead."

I knelt by the trough and began folding the edges of the dough. I'd never seen so much—enough to make fifty loaves or more. Soon, my arms and back were aching from bending over so long. I sat on my heels for a moment, straightening up and rolling my shoulders.

"Lazy bitch! I didn't say you could stop!" the mistress called out loud enough for all to hear. "Keep at it, or I'll take the birch to you."

I'd met women like her before—the sort who liked to bully those unable to defend themselves.

"Go and help her, Ragerta, or we'll be waiting 'till midnight." She scowled.

Scurrying to join me, Ragerta knelt alongside. "Here, I'll take one end of the dough, and you the other. Lift as high as you can, fold inward, then push hard into the middle. It won't take much for Sigrid to punish you, so don't give her a reason."

It was much easier together, and we worked on in silence, aware of hard eyes watching us, until I couldn't help myself.

"Who is she?" I whispered.

"Sigrid?" Ragerta rotated the dough, and we lifted it again. Keeping her head lowered, she spoke into the trough, "—the old jarl's sister."

"Beornwold's sister?" I glanced over. Part of the warp appeared to be wearing thin on the loom and she was intent on twisting new fibres into the upright thread. "And she's mistress here?"

"Always has been. She's a shrew—never happy—but worse since Bretta died."

Bretta. Eldberg's wife. Not for the first time, I wondered about her.

"What was she like, this Bretta?"

Ragerta paused in her kneading but didn't answer.

She passed over one of the long-handled paddles next to the trough. "Fist-sized pieces," she directed. "Pull them off, and roll them in your palm. Sigrid likes them slightly flattened."

Demonstrating, she eased one onto the paddle. "When we've ten loaves on, we'll slide it over the embers."

Again we worked.

From outside came the sound of cattle lowing—passing in front of the longhouse, being led down to pasture.

"Did he love her?"

Ragerta's eyebrows rose. "We all loved Bretta."

Like Asta, I thought. We'd all loved Jarl Gunnolf's wife.

"But what sort of marriage was it?"

Ragerta stared at me, and I felt my cheeks redden. I didn't know why I was asking.

"Arranged of course. Beornwold had no sons and needed an heir. Eldberg joined him as a paid hand at first, on the jarl's trips to raid the Western lands. When Beornwold saw his strength, he adopted him, then married him to Bretta. Their offspring would be sure to continue the line."

"Except that she died."

Ragerta frowned. "It was a terrible thing. Horrible." She seemed to think for a moment, then shook away the image. "Sigrid was mother to her from the start. A bad birthing, you know—"

I did know. I'd seen my share of babes and mothers die. Unconsciously, my hand went to my belly. What if that happened to me? Who would look after this child?

I asked hurriedly, not wanting to lose my chance, "Is there someone you have feelings for, Ragerta? Someone you love?"

"By Freya! What a thing to ask!" Ragerta looked flustered. "There are one or two I let take me outside, and a few I've had to lay with regardless of my choice. I'm not fool enough to think any of it matters. I'm naught to them, nor they to me."

I didn't know what to say. It was a sad thing for any woman to admit—even such as Ragerta, who would spend her days a slave.

"Now, ask Thirka, and you might hear a different answer." Ragerta gave a sly smile. "Thoryn's been sweet on her this half-year past, and he's a better sort than most."

We'd almost reached the end of the dough, and the last of the cows had passed the doorway.

"But naught will come of that," I mused. "Not unless Eldberg frees her."

"True. No thrall can marry a free man, so here she'll stay…" The loaves being all upon the embers, Ragerta made to rise. "For Eldberg has never freed any in his possession. Those who disappoint or anger him, he sells at the slave market—or gives a quicker end."

With that thought in my mind, the room suddenly grew gloomier, the sun falling dim. Looking up, I saw the jarl standing upon the threshold, his breadth and height silhouetted dark against the light.

I was aware of the room falling silent—of Thirka having stopped her work, and Sigrid, too; Ragerta standing openmouthed.

"Come." With a jerk of his head, he indicated that I was to enter his chamber.

He stripped away his own clothing, then mine. Throwing me upon the bed, he bound me as he had that first time, but far tighter, and he lay upon my back. I was pinned beneath, with his cock nestled between my cheeks, his own legs extended to touch the length of mine.

He reached beneath to take my breasts in his hands, kneading them as I had the bread, squeezing their softness in his palms. He kissed my spine but was too impatient to spend further time in preparing me.

"Tell me." His arousal nudged where he'd attempted to claim me the night before.

"I'm ready for you, my lord."

It was neither truth nor lie. My fear was potent, but as he'd tied the sashes about my ankles and wrists, a warm ache had begun in my belly, the snake unfurling once more, hissing its own desire.

"And what am I to do with you?"

"Enter me, my jarl." I closed my eyes. Against my wish, I was his possession, and would submit to whatever I must.

He brought one hand down my belly, then lower, to the swollen part of me. As I moaned for him, his voice, always so rasping, was husky with desire. "You please me, thrall."

Thrusting within me, his fingers pressed to my tenderness, lifting me to meet his rhythm.

"Tell me," he said again.

"Please." With my body jarred by the force of his, it was difficult to speak. "Please." This was what he wanted—for me to beg.

"More?"

"Yes." My voice was strangled, but I could not deny it. I was swollen and wet. "Your seed. Spill inside me, my lord."

Slippery, he drew back and with his next stroke, pushed into my tighter place.

Dear gods! My instinct was to clench against the intrusion, but his fingers delved and caressed, and the snake inside me writhed in rippling waves, its tongue licking hot. As he entered, he lashed with the poison of pain and pleasure combined.

"My lord," I whispered. "My lord."

11

ELDBERG

August 4th, 960AD

Eldberg tore off the last strip of meat, greasy between his fingers, then brought his mouth to suck the juices from the bone.

He was ravenous. Hungry enough to eat another whole trencher of food. Hungry for something else, too, though he'd been consuming that particular delicacy for the better part of the afternoon.

He watched as she made her way to each guest, all seated at two long tables placed along the length of the hall, on either side of the central fire. To celebrate their success in burning Svolvaen, all were welcome. His men were never reluctant to share the abundance of their jarl's table. Several nights of revelry were planned.

As Elswyth refilled cups with mead, the eyes of every man were upon her. She kept her own lowered, no doubt keen to go unnoticed. As if that were possible!

Her gown's slender bodice and low-cut yoke placed her well on display, letting all see her ripeness. Breasts to make even the goddess Freya envious! Silken to the touch, full, and heavy. Nipples of the palest pink, large, and soft like those of a young girl—until they hardened beneath his tongue, yearning to be suckled.

He'd sated his cock well-enough, but he was hard again, thinking of her tightness and warmth, thinking of how it felt to move inside her. It had been satisfying to watch her struggle, to try to deny him, but he preferred seeing her pliant—submitting to acts she found shameful, yet unable to control her response.

She glanced at him, and he saw her tremble.

Good! He took a long draught, draining his cup then raising it. Let her come to him.

Eldberg watched the sway of her hips as she walked—hips made for a man to hold onto. She was a fine piece of womanhood, though she behaved more like a virgin—as if she'd never been touched before, as if his fucking of her was a great surprise, and the ways he took her previously unknown. It hardly seemed likely to be true, but it aroused him—this blend of reluctance and passion.

Only when she stood beside him did she look up, her lips parting as she gazed into his face. Those lips! A little plump. A little bruised.

She hadn't wanted to kiss him, but he'd refused to let her get away with that. A thrall obeyed her master. She'd no right to hold anything back.

As she held out the jug to replenish his cup, he brought his hand around her waist and her scent lifted to him—honey and musk. She squirmed, almost pulling away, but he tugged her closer.

The curve of her breast was before his face. How easy it would be to release that bounty and taste it again. By the gods, he was iron hard! He'd a mind to raise her skirts and haul her onto his lap right here.

"Eldberg!" Sigrid's voice, shrill beside him, intruded. "Did you hear what I said?"

Distracted, he relaxed his hold on Elswyth's waist, and she neatly slipped away.

"What is it, Sigrid? Must you nag me even while I eat?" Eldberg scowled.

No other dared speak to him as Sigrid did. Not for the first time, he berated himself for permitting it. Her shrewish ways made him want to wring her neck, but he owed her a debt. He was a man who never forgot an injury and never forgave an insult, but nor did he ignore the service of those who were loyal.

All those years Beornwold had been without a wife, she'd been lady of this hall, running the household. Moreover, she'd raised his daughter, loving Bretta as any true mother. Only she, of anyone in Skálavík, knew the grief Eldberg had suffered. Without speaking of it, she understood.

He'd not forgotten, either, that she'd tended him through his recovery. The healer had provided salves, but Sigrid had administered them and, through those first weeks, when sleep was impossible without the coming of nightmares, she'd sat beside him.

She deserved a degree of respect and status, and he would not put her from the house, though she oft drove him to the edge of his temper.

Sigrid lowered her voice, but her words were no less scathing. "Are you turning fool, nephew? Letting that trollop tame you? You've done little but moon after her since your return."

"If anything is to be tamed, I wish it were your tongue," retorted Eldberg. "Beware, mistress, lest you stretch your neck too far toward my blade."

"Ha!" Sigrid took a swig from her cup. "That is more like the jarl we serve! A man ready to act when one beneath him oversteps the mark." She placed her hand upon his arm. "Beware yourself, nephew, or you'll have Skálavík laughing at your folly—a jarl who forsakes his duties in pursuit of a hussy!"

Eldberg removed Sigrid's hand and fixed her with a steely gaze. "If I require your advice, you shall know of it. Until then, better we sit in silence."

Sigrid tossed her head, ignoring the warning, though she lowered her voice. "You'll see the truth when it stares you in the face. Until then, make your mistakes."

Gritting his teeth, Eldberg motioned over one of the other thralls, stabbing a piece of mutton from the platter.

"And what is it, good aunt, that's clear to everyone else except me!"

Sigrid leaned in closer. "She's a wanton. Good for nothing but opening her legs.""Is that all the complaint you have of her?" Eldberg barked with laughter. "A man must spill his seed—what care you whose throat or cunt I use for that purpose? She's my bed thrall—nothing more."

Sigrid shifted in her seat. "You agreed she'd help as the others do."

"That she may, when I've no immediate use for her beneath me. If she's lacking, then teach her, but don't grumble to me, Sigrid."

Picking an apple from the bowl, she quartered it with her knife. "As long as she pleases you, 'tis good enough reason for her to stay. I shall say no more about it."

"Odin be praised!" Eldberg went to drain his cup but found it dry. Where was Elswyth? He'd a mind to take a jug of mead, and her, to his chamber.

"Only this…"

Eldberg glared, then sighed. "Very well, Sigrid, speak and be done—but then no more."

"Watch her well, my jarl, for I fear she's one to use her wiles to trap a man. There's something of the witch in her. You must have noticed she looks like—" Her hand came again to his arm. "Perhaps 'tis I who am foolish, but it would be the way of a sorceress to make her appearance familiar to you and worm her way beneath your skin." Sigrid's voice quavered. "I wish not to quarrel—only to show my concern."

"Your words are riddles to me, Sigrid." Eldberg rubbed his forehead. "But we'll have no more dispute. Let this be an end to it." Eldberg looked over at her—his little enchantress—standing at the far end of the hall, beside Sigrid's chamber.

She held her hand to her brow, looking weary. There was a resigned despondency to her.

Perhaps he'd worked her too hard in his bed.

I can do with her just as I like. She's my captive. My thrall. My revenge.

But she was something else, too. There was an element of truth in

Sigrid's warning, for wasn't this a spell of sorts—when a man couldn't take his eyes from a woman?

She was bending to fill Sweyn's cup, her long hair loose-plaited and golden, falling over her shoulder.

Eldberg's attention flickered to the commander of his battle-guard. He'd grasped the end of Elswyth's plait and was drawing her downward, whispering in her ear. Some lewd comment, most likely, for she reddened and pulled away.

The thralls of Eldberg's household were there for the taking, if his sworn-men had lust to abate. He'd never denied them that privilege, though most had their own slaves, and a wife besides.

But Elswyth was not like the others.

She is mine.

Others could look upon her, but she was for his bed alone.

He'd have words with Sweyn. No one was to touch her. He would show his blade to any cur that disobeyed him. Eldberg strode forward. He'd make himself clear and wipe away that covetous leer.

He'd taken but five steps when he heard Thoryn's shout from the other side of the hall. "Thirka!"

There was a scream and commotion as the thrall's platter hit the table, showering food. Her skirts were alight. She screamed again, running back and forth, beating the flames with her hands.

Eldberg leapt forward, sending her to the ground, rolling her back and forth. Yet the fire licked, and the woman shrieked.

"Use this! Cover her!" Elswyth tossed a bundle of cloth at his feet.

With the flames smothered, Thirka's terrified cries subsided to sobs. Moaning, she looked up with wide eyes. Thoryn had bounded over the table. Kneeling at her side, he took Thirka's hand, his face grey. "She stepped backward, coming too close to the embers."

"So tired." Thirka was mumbling. "Just need to lie down."

"'Tis all right," Thoryn whispered. "I'll care for you." He picked her up.

"By your leave, jarl, I'll take her to my hut."

How did I miss that? thought Eldberg. Thoryn was in love with the girl. Under his own nose, and he'd not realised.

"I can make a salve for the burns." Elswyth was beside them, lifting the hem of Thirka's skirt. She winced at what she saw.

"We have honey," said Ragerta. She wrung her hands. "And there's marigold in the herb garden."

"Gather them quickly, and comfrey if you have it." She thought for a moment. "If you have valerian root, we'll steep that for her to drink, and mash the others for a salve."

She turned to Thoryn. "You must spread it thickly on her feet and calves —on her hands, too. Lay Thirka down, and bare her legs. You'll need some linens to wrap her, after you've applied the salve."

Eldberg beheld Elswyth in wonder. Gone were the downcast eyes and her forlorn look. A spark had lit within her, giving her new purpose.

Thoryn swallowed. "Good lady, my thanks, but—"

He looked at Eldberg. "I would have her help. I don't know if I can—" Thoryn's voice wavered.

He touched his forehead to Thirka's. "She is burnt."

Burnt.

Eldberg knew what it was to be touched by fire. The healers had made his salves, with herbs not just from Skálavík but those traded from far lands. Aloe, wasn't it, that they'd smeared over him. Cooling, soothing aloe. A small pot remained, which he yet used upon his eye.

"Sigrid!"

She hadn't moved from her place at the high table.

"The salve for my eye. Fetch it."

Cutting a segment from her apple, she took it between her teeth. "It's costly, and there will be no more until the merchant returns. Are you sure, my jarl, that you wish to use it on this thrall?"

Eldberg clenched his fists. "Fetch it, Sigrid."

He looked from his friend to Elswyth. "Go, Thoryn, and take her with you. Ragerta will bring what you need. There's enough moon for her to see by. She'll find the plants and carry all to your hut."

Elswyth hesitated, as if disbelieving, then hurried after Thoryn.

Only after they'd left did Sigrid come storming over to him, her face twisted in rage.

"That bitch! She dared enter my chamber and took it! My new cape!"

It was a rare thing for Eldberg to laugh, but he felt it rise in him now. The cloth in which they'd wrapped Thirka had been the same red as Elswyth's dress.

12

ELSWYTH

August 4th, 960AD

Thirka had been fortunate, Eldberg's quick-thinking had saved her from greater injury. She'd heal, if her wounds were kept clean. There would be scarring, but she'd walk again. The burns on her hands were superficial, her palms already accustomed to working close to the fire's heat.

Ragerta and I had worked quickly to prepare the unguent of honey, comfrey, and marigold, spreading it thickly, then wrapping it with strips of linen. We used the aloe where the burns seemed most severe—the back of Thirka's knees and her lower thigh. To ease her discomfort, we mashed valerian root, steeping in hot water. This, she was to sip every waking hour. I'd find willow bark when there was more time, for that was the best remedy in subduing pain, and it was easy to chew. Perhaps the forest held witch hazel, too. Once Thirka began to heal, it would aid the process.

"You have my thanks." Thoryn clasped us both by the hand as we reached the longhouse. "If I can repay you, then let me know the manner, and it shall be done."

The night sky was already lightening, the fjord glittering beneath a low-clinging sun. The air was cool, thanks to a breeze blowing in from the sea, and all was hushed. The residents of Skálavík would sleep on another hour, although there was movement in the harbour. The fishermen were early to rise, pushing out beneath those violet-shadowed mountains.

We all needed sleep, but the early morning light was too beautiful to turn from, and I had no eagerness to join the one who awaited me. Ragerta and I stood, watching as Thoryn retreated.

"His mother died early in the spring. He'd been living alone," said Ragerta sadly.

"He has no thrall?" I'd noticed a woman's touch in the woven coverings for his bed and walls, but the cauldron had been empty, and his tunic looked to have gone many days without being washed.

Ragerta gave a small smile. "He sold her. Thirka says he's promised not to have another woman in the house until she can join him."

"Well, she's under his roof, now." I gave Ragerta a nudge. "Perhaps that's where she'll stay."

"If the jarl permits it." She yawned. "A strange night it was, and I'd say the gods had a hand in it. Many are the stories of lovers united after sore trials. Thirka's accident may bring them together."

Aye, if the Beast has a heart and will let her go, I thought. I'd seen little of it until now, but nor had I expected him to act as he had, risking himself for one so insignificant in his eyes.

The two sentries walking the perimeter of the longhouse had made their circuit and paused before us now.

"Best get to bed," said one. "The mistress will be shaking you out of it afore the cock crows twice."

"Unless you'd prefer to tarry with us?" The other gave a wink. "We'll lie you down all right, but I can't swear you'll get any sleep."

"An attractive offer, I'm sure." Ragerta rolled her eyes. "But I'll take my own finger over a poke from you. 'Twill be cleaner, at any rate!"

The guards laughed and gave Ragerta's rump a friendly smack as we turned to go in.

Fleetingly, I wondered if I might have run in those moments we'd been alone. Ragerta wouldn't have stopped me.

Don't be ridiculous. You'd not have made it to the trees.
But my time will come.
Better to be patient.
Watch and learn, and discover the best way.
I'll have only one chance.

Inside the hall, Kellick, the lad who chopped wood and ran other errands, had stacked the trenchers and cups to one side, but they'd not been washed. That job might fall to me, besides many others now that Thirka was unable to help. Sigrid was happy to work her loom, but I didn't imagine she took the dirty work of the household.

Though I was weary, the prospect pleased me. The more I was needed for other tasks, the less time I might spend in Eldberg's bed, and the more I'd learn about this place I'd come to.

I paused at the curtain. Was he awake? The bed creaked, and I heard a sigh and a grunting snore. Would he even know if I didn't join him? I could sleep on a bench in the hall—like the other thralls. But, he would know when he woke, and it served me in no way to stir his anger.

Wearing my shift, I took my place beside him. He sighed again and turned, his arm coming over me, pulling me close.

I stiffened at his touch, but he was still asleep, and dreaming—of something that disturbed him, it seemed, for he cried out, though not loud enough to wake himself.

He tossed and mumbled, then curled back to me once more. And I lay listening, as his murmurs became words I understood: "No" and "Find her".

He pulled me tighter to the curve of his body, and his lips found my neck.

"My love, my love…"

And with his caress, he repeated the name of the woman he dreamed of. *Bretta.*

In the weeks that followed, Thoryn came to the longhouse each morning, escorting me to his home to attend Thirka. In his care, she flourished, healing more quickly than I'd expected.

He'd offered Eldberg twice her value, and they were to wed as soon as Thirka could stand unaided.

The jarl did not speak of it, merely purchasing two thralls to replace her —a married couple of Norse blood and older years, enslaved during a raid to the north. Though Sigrid kept Ragerta and me busy, the work became easier, with more shoulders to bear the burden.

Eldberg's moods were varied—at times angry, at others, considerate. There were days when he kept me in his bed, watching as he caused my tension to build, edging me toward release, making me shudder with passion I could not withhold.

I endeavoured to close my mind against all that shamed me, accepting that a thrall had not the privilege of choice. What shamed me most was my desire to be comforted and caressed. I wanted to defy him, yet fought the impulse to reach out. A strange intimacy had grown between us, and it was as if two different men resided within him.

Despite these thoughts, I didn't forget that I was his captive, and he my master—for as long as it amused him. When that time was over, I knew not what would come. He could dispose of me in whatever fashion he saw fit— selling me in some far-off market, to whoever paid the best price. Selling my child, too, if it lived.

The need to escape remained with me, though I knew not how I would realise such a plan. To stow away on some trading vessel would likely take me from one danger to another. To attempt a crossing of the mountains would be madness. The river which had brought me to Skálavík swept the edge of the settlement only to flow into the fjord. I might follow the water's path as it had brought me to this place, but I knew not if anything remained of Svolvaen.

If my old friends had survived, did they think me dead, or that I'd colluded with Skálavík to bring about the events of that terrible night? It pained me to think of it. The friendships I'd made had been precious to me —hard won as they were.

Astrid. Ylva. Torhilde. Helka… And Eirik. Was it foolish of me to hope they might still live? Hadn't I seen the longhouse set afire and heard the screams of those within? Hadn't I witnessed Eldberg stand over Eirik and plunge his blade into his body?

I oft saw Eirik in my dreams, so vividly—his shoulders squared for battle, his sword raised in defiance.

To reach Bjorgen would be my best chance. Jarl Ósvífur would grant me protection, surely, honouring my position as Eirik's widow. Perhaps, Helka and Leif had survived the attack, and I'd find them safe there, although it hardly seemed possible to hope. If they were alive, wouldn't they have come and bargained for my release?

Still, I needed to believe there was a place for me, somewhere beyond Skálavík.

Wormwood for stomach cramps, milfoil to stop bleeding, burdock to ease aches in the bones, and feverfew to subdue a headache. I touched each plant as I recounted them to myself, then broke off a stem of lavender, rubbing it between my fingers. Lavender for sleep. There were many others I recognised—mugwort, chicory, chamomile, angelica, yarrow, and plantain.

I'd grown the same plants in Svolvaen, using them in so many combinations when I'd been seeking a cure for the disease that plagued us. Little had I known, then, that the answer lay in the caves of the fjord, where a particular seaweed grew thick on the walls.

The herb garden had been Bretta's and had grown neglected, nettles growing through the rows of plants. Not that nettle leaves weren't useful, but they couldn't be allowed to swamp everything around them.

Sigrid shouldn't have allowed it to become overgrown, but it wasn't my place to correct her. Instead, I resolved to tidy it a little each day.

This morning, I was looking for fennel and thyme. With comfrey and marigold, they'd make a good salve for Elberg's eyelid, which still wept and seemed unwilling to heal.

Beyond the little garden, where the grass grew long, I spotted the frothy white flowers of giant cow parsley. Now there was a source of retribution! A drop of sap from its stem into each eye would burn his vision entirely, but it struck me that I would never, now, want to inflict such a thing upon him.

With passing time, the urge to take my vengeance had faded. I might easily have concealed a knife and slit his throat as he slept, but I'd lost the taste for such revenge.

When I fled, I vowed, it would be without blood upon my hands.

Still, I jumped at the feel of Eldberg's touch upon my shoulder.

"Mixing your potions, thrall?" He plucked the thyme from my fingers, raising it to his nose.

"For you, my lord." I held out all I'd gathered. "You've allowed me to help Thirka, and I'll help you, too, if you'll permit it."

"You find my injury unappealing?" The old hardness was in his voice. "I'm not handsome enough for you?" He grabbed me by the shoulders. "'Tis easily remedied, for I may have my fill of you without either of us seeing the other's face."

"Nay, my lord. You're too easily offended. I thought only to ease the discomfort of this wound that's so long in healing."

He let go, and a shadow passed over his features—a fleeting glimpse of remorse, I thought, for his having spoken harshly.

It was not his way to take back words spoken or to apologise, for he was jarl, and there was no necessity to explain himself, but he drew me to his chest.

"I came to find you on an errand of my own, and it shall serve both purposes, if you wish to attempt the curing of me. The merchant who sold us the aloe some months ago has returned, and his ship carries other remedies. 'Twould be well to create a chest of medicines. Thoryn tells me of your skill and, having knowledge, you should help me choose, for I trust your judgement as well as any healer in Skálavík."

It was a great compliment—the first I'd heard from his lips, but I knew better than to appear too pleased, or to set any store by it.

Rather, I tilted back my head, offering my lips, which he took with eagerness, bold and demanding, wrapping me within his arms as he claimed my mouth thoroughly.

It was enough, that kiss, to rouse his manhood and, when he broke off, he was breathing heavily. Shrugging off his tunic, he lay it flat upon the row of chamomile in which we stood, and guided me to lay upon it.

"You cannot mean... not here!" I protested, but he had already loosened the fastening of his trousers, and his hand was beneath my skirts.

"I am jarl, and it's my wish. As for your modesty, worry not, for the plants grow tall enough to conceal us."

And there was no arguing thereafter, for he claimed another kiss and moved between my legs, his flesh hot in mine.

It was with some lightness of heart that I walked by Eldberg's side to the harbour. I'd never been permitted farther than Thoryn's hut—and only then in his company. At other times, I'd been under the watchful eye of Sigrid or the longhouse guard.

Like Svolvaen, Skálavík's heart lay in its harbour—but it was more than a place of fishing. As we descended the headland, Eldberg told me that merchants often visited, trading for Skálavík's whalebone and whale oil, hides and herring, axes and arrow heads, and blades of all description. The forge was worked by six strong men, whose skill attracted many in pursuit of fine weapons. The metal came out of the very rock above the settlement, with many to extract for smelting.

In return, Skálavík purchased amber beads from the Baltic lands, soapstone, salt, silks, other fine cloth, and grain, too. The land here did not lend itself to the growing of such crops, and much barley was needed for bread and ale.

The place was a bustle, people jostling to peruse the many goods on sale. The scent of cook-fire smoke mingled with the pungent odours of fish and livestock, while buyers haggled noisily. We made our way past stalls of meat, nuts, and cheeses, the marketgoers parting as Eldberg approached, making way for their jarl—and eying me with curiosity in no manner concealed. I'd picked out the chamomile from my hair and smoothed myself as best I could, but I felt the shabbiness of my appearance, for the dress I wore had been on my back near three weeks without washing, since I'd no other to replace it.

Our destination was a ship anchored in the bay, from which a small rowboat had been sent, waiting for us at the pier's end. Eldberg jumped straight in and held his hand to help me board.

"This captain prefers to remain on the water with his cargo—it being of particular value." He nodded at the man standing on deck, watching our approach. "It suits me well enough, since it offers more privacy for our transactions."

A rope ladder was cast down the side, enabling us to climb up, hand over hand.

I was surprised at once by the size of the vessel and its orderliness. The deck was broad and mostly clear but for neatly looped coils of rope. The sails had been well-tied, enabling the ship to sit perfectly still at anchor.

"*Selamlar*, Yusuf." Eldberg inclined his head slightly before touching his forehead and heart.

"*Barış seninle olsun, arkadaşım*," the man replied, offering the same gesture of welcome in return.

The captain smiled, his eyes flickering swiftly over me before returning to Eldberg. Behind him stood eight of his crew, each as nut-brown as their captain, with legs planted firmly and their eyes upon us. Though they appeared at ease, each wore a weapon at his belt.

"And peace be with you, my friend," said Eldberg, moving forward to clasp the other's hand.

"You have something special to trade today, yes? A treasure with eyes like jewels and skin of ivory."

A cold wave broke through me, hearing those words spoken haltingly in the Norse tongue. I looked fearfully to Eldberg. Was this the moment after all, when he would fulfil his threat? If so, then there was no greater fool than I, for I'd begun to believe Eldberg would be sorry to lose me, when the day came that I made my escape.

"Ha!" Eldberg answered with clear amusement, the corner of his mouth twitching. "She is mine to sell, but were I able to part with her, I'd ask for sapphires large enough to match those eyes, Yusuf."

"Forgive me." The captain dipped his head. "I merely assumed…"

Eldberg's grand reply was almost as disconcerting as my belief that he might sell me. He spoke, truly, as if I were precious to him.

"In this case, I have silks and bracelets of gold, carried from Constantinople. It is these you come for, yes, to adorn this cherished plaything and make her fit for your harem?"

"You change not a whit, Yusuf!" barked Eldberg, clearly enjoying this game, though my own temper rankled to hear them speak of me thus.

"You may tempt me with your trinkets later, though I warrant you have nothing to offer that can compare to the enticement of her bare skin. She needs no fine garments to make herself beautiful to me. I'd keep her naked all the day and night were it not that I must drag myself to attend other matters occasionally." Eldberg met my eyes, and his own were laughing still, caring not that anger flashed in mine.

"But, of course, a woman's natural state is always most desirable," the captain replied, and I saw a hint of lasciviousness as he looked upon me again, no doubt imagining me without the cover of my gown.

Eldberg cleared his throat and composed himself, asking more seriously, "It is medicines I come for, Yusuf. Like those you traded before, when I was unable to greet you and Thoryn came in my stead." He turned his face, indicating the burns that had healed. "The aloe was effective, and we would purchase more, together with samples of other ingredients you recommend. If they prove potent, we shall buy greater volumes next time you sail to us."

"I see you are not just fortunate in your company but wise, Jarl Eldberg." The captain touched his heart. "And it will be my pleasure to supply all you require."

Turning, he uttered instructions in his own tongue, sending two of his men below deck. They returned with a chest.

Opening it, Yusuf brought forth a ceramic pot sealed with wax. "One silver piece for an amphora of aloe, my friend. For the rest, I shall prepare a small vial of each spice from my personal store and explain their properties. For this, in good faith, I make no charge, but shall return with the spring tides and greater volumes—from which you may purchase as much as you wish. If it pleases you, I would trade for the furs you harvest this winter. Your foxes are particularly fine, and I have buyers who await them back in the east."

Eldberg gave his agreement, and they proceeded about the business, Yusuf decanting small quantities of colourful powders and potions, giving their name and application: turmeric and ginger—to counteract soreness in the body and aid digestion, clove oil for relief of tooth pain, and cinnamon to ease breathing. There were twenty or more, each with its own remedy, which I committed to memory.

"And this, my friend, I'm sure you have no use for." The captain shook a small ball, making it rattle. "It increases a man's ability and sustains his force, for the creation of many children." He gave a small smile. "Though you need it not, I shall place this nutmeg with your other medicines, in case one of the men under your command wishes to test its potency."

Shaking hands, Eldberg thanked him for his thoroughness and opened the pouch upon his belt, counting out the necessary coins. When he'd finished, he held up an extra five.

"What else do you have for me then, Yusuf? Show me your best. Something fit to be worn by my golden queen."

I reddened to hear him call me such, for the jest was at my expense. Whatever he named me, I was still his slave, without any right to refuse him or his gift.

The captain considered a moment before giving instruction again, sending another of his men to fetch what he requested.

There were three bolts of fabric, each of sufficient length to make a gown. The first was of rich green brocade, the next in pale gold, threaded through with silver, and the last a silk of shimmering blue—its hues similar to those of the fjord. In addition, Yusuf produced an arm circlet intricately shaped in silver and studded with pearls, with brooches to match.

I was speechless, for not even the fabric of my own wedding gown had been so fine, and I'd never worn any adornment of value—other than the ivory brooch given me by Asta.

Eldberg nodded. "You have a good eye, Yusuf. Pack everything, and we'll leave you. I wish you a safe journey and shall look for your return."

"*Veda arkadaşım.* Farewell, my friend."

As we rowed back to the pier, Eldberg leaned forward, resting his forearms upon his knees. "You will look most elegant, my Elswyth, but I meant what I said."

"And what was that, my lord?" I looked over the water, not trusting myself to meet the intensity of his gaze.

"No matter how fine your gown, I shall always prefer you out of it."

13

ELDBERG

October 31st, 960AD

The skuas, gulls, and terns had flown, leaving the wind to moan its loss through the crags that hung above Skálavík.

Eldberg raised his face to the rolling pulse of shivering light—flickering green, silent. Even with his eyes closed, the shimmers remained, rippling and breaking—as vivid as the memory of her face.

In his mind, he reached for her.

Do you see me, Bretta?

They'd gathered to mark the rite of *Alfablót*, to honour the souls of the dead and the spirits of the dark—the *Dökkalfar*. Unseen by the living, mysterious, and at their most powerful during the long nights, such forces dwelled in the mountain above Skálavík. Tonight, they would receive their sacrifice, and all men would remember their frailty in the darkness of the unknown.

Sweyn led the young bull within the sacred circle—a stone for each man of Skálavík, and each man behind a stone.

"We call upon our male ancestors to protect us—to speak for us among the dark ones." Eldberg's voice rang out, addressing all surrounding him. "We offer this *blót*, this libation, and we beseech mercy through the winter's long cold, that we may live to see the sun return."

Raising his axe, Eldberg swung it thrice about his head before burying it with a splitting thud in the calf's skull. It was a clean kill, the creature falling to the ground with the blade still lodged in the bone. It gave no bellow—only a sudden jerking and a wide-eyed stare.

Planting his foot firmly against the calf's shoulder, Eldberg released the weapon and gestured to Sweyn. With a shallow bowl placed beside the creature's neck, his sworn-man knelt and plunged his dagger deep, bringing forth a gush of blood.

When the vessel was full, he raised it up and Eldberg dipped his thumb into the liquid, marking the forehead of his commander and then his own. While the bull's life-force soaked the ground beneath their feet, Eldberg brought the dish to his lips and drank.

"Pledged in loyalty, we stand, brother to brother, until we enter that other realm."

"Until we enter that other realm." The response travelled the circle with the passing of the bowl, all drinking and receiving his jarl's mark.

Having completed its journey, the dish returned to the centre of the circle, and each man nodded soberly to his neighbour. There would be revelry later, with the animal's meat roasted and a portion brought back to this place with a tankard of mead. For now, they would depart in silence, carrying the carcass of the beast between them.

The wind was rising, and Eldberg could smell storm clouds gathering.

"I would speak with you, my jarl." Sweyn touched his arm, drawing him aside. "For there is more for us to fear than the forces of the hidden world."

Eldberg surveyed his commander. "You wish to warn me, Sweyn?"

The other squared his shoulders.

"That wench—she has bewitched you." He wetted his lips, hesitating. "And the rounder her belly grows, the more she has you under her spell."

"You're brave, this night, Sweyn." Eldberg fixed him with a hard stare. "You think to tell me whether this thrall deserves the warmth of my bed?"

Sweyn's glance darted away. "She rules not only your bed, my lord. The clothes she wears are finer than Sigrid's, and she no longer performs the duties of a thrall. There are two mistresses now, for the other slaves follow her more willingly than their true lady."

"If 'tis true, then it speaks more of Sigrid's lack than Elswyth's. As to her duties, they are mine to decide."

"Forgive me, my lord," Sweyn dared to raise his gaze, "But the men are saying you let this woman—an enemy of Skálavík—twist you to her bidding, that you neglect your visits to the harbour and the mines." He swallowed hard. "Give her to the men of the guard and you'll be free again, my lord."

Eldberg tasted ashes on his tongue. No man had the right to speak to him thus. No man should dare.

He closed his hand around Sweyn's neck. "You think to judge me?" Eldberg squeezed harder. "You go too far, Sweyn." Slowly, he raised the man in his grip, lifting his feet from the ground. "She has soothed the disquiet of my grief, and her skills have brought healing to my eye; for that I favour her, but I am her master."

"Your eye, my lord!" He spluttered, kicking his feet. "She sent my brother deep into the caves of the fjord, making Thoryn bring back every seaweed he could find. There was one she wanted. 'Tis that she used in the poultice—a type that grows only in the dark, hidden." Sweyn gasped for air. "Her spells use not the medicines you purchased from the Mikklagard Turk. She's no better than the old woman who lives in the mountain, dabbling in things no man should know."

Eldberg let Sweyn drop, his lip curling in distaste.

"You're relieved of your post as commander of the guard. From tomorrow, you'll report to the mine."

Sweyn crawled back, clutching at his throat. "That place! No!" He looked up at Eldberg, his mouth slack, disbelieving. "I've served you faithfully. I've done all you bid." He shook his head. "I don't deserve this."

"You've served yourself." Eldberg touched the hilt of the dagger sheathed at his waist. "I release you from your bond. You're a free man. Go where you will. If the mine doesn't suit you, find your fortune elsewhere."

Sweyn scrambled to his feet, eyes dark with hatred. He went for the blade at his own belt, but Eldberg was too quick. His weapon slashed the back of Sweyn's wrist before he could draw.

Stumbling back, Sweyn cried out, clutching the wound beneath his arm.

"I have your answer." Eldberg wiped clean the blood from his dagger. "Know that I let you live only in token of your past service. Tomorrow, you'll leave. I care not where you go. If I see you again, my blade will open your throat."

Sweyn spat on the ground. "Curse you to the mouth of Hel, and that bitch!"

Eldberg took a single step forward. It was enough. Sweyn ran, down the headland and away, toward the longhouse.

Rain was falling. He ought to get inside, join his men, but a stronger desire was calling to him, beneath the shadow of the mountain.

He wanted to see the wise woman, Hildr. It was an auspicious night—*Alfablót*. The night of the dead.

What better time to consult those unseen forces? To seek out the seer who existed between the dark souls of the mountain and the world of men.

He'd only once visited her cave. When Beornwold had first taken Eldberg as his commander, offering him a permanent home, he'd insisted on Hildr casting the runes.

She'd spoken in riddles, of course. He'd been impatient, wanting to know what she beheld. Those white-shaded eyes had unnerved him; blind, yet seeing something others could not. She'd touched his left side, then pulled her hand away. Too hot, she'd said. Then, covering his eye with her palm, had mumbled something about Odin's mark.

It had seemed nonsense at the time.

He knew better now.

Eldberg pulled his wolfskin closer and turned his face to the mountain.

His memory hadn't failed him. Though the entrance was overhung with vines, the patch of ground in front bore evidence of feet; those of the crone and those who visited her.

There was a flapping of wings and an owl swooped low, coming to rest in the tree to one side of the entrance, turning its slow-blinking gaze upon him.

Inside, the cave was as he remembered it. Twigs and stones sat in piles, runes were scratched into the walls, and there were the rudiments of living —bundled blankets, a cooking pot, knives, and an axe.

The scent of her fire—pine branches and moss—was strong, but the cave was cold, despite the well-stoked flames, brought high by a draught from above. Smoke curled upward, drawn through a crevice in the upper rock. Water dripped somewhere in the back.

Hildr lifted her head, sniffing the air, her clouded eyes turned in his direction. She was more bone than flesh, sinew wrapped in rags.

"I've been waiting for you." She gestured with her hand. "Sit. Drink with me." There were two cups.

Eldberg brought his nose cautiously to the brew; fungi and twigs. He grimaced and heard her chuckle.

"Nothing to poison you—only to help." She sipped from her own cup. "You'll live long yet, but you've not come to ask that, have you?"

"Nay." Eldberg took some of the liquid into his mouth, making himself hold it there, ignoring the bitterness.

The runes were laid out beside her: fragments of bone—some carved, beaks and claws, an owl's feather. She touched them lightly with her fingertips. "But you have a question."

"Perhaps."

"Then tell it to the dark ones." Her voice, previously as frail as a moth's wing, was insistent. She reached for him, taking his hand, placing it within the runes. "Picture all in your mind. They will hear."

He enclosed the fragments between his two palms, rattling them as he'd done the first time, then tossing all upon the ground. They scattered, falling randomly. He peered, looking for some pattern, but there was none. Nevertheless, the seer bent forward, her fingers trembling over the pieces, feeling for where each had settled.

"Yes," her voice crooned. "I saw it even before you came."

"What?" Eldberg had to stop himself from shaking her. "What do you see?"

"Two claws are touching. There is conflict. In your past, in these days you are living, and more to come. The beak is upward—sharp, dangerous, the threat of wounding. Life hangs in the balance. Someone wishes ill upon you. There is envy. There is betrayal."

Eldberg hissed. "This I know without you telling me. What else, old woman?"

Revealing more gum than tooth, Hildr smiled. "What you desire will not bring you happiness."

Eldberg closed his eyes, suddenly weary. His journey had been wasted. She'd told him nothing of value.

"You do not wish to hear, but you must learn." Carefully, she gathered up the runes, placing them as they had been, each in their allotted place. "You are the spider in the web and the fly. Each movement determines what will come. Much is written, but there are many paths. You must choose."

Eldberg sighed. He'd heard enough.

Only as he stood, did she crawl forward, her fingers grasping, hooking through the crossed laces that held the fur about his leg.

"Leave the dead to rest." Her voice rasped. "And look to the living."

Her head jerked up, her eyes staring beyond him.

"In the forest! Find her!"

14

SWEYN

October 31st, 960AD

The hall was full—people lounging on the long benches, joking, and laughing. An arm wrestling contest had begun at the central tables. Slabs of beef were already searing on the roasting griddles, the calf having been promptly butchered. The rich scent of stew carried over the fire's smoke.

Sweyn sidled up to where the wench was supervising the opening of a new barrel of mead. He tugged on her sleeve. "The jarl has asked for you. He's waiting." She seemed not to hear him above the merriment around them, so he jerked his head, mouthing the word clearly. "Outside."

Elswyth frowned. "Isn't he coming? They're all waiting for him."

Sweyn glanced about. As far as he could see, no one was waiting for anything—except more mead.

"You're to come with me." Sweyn placed his hand under her elbow, guiding her from the barrel.

Warily, she let him lead her onward.

Across the room, Sigrid caught his eye and glowered. She'd become sourer by the day, displaced, and disgruntled. Before Sweyn had gotten Elswyth to the door, Sigrid had intercepted them.

"She has things to do here. We all have. Where's she going?" Sigrid barked her question, grasping Elswyth by the other arm.

"Jarl's orders." Sweyn shrugged. "She's to join him on the headland. Some part of the ritual he wants her to take part in—favoured as she is." He gave a sickly smile, knowing the request would rile Sigrid.

"More of the same! And when we need all the help!" Sigrid spat her retort. "Go on then." Her lips rose in a sneer, squeezing the girl's elbow sufficiently to make her wince. "Perhaps it's your blood he wants, my dear—a more powerful *blót* for the dark ones."

"Nothing like that, I'm sure." Sweyn cursed Sigrid for her cruel tongue. He'd seen the jarl striding into the trees rather than following him down, but he didn't know how long it would be until Eldberg joined them. If his plan were to work, Sweyn needed Elswyth to come quickly.

"I'm hardly dressed…" She indicated her gown—a flimsy thing of bright blue silk, worn over a simple shift of white. It was better suited to the summer months gone, but it grew hot in the hall when so many came together. The men would have their chests bare before the night was out.

"We'll not be long." Sweyn tugged her again. "Don't keep him waiting."

Sigrid gave a final scowl as he bustled Elswyth outside.

There was definitely colder weather blowing in, spits of rain falling persistently. The guard of two passed on their perimeter walk, shoulders hunched against the wind, and Sweyn called them over. "You're to go in and get yourselves a cup of mead. The jarl bids you well. Come out as soon as you've drunk it, mind!"

They didn't need to be told twice.

Sweyn breathed easier. He just needed to get her to the treeline, and they'd be out of sight.

"My cloak!" Elswyth tried to pull back. "I'll fetch it."

Sweyn cursed again. "Nay. 'Tis not cold enough for that—and the thing is scorched. 'Twould shame you to wear it for what the jarl has in mind."

She seemed to consider. Thoryn had returned the cape in the days after Thirka's accident, and Sigrid had turned up her nose, the inside now blackened from the flames. Eldberg had promised Sigrid a new cape of fur once the hunting season began, and the same for Elswyth—to Sigrid's disgust.

Sweyn could see the girl thinking. She'd been wearing it the night Sweyn had abducted her. She seemed suddenly to grow aware of how tightly he held her arm, how persistently he was dragging her farther from the door.

"Stop! I don't want to go. This isn't right. I don't believe you!"

In a single motion, Sweyn struck her forehead with his own. She crumpled immediately and, with a last look about him, he hefted her onto his shoulder. Even with her rounded belly, she was an easy weight to lift.

He skirted the edge of the longhouse and made for the forest's edge.

☙

Sweyn carried her as deeply into the trees as he dared. Too close and they'd be spotted; too far, and he'd waste precious time.

By Fenrir's teeth, he hated that berserker scum. He should've died in the fire, and everything would have worked out differently. Sweyn had kept things running while that ungrateful bastard had lain at death's door.

Who else but him would have become jarl in Eldberg's stead? Even that miserable bitch Sigrid would have given her blessing.

Now, if he wanted to keep his head on his neck, he'd have to leave. Eldberg had recovered from injuries that would've killed an ordinary man, and he remained the strongest among them. No one could stand against him in single combat and expect to win.

But he'd give Eldberg something to remember him by—and he'd be back all right. No one treated Sweyn like this and got away with it.

As for this one!

Sweyn knelt over Elswyth, gripping her face with one hand. She was coming round slowly, not fully conscious yet.

Bringing her to Skálavík had been a mistake.

It was true she'd distracted Eldberg in those first weeks—an unexpected boon, all things considered—but her influence had changed him in ways Sweyn couldn't have predicted.

Eldberg's temper had always been savage. Coupled with his warrior strength and skill with the sword, it made him undefeatable. During his marriage to Bretta, a change had been apparent. He'd determined to see Skálavík thrive as a trading port. His legacy, Eldberg had called it—his desire for them to one day rival Hedeby as a place for merchants to gather. Instead of plundering other lands for riches, wealth would flow into Skálavík through commerce.

Bretta's death, and that of Eldberg's unborn child, had near broken the jarl, his grief reducing him to the barbarian he'd been all those years ago. Sweyn had rubbed his hands gleefully to see it, for it eased the path to his own ambitions. Eldberg had survived the fire, but he'd bring about his demise—one way or another.

These months past, Elswyth had soothed the savage beast, taming him once more. It had stirred much talk—and not in criticism of the Svolvaen whore. Far from neglecting his duties as jarl, Eldberg had embraced them with greater vigour, expanding the output of the mine and the number of men trained in the forging of weapons. Meanwhile, his harbour guard ensured the smooth running of the market and the safety of all vessels entering Skálavík's fjord.

Even if Eldberg hadn't realised it himself, Sweyn could see what was coming. The jarl would free Elswyth as he had Thirka, once she'd delivered her child—perhaps sooner. Then he'd marry the wench and sire his own heir.

Sweyn's ambitions for himself had been thwarted, but there was one part of Eldberg's future Sweyn could ruin. With any luck, the discovery would send their jarl hurtling back to the chasm from which he'd climbed.

Elswyth's lids flickered as Sweyn took hold of her neck. He'd crush her throat quick and easy, and then he'd be gone.

But, looking down at her, he was reminded of why he'd taken her in the first place. The flimsy gown she was wearing had gotten damp from the rain. It clung to her breasts—even more voluptuous in her ripe condition. The cool air had tightened her nipples. He dropped one hand to squeeze her flesh. Between finger and thumb, he pinched the peak, and she whimpered, though did not fully stir.

It was enough to send a jolt of heat to his groin.

By Thor and Odin and all the gods, this one wanted Skálavík cock and, before he broke her pretty neck, he'd give it to her.

Hungrily, he brought up her skirts, shoving her legs apart with his knee.

She was a captured slave, and he'd fuck her like one.

Grasping her hips, he delved his fingers into her sheath. She was ready enough for the piercing. There would be nothing to stop him entering to the hilt.

Her hair fanned loose about her head—golden silk upon the half-rotten leaves and moss. Her lips, full and soft, invited him. Everything that Eldberg had enjoyed would be his.

He bore down upon her, plundering her mouth while his arousal nudged her wetness.

Too late did he realise his folly.

As her teeth clamped down on his tongue, Sweyn's mouth filled with blood.

※

E *lswyth*
    I roused to pain in my forehead, to an inability to breathe, to the heaviness of him upon me. Instinct made me bite the probing thing in my mouth, and his bellow broke through to awaken me.

He sprung up, cursing, and the lifting of his weight enabled me to scrabble away from him.

Sweyn!

Gulping, I screamed, but he was upon me immediately. A hard slap sent me sprawling into the leaves. He leapt upon me then, holding both my arms tight to the ground.

"Do that again, and I'll snap your neck."

Through eyes filled with tears, I saw the fury in his. Breathless, I forced out my words. "Harm me, and Eldberg will kill you for it."

"I'll be long-gone." His snarl was that of a wild creature.

"And when they find my body? Eldberg will know it was you, Sweyn."

"He might." A wicked gleam lit his eye. "Or the beasts will make short work of you, and there'll be no evidence. He'll think you ran away."

I gulped back my fear.

It was true. It's what they all would think.

I had to keep him talking. Eldberg might be out here. He might have heard me scream. I just needed time.

"What have I done, Sweyn?" I spoke softly. "What makes you hate me? Why are we here?"

"Why?" Sweyn hurled the word back at me. "You think you're so special? It's him I want to hurt!"

I didn't understand. My head was throbbing. Had I hit it when I fell? Nothing made sense. Sweyn had authority, status, and respect. Why was he doing this?

I made my voice calm. "You won't harm me, Sweyn. You know it's not right. You'll be killing the baby as well as me. What do the gods say about that? What do the ancestors say? Aren't they close tonight? Aren't they watching?"

"Shut up!" Sweyn leaned on my arms more heavily, and I cried out in pain. "You know naught about it. You don't belong here. You're nothing!"

Of all the things he might have said, this cut deep.

I'd spent a lifetime not belonging.

But I wasn't nothing.

I looked into his face, summoning all my strength to speak clearly. "They tried to kill me in Svolvaen, but they couldn't. They bound me to the pier, but I escaped. I lived in the caves, and I climbed up through the cliffs. Do you believe an ordinary woman could do that? If I was nothing, do you think I'd still be alive!"

Sweyn's eyes narrowed.

He was unsure; I felt it.

Some had believed me an enchantress. I had no magic. I wove no spells. But I had other power. That of a woman who refused to be cowed. No matter what happened, I knew myself. I'd made mistakes and paid for them, but I was a survivor.

If I could make Sweyn fear me, I might yet live.

"I vow by my own god and all those that govern here, harm me and I'll curse you. Every foul pestilence I'll visit on you, until you'll wish yourself dead and that you'd never laid eyes upon me!"

He let go of my arms, leaning back.

He was afraid.

From somewhere in the bushes, there was a rustle. I doubted Sweyn would have noticed before, but his attention darted up, ears straining.

"Go quickly while you have the chance. Go, Sweyn! Leave me here to the animals of the forest if you like, but run while you can."

"You think to fool me with such nonsense?" He frowned.

Somewhere, far off, an owl hooted.

"So be it."

I froze as he pulled his knife from its sheath. After all I'd said, was he still going to take my life? I watched in horror as he took the blade to the hem of my gown, tearing off a long strip, then another.

The first he used to bind my ankles. The second he wound around my wrists, placed behind my back.

"If the creatures take you, it won't be my doing. You're in the hands of the gods now. Let them save you."

I feared he was right.

My fate lay in who would find me first—Eldberg or the predators who roamed this dark place.

15

ELSWYTH

October 31st, 960AD

No matter how I twisted, my fingers wouldn't reach the cloth that bound my wrists. I refused to give in. I knew not in which direction Skálavík lay, but I believed some force watched over me. I had faith in that guiding power.

Drawing my feet under, I managed to stand, but the bindings round my ankles were too tight. I lost balance, pitching forward into the damp leaves. Again I tried, and again, but succeeded only in scratching my arms and face on brambles.

How often I'd imagined escaping; had thought of which path I might take through the forest's edge and down to the meadows, finding the river and following it back to Svolvaen.

I'd wondered how I might evade detection.

Now, I needed to be found.

I needed Eldberg to come for me before wild beasts sniffed my blood.

Rolling to place my back against a tree, I sat cold and shivering, peering through the gloom. How many eyes were watching me? I listened for the breath of the forest's creatures, imagining movement where there was none.

Should I call out? If Eldberg were nearby, it would help him find me, but what of those other beasts? Would if I summoned them also?

I closed my mind to what else might be lurking—entities for which I had no name. I'd brushed against the unknown things of the otherworld before, when Asta's restless spirit had reached across the veil.

Curling small like a child, I buried my nose to my knees—as well as my belly would allow.

Time passed, the shadows grew darker, and then I was certain I heard breaking twigs.

Something was in the bushes.

I looked about. Was there a branch I might grasp to defend myself? Nothing was close. In any case, my hands were bound.

Whatever it is, let it not see me. Let it pass by.

I sat very still, breathing shallow. My pulse galloped in my throat.

When the thing exploded from the undergrowth, I shrieked. Wings flapping, squawking, whirling away—a pheasant of some sort. A creature as startled as me.

A sob stuck in my throat, making me laugh and cry.

Only a bird, nothing to hurt me.

Through the gloom, something was staring at me, no more than twenty footsteps away. I peered harder and saw bright eyes gleaming. I saw a flash of tusk. A boar! Those rough-bristled swine had vicious tempers. A single gore could tear a man in two.

"Go away!" I shouted, then again.

I growled. I hissed. I barked like a dog.

Still, the creature watched. I heard its grunt, and it emerged from the bracken, swinging its head, snorting, making ready to charge. It pawed the ground, throwing up leaves and chunks of moss.

I screamed, drawing back against the tree. My time had come.

But there was another sound—a soft footstep?

The beast raised its snout, nostrils twitching, sensing some other presence. I couldn't see and hadn't the courage to turn.

A wolf? Or more than one?

Would they fight over which was to make a meal of me?

And then a steady voice, low and firm, commanded me. "Be still."

Briefly, I saw the glinting blade. Eldberg threw his axe true, driving it into the boar's neck. The creature thrashed and squealed, blood gushing. In fury, it lowered its head and rushed to meet its attacker, but Eldberg's dagger was ready. As it was almost upon him, he sank it through the boar's snout.

The beast fell immediately. It rolled to its side, pawing the air, and Eldberg acted swiftly, delivering the final thrust to end the creature's pain.

I closed my eyes, not wishing to see more, my heart still racing. I was aware of Eldberg freeing me—first my feet and then my hands.

His palm was upon my forehead, then his lips, and his arms came around me. Limp and numb, I gave in to exhaustion.

I wished the bed would stop tilting back and forth. Tentatively, I touched my forehead. What had happened? The events of the night seemed unreal, though my aches and bruising told me otherwise.

It had been my barking that had brought Eldberg to my exact spot. Of Sweyn there was no sign. The harbour watch reported that he'd taken a small fishing boat and left the fjord not long ago. The vessel might carry him some way if he avoided wrecking on the coastal rocks.

Eldberg helped me out of my filthy clothing, rubbed dry my hair, and wrapped me warm in his bed. He pulled the furs to my shoulders, but still I was chilled.

Ragerta brought warm buttermilk, and he bid me drink, though slowly. He paced the chamber, then folded his arms. His voice was stern. "Promise me that you'll never leave."

I was too weary to argue, but neither did I wish to tell him a falsehood. "You know that I did not. Sweyn took me."

He waved his hand dismissively. "Of course, since you would hardly have devised to bind your own hands and feet. I ask because I wish you to say it."

He came to sit beside me, taking my hand. "You could have died."

It was true. I'd prayed for Eldberg to come, and he'd done so, but I could never promise to abandon hope of my freedom.

Instead, I asked, "Why did you risk yourself for me?"

"Because you're mine—and a man protects what is his."

I hadn't the strength to tell him again that I wasn't his. I'd long ago exhausted such reasoning. An uneasy peace had fallen between us, his early brutality having spent itself, and there was much for which I was indebted.

Ragerta had brought some of the aloe. Turning over my hand, Eldberg dipped into the pot and touched the soothing balm to the welts on my wrist.

"You haven't promised yet."

"I..." The words stuck in my throat. If I said it, what resistance was left?

"Elswyth." His voice was enticing. He looked down at my hand resting in his, then raised his eyes, locking me in his gaze—liquid dark. "Your lips are trembling." He spoke softly, leaning in, until his mouth was close to my own.

"No..." I said, knowing it was a lie.

"You're fevered with need for me—as I for you."

I wanted to turn away from his kiss, to close my eyes against him, but I couldn't. I was no longer struggling.

His lips were soft on mine, coaxing me with gentle tugs and nudges, until my mouth was fully open and his tongue slid upon mine. I lost myself in the desire to be caressed tenderly.

I told myself to no longer think; to set aside what I'd been before, to set aside the past. There would be only now, and the kisses of a man who was both strong and vulnerable. Weren't we the same? Selfish. Cruel. Hurting. Yet needing to be loved. He was my enemy, and he was myself.

And yet, I was compelled to speak my mind. I broke the kiss, saying, "Give your promise—to release me from thraldom, so that my child will be born free."

"You need fear nothing."

I wished it to be true—to be sure that his feelings for me were stronger than his desire for revenge. Eldberg had destroyed everything I'd cared for. Such a thing could not be easily forgiven, but I wanted to set aside that anger. It had eaten at me for too long.

He reached for both my hands. "I wish to be whole again and take you to wife."

His expression—always so mocking—was no longer so. I'd witnessed him in every mood, but never this—so intense, so sure.

He turned my palm, bringing it to his lips. "If I enslave you, it shall be through love."

The words were enough, and I pushed down the furs, bearing myself to him. "Touch me, my lord." It was a demand but softly made.

Gently, he obeyed, trailing his fingers across my breasts, across the full-roundedness of my stomach, hard with the babe, until he fingered between my curls, slipping his finger where he knew I would be wet.

No other command was necessary. He brought himself naked to me, and I embraced the body I'd come to know so well—the tight curve of his buttocks and powerfully muscled thighs, the firm contours of his back.

As he moved within me, the expression in his eyes stilled my breath—for it was as if he were searching for my soul, thirsty for more than the oblivion of shuddering surrender.

It was a yearning that haunted us both.

16

EIRIK

November 1st, 960AD

He became aware of voices and clattering somewhere, far off. All was dark, for he wasn't ready to open his eyes, but he stretched his fingertips, rubbing at the weave of the cloth upon which he lay.

He tried shifting a little, reaching out for Elswyth, but his arms were heavy and wouldn't obey, as if only his mind had woken and not his body. Not yet.

If only he could move, he'd find her. She would be there, next to him. He wanted to kiss her. His wife. To draw her close, his fingers tangled in her golden hair.

"Elswyth." His lips moved to form the word, but his mouth was too dry to make the sound. He tried again, to no avail.

Someone squeezed his hand, and a feminine voice asked, "Are you awake?"

Of course he was. He could hear her—Helka.

He returned the pressure of his sister's touch.

"Thank the gods!"

His hand received a sharper squeeze and was lifted to his sister's cheek. Had she been crying? What was the matter?

A man was allowed to sleep late on the day after his wedding, surely. He couldn't remember getting to bed, but it wasn't the first time another had carried him. If a man couldn't get drunk on the day he married the woman he loved, when could he?

Though his throat was parched, his head was free of the ache that usually accompanied a surfeit of mead.

"Drink this."

A cup touched his lips, wetting them, and Eirik swallowed gratefully. He wanted to open his eyes, but it was so difficult.

"What do you remember?" Helka's lips pressed to his forehead.

Eirik fought to recall. The wedding feast, and Elswyth looking beautiful in her crimson gown, her diadem not of hammered gold but of meadow flowers. And the room hung gloriously with boughs of blooms. Bride and groom, they'd paraded, then been carried from one end of the hall to the other, passed above the heads of their guests. How loudly everyone had cheered.

There had been games, riddles, and wrestling, and enough meat to fill a man's belly thrice over.

Later, Elswyth, overcome by the warmth of the room, had gone to take some air—and Olaf had challenged him to a drinking contest. Ten horns they'd supped dry. "Climb on the table," Olaf had said. "Whoever reaches the end first, without falling off, will be the winner."

But he'd heard a scream. Then shouting.

Fire!

He'd looked up. The roof was crackling, amber licking between the timbers, eating the turf—dry from the good weather. Chunks were falling through.

Eirik's heart leapt in panic.

There were flames!

He squeezed Helka's hand fiercely and drew a deep breath, filling his lungs with air.

"F-fire!" He forced out the word. "Fire!" He gulped down more air. "Helka! Fire!"

He needed to waken properly and open his eyes. He needed to warn them. Get everyone to safety. His shoulders lifted a tiny fraction, but it was as if a great weight were pressing him back. He fought to sit up, and a terrible pain bolted beneath his ribs.

"Shh, calm yourself." Helka's hand touched his chest. "We're all safe. The fire's out now."

She paused momentarily. "What else, Eirik? What else do you remember?"

He'd leapt down from the table. Flaming torches flew through the doorway, but still people pushed, stumbling, calling to each other, running to escape.

Helka was nearby, coughing through the smoke. Grabbing her, he rushed forward, and they were out, but the hem of her gown was alight. To smother the flames, he pushed her to the ground.

It should have been dark, but the fire lit everything in its glow. Where was Elswyth? Was she safe?

And then he saw. Amidst the smoke and the shouts and the rush of bodies, there were others. Standing, watching. A shout of command and a glint of steel.

Instinctively, his hands reached for his sword, but there was no scabbard at his belt. Only his ceremonial dagger hung there.

He barely had time to clasp its jeweled hilt when he was pierced by pain. He saw the blade thrust clean through. Blood bubbled into his mouth; the dagger slipped from his hand. And then he was on his back, the ground strangely soft, and a figure loomed above.

Someone called his name.

The violet sky grew darker and the shouts around him faint, until there was only the ragged rattle of his breath.

The far-off voice was no more.

And the light, too, faded.

Helka

"Eirik!" Helka pinched his cheeks.

It had taken more than three phases of the moon for her brother to wake. She wouldn't allow him to slip away again so soon.

In the first days, she'd thought him lost. The injury was too severe; how could he recover? But her brother was strong. More than any other man she knew.

The Norns had woven a cruel fate for Svolvaen that night, but the blade that pierced him had only nicked his lung, penetrating beneath his ribs. He'd spilled much blood and fought a fever, but it had passed—the wound healing well, though he'd remained unconscious.

She'd never given up hope that he'd return to her, insisting that she tend him in her own hut. Propping him up, she'd spooned tiny amounts of broth between his lips, massaging his throat to make him swallow.

At last, one eye fluttered open.

"Elswyth." This time, he spoke her name clearly.

Helka gestured to Leif standing by the door, signaling for him to fetch the others.

Eirik needed to know. She had to tell him. "Svolvaen was attacked." She swallowed. "Leif escaped with others through the opening to the rear of the longhouse."

"I'm glad of it… but Elswyth?"

"We looked everywhere she might have run to, everywhere she might have hidden."

"You didn't find her?" Eirik's face was pale.

She took his hands in hers. "The two guards who'd been on watch had their throats slit." She took a deep breath. "Both had 'Skálavík' carved into their forehead."

Eirik started, struggling again to sit up, only to fall back on the pillows. His face contorted with pain. "She's been taken—as our mother was."

"No message was received for her ransom, but I'm convinced you're right."

"We must send an emissary, ensure her safety," Eirik's voice was pleading.

"I wished to do so, but there were so many wounded. Anders volunteered, but I couldn't spare him. I needed everyone."

"All this time…" Eirik stared upward.

Neither spoke.

If Elswyth were alive, what would she have suffered? If she returned, like their mother, would she be broken in ways that could not be mended? The Beast of Skálavík had earned his name not through gentle hospitality.

"I just need a few days to get on my feet, then I'll take a boat. I'll bring her back—and if Eldberg has harmed her, he'll pay with his life."

Helka nodded. For now, she would pacify him. She and Leif had already made plans. They couldn't ignore Skálavík's act of aggression. Leif was to ride to Bjorgen and return with enough warriors to man Svolvaen's boats. They'd show Skálavík they weren't without allies.

"Elswyth is strong," Helka said what she knew Eirik needed to hear. "She'll endure."

Eirik returned his gaze to the rafters. It was too much for him to take in, Helka knew. She'd had many weeks to accept what had happened; weeks in which she and Leif had helped Svolvaen's survivors band together. The younger children, at least, had not been in the hall that night. And their attackers had ignored Svolvaen's stores, which they might so easily have razed.

"There is something else." Though Eirik looked wretched, Helka wanted him to know as much as possible. "Gunnolf sent someone to Skálavík, while we were in Bjorgen. We have a witness. He arrived but yesterday, claiming our man set alight the Jarl's hall at Gunnolf's order. Many died, including Jarl Eldberg's wife."

Eirik turned to her in alarm. "Just the same…" The significance was not lost upon him.

Helka nodded. "And there was only one objective in the attack upon Svolvaen."

"Revenge." Eirik's expression was frozen. He licked at his lips, and Helka offered him the water again. "Who is this witness?"

Helka turned to the door. Leif was waiting, the stranger behind him flanked by Olaf and Anders.

Helka nodded curtly. "His name is Sweyn, and he has his own score to settle."

17

ELSWYTH

December 1st, 960AD

As the cloak of winter fell, the mountains turned to ice and the world beneath huddled against bitter winds. The sun had retreated so far that it seemed gone forever. The long nights were upon us.

Skálavík's stores were richly laden—with its own harvest and an abundance traded. Eldberg and his men made many hunting trips, provisioning us with furs to be traded when the merchants returned, and with game, which we smoked and salted.

Within my belly, swollen high and round, the babe punched restless fists and feet, and I thought of how I would have placed Eirik's hand to feel its movements. It was Eldberg, instead, who watched life grow within me.

He'd a cradle made, finely carved and made to rock, though it would be three more moons before we held the child.

He had no wish to wait, but I needed time to put aside my memories, and we agreed the new year would see our marriage. On that day, I'd gain my freedom, and stand beside Eldberg as his equal. I mourned still, but I wanted to believe Eldberg had changed—that he could look to what lay ahead rather than behind.

As the season of Jul began, the longhouse welcomed all. I thought back to the year now passed, of how we'd decorated Svolvaen's hall, of Helka balanced upon Eirik's shoulders, fastening the festive boughs under which our people had made merry. It was another lifetime.

In Skálavík, too, the men gathered mistletoe and wreaths of green, swathing the rafters, and it became a place of merriment and games, feasting and drinking. We women took our part, for the thralls couldn't have prepared everything alone, and there was pleasure in working side by side to fill the platters every one of us would enjoy. Many were reluctant, at first, to accept me as anything other than what I'd been, but they saw the status Eldberg afforded me and thought it wise, I supposed, to show friendlier faces. I would soon be their jarl's wife, sharing in Sigrid's bitterness would bring them no favours.

Ivar had taken to recounting a different story of the gods each day—of Loki's mischief, and Odin's cunning. He was a fine skald, assembling many about him as he assumed each voice, using gesture and song to illustrate his tales. It mattered not that the stories were already familiar. The time passed quickly.

He was beginning the tale of the Wild Hunt, telling of the army of the dead riding through the night, headed in their chase by mighty Sleipnir, Odin's eight-legged steed.

From across the room, where I helped Ragerta in seasoning joints of meat, I caught Eldberg's eyes. He'd been talking to Rangvald but gave me his slow smile. I knew well that look—that he wished to return me to his bed and make our own entertainment.

Casting his gaze briefly about the room, he rose and entered our chamber.

Wiping my hands, I made to join him, but had taken no more than a few steps when I saw that Rangvald followed our jarl.

'Twas a strange thing, for Eldberg rarely summoned his men for private meetings. Curiosity stirred within me, and I wondered if they planned together for the coming rituals of Jólablót, when our marriage was to be celebrated.

Joining the outer edges of those who listened to Ivar's story, I placed myself near the divide of our jarl's chamber from the main hall. I could barely make out their words, for they spoke low. But with my finger pressed to one ear and the other directed toward the curtain, I discerned bits of their conversation.

I heard mention of Ivar's name—that he'd been sent somewhere and recently returned, and had been travelling as a skald.

I frowned at that. It didn't make sense. Ivar worked as a carpenter and had a family in Skálavík. He was one of Eldberg's men. Regardless of his cleverness with words, why would he wish to roam other settlements?

Rangvald spoke: Ivar had disguised himself, hunched and cloaked. He'd stayed only one night; it had been sufficient to learn what they needed.

What was this?

The next words I heard brought an icy fist to my chest.

Svolvaen.

Ivar had been to Svolvaen?

I leaned forward. What had Ivar been doing?

"He's there," Rangvald hissed, "…with a purpose…ingratiate himself with lies…led them here."

Eldberg swore. "They have allies?"

"The sister married a Bjorgen man."

Helka! They must mean Helka.

Was she alive?

"We'll be ready. None can approach unseen… double the guards on the river and the harbour… alert the watch on the headland."

They thought Svolvaen would attack? Impossible! Helka would never be so foolhardy—unless she was ignorant of Skálavík's strength.

Rangvald again. "The jarl…"

His voice dropped low. I couldn't hear.

What of the jarl?

Eirik was dead. Some other had taken his place. Olaf perhaps? Had he survived? Or Anders?

"Woken up… long time…"

Woken?

Eldberg spoke. "…come to his own slaughter… Bloodeagle…"

I clenched my nails into my palms.

Helka had told me of the bloodeagle—that Gunnolf had once inflicted it upon someone who'd refused to acknowledge him as jarl, having accused him of murdering Hallgerd.

 The man had been restrained face down, having the shape of an eagle with outstretched wings cut into his back. His ribs had then been hacked from his spine with an axe, one by one.

I sickened at the thought of it.

And there was worse. For the bones and skin on both sides had been pulled outward, followed by his lungs. Spread out like wings, Helka said, fluttering as he gasped his last breath.

No man deserved such a death.

"…blood must satisfy blood."

"Aye, my jarl."

Feet approached the curtain. Rangvald's voice was clear. "This Eirik shall pay Svolvaen's debt."

I clutched at the curtain to prevent myself from falling.

It could not be!

Eirik—alive?

18

ELSWYTH

December 1st, 960AD

For so many months I'd thought Eirik dead. I'd grieved, had spent my anger and had, at last, accepted. I'd believed him gone, and I'd bargained myself to Eldberg—to save myself and my unborn child.

Could I allow myself to believe Eirik alive? Suppose Ivar were mistaken. If my husband lived, then who else had survived that night of flames and ruin?

Would they come for me, as Eldberg seemed to think, or would they believe I'd gone willingly—a traitor to my people? There were some in Svolvaen who'd never trusted me. Would they poison Eirik's ear?

He'd forgiven me for having taken Gunnolf as my lover. He'd understood I'd thought myself forsaken. How little faith I'd had, but Eirik had borne no malice—had blamed himself. It was I who'd doubted, never him. Even on our wedding day, I'd kept my secrets—had failed to share my fear that the child I carried was his brother's.

And now? If we were reunited, could he accept what I'd become here in Skálavík? Could he pardon this betrayal and forgive?

If we found each other again, I vowed I'd hold nothing back. Only that, surely, would earn his trust. Only then could we be reconciled as man and wife.

And Eldberg?

I feared him, and I raged. I hated him.

But I loved him, too, for something connected us. When I looked into his eyes, I recognised his pain.

And what of his feelings for me?

He'd professed love, but was I no more than a possession? A symbol of his victory over those who would destroy him?

There would be no use in begging him to abandon his thirst for revenge. I'd told him many times that Gunnolf—of unsound mind—must have sent the man responsible for Bretta's death; that Eirik sought only peace, and Svolvaen had instigated no aggression.

At least, that had been true before. If Eirik lived, as Ivar reported, and came for me, what then? Skálavík's warriors would be watchful. They held the advantage. Even with Bjorgen men behind him, could Eirik hope to subdue Skálavík?

I feared he'd be walking into a trap.

Somehow, I had to warn him and all Svolvaen. If I could but find my way back, how much bloodshed would be avoided—for Svolvaen and Skálavík.

To wait was torture, but I knew that my only hope of slipping away would come while Eldberg slept. I'd dress as warmly as I could—a woolen gown over both my underdresses, my cloak from fox furs Eldberg had lately given me, and foot and leg coverings I'd sewn from the same.

Through the evening, I oft refilled Elberg's cup, needing to be certain that he wouldn't wake when I rose, and ensured his trencher was laden. With belly full of mead and victuals, he'd sleep most deeply.

He gave no indication of what he'd spoken of with Rangvald. Had I not overheard, I would've been none the wiser, though I felt his eyes upon me more than usual.

"Come, Elswyth, kiss me." He drew me onto his lap and cared not who witnessed as he embraced me.

Even Sigrid seemed to accept his plans, allayed somewhat by the gifts he'd given her. Tonight, she wore a fur caplet over her gown. It occurred to me that she'd never married, running first her brother's household and now Eldberg's. Had she never wanted a man of her own? A family?

She'd had the care of Bretta, of course.

Eldberg whispered endearments to my ear. "Not long till the gods bless our wedlock, and I shall call you not just the woman I love but wife." Though I was large in the belly, his arms still reached about me. He locked his fingers at the indentation of my waist and nuzzled his mouth to my neck.

"The rest shall be forgotten. There shall be only our pledge, forsaking all others."

Had I not known all I did, I'd have thought him merely amorous, but I heard the double-edge of his words, for he believed Eirik alive, without intention of telling me. He would marry me without offering me the knowledge that would bring choice.

Despite his fine words, I was a prisoner still, for I wouldn't be permitted to return to Svolvaen. There would be no question of that.

"Aye, my lord." I touched the newly healing scars around his left eye, and those covering his cheek. "And both of us shall forgive—for naught good comes from twisting wounds, nor can love grow when we harbour deceit."

His lips twitched, but he said nothing, merely bringing my palm to his lips.

It pained me to offer a lie, but it was no less than he deserved, and I tried not to think of the betrayal Eldberg would feel when he discovered me gone.

If Eirik came to Skálavík, Eldberg would finish what he'd begun and kill the man I loved. That I would not allow, not while I had strength to prevent it.

As the hour grew late and our guests' heads nodded on their chests, I rose to speak to Thirka. Now Thoryn's wife, she looked radiant, though she'd sat shyly beside him through the feasting. Having served in the longhouse so many years, it must seem strange to be there other than as a thrall. I wondered if her mind travelled to the night upon which the fire had leapt around her and near cost her everything.

"You're happy, Thirka?" I squeezed her hand. "Thoryn is a considerate husband, and the healing continues well?"

"Oh yes, my lady." She smiled, truly. "With much thanks to you." She sighed. "I never thought to be so happy."

"It brings me pleasure to hear it." I drew her farther from the table, nodding to those who sat on either side.

"You wish the same contentment for me, I think." I kept hold of her, ensuring she stood close.

"Of course." She looked uncertain. "And you are so, I hope, now that the jarl is to marry you. 'Twas not easy, but…" Her voice trailed away.

What could she say on that subject? I'd been his slave and still was, but now he wished to call me wife. Thirka knew the truth of that as well as I.

"And you would help me, Thirka, if there was some small thing I asked?" I lowered my voice, for none other could hear what I wished to tell her—not yet at least.

"In whatever way I can." She returned the pressure of my fingers.

My heart warmed. I'd no desire to imperil her, for even Thoryn would be unable to prevent Eldberg punishing Thirka if the jarl thought her complicit in my escape. But she would say whatever I asked, and willingly.

"Before I pledge myself to our jarl, there's a cleansing ritual I want to perform. I need to go alone and wash my feet in the river."

Thirka looked anxious. "But it's so very cold, my lady." She glanced down at my rounded belly. "And—"

"There's nothing to worry about." I tried to sound reassuring. "It's the way we did things in Holtholm—where I lived before. It's very… refreshing! And I'm hot all the time anyway with the baby growing. I'll wrap warmly—and it's just my feet. I'll be in and out swiftly."

"You want me to go with you?" Thirka asked.

"You're very kind." I sighed. "But the ritual has to be conducted alone—

and there are other elements to it." I thought on my feet, making up the details quickly. The plan wouldn't work at all if Thirka wanted to accompany me.

"There are words to be said, and I'll be addressing my old god, as well as those we all revere here in Skálavík."

"Oh!" Thirka was taken aback, suddenly uncomfortable. "And what does the jarl say?"

"It's for this that I need your help." I looked about. No one seemed to be paying attention to us. "He's very protective, and with the frost so hard, he won't want me to go."

"He'll try to stop you."

"Exactly." I inclined my head. "Carrying out the ritual is important to me, so I'm going to leave the longhouse early in morning and make my way to the river. When Eldberg wakes, he'll wonder where I am."

"You want me to tell him where you've gone?" Thirka chewed at her lip. No doubt, the thought of saying anything to the jarl filled her with apprehension.

"Yes. Tell him, Thirka—just as I've explained to you. Let him know that I wouldn't let you come with me. Tell him I didn't want him to worry." I swallowed, hating myself for what I was about to say. "That I'll return later, when the ritual is complete."

It would give me more time, I hoped, before Eldberg came looking for me. By the time he did, I'd be well on my way.

19

ELSWYTH

December 2nd, 960AD

The longhouse was warm, and few wished to venture outside. At last, our guests fell asleep, lying upon the benches. Eldberg swept me to our bed with amorous intention but had drunk too much to be capable; I'd seen to that. He slept soundly, his snores as loud as any in the hall. The fire had died to glowing embers.

I cracked open the door, listening for the guards. They walked the perimeter of the homestead.

The moon shifted between passing clouds and the ground glowed white, reflecting what light there was. It wasn't long before I heard voices and stamping feet. They were complaining of how cold it was. They approached, then drifted away, and I stepped outside.

I'd thought myself well-clad, wrapping my hands and head—even my face—but the rawness of the night struck me. Snow was falling, though lightly. I'd have to keep moving.

I made for the forest's edge. There, I'd be hidden from view. If I kept to the shadow of the trees, I could make my way down the slope of the hill. From there, I'd use the river as my guide, but not along its banks. Instead, I'd climb upward to where the forest hugged the crags, keeping the water in sight.

At some point, I'd need to descend, to follow the river again, but that would be another day's walk. How long would it take to reach Svolvaen? By boat, the journey had taken most of the night and the morning hours. On foot, I guessed three days.

Eldberg would seek me out, I'd little doubt, but he'd be some hours behind, and there would be no tracks. The snow would see to that.

I'd promised not to flee, but what did such a promise mean between my enemy and I? Hearing Eldberg speak so full of hatred still, his intent for vengeance remorseless, how could I remain?

I just needed to keep walking. All would be simple—as long as I avoided falling into the chasm, or freezing to death, or running into wolves.

Even if I were torn to pieces by some creature filled with winter hunger and met my end tonight, I would know that I'd tried. For too long I'd accepted my fate, thinking that Eirik was dead. Now, I had a reason to attempt the path back to Svolvaen.

Concealed within the trees, I reached the water, then headed upward, through the forested slopes. Keeping the sound of the river to my left, I pushed on, my cloak wrapped tight to avoid the snagging brambles.

In autumn, the forest had been full of sound. Now, it was snow-deadened, but for the wind moving far above through creaking branches and the distant rush of the river, travelling through the chasm below. The canopy gave some protection, but the flakes still fell, coming to rest on my eyelashes and nose.

One step and then another, I told myself—each footfall a soft crunch.

Drawing down the wrap from my face, I focused on my breathing—in, then out, watching the plume of white leave my mouth.

I kept moving but stopped seeing my feet, stopped listening. Tripping over a tree root, I sank to my knees, hands planted in white. Jolted to awareness, I realised that I couldn't hear water any more. I'd let myself wander blindly. And for how long?

It was too early for the sky to lighten; it would do so for only a short time in the middle of the day. How then, would I know in which direction to walk? I might only take myself farther into the forest.

I'd rest for a little while—not to sleep, but to regain strength. As soon as the sky lightened, wouldn't I be able to see more clearly where the trees gave way to the chasm?

I drew out the skin of water I'd thrust into my deepest pocket and touched it to my lips, wanting to gulp at it greedily, but the liquid was too cold against my teeth.

I had some bread. Not much, but enough. I tore off a piece and held it on my tongue, softening it. There was cheese, too—the chunk half the size of my palm. Biting into it, I closed my eyes, savouring its tang.

With my cloak under me and the cloth wound close to my face, I crouched against a fallen trunk, brushing off the snow to reveal moss, and made a crook of my elbow in which to place my head.

I hadn't intended to sleep but woke to the low call of some nearby bird. An owl on its last nocturnal hunt? The sky was lightening, and I'd been right; to one side, the trees appeared denser, the shadows far darker. To the other, they seemed to thin, revealing daylight. The chasm had to be that way.

There was no time to lose, but the frost had entered my bones. With great effort, I unbent my knees, pushing up from the log. The pain of standing made me gasp, and I cursed myself for having lain still so long. Had I slept longer, perhaps I wouldn't have woken at all.

Which heart would have stopped first? Mine, or that of the babe inside me, nestled unknowing in warm flesh?

With faltering steps, I shuffled forward, knowing that I must keep moving—must stir my blood to warm me and make my limbs useful again.

I imagined Eldberg swinging into the saddle and setting off at a gallop, sweeping for signs of my trail, bending low with piercing eyes. I glanced back, half expecting to see him, but I was alone still.

Think only of what you must do.

Soon, I heard the rush of water again, growing louder as I approached. Reaching the edge of the trees, I grasped a branch and looked down. There it was—the river, and the sunlight, and a sky clear now of clouds.

My progress was slow but feeling was returning to my limbs. I struggled on and, before long, realised the ground was shelving downward. The sheer walls of the chasm were retreating, giving way to softer contours, the forest sloping to meet the water's edge.

I might have remained within the trees but wanted to feel the sun's warmth—what little of it there was. I'd descend to walk as close to the river as I could. Continuing upstream, there'd be no chance of becoming lost.

Carefully, I proceeded, keeping hold—one branch to the next. It had become much steeper and slippery with it, the frosted depth of powdered snow and leaves parting as my weight came down. Suddenly, I was sliding, scooting on my behind, skidding faster toward the brink, where the bank dropped away to the water. Fearful, I spread my arms, digging in my heels, needing to grasp something to stop my tumbling. Shooting past ferns and bracken, my cloak whipped from under me and my skirts rode up. I was grabbing handfuls of nothing that would prevent my fall—and the river was rushing closer.

Then, there was a jerk, and I shrieked, pulled so suddenly to a halt that I lost my breath. My cloak had caught on a stump, leaving me dangling.

I lay there for a moment, wanting to cry and laugh. I was winded and bruised and I'd scraped my hands, but I was unharmed. I just needed to gather myself. Lying here, I'd only become cold. I needed to sit up, to untangle my cloak.

The river was very close, the water rushing below my feet. I'd be able to walk here safely enough. I might even slither down and make my way directly along the river. Weren't there stones and shingle on either side, along some stretches of the water, beside the shallows?

Rolling onto my side, I looked back toward the depths of the forest and the slope above me—so much steeper than I'd realised. I'd been lucky not to truly hurt myself.

I twisted, propping myself on my elbows, and the cloak pulled taut, straining at my neck. I fumbled at the brooches pinned on either side and the strap of leather between them. But as the thong pulled free, I was suddenly falling, staring back at my cloak, still hooked on the fallen trunk. I was clawing at fistfuls of snow and rotted matter, and then there was nothing beneath me at all.

As I hit the water, a thousand icy needles pierced me.

Gasping, I came to the surface, splashing in fright, my feet scrabbling for purchase on the riverbed. It seemed my lungs would burst, so cold was the water and the air. It seemed to freeze as it entered my body.

The rushing, icy torrent robbed me of movement, of thought. It robbed me of breath.

I'd landed just beyond the shallows, the water no deeper than my chest but the current was strong, sweeping back the way I'd come. With the rocks slick beneath, I fought to stand upright.

Got. To. Get. Out!

I made myself look at the bank and told myself to push, to swim, but my limbs were already numb.

In warmer water, without my heavy skirt, I might have managed, but my gown dragged heavy. Slipping sideways, I went under again, pulled along, tumbling in the churning water until I struck against a boulder on the river's bend and emerged choking.

I clung, spreading my arms. Grasping the rock to my chest, I coughed the water up I'd swallowed, and sobbed at my foolishness, for now I would die —too weak to escape the river.

If I let go, all would be over. The babe I carried would never draw breath. I'd never see Eirik again. I was afraid to do so—to be swept from this life.

And then, above the rushing around my ears, I heard the whinny of a horse and a man's voice, stern in command. A stallion was upon me, kicking up spray from the shallows, its rider swathed in coarse fur—and the face that looked down was filled with fury, barely contained.

Guiding the horse into the deeper trench, Eldberg leaned over to wrench me upward, clasping me under the arms to sit before him in the saddle.

Without uttering a word, he turned us back to the shallows and urged the stallion into a canter. Shivering, I laid my head to his chest. I had nothing left, and my tears fell silently as water streamed from my sodden clothes and hair.

It was over.

Eldberg

Since before first light, he'd ridden upstream, looking for signs of her passing, for where she was perhaps hiding, or where she might have left the river. There were crevices all along the chasm which could be climbed, leading into the forest.

Thirka had come to him, Thoryn at her side, to explain Elswyth's absence, and had seemed to believe what she'd told him—that Elswyth had risen early to perform a cleansing ritual. But he'd been suspicious at once. A blizzard had blown through during the night, and she was close enough to her time of delivering the child to make such an outing foolhardy.

If she'd heard Rangvald or Ivar talking, or what had passed between himself and Rangvald, it would be reason enough for her to make for Svolvaen.

Still, to find her gone had enraged him. She'd come to him as a captive, and he'd used her with little mercy in those first days, but hadn't he shown her how his feelings had changed? Hadn't he showered her with gifts and made her life one of ease? More than that. He'd bestowed the highest honour in asking her to be his wife—and she'd thrown all back in his face. She'd forsaken him and betrayed him.

Now, he carried her, wet to the bone and shivering, into the bathhouse. He'd left instruction with Ragerta to stoke the fire and fill the barrel deep. Swiftly, he pulled off Elswyth's sodden clothing, then his own.

She offered no resistance as he lowered her in, limp in his arms. Beneath the water, he attempted to rub life back into her body. Her teeth continued to chatter, but she looked at him, touching his chest.

There was much in her expression, though she said nothing as he kneaded the length of her limbs, her hands and fingers, feet and toes. Her lips were tinged blue. He saw again the resemblance—those eyes looking up at him…so very like…

Dipping her, he let the water cover the back of her head, her hair fanning out. When he raised her again, he noticed blood trickling—a gash which the warmth had opened up. Turning her head, he looked behind her ear, where he'd so often kissed, just above the little mole. Lifting her hair, he saw the wound; it seemed small enough not to need sewing.

He parted the hair on either side, checking that he hadn't missed anything more.

Beneath his fingers, he felt them before he saw them. Two more moles. With the one just below her hairline, they formed the familiar shape.

His fingers trembled.

How had he missed this?

How had he not seen?

So many times the likeness had struck him, but he'd pushed it from his mind. Now, he understood.

The same mark, given at birth, worn by all of Beornwold's line—a triangle behind the ear. Beornwold's had been dark and prominent. Sigrid's were fainter. Bretta's had been the same as those on Elswyth's skin, barely raised. Elswyth's hairline had covered the other moles, but they'd been there all the time.

And those eyes—so like Bretta's.

Who was she?

20

ELSWYTH

December 3rd, 960AD

Eldberg held my face in his hands.

I'd expected him to berate me; at the very least, to scold me for foolishness. But his initial anger had dissipated, replaced by intensity of a different sort—as if he perceived something he'd been unaware of before, and were seeing me for the first time.

There was hesitation in his growling voice. "Elswyth, I must know…"

Just then, the door flung wide.

Thoryn stood on the threshold. From beyond, there was shouting and a rush of movement. "A raid, my jarl!" Thoryn was breathless. "They were spotted on the uppermost cliffs, where the forest meets the mountain. The headland guard has been struck down! I've commanded men to remain at the harbour and along the river, in case this is a diversion, but we're rallying all to arms to meet the attackers."

Eldberg had risen from the water, dragging on his clothes. Though his axe and short dagger hung from his belt, he was without longer blade.

"Give me your sword."

"My jarl?" I'd never seen Thoryn falter in obeying Eldberg, but a man's sword was an extension of his arm. With reluctance, he unsheathed it. Thoryn's had the *Valknut* carved into the hilt: Odin's symbol—three interlocking triangles with the power of life over death.

"Stay here, Thoryn. Protect her. Hide her in the forest if necessary—but she's not to be taken."

Eldberg flung one last look upon me and was gone.

Thoryn stood frowning, evidently displeased. Casting about, he saw first my wet clothes upon the floor and then another gown, dry and clean, folded to one side. Ragerta must have left it for me.

He threw the towel. "Be swift, Elswyth. I'll guard the door while you dress."

I felt as if I could lay down and sleep for a whole day and night, but I worked as quickly as I was able. My fingers tingled strangely, still partly numb, and my hands shook as I laced my bootlets; they were damp from the river, but I needed to be ready. At any moment, Thoryn might insist on moving position, and I'd no wish to go barefoot through the snow.

Outside, the shouts grew louder. I recognised the ring of blade hitting blade. Was it as Rangvald had warned—that the survivors of Svolvaen had called their Bjorgen allies to aid them? And for what purpose had they come? If Eirik were alive, as Ivar had said, was he here? I could scarcely let myself believe it, and yet I hoped.

Thoryn drew out the shiv from his belt, passing it by the hilt. "Take it, and be prepared to use it."

I'd only used a knife to prepare meat, never to kill anyone. And why would I now? The men of Svolvaen would know me and would never harm me.

But what of Bjorgen's warriors? They, you've never met.

I touched its slender spike.

"Under the ribs, here." Thoryn pointed. "Push hard, and it'll go straight through. Or behind if you need to—just the same, into the soft organs."

He clasped his axe. "I must see how the fight goes. I won't leave you, but you must be prepared."

He nodded to me before easing up the latch. Bringing his face close, he peered out through the opening but, in the same instant, the door flung back.

A figure leapt into the room, silhouetted against the fading light, his shield blocking the swing of Thoryn's blade. The two wrangled, their axes locking as they pushed against one another. Then, Thoryn shouted in surprise. He fell back, lowering his axe.

"Sweyn!"

"Aye, little brother. 'Tis me!" He kicked the door shut, and his gaze passed over me.

I'd shrunk to the far wall, the shiv's handle tight in my palm, its steel cool, flattened against the back of my wrist.

"Just what I've been looking for."

Thoryn, uncertain, looked from Sweyn to me and back again. "You disappeared without a word. Why, brother? Were we not worthy enough—the men who've stood by your side since we first held our wooden swords? You wished so badly to leave us?"

Sweyn narrowed his eyes. "You ask me that? Where was your loyalty when Beornwold died? I was his favourite until Eldberg came. He would have chosen me to take his place—chosen me to marry Bretta. I was our jarl's second before that berserker scum gained the old man's trust, but none in Skálavík spoke for my claim. Where was your brotherhood then? Or was that your own jealousy? You'd rather see a stranger rule than bow to me?"

Thoryn shook his head. "So much anger, *bróðir*. Don't the gods show us the folly of kin turning on kin?"

"And this one." Sweyn jerked his head in my direction. "She's no kin at all, but that matters not. Eldberg knows no loyalty, and nor does she—a whore who makes her bed where it's softest."

A dawning awareness seemed to come to Thoryn. "You were looking for her? Did you not think her dead, Sweyn—since you left her so?"

"I had to be sure." He curled his lip. "Before I slit the throat of the last man of the headland watch, I found out what I needed to know—that the bitch yet lived."

Thoryn held his axe aloft again, but his face was full of sorrow. "You betrayed us."

"Aye! And 'twas easy! Those Svolvaen fools believed readily enough that I'd tried to help their precious Elswyth." His face contorted in a mocking sneer. "So sad that we were separated in the forest!"

Sweyn tossed aside his shield, placing both hands on his axe.

"I'd thought only to find shelter there, but they're stronger than we realised with their Bjorgen friends. There's enough of them to take Skálavík — and it's I who'll be given command when they do."

Thoryn was nimble, swinging his axe towards Sweyn's chest, but his brother was speedier, arresting the blow and sending his own blade into Thoryn's upper arm.

I cried out as Thoryn crumpled. He slumped to the floor, groaning and clutching the wound.

Sweyn gazed down at him. "'Twas my bargain, brother—to lead them here, bringing them up through the chasm in the cliffs. You must remember how we discovered the crevice leading to the cave, and the pact we made to keep all secret? Our special place, that no other knew of."

Pulling his arm into his chest, Thoryn winced. "You're no brother of mine but some changeling, sent to destroy what we've built."

Sweyn pushed him lightly with his foot. "If you be right, then I truly owe Skálavík nothing and shall take from it what I see fit."

Tipping back his head, Thoryn grimaced. "And you helped our enemy all along, I suppose, with that worm who set the longhouse blazing."

"Oh no! That you have quite wrong." Sweyn's laughter was mirthless. "I found the sorry cur spying on us, right enough, on the edge of the forest, but it was I who shot those arrows. A rewarding hunting trip, indeed, for I caught a scapegoat for my misdeed, and broke his jaw before dragging him to our jarl."

Hearing those words, the room swam before me. All this time, Eldberg had believed Gunnolf's man responsible for the fire that killed his wife. On this basis, he'd attacked Svolvaen and blamed Eirik equally with his brother. But Sweyn had been the viper, waiting to send his venom to Skálavík's heart.

Thoryn closed his eyes. "And what now, Sweyn? You must kill me, for I'll not permit your foul villainy—not while I live."

"Aye, brother, you'll die, and the whore with you. Look how she quivers." His voice dripped with contempt. "There shall be none alive to contradict my story."

As Sweyn bent to Thoryn, placing his hands about his neck, I took the one chance I had. Flinging myself across the room, I plunged the shiv with all my might deep into Sweyn's side.

He screamed in agony—in rage. Twisting, he tried to pluck it out, but I leapt forward again, jerking the blade free. He lurched to one side, disbelieving as the blood spurted from the wound.

I glanced at Thoryn. He was pale, but his lips moved, urging me to act.

On his knees, Sweyn was groping for the axe he'd let drop. Steeling myself, I jumped upon him and drove the shiv home again, clear through his neck.

With a cry of horror, I recoiled, watching as Sweyn fell. This time, there was no scream—only the gurgle of a man trying desperately to breathe. He struggled briefly before his head fell back, and he moved no more.

"Elswyth." Thoryn's voice rasped. "Help me!"

His tunic was stained crimson. He was weak, but conscious still. Where the blade had entered, the fabric was ripped and I tore it farther, to better see the wound. It was deep and the blood rising dark.

Grabbing the towels, I wadded one, pressing it to the open flesh, bidding Thoryn hold it while I brought the other cloth around, binding all tight. Pulling Thoryn, I brought him more securely into the corner. Even if he fainted, he would remain upright. It would give him more time. Though, if he lived, it would be the gods' will, for I could do nothing more without needle and thread.

To find those, I'd need to leave where we were.

I'd need to reach the longhouse.

21

ELSWYTH

December 3rd, 960AD

Since Sweyn had entered, I'd paid no heed to the commotion outside. Now, I heard again the clash of metal and the screams of men slain—not immediately outside but farther down the hill. I was fearful to confront what lay beyond the door, but I needed to help Thoryn, and myself.

I wiped the shiv clean on Sweyn's tunic and took a deep breath.

The cold was cruel after the warmth of the bathhouse, and I'd no cloak for my shoulders, but there was little time to think of comfort—only of action.

Wounded men, the dead and dying, lay between me and the longhouse but none to prevent me reaching it. The snow, falling gently, was already covering the bodies, the snow stained scarlet beneath them.

In twenty paces, I reached the great hall and paused for breath, leaning my head against the frame of the open doorway. From inside came the sound of furniture pushed aside.

Someone was there—moving through the space.

A Bjorgen warrior, greedy for spoils while his brothers fought? Or a Svolvaen man, who could lead me to Eirik?

Holding the shiv before me, I darted within, pressing my back to the wall.

They were in the far chamber.

"Take what you like. I won't stop you!" It was Sigrid, frightened, discovered in her hiding place. There was a clatter of something overturned, then a shriek. "Don't hurt me, please!"

I cursed. For all that I disliked Sigrid, I couldn't stand by and allow her to be harmed. Swiftly, I made my way across the space, pausing where Sigrid's loom hung. Beneath were several sacks of wool, yet to be spun, and as I stopped, one toppled over. There was a squeak, then a low mumble. Two pairs of eyes peeped out.

Ragerta and Thirka!

Seeing me, they crept out, grasping my hands, drawing me into their embrace. They were as pleased to see me as I them, but there was no time to waste. With my finger pressed to my lips, I pointed toward the cooking knives.

"I don't know anything!" Sigrid screeched from beyond the curtain.

Wielding our weapons, we yanked aside the cloth.

On the floor, her assailant was twisting Sigrid's arm behind her back. The torturer looked up and, seeing me, gave a snort of surprise.

"Helka!" I dropped the shiv and rushed to her.

The next moment, Leif appeared, locking Thirka and Ragerta about the neck.

"'Tis all right." I motioned the women to lower their blades. "We're friends here."

"We've come for you, Elswyth, to bring you home." Helka stood tall, her eyes glinting fire. "And to avenge those who died in Svolvaen, the families who've been torn apart. We'll make Skálavík pay!"

"No!" I couldn't bear it. This fighting must cease before more lost their lives. "Skálavík was betrayed!" Taking Sigrid's hand, I pulled her up. "It was Sweyn. He's deceived everyone. He set the fire that killed Bretta!"

Sigrid's hand flew to her mouth and her face crumpled, but then she shook herself. "I don't believe it! You're up to your cunning tricks again!"

I could have shaken her for such stupidity.

"Thoryn knows. He heard Sweyn confess."

Thoryn!

I turned to Thirka, telling her to go to the bathhouse and take everything necessary. Ragerta would help. If they could stop the bleeding, he had a chance.

"This Sweyn, who led us here—" Helka made me look at her. "He said naught of this—only of his grievances, and that he tried to help you."

White hot fury surged through my veins. "He wanted to kill me. He's without honour or truth, serving only himself. All this—" I found, suddenly, that I was crying. "Everything. It's his work."

"Come, Leif, we'll tear each limb from his body and fling him from the cliffs!" Picking up her weapons, Helka pushed past Sigrid.

"He's dead already, Helka." I held up the shiv. "By my hand."

Helka stopped immediately. Turning, she stood for a moment, only looking at me. Then, her gaze dropped to my belly. Her eyes grew wide, and she clasped me to her again.

"Always fighting for your life, brave one." She buried her face in my hair.

"Eirik?" I had to know. "He's alive? He's here?" My heart pounded.

Eldberg was possessed by hatred that would brook no outcome other than Eirik's death. If he found him, he would kill him—even if it brought his own end.

I could not deny that I loved them both—in different ways.

To think of either being hurt or dying!

I couldn't bear it.

She nodded. "We'll find a way to stop this madness."

Unstrapping the crossbow from her back, Helka passed it to me. "You remember how to use this?"

※

Eirik

Eirik gripped his sword—the weapon that had served him through all time, his Heart of the Slain. Raising his prayer to Thor and Odin, he asked for their strength.

There was but one man Eirik sought.

If Elswyth were alive, only this man's death would free her.

He'd heard of the cruelties of his adversary, and the brute strength which brought annihilation to his enemies.

Running to meet the advancing foe, Eirik sent his blade into a man's stomach. His axe sliced through another's neck. Amidst skewered flesh and splitting skulls, he was aware of his warrior brethren and the Bjorgen warriors fighting alongside, but was single-minded in his purpose.

Eldberg!

Who'd brought vengeance to Svolvaen for a crime laid only at Gunnolf's door. Who'd killed men and women innocent of misdeed. Who'd kidnapped his wife, degrading her as his bed-thrall!

Across the fray of screams, Eirik saw him—taller by far than anyone else, his head without helmet, his hair a wild mass of copper, and his face scarred upon the left side.

The throng of battle seemed to part as Eirik gazed upon Skálavík's jarl, and his voice rang clear. "Time to taste my blade, Eldberg!"

Those about them fell back, making way for the two whose encounter would shape all that was to come. Through the fading light, each took measure of his foe. It was a meeting long coming.

"Or have you bravery only for skulking in the night, abducting women—like Beornwold before you."

In reply, Eldberg thundered forward, his sword raised fully above his head, bearing down on his enemy. Fury boiled in his fearful war cry—the wrath of a man who'd suffered pain and loss, and would fight unto death to exact his vengeance.

Eldberg charged and swung, delivering a stroke that might have felled Eirik before he'd offered a single blow, but Eirik threw himself to one side, rolling away. Leaping up, he raised his shield to ward off the next strike. It was swift in coming; Eldberg's sword ringing from the metal edge.

Eirik kept his feet firm but managed not a single thrust in retaliation, barely defending himself against the attack Eldberg rained down upon him. He was tiring, straining to withstand his adversary's onslaught. Helka had warned him; his strength was not as it was.

Despite the freezing air, sweat drenched his body, but he needed only one sure hit—a quick motion, stabbing under Eldberg's raised arm, into the tender, unprotected flesh.

As Eldberg's weapon fell again, Eirik levelled his sword. Now was the time to strike—between his enemy's blows, but Eldberg seemed to anticipate his move.

With a groan, Eirik blocked the weight of plunging steel. He staggered, faltering, then dropped to one knee.

Snow had begun falling again, light flakes upon heated skin.

In silent horror, Eirik witnessed Eldberg's sword enter his shoulder, slicing through muscle, flesh, and bone. The force broke the blade in two, leaving him impaled.

Elswyth, my love, where are you?

From far away, there was a scream.

Eldberg

Eldberg pulled out the sword and flung it away, then pushed Eirik flat beneath his booted foot. Drawing up his enemy's tunic, he laid his back bare and, from his belt, took his axe. He'd promised bloodeagle, and this he would deliver. First, the skin peeled back, then the ribs hacked from the spine. As he plunged his hands in this man's blood, he'd offer the death to Odin. As to the lungs, he'd burn them and let the smoke carry to Valhalla as proof of his victory.

Standing, he raised his axe high above his head and bellowed his triumph.

Many of those who'd been fighting had already fallen back, seeing Svolvaen's jarl at the mercy of the Beast.

Eldberg looked about him, reveling in his conquest.

Let all behold and fear!

None would take what was his. Skálavík! Elswyth! And his true revenge! He would be denied nothing.

Elswyth

Helka would never reach them in time. I had to shoot and pray that my aim was true.

Only as the arrow pierced his shoulder did Eldberg see me. The axe dropped from his grip, and his face turned full to mine. It showed first disbelief, then agonized sorrow, as if a searing light had been extinguished.

I had betrayed him.

He staggered, crumpled, and pitched forward.

22

ELSWYTH

December 3rd, 960AD

I loved them both.
 I didn't know how this could be, but it was true.
 Eldberg refused at first to look at me, though he allowed me to clean and bind the wound. I'd made my choice clear, in taking arms against him. The injury I'd inflicted might forever pain him.

"You loved your wife. You must understand." I sat beside the bed we'd shared.

Whatever Eldberg imagined he felt for me, it was not love. A desire to possess or to see in me what he'd lost. But I would never be Bretta, and he was not Eirik. He wished me to love him, as he had come to yearn for me, but this would never be.

Eirik was the husband I'd chosen.

"There is much you do not know." He regarded me warily, as if it was too painful, or too dangerous to keep my gaze.

"The gash behind your ear—"

I touched it, gingerly. It had scabbed over but remained tender.

"You have a mole—" He paused. "There are two more, within your hair. Three altogether."

"What of it? Many have such marks on their skin."

"Not like this."

Eldberg told me then of his conviction, that I was of Beornwold's line, that the babe I carried was Beornwold's grandchild, that Bretta had been my half-sister. I'd told him long ago of how I was conceived—by rape of my mother during a Viking raid. It had been more than twenty years ago, before Eldberg joined Beornwold's service.

"So many times I saw her in you. Wishful thinking, I believed, but there was more to it than that. Sigrid saw it, too, though she didn't want to accept."

I'd always known that I belonged elsewhere. After all that had happened, all that I'd endured, to find that Skálavík was that place! That my father had been here all along. And a sister…

It changed nothing between Eldberg and I, but it provided a stronger reason for Svolvaen and Skálavík to put aside their blood feud. The clans were already joined, through Ingrid of Skálavík, Eirik's grandmother. Now, the child I carried would join the two again.

"You'll speak with Eirik. You'll agree to a truce." I told Eldberg of what Sweyn had boasted—that he was responsible for the fire, that his ambition was stronger than loyalty to his own.

Gunnolf, half-mad as he'd been, had not planned the attack.

Thoryn gave testament, having heard every foul confession from Sweyn's lips, and Eldberg nodded in acceptance, as if having always known the truth of it. He'd retaliated against Svolvaen when no blame lay among its people.

"For my sake, for whatever love you bear me, you'll set aside the past?"

He nodded wearily. "Not just for your sake, but for Bretta's. 'Tis fitting that you wielded revenge on he who took her life. I shall never forget, nor forgive, but 'tis a door I must close or I shall lose my reason—and my will to remain in this world."

I brought his hand to my cheek.

There was good in him; that I believed with all my heart.

Many had been injured, and many killed. The longhouse was filled with men needing treatment. Sigrid helped, with Ragerta and Thirka, though she would not speak to me.

She'd shown me nothing but ill-will, viewing me as an interloper. When Eldberg told her what he knew, perhaps her manner would soften. Meanwhile, I was content with friendship borne of true kindness, which those of gentlest heart had offered freely.

Thoryn was regaining his strength, and Eldberg, too, though neither would wield a weapon as they once had.

It was Eirik's bedside I kept through the coming weeks—Eldberg having granted haven to all Svolvaen's wounded. He'd come too soon to battle and had barely strength to endure this fresh wound, but I believed he would recover. My indomitable Eirik!

A signal had been cast from the clifftops soon after the battle, calling the waiting ships into the fjord. Leif and Helka sailed without delay, with those fit to take oars, returning them to Svolvaen and Bjorgen.

Our treaty was struck—for Skálavík to retain its independence, though the Bjorgen forces had brought those of Skálavík to their knees. Ships of both Svolvaen and Bjorgen would be welcomed in the harbour and given preference in all terms of trade. In times of need, we pledged each to come to the others' aid.

I'd told Eirik of my capture and the bargain I'd made with Eldberg to keep myself alive. In the name of the peace that must be, for the good of Svolvaen, he accepted what was done, though I saw it ate at his heart.

As to the babe growing within me, once his wonder had passed, I saw the uncertainty that burdened him.

"There is something between you and Eldberg?" he asked. "You must tell me, Elswyth. If there is love—" His face contorted, for he could not speak all his fears. "And this child…"

"Nay, husband." I brought my lips to his, letting him feel my love through my kiss. "Only you have my heart, and the babe is due but two moons from now."

At once, hope replaced despair, but there was more to be said. I had to tell him everything. We could not build a future on half truths. "Almost a year ago, you went away, and much happened that brought me sorrow."

"You told me of it," Eirik replied. "Of Gunnolf's cruelty and his demands of you. Had he lived, I would have challenged him to the death for how he treated you. As it is, the gods delivered their own justice for his betrayal."

I shook my head, my eyes stinging. "But, the child—" My bravery failed me. "What if—"

Eirik spread his fingers wide over my stomach. "I will love the child, whether it bears my brother's blood or my own." He managed a weary smile. "I'll teach the boy to be a brave warrior—that he may take the mantle of Svolvaen's rule."

"And if we have a daughter?" I raised an eyebrow, pushing away my tears.

"I'll teach her just the same. She'll be like her aunt, Helka."

I pressed my hand over his, filled with new joy. Life was growing inside me. A child we'd raise together. Much had been lost: my mother and grandmother, and the boys with whom I'd grown up, my first home left behind, my lady Asta, and so many of Svolvaen.

Life was fragile, and happiness too precious to throw away. It was worth fighting for. I didn't know if we could put aside all remorse, but I knew we must try.

"You can forgive me—for all that has happened? You believe me worthy of taking my place beside you as your wife?" I was almost afraid to meet his gaze, for I knew nothing would be hidden there, but he looked truly into my eyes.

"You're stronger than any woman—even than Helka! By Odin's blood, what you've endured! You've the determination of ten men! You've always been enough, just as you are. It is I who must strive to prove myself worthy of you."

He buried his face against my belly. "I thank the gods you're still alive, and beseech them that nothing shall part us while we yet walk this earth. There is no peace for me in a world without you."

We kissed then, tenderly and long, remembering the feel of each other's lips and the wonder that was our love. It would only grow stronger, for we had both learned what was real—belief and trust and belonging.

I touched the old scar that ran down Eirik's brow and cheek. There were many more, across his torso and back. Of my own, most were hidden deep inside, but they were as real as Eirik's. Once, I might have wished them away, but I knew better now. The scars were reminders of all we'd lived through. They were reminders of what we must learn if we were to carry on and start anew.

EPILOGUE

February 2nd, 961AD

I clutched Eirik's hand, bracing against the rising swell of pain.

"Save your strength, my lady." Ragerta passed a cold cloth over my forehead. "'Twill be some time yet."

Thirka nodded as my features eased. "And the jarl, he might take some air."

Eirik looked haggard but said, "I'll not leave."

Through the night, the two women wet my lips with water and murmured prayers over me, but my fortitude waned, until I could barely cry out against the spasms, my breathing growing shallow with the lamp's dimming flicker.

It was near dawn when Ragerta shook my shoulder.

"'Tis time. You must bear down and push the child."

"No more... Just sleep..." I wished to close my eyes again, but Eirik rubbed my hand between his own. He looked so pale.

"You must, Elswyth. Soon we shall have our child, and our lives will begin a new season. But you must fight!"

Moving to the top of the bed, he brought my shoulders to rest upon his chest.

"Together, we shall do this, wife. You have my strength and your own."

I did as he asked, straining, grunting, forcing all my will into the child.

"The head!" Thirka shouted. "Again, Elswyth, and the babe is here!"

Eirik's arms were firm about me. "My brave wife, you can do this!"

Again I strained, forcing the pain downward, and was repaid with the sensation of a great shifting—of a weight moving within me.

I gasped and fell back into Eirik's embrace, his cheek pressed to mine.

Ragerta lifted the child for us to see, and there was a lusty cry. "'Tis perfect—a fine daughter!"

She laid the babe on my chest, and tears sprang to my eyes. Through all the sorrow of these seasons past, I was delivered of the child I'd longed for—the most precious treasure. She was the creation of my body, miraculous, and belonging to me as nothing else had ever done.

As she nuzzled to my breast, Eirik pressed his mouth to my ear, whispering, "I have everything." He lifted her tiny hand, and I saw the pride in his face—that he felt it, too.

Her hair was pale, like my own. Like Eirik's. If she was Gunnolf's, there was nothing in her appearance yet to show it. Perhaps we'd never know. Perhaps it would never matter.

She was mine and Eirik's—and I prayed she would know, always, what it was to be loved.

Doesn't Eldberg deserve his own 'happy ever after'?
I'd say so.... and I'll be writing this for him next year.
I've a heroine planned who is more than his match.

Want to be first in the know when that releases?

Just sign-up via Emmanuelle's website, to receive news to your inbox.
www.emmanuelledemaupassant.com

ABOUT THE AUTHOR

Emmanuelle de Maupassant lives with her husband (maker of tea and fruit cake) and her hairy pudding terrier (connoisseur of squeaky toys and bacon treats). She likes sushi, and marzipan, and the Scottish Highlands.

Visit Emmanuelle's website to sign up for her newsletter: gossip, giveaways, and behind the scenes chat, delivered to your inbox.

www.emmanuelledemaupassant.com

NINE CONQUERING REASONS TO SURRENDER

Ashe Barker, Lily Harlem, Felicity Brandon, Gianna Simone, Vanessa Brooks, Sassa Daniels, Sky Purington and Jane Burrelli, join me - Emmanuelle de Maupassant - in creating a shared-world of supreme alpha hotness, guaranteed to have you page-turning into the late hours.

Delivered into Viking hands, the brides of Achnaryrie now belong to their conquering masters but, as wedding nights bring surrender to duty, will fierce lovers also surrender their hearts?

The Highland wilderness is savage, life is perilous, and the future uncertain, but each Viking has sworn protection, and there are no lengths to which a man will not go to safeguard the woman he loves.

Discover the **Viking Surrender** series

Printed in Great Britain
by Amazon